CW00351551

SPIRIT DAUGHTERS

A NICKY MATTHEWS MYSTERY

CAROL POTENZA

Tiny
MAMMOTH
PRESS

Published by Tiny Mammoth Press, LLC

website: www.carolpotenza.com

LCCN: 2022912087

Names: Potenza, Carol, author.

Title: Spirit daughters / Carol Potenza.

Description: [Las Cruces, New Mexico] : Tiny Mammoth Press, [2022]

Identifiers: ISBN: 978-1-7363262-8-2 (hardback) | 978-1-7363262-5-1 (paperback) | 978-1-7363262-4-4 (ebook) | LCCN: 2022912087

Subjects: LCSH: Policewomen--New Mexico--Fiction. | Pueblo Indians--New Mexico--Fiction. | Infertility--Treatment--Fiction. | Medicinal plants--New Mexico--Fiction. | Murder-- Investigation--Fiction. | Mothers and daughters--Fiction. | Spirits--Fiction.

Classification: LCC: PS3616.O8435 S65 2022 | DDC: 813/.6--dc23

EDITOR: COLLEEN WAGNER

PROOFREAD BY GILLY WRIGHT

SENSITIVITY READER: SCS

COVER: BRANDI DOANE MCCANN

DEDICATION

For my dad, who raised three daughters and told them they could be anything they wanted to be.

SPIRIT DAUGHTERS

CHAPTER ONE

Bernalillo
    New Mexico, USA

IN THE DARKNESS, Nicky Matthews lay on her bed and stared up at the ceiling, fingers laced and cradling the back of her head.

The phone rang, interrupting her contemplation of the slowly rotating fan and whether a run would tire her out enough to get a few hours of sleep. It had worked the night before.

She picked up her cell. Fire-Sky Dispatch. 2:34 A.M. She pressed the green icon. "Matthews," she answered.

"Sergeant? We received a call reporting a burglary about, uh, thirty minutes ago from inside the Isgaawa Cultural Center and Museum. The caller hung up before I could get any more information. Officers Valentine and Aguilar responded and report the electricity is out and front door unlocked."

Nicky sat up. "Dr. MacElroy?" Dean MacElroy, the museum director, was a close family friend.

"No contact, either by phone or when they checked his house."

Her stomach dropped. She swung bare legs to the floor and strode to the bathroom across the hall, Saltillo tiles cool against her feet. "Send backup. Who's on tonight?"

"José and Garcia…. Wait. Unavailable. Out on a loud-party call. Waconda and Yepo." There was a pause. "I don't know, Sergeant. They're pretty traditional, and that museum…" The dispatcher tutted over the line. "I mean, I wouldn't go out there at night. Too many ghosts in all that dug-up ancestors' stuff."

And Officer Manny Valentine, already on scene, would be lead. Besides the fact that Nicky didn't like or trust Valentine, he tended to loaf unless a superior was present.

"Send Waconda and Yepo," she replied. "I'll head in, too."

"Officer Matthews?" The dispatcher's voice was tentative. "Agent Martinez is on call tonight for Conservation. You've partnered with him in the pa—"

"No. I don't need him." Nicky pulled in a breath and relaxed her grip on the phone. She glanced at the time. "ETA forty-five minutes. Matthews out."

The harsh bar of light above the sink hit her senses like a slap. In the mirror, tired brown eyes smudged purple underneath stared back from a pale oval face. She yanked the elastic band from her straight dark hair and turned on the shower before she stripped and stepped into the lukewarm spray, her worry for Dean MacElroy wiping away any thoughts of sleep.

Motion-activated security lights popped on as Nicky swung open the side door into the carport and hit remote start. Her unit rumbled to life, billowing puffs of white. Coffee in hand, she locked the door behind her and jogged down the short flight of steps. Cool, damp air bathed her cheeks and chilled the neck below her tightly wound bun. She shimmied between her truck and her mother's car and climbed into the SUV.

As the waist-high gate across her home's access rolled open, she called Dispatch. Electricity was still off at the museum, but police on scene had awakened maintenance personnel. She updated her ETA and reversed out of her gravel driveway onto the two-lane road fronting her house. Mist drizzled the windshield, and the wet street glimmered with oily black-cast rainbows. She shifted her car into drive, swung the nose toward the interstate ... and stopped.

A lone figure—male, dressed completely in black, head hooded by a bulky jacket—jogged toward her on the opposite side of the street. Reflective strips on his running shoes caught the edge of her headlights, glinting with each step. She flashed her brights to let him know she was watching. He raised a gloved hand in acknowledgement, but it shielded his face, then he pivoted onto the berm of an acequia and disappeared into the tangle of weeds and leafless saplings that enfolded the houses, tired duplexes, and trailers that made up her neighborhood.

She wasn't buying his act. It was way too early for a casual morning jog, except... Her lips quirked. She'd been out this early on runs at least ten times that month, chasing sleep. Nicky dialed the Bernalillo police and requested a patrol in the area. Then she drove the winding street toward I-25.

Traffic on the freeway was sparse, mostly big rigs avoiding the daytime crush of cars through Albuquerque. Once she took the turnoff to the museum, she was alone again. She turned up her radio for company, listening to chatter on the museum break-in: one injured, non-life-threatening. Fire and paramedics on scene. Backup en route.

At a T-stop, she pointed her unit toward a two-lane road cut into the side of a towering mesa—the only way to the museum except for a hiking trail. The mesa wall buttressed the ascent, leaving the precarious drop-off edging the opposite lane. Nicky clutched the steering wheel and slowed. On clear days, this road served up breathtaking views of vast swaths of the New Mexico high desert. But it was treacherous as hell at night, winding and narrow and dark. Vehicles that plunged over the edge rarely saw their passengers survive the accident.

When Nicky reached the canyon that housed the Tsiba'ashi D'yini Pueblo's Isgaawa Cultural Center and Museum, she parked her unit in the dirt lot near the entrance. After a call to Dispatch to report her arrival, she tucked a small notepad and pen into a pocket and took a quick sip of coffee. Cold drizzle spattered her face as she exited her SUV, sending a shiver down her back.

Thin light shone from a single fixture above the towering entrance doors. Solar ground lights lined the cement walkway, so weak as to be worthless. All of the museum windows were dark, which meant the electricity was still out. The occasional flicker of a flashlight beam grayed the glass.

Nicky adjusted her belt, hand resting briefly on her holstered weapon before she tugged her jacket closer. She wove between vehicles, footsteps brittle on the gravel, and headed toward a shadowy knot of uniformed personnel, their faces lit by cell phone screens.

She scowled. Sometimes, there was no worse gossip than a cop.

One man looked up, leaned into the group, and whispered a sibilant "*Sergeant.*" Phones were hastily shoved into pockets, and the men scattered, leaving two officers. Cyrus Aguilar was one of a growing number of Tsiba'ashi D'yini—Keres for "Fire-Sky"—tribe members on the force. In his early twenties, he stood trim and sharp in his dark blue uniform, his long hair wrapped into a regulation bun. Ambitious and smart, he'd once half joked he'd have her job one day. Maybe, if she could just get him to stop feeding the pueblo gossip mill about the crimes they worked. The other, Manny Valentine, tall, broad-shouldered, with close-cropped brown hair and a luxuriant mustache, pivoted toward her. He crossed his arms, his stance confrontational, his face a dark mask.

"Well, well. Sergeant Matthews taking a call. I guess your newfound wealth doesn't make you all that special, does it?"

This guy never seemed to learn.

Nicky planted herself in front of Valentine.

"Nothing to do, Officer? Then why don't you head up to the entrance of the canyon for traffic control. Judging by the number of cell phones I saw in your little gathering, I'm sure this news will spread fast, and I don't want any civilians slipping in to mess up the scene."

He opened his mouth, but Nicky turned her back on him. Valentine might not like her orders, but he knew better than to disregard them. The last time he had, she'd suspended him two days without pay.

"Officer Aguilar," she said, sharp-edged.

"Sorry, Sarge. About the phone."

"Then don't do it again. What do we have? You and Valentine were first on scene?"

"Yes, ma'am." He matched her stride as she walked toward the open doors of the museum, the darkness inside like a cave. "Dispatch put out the call at two-oh-one," he said. "I arrived at two twenty-three, Valentine right behind me. No vehicles leaving the scene, no vehicles in the lot. We did a quick walk around. Officer Valentine found the junction box open—it's out back. Looks like they used a crowbar and bolt cutters. Don't know the damage. The front door of the museum was unlocked."

Nicky stopped in the quiet vestibule next to the welcome desk. Two tiled halls ran left and right from the entrance. Behind the desk, a third corridor led to a small café and dining space. The dark stairwell off the left-hand hallway ascended to the second floor. Aguilar flicked on his flashlight and pointed it down the right-hand corridor. She walked beside him toward a series of connected galleries, but he skirted the entrance and headed to the conference room and class-rooms lining one corner of the structure.

"You did an initial walk-through?" Nicky asked.

"We checked the café and plaza." A large open-air courtyard for ceremonies and dances was nestled in the middle of the complex, surrounded by the building. "Valentine cleared the upstairs office and Yepo and Waconda the gift shop and restrooms."

An incomplete answer. She'd circle back later. "There was an injury?"

"An attack, actually. The intern working late heard a noise."

She frowned. "He didn't notice the lights popping off?"

"She. And no, ma'am, she said she didn't. Something about solar panels and batteries powering her office and computer. When she came downstairs to investigate the noise—she said it sounded like a door slamming—the perps, she thinks there were at least two, knocked her in the head and tied her up. We heard her kicking against the door of a maintenance closet once we got inside."

"She okay?"

"You'll want to talk to the paramedics. They're with her now," he said. "We found blood on the floor at the bottom of the stairs. Probably hers. Contusion on the back of her head and some bruises on her arms. She wanted to know who was in charge of the investigation." He stopped at the glowing threshold of a room at the end of the twisting hallway. "Guess that's you."

Nicky peered inside. Two portable lanterns illuminated the space with brilliant white light. It was a break room, clean and cold, with a couple of vending machines and scattered tables and chairs. A slim woman sat quietly, one of the med-techs standing behind her, his blue-gloved hands parting wavy hair and dabbing her head with gauze.

Nicky stepped back into the corridor. "She the only one here?"

"That's what she said. Valentine and I checked the staff houses. Only Mike Shiosee answered. He's in the back with Fire personnel trying to fix the power."

"Did she alert Dispatch to the break-in?"

"No, ma'am. She was tied in a closet, Shiosee had to be woken up, and Dr. MacElroy is absent."

"Who made the call reporting the break-in?"

"Dispatch said the guy wouldn't give a name, but it came from the extension in the gift shop."

"So, it could have come from the perp." Nicky pinned Aguilar with her gaze. "Let me ask you again. Did you search and clear the museum?"

Aguilar shifted on his feet. "We figured they'd gone before we got here. I mean, if they left right after the call, they could make it off the access road, and we wouldn't have seen their vehicle. Valentine said they probably didn't expect anyone in the building and called because they felt guilty about the intern."

Still not an answer. Nicky set her teeth. "Officer Aguilar, has the building been cleared?"

Aguilar hesitated, then grimaced. "No, ma'am. None of the traditional officers felt comfortable searching the galleries." He squared his shoulders, but he wouldn't meet her eyes. "There've been reports— well, not reports, but ... Some of the people have seen something. The war chiefs came in to bless the rooms, but it's still there. You know what I mean." His gaze flicked back to her. "You see them, too. Right? Ghosts and spirits, even though you're not Native, not Fire-Sky. So, Officer Valentine said we should wait for you."

CHAPTER TWO

NICKY PRESSED the release on her holster and brought the Glock 23 up, arm relaxed, finger laid across the trigger guard. She didn't have an under-barrel light, so she clicked on her flashlight and strode through the opening into the first series of galleries.

The museum had been built as a rambling rectangular structure that mirrored the ancient, stacked adobe homes of Little Aquita, Sky City, and Taos Pueblo, only the rooms were bigger, the ceilings at times rising two stories. Smaller exhibition spaces and niches were tucked behind walls and off corridors, making the structure mazelike. Excellent places for an intruder to hide.

Protocol dictated she wait—have a partner for the search—but the vast expanses of the reservation and limited number of police and conservation officers meant going it alone most of the time.

That suited her. She would do this by herself.

Besides, she'd made the mistake of sending the only non-Native officer to guard the road leading to the museum. She could replace Valentine with one of the other officers and partner up with him for the search. Her lips twisted. No way. She didn't want him at her back. Instead, she'd assigned Aguilar, Yepo, and Waconda to stand in the vestibule in case she flushed out a perp. She doubted anyone was left inside—what Aguilar had said made sense—but her frustration at what amounted to the refusal of the traditional cops to search the building was an ongoing problem with Native hires. The galleries were filled with ancient tribal relics whose purpose had been lost in time. When the museum was proposed, some members of the pueblo had objected to the display of these artifacts. They warned that ancient spirits and ghosts could still be attached no matter how many times the building was cleansed by medicine men or war chiefs or blessed by Catholic priests assigned to village parishes. Which meant those spirits could bind themselves to anyone who came through the rooms and follow them home.

And she was sympathetic—most of the time. But when tradition interfered with law enforcement and crime scenes... She drew in a breath to dissipate her frustration. She needed to focus.

Nicky cleared the first gallery and stepped into a hallway splashed with colorful murals, its length punctured with half a dozen entrances to smaller permanent displays. She stood in each opening, painting the rooms with her light, stepping in only to circle plinths holding fragile pots or frayed cloth, rock tools, flaked arrows, or spearheads, listening for a presence. The silence was intense. No shush of airflow through vents, no buzz of lights. No sounds of recorded birdsong, wind, or rain played as soothing background noise.

She spotlighted a bronze plaque embedded at eye level in the wall. The Siow-Carr Gallery was the premier space in the museum. All major shows were held there. The *Wedding and Fertility* exhibition—one Dean MacElroy had raved about—was even now being installed. Nicky clenched her jaw, anxiety welling up inside. *Where is Dean?*

The carved wood double doors into the gallery, normally open, were closed with a DO NOT ENTER sign posted in English, Spanish, and Keres—the native language of the Fire-Sky People. A narrow hall bypassed the gallery, hung with beautifully displayed childhood reminiscences of tribal elders. Nicky shined her light down its length. Clear.

She holstered her gun. With a deep breath, she stepped back to the doors and curled her fingers over the cold metal handle. A press downward, the tick of the latch, a tug, and the door swung toward her on silent hinges. Cold air oozed through the threshold. Nicky stilled her movement and once again listened. She was met by complete quiet. She suppressed a twinge of disquiet that accelerated the thump of her heart. The room was large. If someone hid on the other side or Dean lay injured or worse …

She took a steadying breath and crossed into the gallery, slowly moving the beam of her flashlight over a myriad of displays, their silhouettes hard and sharp, their glass covers fracturing the light. No movement, no sound. And no feeling of anyone present. Another step. She climbed her light up the far walls, chasing shadows up to the black-painted ceiling, and the edge of the door slipped from her fingers. It banged shut.

Nicky wheeled, her light a narrow circle on the wood. No handles. The surface was smooth. She pushed against the doors, dug finger-nails into the tight gap between. They didn't budge. She was trapped. Releasing a shaky breath, she tugged her radio from her belt.

"Two-one-three to five-seven-seven. Aguilar, do you copy?" she asked, voice low and urgent. The shirr of static was the only response. "Waconda, Yepo. Request eighty-two PD, Siow-Carr Gallery."

The radio went silent.

Dammit. Nicky tucked her flashlight under her chin, fiddled with knobs, pressed buttons, shook it—nothing. Her body tensed then relaxed.

She hadn't checked her batteries before the search. And she wasn't trapped. The exit doors were directly across from her. But she still needed to make a thorough search of this space. She holstered the radio and tread farther into the room, walking a slow zigzag pattern to cover every inch of the gallery, lighting up each display plinth and case. She spotlighted square glass enclosures of two-spouted wedding vases decorated with vines, fantastical animals, and geometric lines and shapes. Huge clay basins used to wash newborns nestled on woven reed mats, walls so thin they were almost transparent. Herb bundles, harvested from traditional medicine-wheel gardens scattered around the pueblo, were tucked next to metates and manos, ready to be ground and mixed into wedding teas or fertility medicine. Nicky bent over a table, flashlight beam scanning the dried plants. Before she'd switched to the criminal justice degree at New Mexico State, she'd done research on specific organic components found in medicinal plants, following in her mother's foot—

Plink.

Nicky straightened, arm hair on end, muscles tight. *Stupid.* She'd gotten distracted. Berating herself, she stilled and listened.

The sound, a faint melodic note, repeated. Then again—high-pitched, almost metallic. Nicky swept her light. It glanced off the sheen of water on stone, and her shoulders relaxed. Of course. No fertility exhibition would be complete without a traditional birthing niche. Still carefully searching each display, Nicky crept toward the back of the room. She played the beam over water trickling down the slab of rock and filling the spring at its base, each drip of water creating a gentle circular ripple that expanded to the edge of the pool, a never-ending spiral representing water in the Fire-Sky culture, just like the one carved into the center of the stone. Nicky squatted, curious. The electricity had been off for hours. Any residual water should have drained. Yet a pulsing rivulet continued to emerge from the top of the stone and run into the pool. As she stared, the drops came faster and faster until they merged into a stream.

That was weird.

Static crackled from her hip. She jerked to her feet and fumbled to turn down the radio's volume. The sound faded to a whispered *shush.*

But it didn't come from the radio. Not this time. It … moved.

Nicky twisted her head to follow the noise, then spun as it swirled behind her, now above her. Air through a vent? Had the electricity been restored? The room was still dark. Were lights turned off in this gallery at night? Nicky backed away from the birthing niche, bumped hard into a display, pointed her flashlight upward. A faint wisp of cold air brushed past her cheek. She breathed in relief. *Air-conditioning.* The power must be back on.

Her light flickered and died. *No.* She pressed the button on the shaft, clicking over and over. Nothing.

Absolute blackness closed in. Prickles ran down her arms and legs.

The musical notes of the gurgling spring changed to the tinkling of childish laughter. But it didn't stay in one place, either. It bounced around the room. Mist-laden air swept over her bare neck like a touch, swished past her ear. Sounds held within a breath of suddenly icy air whispered, *"Guw'aadzi, sha'au. Key shro'kch."*

Hello, sister. I see you.

Nicky dropped her flashlight, pulled her Glock, and crouched on watery knees. The tinkling laughter changed to the bleating cries of a newborn, only to morph into the sobs of a woman, muffled and inconsolable. The sound circled around her, spiraling closer. Nicky tracked it with her gun, her finger slipping to the trigger.

The gallery lights snapped on.

Half blinded, she swung in a jerky pirouette. The noise, the chill, the brushes of cold … gone. Except…

The spring at the base of the birthing stone roiled, a swirling black mass blurring its surface. An odd sense of déjà vu flashed through her.

Releasing one hand from her gun, then the other, Nicky swiped at her eyes.

Wet stones came into focus, concentric ripples the only thing marring the dark blue pool. The soothing notes of water filled the room.

"Five-seven-seven to two-one-three, copy?"

Aguilar's voice snapped her gaze to the radio. Nicky took a steadying breath and holstered her gun. She scooped up the radio with trembling fingers.

It had died moments ago. Hadn't it?

"Matthews, copy. Over," she replied, her voice steadier than she'd expected.

"Everything okay?" Aguilar asked. "You've been gone a long time."

"Yeah." She took a deep breath, willing her pounding heart to slow.

"Officers José and Garcia are here. What would you like them to do?"

"Clear the museum from the right-hand corridor. I'll meet them.

And Aguilar?" She stared hard at the birthing niche, her throat tight. "You were right."

"About what, Sarge?"

Nicky hesitated. "About the perps being long gone. Over and out." She secured the radio and strode to the exit.

CHAPTER THREE

NICKY STEPPED through the threshold of the break room. The two med-techs were still with the injured intern. Milo Juanito tipped his chin up in greeting. She beckoned, and he hurried over, a barrel-chested man with bowed legs, shaggy hair, and a chubby acne-scarred face.

The intern's head came up, and Nicky sucked a quiet breath. The woman's eyes were startling—a piercing light green. Her face was wan and tight, mouth pulled down and trembling. She bit her lip and stared hard, almost pleadingly. Nicky gave her what she hoped was a reassuring smile before she tugged her gaze away and turned her attention to Milo.

"Report," Nicky said.

"Charlotte Fields, age twenty-seven. Abrasions on her wrists and around her ankles. Fingerprint bruising on her arms and legs. Seems pretty shaken up," Milo said. "Whack on her head caused a shallow split in her scalp—it almost looks like a knife cut. Said she was knocked out." His eyes darted back to Charlotte. The woman stared down at her fidgeting fingers. He lowered his voice. "I'm not so sure."

Nicky absorbed his statement. Her gaze found rope piled on a table near an open door across the room. A yellow mop bucket stood tucked next to the wall, and a couple of brooms had been propped in a corner. "Why?"

"Lump's there, sure, but it takes a lot to knock someone out. Not like in the movies. More likely, she fainted, I guess."

"I need to ask her some questions."

Milo's gaze swiveled toward the woman on the chair, his dark brown eyes narrowed. "I think she's fine for questions."

He'd been on the job for almost fifteen years. He was good at what he did, probably the best med-tech on the rez. Nicky trusted him, trusted his instincts.

"Milo?" she said, her voice soft. "What's wrong?"

"I don't know, Sarge. It's just…" He hesitated. "Do you sometimes get the feeling there's more to something than meets the eye?"

Nicky snorted. "All the time. You think she's exaggerating her injuries?"

He shrugged. "Should I give the crime-scene techs the swabs I used to clean her scalp? Maybe they can do a DNA test? Could be justified to eliminate her as a suspect."

"We'll have to do one on the blood in the hall. Your swabs would have provenance. Go ahead and fill out the verification paperwork."

"Got to do that anyway." Milo grinned and winked. He nodded to the second med-tech, who was cleaning up and packing away. "Me and Wiley'll stay a while longer, Sarge, in case you need us."

She thanked him before she once again turned her focus on Charlotte Fields. The woman's gaze had snapped to Nicky and, as she came closer, roved her face, almost appearing to catalog her features. Nicky studied her just as closely.

Ms. Fields was pretty in a muted sort of way. Slim, with an air of fragility. Reddish-brown hair tumbled in waves over her shoulders. Tiny turquoise dot earrings nestled in her lobes. She was dressed in heavy leggings, a bulky sweater, and brightly colored athletic shoes. Her face was a soft oval with clear pale skin, feathery brows, and eyelashes so long and thick they looked tangled. A thin, straight nose topped pale pink lips, the bottom one probably swollen from the way she nervously bit at it. But her eyes, a clear crystalline green, made her memorable. Large and luminous, they suddenly welled with tears. With the fright and trauma she'd been through, her burst of emotion was no surprise.

"Hey, hey. No need for tears. You're safe now." Nicky pulled a chair close and sat, knees almost touching, and picked up the woman's cold hand. She rubbed it gently. "I'm Sergeant Monique Matthews of the Tsiba'ashi D'yini Police. Do you feel up to answering a few questions?"

"Monique Matthews." The woman's voice was high but almost musical, with a breathiness that could be because of circumstances. She smiled tremulously. "Please, call me Lottie. Your friends call you Nicky?"

Nicky's mind scrambled. "Have we met?"

"No." She blinked away moisture and squeezed Nicky's hand. "Dean—Dr. MacElroy—calls you Nicky. He talks about you all the time." Her lips lifted into a small smile.

Nicky's brows raised slightly. Why would Dean talk about her to this woman?

"What's your position at the museum, Ms. Fields?" She pulled out a small notepad and pen.

"Lottie, please. I'm a rotating graduate student. From the University of New Mexico? I just started my ethnology PhD program when the internship came up. The previous intern couldn't come because he got hurt, and Dean—Dr. MacElroy—needed someone with training because of the fertility exhibition opening this fall. I have a museology masters and curation experience."

"You were working alone in the museum?"

"Yes. I have a lot to catch up on, coming in so late in the planning of the exhibit. Plus my own work."

"I need to ask you a few questions about the attack. Where were you before it happened?"

Charlotte nibbled her lip, brows knit. "Upstairs in my office, transcribing provenances to the computer. You wouldn't believe how many of the pieces and artifacts come with handwritten histories."

"How long had you been working at your computer?"

"Well"—she rubbed her temple with trembling fingers—"Dean and I were back and forth between the gallery and vaults all day moving pieces for the exhibition. We both went home for dinner about six, and I came back at eight."

"Where is home?"

"I've been assigned to a staff house here in the canyon—the middle one—for the semester."

"Do you live alone?"

"Yes."

"Would you give us permission to search your house?"

Charlotte hesitated. She grabbed at her bare neckline before her hand fell away. "It's a little messy. My key's in my office."

Nicky nodded. She wouldn't need it. The house was tribal-owned, so Mike Shiosee would have the master.

"You have a key to the museum?" Nicky asked.

"No. A code for the staff entrance. I came in that way."

"And a code for the alarm system?"

"Yes." Charlotte's face blossomed red. "I, um, disarmed it when I came back after dinner. I was going to rearm it when I left."

That explained why there'd been no alarm.

"Was anyone else here when you came back from dinner?" Nicky asked.

"No. Mike usually does his final walk-through around seven, seven-thirty. It depends when the cleaning staff finish. They start immediately at five o'clock. They don't like to be here after it gets dark. Superstitions about ghosts attached to some of the artifacts."

Nicky didn't like the derisive twist on Charlotte's lips, but it wasn't like she herself hadn't been frustrated by the traditional officers' reluctance to do an initial search. After the weirdness in the exhibition gallery, they had a point.

"You told one of the officers you heard a noise. About what time was that?" Nicky asked.

"One-fifteen? One-thirty?"

"You didn't notice the electricity was out?"

"Not right then. To save energy, Mike shuts off all the lights in the evening. The museum was designed to give us the option of using solar power stored during the day if we work at night. I only had one light on—a desk lamp—and my laptop."

"What about the ventilation system? It's controlled for artifact preservation, right? Is it run by solar at night?"

"I don't know."

"It's pretty loud." Nicky paused and looked up at a ceiling vent as the air kicked off. The background of faintly buzzing light fixtures filled the space.

"I had my headphones on," Charlotte said, "listening to music."

"Headphones." Nicky made a note on her pad. She looked up, eyebrows raised. "You heard a noise…"

Something like chagrin passed over Charlotte's features. "More of a vibration. Like a door slamming. I thought it was Dean, coming to shoo me out. I went downstairs, and … and…" Her eyes flooded with tears. "I woke up in that closet, my hands and feet tied. I started to scream and yell and kick the door. The two policemen rescued me."

"You told Officer Aguilar you thought there were two people. Did you see them before they hit you?"

"Oh, yes." Crimson rose on her cheeks. She put a hand to the back of her head and winced. "I mean, no. I'm sorry, I'm just a little—"

"It's okay. Take your time."

"I must not have been completely out when they put me in the closet, because I thought I heard two different voices. Men, but I couldn't make out what they were saying."

"Ms. Fields, do you know where Dr. MacElroy is?"

"I thought he'd be here with all this fuss."

Nicky's radio buzzed.

"Four-six-eight to two-one-three. Do you copy?" Officer Garcia. An urgency in his voice that shifted Nicky's attention.

"Stay here," she said to Charlotte and strode into the hall before she replied. "Two-one-three, copy."

There was a burst of static. It cleared, and Garcia said, "I need you out back, Sarge, by the horno ovens, er, on the south side of the building. We think we've found blood."

Nicky bolted out the open front door, the damp, chilly air stinging her cheeks. Keeping to the sidewalks, she raced around the building. Headlights from a large white SUV almost blinded her. *Dammit,* she'd told Valentine to restrict entry. Dean was missing and—

She cut off that thought as the bulky mounds of the ovens appeared in the graying morning. Two men squatted on a short sidewalk leading from a flat metal side door. They both stood as she pulled to a stop.

One was Dennis Garcia, expression grim, the other a firefighter, Ryan Bernal, one of her best friends on the pueblo.

"Drops of blood on the cement. Didn't see them at first because of the damp." Garcia played his flashlight beam over dark diffuse spots staining the concrete. "Unknown footprints Bernal here tracked in from the direction of the trailhead. And drag marks. Something heavy." He speared the door handle with his light. Blood smeared the metal fixture.

"Garcia, secure this area and wait for CSU. Lieutenant Bernal, with me."

Ryan eyed her. "What's the matter?"

"We can't find Dean MacElroy, and the blood..." She felt sick.

"His car's not at his house?"

"He doesn't drive."

She and Ryan jogged into the vestibule. Charlotte Fields stood in front of the welcome desk, hands clasped tightly. She was taller than Nicky had first estimated.

Nicky stopped. "Ms. Fields, can you take us to the door leading outside to the horno ovens?"

"Of course. But please call me Lottie." Charlotte peered around Nicky. "Hi, Ryan."

"Hey, Lottie."

Nicky stared between the two of them. They knew each other? "The door, Ms. Fields?"

"This way." She led them into a series of still-darkened galleries, through an archway, past the bathrooms. "Down this hall. There's the light switch."

Nicky flipped it. Overlapping cones of white light illuminated the empty hall. She unzipped a pouch on her belt, tugged out a pair of blue nitrile gloves, and snapped them on. Ryan did the same with ones he pulled from a pocket.

"Step back, please," Nicky said.

Charlotte inched away, eyes wide.

"You, too, Ryan." Nicky crept forward. The hall ended in a double metal door, a green EXIT sign above it. On the tile floor, blood drops led a path like breadcrumbs to another closed door halfway down the hall.

"Ms. Fields? Do you know what's behind that door?" Nicky asked.

"It's a maintenance closet with stocks for the restrooms." Charlotte's breath caught sharply. "Is—is that blood?"

A glistening pool of red was visible from underneath the doorjamb, gelation at the edge.

Nicky's knees wobbled. *No, no, no, please.* What if Dean was bleeding in this closet? What if he could still be alive? She twisted the handle, not caring that she might destroy evidence.

The body of a man fell in a crumpled heap to the floor, arms pulled behind his back. A woman screamed. Nicky knelt and turned him faceup.

Skin gray, eyes half opened and beginning to cloud. Dirt smudged one side of his face and powdered his blue-black hair. *Not Dean, thank God.* The dead man's jaw slid to the right as his head rolled back. Throat cut, severed almost to the bone, the wound gaping. Nicky squeezed her eyes shut a few seconds to center herself.

She grabbed her radio. "Garcia? Pull everyone back for now. Call the FBI. We've got a homicide. Over."

"Who, Sarge?"

She studied the face of the dead man. "I don't know."

From behind her, a familiar voice said, "I know."

CHAPTER FOUR

NICKY RECOGNIZED THE VOICE. "Howard? What are you doing here?"

Howard Kie stepped forward, his eyes magnified by black-rimmed glasses too large for his narrow face. He was dressed in rumpled black trousers and an immaculate white button-down shirt covered by a creased Members Only jacket. Did they even make those anymore? An inch of white tube sock showed above his ubiquitous Keds high-tops. He clutched a box of candy in one hand, knuckles white. They'd met for the first time that year, back in April, when she'd been investigating the disappearance of Howard's friend Sandra Deering. He'd been key to solving the case. But he also had a low tolerance for blood and gore. A *very* low tolerance.

He swayed, eyes riveted on the dead man's face. "I'm a driver. For PonyXpres."

Great. The worst driver on the pueblo worked for the American Indian equivalent of a ride-sharing service.

"You know who this man is?" Nicky stood slowly.

"He stays at the casino. The nice one. A lot."

Fire-Sky Resort and Casino. She'd need to get an officer over there and make enquiries.

"I just picked up Dr. MacElroy from there," Howard said.

"Dean? He's okay?" Relief swept Nicky.

Howard jerked his chin over his shoulder, eyes wide and riveted on the dead man. "He's there, with that ku'yoh who's mean to me. Uh…" He swallowed. "That guy's got no hand."

Nicky whipped around. She fumbled with her flashlight, remembered the batteries had died. "Ryan, give me your flash—" Her light clicked on. Nicky clutched it tightly and hissed out a breath.

She pointed its beam to the body on the floor. He was half on his back, twisted awkwardly. His arms must have been tied together, probably at the elbows, because the left forearm peeking out from underneath him ended with a ragged amputation. She couldn't see the second arm.

Her radio crackled.

"Sergeant Matthews?" Officer Garcia said. "I put in a call to the FBI. They'll have agents here in about an hour. You got time to come back outside? The back of the museum's been tagged. Looks like Crybaby gang graffiti. Mike Shiosee said it wasn't there yesterday. Over."

Nicky's jaw tightened. If this guy was a Crybaby victim, that would mean the other hand was gone, too. Classic retaliation for someone who betrays or steals from the gang.

"Crybabies." She suppressed a curse. "Be out in ten."

Led by the notorious Chen Cano, the Crybabies were an Albuquerque gang—vicious and vindictive. For years, they and other gangs had used the vast fields below the museum to dump their murder victims. But why the hell would they break in, stuff a body in a closet of the Fire-Sky Cultural Center, and leave a potential witness—the intern—alive?

A crowd had gathered at the end of the hall, including a couple of her officers leaning over their cell phones.

"Put your phones away," she ordered. "I want a complete blackout on this crime scene. If anyone talks, one-month suspension with no pay. Everyone else, stand down until forensics arrives. I don't want to compromise the scene any more than we already have."

Officers dispersed, revealing EMTs in the middle of the vestibule hovered over the prostrate body of Charlotte Fields. She held a thick white towel to her head and appeared to be gesturing weakly and speaking to someone, but Nicky's view was blocked. Ryan stood behind Howard, his expression grim.

"Howard, you said you recognized this man," Nicky said. The bloody gash along the neck glistened hideously. "What's his name —*Howard?*"

Howard's eyes spun up into his skull. She darted forward but couldn't catch him before he clunked to the floor in a dead faint. Red pellet-shaped candy spilled from the box in his hand, ticking and rattling across the tiles. Ryan, his expression impassive, nudged Howard's shoulder with the toe of his boot. When there was no response, he motioned to one of the EMTs, then stepped over the prostrate form, kicked away some of the candy—Hot Tamales? *Seriously?*—and hunkered down next to the corpse.

Hands on her hips, Nicky stared back and forth between Howard and Ryan. "You could've caught him."

"Yep." Ryan gave her the faintest of smiles, but his hazel eyes were flat. His half-Jicarilla Apache, half-Swedish heritage blended to form stark, handsome features. His long golden-brown hair, usually tightly braided down his back, was twisted in a traditional bun on his neck as per regulation. "But I still owe him for crapping up my life. Let's see if this guy still has his wallet. Then you won't have to depend on that dyeetya for ID." He spat out the Keres word for "rabbit," his nickname for Howard. "Got a fresh pair of gloves?"

Nicky handed Ryan some gloves and crouched beside him. The brushed silver of his wedding band gleamed dully in the fluorescent lights before the blue nitrile covered it up.

Nicky knew Ryan was deflecting. He was having a hard time forgiving himself for his precipitous actions earlier that summer. Actions that had deprived him of the woman he'd loved unconditionally for over five years when he chose to marry someone else out of pity, need, and despair. Maybe Howard did bear some responsibility for what had happened, but there was plenty of blame to spread around.

Ryan dug into the dead man's trouser pocket.

"Find something?" she asked.

"No ID, but he was carrying this." He held up a plastic zipper bag. "Maybe it's the Crybaby connection."

Inside was dried plant material crushed into small enough pieces as to be unrecognizable.

CHAPTER FIVE

The sun had risen above the Ortiz Mountains, its light slanting through a V-shaped notch of rock in the side of the bowl-like canyon that held the Isgaawa Cultural Center. From the opening, a trail descended into an undulating plain stretching all the way to I-25, the interstate linking Santa Fe to the north, Albuquerque to the south, and that ran through a section of the Fire-Sky Pueblo.

Nicky stood at the base of the notch, clutching a bag full of evidence markers and fighting annoyance. Ryan and the two FBI agents out of Albuquerque fanned out around the trailhead. In the distance, a large coppery-brown oval of water marked a tank dug into the earth to capture runoff for livestock and game. As if trying to make amends for its absence during the long hot summer, clouds building to the south promised more rain.

"Blood and drag marks originate from this track," Ryan explained, "so there could be a secondary scene, possibly the actual murder site or—"

"Thank you, Lieutenant, um, Ryan. You've been a great help." Djimond Headley, assistant special agent in charge, smothered a huge yawn with the back of his hand not holding his coffee. Tall, deep-chested, with a bull neck and powerful arms but legs like carnival stilts, he looked oddly unbalanced in his charcoal-gray suit and subdued silk shirt and tie. He scanned the steep walls of the canyon from behind the ubiquitous dark glasses all those guys seemed to wear, morning light catching in the tight silver curls peppering his close regulation haircut.

Nicky eyed him narrowly. "Bernal," she corrected. "Lieutenant Ryan Bernal. Since the lieutenant is one of our best trackers, he and I will head dow—"

"I think it's best if we divide up our skills so we can get the official investigation started," Assistant SAC Headley said.

The slight emphasis on *official* set Nicky's teeth on edge.

The younger of the two FBI agents, Sylvia Song, inched through the notch's narrow stone passage and stared down the rocky trail. Although Nicky and the agent were about the same age, Song was a couple of inches taller. It gave her the irksome ability to stare down her nose at Nicky, which she'd been doing since the two agents had arrived at the museum.

"This place is weird. A canyon on top of a mesa? I mean, is it like an extinct volcano or dried lake or something?" Song bent to swipe at dust and dirt on her trouser cuffs, obviously not expecting an answer. Nicky tried not to grind her teeth.

Cool and sleek, Sylvia Song resembled an actress cast to play an FBI agent in a made-for-TV movie, which wasn't completely fair. The woman was efficient and smart. But like a lot of the FBI agents Nicky had worked with in the past, her arrogance showed. She also wore sunglasses and a tailored suit, her straight black hair wound into a perfect bun at her neck, nothing out of place. Nicky shoved her free hand in her pocket to stop from smoothing her own hair. No telling what it looked like now.

"Sergeant Matthews, you sent our witness to the hospital." Headley pinned Nicky with a glare.

Well, it could have been a glare. Who could tell behind the Ray-Bans?

"I sent Ms. Fields to the Fire-Sky Clinic," Nicky countered. "And I made that decision because you guys decided to stop for coffee and pastries on the way to a murder scene."

Headley's silence was glacial.

"We offered to bring you some," Song said from behind her. "Shoot. Did I step in—?" The woman scraped the bottom of her shoe on a rock.

"I received a text that Ms. Fields is on her way back to the museum," Nicky said. "An empty office upstairs has been cleared for interviews, and Dr. MacElroy is doing a room-by-room to see if anything was taken. Here's a list of employee names and information on possible whereabouts at the time of the break-in." Nicky dropped the markers at her feet and tore a sheet of paper from her small notebook. She held it out, then pulled back a little. "Unless you two would prefer to follow the drag marks down to the mesa?"

"Contact us immediately if you find anything." Headley took the paper from her hand and walked away. Song scraped her shoe one last time and strode after him.

"Why do the Feds always send their burnouts to Indian Country?" Ryan said.

Nicky's gaze followed Headley's broad form and the lithe figure of Song back to the museum. "Song isn't a burnout. She's here for her six-month field rotation. I think she's smarter than she acts."

"I think she's Native," Ryan said. "Hides it or the FBI would make sure everyone knew. Too much of a feather in their bonnet." He winked.

"Not touching that," Nicky said. She squatted down beside the drag marks. "What do you see?"

"Two people—by their shoe size, probably men—hauled something from this notch to the museum on a tarp or blanket." He squinted against the sun. "But they didn't drag anyone up that trail. All of this is faked."

CHAPTER SIX

"YOU DIDN'T TELL THE FBI," Nicky said.

Ryan shrugged, a glimmer of malice in his eyes. "Didn't want to overload them with information."

She stared at him, mind working. "So, the perps didn't drag the body up the trail?"

"My guess is they broke into the museum, conked Lottie, left her in the closet, dropped off the dead guy, then used some of those metate grind stones round back of the museum to make the drag marks. They loaded up stones on a tarp, dragged them here, then turned around and dragged them back, leaving a trail in the mud."

"With boot prints in only one direction?"

"They're blurred from being stepped over. Like this." Ryan walked backward, arms stretched out in front of his body, pretending to pull something, then he extended his arms behind his back and walked forward, stepping in his tracks.

"Right. No mud on the floors means whatever they used to transport the body into the museum wasn't muddy yet," Nicky said. "Still, they had to go back inside to make that phone call. With all the rain, why didn't they track mud in later?"

"Maybe they took their boots off or mopped up after themselves. They were in the custodians' closets."

"Tidy murderers. But cleaning up a crime scene isn't uncommon," Nicky said. "If any of this is true, that means the blood drops on the sidewalk and down this trail were probably planted. Pretty elaborate. Why?"

"We won't know until we follow their breadcrumbs," Ryan said.

"Then let's get some *official* work done and head down the trail they left us," Nicky said and rolled her eyes.

Ryan grinned. "Hey. Don't let that *ass-SAC* get to you."

She smiled and shook her head. Bending to retrieve the nylon bag, Nicky pulled out numbered markers and placed them by two obviously different boot tracks. She snapped photos, then radioed one of the evidence techs to make plaster casts before she and Ryan edged through the notch and started down the side of the mesa.

Nicky dropped another marker beside a splatter of blood, then a second one about ten steps farther down.

"Yep. Breadcrumbs. I doubt they lead to a gingerbread house. There's another one." She clambered down the path and dropped a third marker. "They sure were lucky the rain didn't wash these away."

"If it had, they'd have found another way to get us down here," Ryan said.

The sun had silvered thin creeping clouds above them by the time she and Ryan reached the bottom. Behind them, numbered yellow markers marched up the hill, spaced almost perfectly.

Nicky stood, hands on hips. "Whoever did this made sure even I could track it. I almost feel insulted. Drag marks head to the tank." She smiled at Ryan. "I know you're off shift. I'll radio Aguilar to spot you if you need to get home to Jinni. You can take my unit."

"Nah. I already told my captain I'd stay. Besides, we could use the extra overtime money. Not that you have to worry about that anymore." The last was said under his breath.

Nicky's smile dropped. First Valentine, now Ryan. Everyone seemed to envy the money, like it was some kind of windfall. But she'd earned every penny of the settlement from the tribe because the weird organism that had infected her—had almost killed her—was something she'd picked up on the job. No one ever seemed to remember those little details. And she didn't need this right now, especially from a friend.

They trudged forward, Nicky biting her tongue to keep from snapping back at Ryan. When she spoke again, her tone was determinedly light.

"How's Jinni doing? I haven't seen her in a while. I'll bet she's ready for the baby to come. She's due when?"

"First week in November. And you haven't seen her in a while because you're avoiding us—me, Jinni, Savannah." Ryan slanted her a look. "Franco."

"I've been busy." A knot formed in her gut. Probably guilt. Maybe some anger. Definitely hurt. "How do you know Charlotte Fields?" Another attempt to change the subject even though she knew it wouldn't work.

"Lottie attends a Keres language class Savannah teaches at the FEMA trailer. Says it's for her degree. She somehow wrangled an invitation to a Friday-night dinner. Jinni and I met her there." He pointed out another blood splotch. "Savannah says she's going to stop inviting you if you don't come soon. That's a lie, but she's pretty hurt."

The knot tightened. Friday dinners at Savannah's home had been a staple in her life for the five and a half years she'd worked at the Fire-Sky Pueblo. Savannah Analla had taken her under her guardianship on Nicky's second day at work at the Fire-Sky police. Saved her from sure humiliation when her fellow officers had sent her out to settle a family dispute involving a decades-old feud and a bad-tempered goat. They'd been best friends ever since.

Nicky stopped to mark more blood droplets. "My not coming to dinner has nothing to do with her."

"She thinks it does," Ryan said.

"And Savannah told you this. Right."

Ryan's lips compressed. "No. Savannah told Jinni, and Jinni told me. They're pretty good friends now. Savannah thinks you're mad at her for leaving the rez right after…" He shrugged uncomfortably. "You know."

"Yeah. Right after Savannah found out you and Jinni were getting married and she cried for two days straight. I doubt she told Jinni that." Nicky dropped a marker.

Ryan stayed quiet for a few more steps. "Savannah thinks you're mad at her because she left so soon after what happened between you and Franco. That she should have stayed and given you support."

"There *was* no me and Franco, so there's no reason for me to be mad at her for leaving. She needed a break, especially after what you —" Nicky bit off her words. She stopped and straightened, shading her eyes and scanning the area around the earthen tank. The drag marks led directly to it. "Especially after what happened with her father," she finished.

Ryan stared at her.

She marched past him, heading for the berm walls—the tapered, U-shaped dam curving around the deepest section of the pond.

"This isn't just about Franco and Savannah, is it?" he said. "You're pissed at me, too."

"You shouldn't have done it, Ryan," she said over her shoulder. "You shouldn't have married Jinni. You know it, I know it."

"She needs me. The baby needs me."

Nicky wheeled on him. "You barely knew the woman. Barely know her now. You're not even the father. You should have waited for Savannah." She turned and strode forward.

"I waited long enough," Ryan said, matching her stride. "I needed to get on with my life. And I'm trying to make my marriage work. I'm not the one cutting myself off from friends, completely ignoring Franco's existence. You and he are so much alike. Hiding behind—"

"Is that what he told you?" Nicky said. "That I ignored him? That I didn't try to talk to him? Explain? Apologize? Because I did, and he looked through me like I was glass."

There was a long silence.

"Then you need to try again," Ryan said quietly.

Nicky threw up her arms. "Sure, no problem. I'll just keep flinging myself against that wall until I'm one huge bruise. Why does it have to be me anyway?"

"Because you're stronger than him."

That stopped Nicky in her tracks.

"Because he thinks it's over," Ryan said.

She stared at the horizon, lips pinched. The dark clouds in the distance looked like a giant black wave. "That's where he's wrong. He didn't trust me enough to even let it start." She began walking again. "And I don't need a lecture about hiding and avoidance from *you*. You used Jinni and her baby, and now you feel so guilty about it you're never home."

"Our baby. We've already got adoption papers ready for me to sign after the baby's born."

"What about the real father, Ryan?" Nicky asked. "Did he give his consent for you to adopt his biological child?"

"Real father, Nicky? Like mine? Or yours? Men who abandoned us."

The sand was deep and loose, and her thighs burned with effort.

His jaw clenched. "Jinni won't tell anyone who he is. Says he's dead."

"You know she's lying." Nicky detoured left, hit the steep side of the berm around the earthen tank, and powered upward.

"And you're changing the subject. Again. You and Franco need to talk. Clear everything up, apologize—"

"I *did* apologize. *He's* the one who jumped to conclusions. *He* needs to apologize." She topped the berm and stopped on an indrawn breath. "Aw, *crap*."

Ryan scrambled up beside her and followed her gaze.

Along the gentle slope on the opposite shore of the tank, a darkly clothed body lay sprawled on its back in churned-up mud, arms flung out, head canted back, a shiny red-black puddle underneath. A few flies braved the cold, crawling over the gaping wound in his neck.

"No hands," Ryan said. "Do you think they're in the tank?"

"Look down," Nicky said.

Below them, a pale hand bobbed at the water's edge, fingers

splayed on the bank. Tiny shadowy creatures roiled the brown water around the severed wrist. It was a left hand, a wide gold band circling the ring finger.

Nicky tugged her cell phone out of her pocket.

"Dispatch? This is Matthews. We have a ten-seven subject— Rhyerson Tank. Notify supervisors. Start me ten eighty-two. And tell backup to keep this off the radios. Over."

CHAPTER SEVEN

THE CRIME SCENE Unit cast multiple sets of tire tracks, two of them fresh, and five sets of footprints, one belonging to the dead guy on the shore, two matching the museum tracks, and two unknowns.

The FBI had come and gone. Assistant SAC Headley had muttered something about another gang slaying, Agent Song piping up that the body up at the museum was probably a gang initiation killing.

Nicky again offered to call someone to replace Ryan, but he refused to leave. Like Nicky, he volunteered to search the opaque brown water for evidence with rakes and metal detectors. The large tank, scraped into the ground by a bulldozer, was maybe thirty feet in diameter and sloped deeper into the ground toward the berm end. The displaced dirt and sand had been pushed into an earthen barrier that rose out of the water about five feet high and hugged the back of the tank. The earthen barrier tapered on two sides toward the front. A few scrubs and trees dotted the backside of the berm, but the owner kept the wide, flattened trail around the top clear. Runoff from rain or melting snow collected in the tank, which was well-used by cattle, wild horses, deer, and elk. Smaller tracks—stray dogs, coyotes, a bobcat, rabbits, birds—were also pressed into the wet ground. Normally, the earthy smells of cow flop and urine rose over the muddy scent of water. Now the tang of blood predominated.

Nicky and Ryan donned rubber waders and worked quadrants under the supervision of the remaining CSU team member. Along with the wedding-ringed hand, the young woman carefully and excitedly bagged up the evidence they found, including a machete and two more severed hands—a matched set. The tech had been less enthusiastic about the trash retrieved: two old soda cans, a discarded Coke bottle, and various plastic articles. They worked until the tank's muddy bottom and depth stymied their search.

They were still missing a hand.

The CSU tech leaned against her vehicle, scrolling through her phone. Ryan finished his call and tucked his cell back in Nicky's unit. One of her officers had retrieved her truck from the museum.

Ryan yawned hugely. He slipped off his waders and slung them over the hood next to hers to dry. Bloodshot eyes surveyed the surroundings. Nicky imagined she looked just as exhausted.

"The owner's Fire-Sky, but the land isn't," he said. "Conservation can't convince him to let us drain the tank, and the tribal council is backing him up. They say to use other means. Draining is a last resort."

"We've been getting so much rain, it would probably fill up again before spring." Nicky waved a hand at the thick black clouds bearing down on them. "We need to find that hand before it starts up again."

"You contacted the State Police Dive Team?" Ryan asked.

"Yeah. They won't come if it can be drained." Nicky shivered. Even though it was noon, the air was damp and cold. "What do we do?"

Ryan hesitated. "Conservation has a suggestion. You know they do a fish census in some of the mountain lakes and streams every summer. It's also a cleanup. They pull all sorts of trash out with the nets. A couple of the agents are willing to come out and see if they can cast up the missing hand or anything else in the deep end. Actually…"

Nicky jerked her head around at the sound of a truck motor. A white single-cab conservation vehicle bumped down the road with two men silhouetted in the seats. A slight man occupied the passenger's side, while the driver was large with wide, bulky shoulders. *Franco Martinez*. She whipped her head around and glared at Ryan.

"Look at that," he said, lips twitching. "Here they are."

NICKY IGNORED FRANCO, as he did her, maintaining an icy silence. He pulled on chest waders while he chatted with Ryan and the flirtatious CSU tech and shook out his cast net. Now he was waist-deep in the muddy water, re-searching territory she and Ryan had already covered. A slight breeze had kicked up, riffling the surface of the water, and fat clouds swept across the sky above them like scouts sent from the storm gathering to the south. Muted blue and white reflected off the muddy surface of the tank, making it almost pretty.

Pep Katina, Franco's partner, stood on top of the berm, his slicked-back hair twisted into a tapering braid instead of the regulation bun. Older than Nicky by about ten years, he'd never moved up in the ranks of the Fire-Sky Conservation service, seemingly satisfied with his position as agent. He was stocky, his shoulders narrower than his waist, with a face and hands a rich brown color compliments of his job outdoors and genetics. He had a ready smile. Pep was too short to wade into the tank and throw the net, something he readily admitted.

"Let the tall medagaana and Chishe do that. I'd just as soon fish off the bank."

He winked at Nicky. Then, net thrown over his arm, he slipped and wobbled down the steep slope of the berm toward the edge of the water where they'd seen the first hand. He unfurled the cast net, twisted, and with a graceful swinging motion sailed the net into the air. It ballooned into a diaphanous circle, its edges dotted black and white with weights. Like a dusting of frost, the net floated on the water's surface for the briefest moment before the weights rolled it under. He was clearly a master of the cast net, and both Ryan and Franco stopped to watch. Pep smoothly spooled out nylon rope as the net sank, paused, then carefully pulled it back in. Lines running from the nylon rope to the lead weights pouched the net into a floppy donut shape, trapping a few small, denuded branches and a disintegrating plastic grocery bag. He deftly untangled his catch, handing everything up to Nicky, who discarded the sticks down the side of the berm and motioned for the CSU tech to come retrieve the bag. Pep continued his casts, methodically moving along the berm, wobbling every once in a while in the soft, wet sides. All he caught were more branches.

"Hey, Nicky. Want to try?" Pep grinned and retreated up the tapered end of the berm onto more solid footing. "You found the first hand; maybe you're the only one who can find its match."

"All right," she said. "But I have no idea what I'm doing."

"Eh. If I can teach Franco, I can teach anybody. Ain't that right, Franco?"

Nicky spun around. She'd been so focused on Pep, she hadn't noticed Franco had come up the other side of the berm and stood behind her, almost within touching distance. She turned away to search for Ryan. He was next to her unit, on his phone.

"Calling Jinni," Franco said, his face impassive.

"Okay. Stand here," Pep said. "Yeah, we're a little high up, so don't step off the top and fall in. Slip the loop around your wrist. Now spool up the handline."

Nicky nodded. The nylon rope threading through the center of the net was wet and rough on her exposed skin.

"Now hold the net up until the lead touches the ground and grab the mesh waist-high. Right there, right there. Good."

Pep led her with step-by-step directions. He retreated as Nicky swiveled and threw. The net spread in a crumpled circle on top of the water.

"Not bad for her first time, right, Franco?" He leaned in, eyes almost squinted closed from a huge grin on his face. "Franco's first time? He released ... *prematurely*." Pep slapped his knee and almost fell over laughing.

Nicky rolled her eyes, lips twitching into a smile. She darted a glance to the nearest figure, unconsciously wanting to share in the jest, and caught Franco's gaze. He stood even closer, feet spread to shoulder width, thickly muscled arms folded over a wide chest made bulkier by the waders. Much better proportioned than Djimond Headley—

Her smile dropped, and her fingers strangled the nylon rope.

Still laughing, Pep excused himself. "Goin' around back to, uh, water the flowers. You take over, Franco." He scurried to the end of the berm and out of sight.

Nicky pulled in the net, mentally stepping through Pep's directions, and made a second cast. This time it sailed out in a graceful circle, settled on the water, and sank. She spooled out rope, until the line became slack, and waited for a count of five. A teasing breeze rippled the water. It sighed over Nicky's cheeks and neck, suddenly chill and sharp. She shivered. Maybe it was time to give up. Carefully, she pulled in the rope, hand over hand. The line went taut. She tugged, but the rope only tightened.

"I think I'm snagged," she said.

A harsh rush of damp air tattled and moaned through the bushes down the dam's back. The milky sunlight reflected on the water snuffed out, and the day darkened. Once-distant storm clouds covered the sky, roiling black and ominous. Thunder rumbled. She moved a few feet along the berm's top to get a different angle, intent on untangling the line. A gust of wind pushed at her, sweeping up and tapping particles of sand over her boots and legs. Small waves lapped the shore below. The wind played over the water, whistling and humming. The distant crying of a baby jerked Nicky's head up.

And the net pulled back. Hard.

Rope spun from her hand. She grabbed at it and cried out at the burn. The line, now buried in the deepest part of the tank, bucked. Another brutal tug. The loop around her wrist lynched tight. Nicky fought to hook a thumb in the slipknot. She strained back, boots digging into the crumbling dirt at the edge of the berm. Below her, the storm-dark water boiled, a large shadowy shape right below the surface. Her breath caught. The line jerked, and she pitched forward.

Arms like bands of iron cinched around her waist and yanked her backward. The nylon rope binding her wrist immediately loosened. She thrust off the loop before she reeled over the back of the berm, twined with Franco. Nicky twisted around to grab his shirt as the world tilted sideways. They barrel-rolled down, over and over, onto the flat behind the berm, her eyes pinched tight, her head cradled in the crook of his shoulder.

They stopped, Nicky's back and legs pressed into the sand. Her hair had finally come undone, strands lacing across her cheek and mouth. She stared up into Franco's startled face. Breathing hard, he lay on top of her, chest to chest, hip to hip, his arms encircling. He was heavy.

She didn't mind.

Franco's brown eyes darkened, tiny flecks of gold and umber submerging under dilated pupils. Granules of sand dotted one of his cheeks, clinging to stubble. The hard line of his jaw bunched and flexed. He tugged an arm from underneath her and brushed the hair from her lips, tucked it around her ear. The fan of laugh lines at the corner of his eyes softened.

What did he see when he looked at her?

Crunching footsteps hurried from two directions, and his face closed. He levered off her and stood. The cold spatter of rain hit Nicky's face. Franco extended a hand, but Nicky pretended she didn't see it and rolled to her feet. She brushed herself off as best she could, hiding behind a curtain of hair, her gaze bent to the ground. Tiny droplets of moisture stood on the sand for a moment before the earth drank them in.

Had Franco seen the blackness underneath the water? She glanced at him and froze. His gaze sliced into her.

"Oh, my gosh! You got it."

On the berm above them, the CSU tech raised the cast net. Inside was the missing hand, fingers twisted in the mesh.

Ryan and Pep appeared next to Franco, rain now blossoming in dark spots on their shirts. Pep was shaking his head. Nicky gathered tangled strands of hair in her hand and started picking out dead leaves and twigs.

"What'd I tell you?" Pep said. "Premature release."

CHAPTER EIGHT

NICKY COVERED her mouth with the back of her hand and yawned, eyes gritty from watching hours of autopsies deep in the bowels of the morgue. She leaned sideways in the padded office chair so Dr. Julie Knuteson, a good friend and senior medical examiner at the Office of the Medical Investigator in Albuquerque, could hear her in the hallway outside the office.

"Just got an email. Fingerprints confirm IDs on both bodies," Nicky called before she slouched back and slid a finger up the screen of her phone until she found the victims' names. No one she recognized.

Julie bustled into her office with two cups of coffee, the rich scent masking the stringent chemical smell lurking in the air from the overhead vent. Julie handed one to Nicky, her diamond engagement ring glinting under the fluorescent lights. She sat behind her desk, turquoise scrubs hugging her full curves. She'd showered and slicked back her short brown hair, accentuating a fresh, girl-next-door look. Her office was simple, tidy, and sterile, with what was supposed to be a soothing color on the walls that Julie called dead-man gray.

"Sweet'N Low, right? By the way, you look like death warmed over." Julie half smiled and took a careful sip of her coffee.

"Guess I'm in the right place," Nicky quipped back. "I've been up since two-thirty this morning." Even earlier if she counted her inability to sleep last night. "What time is it now?"

"Close to midnight." Julie rolled her shoulders and stretched. "Okay. Let's do a quick postmortem, then I have a personal request."

Nicky straightened. "Personal." She couldn't keep the wary edge out of her voice.

"Oh, no. When you're completely distracted by my brilliant deductions from the autopsies, I'll pounce. You going to record our conversation?" A smile played around her mouth as she moused on her computer.

"Yes." Nicky sighed and pulled her chair around. She pressed the record icon on her phone.

"All right. Identifications. I got them, too." Julie clicked her mouse, attention focused. "Cow-tank man is Durwin Angel Benevidez, age twenty-three. Street name, Angel de Muerto. Angel of Death. Why are these guys always a walking cliché? Arrested multiple times for drug possession, let out by the judicial system's revolving door, and, based on his autopsy, had a serious case of meth mouth. I took tissue samples for analysis, but there's no doubt in my mind the guy's an addict. He also had some fabulous gang-affiliation tattoos. Looks like he was a member of the Crybabies." From a photo of Benevidez's narrow chest, Julie enlarged a stylized skull, a single teardrop below the left orbit.

"The same image was tagged on the back wall outside the pueblo's museum," Nicky said. "Official cause of death?"

"Exsanguination from a deep, oblique, and long incised laceration to the throat, right to left, perp standing behind the victim. Started below the ear at the upper third of the neck and deepened gradually with severance of the right carotid artery. The left-sided end of the injury was at the mid-third of the neck with a tail abrasion. So, your perp is probably left-handed." Julie swirled her coffee. "Lungs showed aspiration of blood, but no evidence of air embolism in the heart. Hands severed perimortem—probably postmortem because there wasn't a lot of blood drain. Everything happened within a short time frame. You found the hands in the tank? What about his junk?"

"His *what*?"

"Mr. Benevidez had his penis chopped off before he was taken to the tank and killed. He was wearing an adult diaper to catch the blood."

"Which usually means punishment for rape," Nicky said. "Any evidence the machete we found was the murder weapon?"

"I've sent it to forensics, but don't expect it to lead you back to someone special. I think the Crybabies buy 'em in bulk," Julie said. "Was this the second or third body found in that field below the museum?"

"Third this year," Nicky answered. "The first two were dumps—only one had his throat cut. Another guy was shot. Neither linked to the Crybabies."

"Popular venue. It was pretty easy to match the hands to each of the men, considering Mr. Benevidez's were tatted up," Julie continued. "He obviously watched *Stand and Deliver* at some point in his life, because he had the same charming letters across his knuckles." She took another sip of coffee. "Meth and death. Such a waste."

"A standard message killing," Nicky said. "Don't snitch or steal, because this is what will happen when you do."

"Remind me never to join a gang," Julie said. She opened a photo of the second murder victim, the one found in the closet at the museum. "This guy is Rémy Tioux, forty-three years of age, married with a kid. Good health, great teeth, very nice suit—pure silk. Handsome man, considering. Couple of tattoos, but discrete. Wedding ring on his left hand—I'll come back to that—ear piercings unoccupied. The modus operandi for Mr. Tioux *looks* similar to that of Mr. Benevidez. Deep throat laceration—this time, left to right, both carotids severed and the cut extending to the bone. The third cervical vertebrae, to be exact. So probably a different killer unless he or she—don't want to be sexist—was ambidextrous. But *this* is where it gets interesting." Julie selected a file, and the X-ray of a head and neck appeared on-screen. "Our Mr. Tioux died because of this." She picked up a pen and pointed to a vertebrate. "Broken neck."

Nicky leaned forward, tiredness gone as she studied the photo. "Could this have happened at the same time his throat was cut?" She grimaced in sudden realization. "There wasn't enough blood on his suit. He was already dead when they cut his throat."

"Got it in one." Julie brought up two side-by-side photos. "This is Mr. Benevidez's shirt." The front of the white T-shirt was drenched in drying blood. "And this is Mr. Tioux's." The white dress shirt was bloodied only around the collar and on one shoulder. "Complete lividity hadn't set in when Mr. Tioux was placed in the closet. That's why there were blood puddles on the floor."

She brought up a picture of Tioux's hands. "And his hands were not hacked off like Mr. Benevidez's. The perps took a couple swings. There were secondary cuts on one arm and on one of the retrieved hands. I'd say this person was an amateur compared to Angel's executioner."

"Hesitation wounds? One of the theories is these murders could be part of a gang initiation," Nicky said. "Maybe whoever did this was a first-timer. Did they use the machete?"

"I'd say an ax instead. Neck, too. Used it like a blade." Julie made a cutting motion across her neck. "Awkward, since he was probably dead already."

"We didn't find another weapon when we searched, so it could still be there."

Julie yawned and shrugged. "Okay, let's see what else. The rope binding Mr. Tioux's arms CSU identified as a climbing rope. I'll email you the brand and manufacturer. It's being processed for DNA, but don't hold your breath for results any time soon, even though the FBI assured me they would expedite the tests. Labs are pretty backed up. I also sent along the baggie of plant debris, but I don't think it's pot just by the smell." Julie paged through photos as she spoke.

"Mr. Tioux's ring finger. The knuckle was abraded. I would have said the perps wanted his wedding ring—it's eighteen karat gold."

"Yeah, that hand was the first thing I saw," Nicky said.

Julie shivered. "You took a great pic. Like the hand's trying to claw its way up the bank."

While the other hand tried to pull her in. Nicky took a cleansing breath and shook off the image of boiling black water.

"It has an inscription." Julie zoomed in on a photo of the ring. "'*H-M-X-H-M* Till death do us part.'" Her tone was sepulchral. "Creepy. Not Rémy Tioux's initials. His wife's name is Kristina, so not hers, either. Roman numerals? *X* is ten, *M* a thousand." Julie grimaced. "But there's no *H*."

"I know this sounds weird, but the *X* might mean 'crossed,' like in Mendelian genetics. You know, peas. Wrinkled-green crossed with round-yellow." Nicky shifted on her chair, shrugging. "When I was little, my dad used to call me *figlia mia numera una*—my first daughter. The progeny of a cross between my mom and him." She stared at the photo of the ring on the computer screen, swallowing at an unexpected tightness in her throat. Ridiculous.

Julie tipped her head to one side. "First time I've ever heard you talk about your dad. Sorry. We're still recording. It's an unusual ring, the way the gold's hammered instead of polished. Looks old. Something Mr. Tioux inherited? Could explain the inscription."

"Can you enlarge the image? The ring seems familiar for some reason." Nicky said. She couldn't place it, but that might be due to fatigue. "Do you have an estimated time of death?"

"Best guess? Midnight, give or take a couple hours. For both of them. Mr. Benevidez was found at the tank, right? And Mr. Tioux was found in your museum's maintenance closet."

"We don't think he was killed there."

"Look for a place with pine trees. I found dried pine needles in his socks," Julie said. "But whether he picked them up before, during, or after his death is up to you to figure out."

Nicky cradled her coffee mug. "Based on the autopsy, what's your theory behind Mr. Tioux's death?"

Julie hesitated. "Don't quote me, but because of the broken neck, I'd have to say the mutilations—neck and hands—were done to make it look like a Crybaby killing. I have nothing to back that up, though.

It really could have been botched because it was an initiation. I think you'll know more when you find the actual murder site."

Nicky nodded. The Crybaby MO was well-known thanks to an accommodating local press. It had even been national news when two Crybaby gang members arrested during a truck-stop sting that summer had their throats cut and hands severed while in protective custody at the Bernalillo County lockup.

Julie leaned back in her chair, eyebrows raised. "I know that look. Your mind is working furiously on connections and holes in this case. You're at peak distraction. Go time." She pressed the icon on Nicky's phone to stop the recording. "Nicky, my fiancé's best friend in the whole world is coming for a visit Friday. He's single, gainfully employed, not bad-looking, and *you*—"

"No."

"—are single, gainfully employed, desperately lonely since Franco Martinez dumped you."

"We went out one time! And I'm not desperately lonely. And he should have trusted me." Nicky clamped her jaw, hurt welling up. "He should have trusted me."

Julie placed a warm hand over hers. "But he didn't. And you've isolated yourself and are living like a nun."

"I am not living like a … a … *nun*." Nicky's insides churned at the analogy. She exhaled and slowed her breathing in an effort to calm herself.

"Yes, you are," Julie said. "You have for years, ever since your nasty breakup with Dax Stone. And it's only gotten worse. I'm worried about you."

Nicky dropped her gaze, hating the pity in Julie's eyes. She stared unseeingly at the soft unraveling of steam above her coffee mug.

"Now," Julie continued. "Let's try this again. Brian's best friend is flying into Albuquerque on Friday. Would you please come out to dinner with us so you can meet a very nice guy?"

Though she maintained a calm exterior, Nicky's chest remained tight.

"When?"

"This Friday night. I'll text you more details. Hey, don't look like the world's gonna end." Julie squeezed Nicky's hand. "It'll be fun. I promise."

"I'll think about it," Nicky said.

NICKY STALKED TO HER UNIT, mind still agitated from Julie's statement about her loneliness and continued isolation from friends. Julie had chosen the exact right words to prod Nicky into something she wasn't ready for. Didn't want to do.

Especially with the memory of Franco pressed against her after they'd fallen at the earthen tank.

Living like a nun.

She stopped dead in the near-empty parking lot, in a place where the light from the halogen street lamps didn't penetrate and dropped her head in her hands. Wasn't this exactly how her mother had reacted when she'd learned of her husband's—Nicky's father's—infidelities? He'd shattered her mother's trust with his affairs, and she'd run away from her life. Left Nicky to be raised by her grandmother.

Was she so much like her mother that she was falling into the same dark hole?

Her fingers pressed into her temples as she cleared her mind. Her list of tasks for work and this bizarre double homicide were too long and too important for an unproductive welling of self-pity.

Squaring her shoulders, she breathed in the chill night air and listened to the rumbling hum of semis, motorcycles, and cars on the nearby interstate, a doppler of sounds as their occupants went on their way, pursued their lives with purpose. Like she should be doing. Head home, get a good night's sleep, go to work in the morning. Purpose.

She slotted personal thoughts away, focused on the autopsies' preliminary findings, and walked toward her truck, which was parked directly under a circle of yellow light. Keys in hand, she beeped it open, reached for the driver's side handle …

And stilled. A square envelope was tucked in the window.

Nicky dropped her hand to the butt of her gun. Turning in a slow circle, her gaze probed the shadows edging the lot.

She saw nothing, but that meant squat.

She slipped the envelope from the glass, opened the flap, and pulled out a business card. It contained a single inked line of instructions:

Tomorrow Starbucks Bernalillo 7:00 am

So much for a good night's sleep.

CHAPTER NINE

NICKY ARRIVED at the coffee house ten minutes early. It was busy, cars bumper-to-bumper in the drive-through wreathed in exhaust steaming from tailpipes. The line inside snaked around sales displays, and the buzz of conversation and music mixed with the rich scent of coffee. There were no empty tables, so she grabbed her cup and slipped outside to the concrete patio. She'd be found by the note-writer, and she'd be safe. The place was too crowded with potential witnesses.

She sat on the cold metal chair and tucked her black jacket tighter against the chill. With studied casualness, she pulled out her phone to check her emails. There were a few other brave souls outside waiting for the sun to rise over the wall of mountains to the east, reading on their tablets or talking in low voices across the lacy mesh tables. Nicky sipped her coffee and scanned the crowded parking lot.

There. A black late-model SUV drew into the lot and crawled forward. Nicky took in the details without visibly seeming to, her finger continuing its own slow crawl up the face of her phone. Darkly tinted windows, make, model. She pressed her camera icon and snapped a surreptitious series of pictures as it passed. The vehicle crept toward the corner of the building. Nicky checked the time. Six fifty-nine. She lifted her head to follow it.

"Nicky? Sorry, sorry. I mean, um, Sergeant Matthews?" A woman in a bulky blue parka and black slacks stepped into her line of sight, her teeth nibbling her lower lip. The cold added pink to pale cheeks, and light green eyes gazed down with earnest intent.

"Ms. Fields?" The intern from the Isgaawa museum. "Did you leave the note on my truck?"

"Note? Uh, no. Sorry. And it's Lottie, please. I just saw you out here and thought I'd come ask about—I mean, I'm sure you can't talk about that ... man, but—" Her smile was pained. She clutched a cup of coffee in her hands, slim, bare fingers tightly woven around it. "Dean —Dr. MacElroy—said you'd be coming back out to the museum today for more questions, even though the FBI was pretty thorough."

Nicky glanced behind Charlotte. The SUV was out of her line of sight.

"I-I'm so sorry. Are you waiting for someone?" She skimmed the patio, her expression tightening with something like worry.

"No." Nicky forced a smile. "Won't you sit down? How are you feeling?"

"I'm fine, actually. Headache yesterday, but it's gone now. Fast healer, I guess." Lottie scraped back a chair and perched on the edge. "I can't stay. I have an appointment at eight-thirty with my principal investigator at UNM, and the traffic is so bad. Thought I'd get some caffeine first." She brought her cup up in a mock toast and wrinkled her nose. "Sorry. Captioning the obvious here." Her voice dropped almost to a whisper. "I heard about the second man. I couldn't sleep last night. I mean, for some reason they let me ... live, while those other two..." She touched the side of her head where she'd been hit and grimaced. "Did you find out who did it?"

Her eyes really were stunning. "We're still gathering evidence. Dean said four o'clock today would be okay?"

"Yes. That should be great." Charlotte worried her lip, took a sip of coffee. "Um, we're still doing inventory, checking to see if anything was taken."

Nicky checked the time. Six minutes after seven. When she looked up again, Charlotte, with her mouth open, blinked and looked at the phone in Nicky's hand. Her cheeks flooded pink. She sat back and fluttered her hand. "I've interrupted your morning. I-I need to go anyway."

Nicky exhaled, guilt niggling her. She'd let her impatience show, and that wasn't fair. Charlotte Fields had been a victim of a crime, too, and deserved her attention and compassion. She gave the woman a reassuring smile.

"Anything you find would be helpful to the investigation. I appreciate your efforts."

"Thank you." Charlotte's gaze searched hers. Whatever she saw she must have liked, because her face relaxed into a wide smile and her eyes brightened. "Okay. Well, I should go." She pushed her chair back, and it bumped into a baby stroller. "Oh, s-sorry! Then I'll see you this afternoon. Sergeant Matthews? You know, uh, my mother and father were archeologists, too. Maybe when your investigation is over, we could meet for coffee or something?" Her cheeks blossomed pink again. "But I don't want to impose."

Because Julie's statement last night about how she was isolating herself still stung, Nicky said, "I'd like that. It'd be nice to hear about your work." It wouldn't hurt to explore a potential new friendship. Maybe they had more in common than first met the eye.

"Dean mentioned your background and who your—your mother is." Charlotte backed awkwardly toward the parking lot, knocking into tables and chairs, apologizing to patrons. "I'm a huge fan of her work, so ... so, great!" When she was beside her car—it was parked right next to the patio—she grinned and rolled her eyes self-deprecatingly. "Such a klutz. Not good when you handle as many priceless ceramics as I do."

Nicky had to smile.

"See you this afternoon." Charlotte waved, slipped into her white compact, and drove away.

Nicky waited until Charlotte's car made it through the light onto the main thoroughfare before she retrieved the baby toy next to her foot. She scooted her chair over to the stroller and peeked inside.

A little boy—just one year old—sat swathed in soft fuzzy blankets. Han Guerra grinned in recognition, and her heart melted. Chocolate-brown eyes bright, he held out his arms to be picked up. Nicky raised her eyebrows at the boy's mother, and the woman nodded her assent, her artfully arranged blond curls bobbing—a wig expertly covering her dark hair. Nicky untangled the child from his blankets and snuggled him in her lap.

"He's grown a couple of inches since I last saw him," Nicky said. "But he's slimmed down, too." The little boy cooed and patted her cheeks with his hands.

"I buy new stuff, and he outgrows it before he wears it twice. And he is now flaco because he runs everywhere." Luna Guerra's eyes were covered with huge gold-rimmed sunglasses. She was slim, elegant, perfectly made-up, and unrecognizable. "I was almost afraid we wouldn't be able to meet because of your new friend."

Nicky cooed at the little boy, tickled him gently, and smiled at his squirming chortle.

"I also heard your friend was struck in the head by the people who broke into your museum and left a dead man in the closet," Luna said.

Nicky's smile dropped. Some of those details hadn't been released to the press. Two explanations: the mother of the sweet little boy in her arms had sources everywhere because of her position as leader of the Crybaby gang, or she'd ordered Tioux's murder and had the infor-mation firsthand. Nicky and Luna had met on the Stone Fetish murder case a few months ago. Luna had broken into her home and threat-ened her life. Funny the people who become your friends. But Luna Guerra, alias Chen Cano, was someone she couldn't tell Julie or anyone about when pressed on her lack of a social life.

"There was a second murder at Rhyerson Tank," Nicky said. "The FBI is convinced both were carried out by your men."

"The graffiti." Luna sighed deeply. "The FBI have no vision. They think in clichés. And you? I hope you would know better." She dug in the diaper bag and pulled out a biscuit for Han. He snatched it up and shoved it in his mouth. Luna smiled, the love for her little boy apparent in her eyes.

Nicky bounced one knee gently under the baby. "I believe at least one of the dead men can be attributed to you."

"Angel. Well … let's just say he won't break into any more homes or wrap plastic bags around any more heads or rape any more grand-mothers."

Nicky gave her a sharp look. That case had been all over the Albu-querque news a couple of months ago.

"He was a thief and snitch, too?"

"He gave a couple of his friends information, and they killed two drivers down south and stole merchandise—mostly for personal use." Face pensive, Luna stared at her son. "Angel never had a chance, you know? He had a terrible childhood. His demise was inevitable."

Nicky sat silently and absorbed Luna's regret. "His partners?"

"They ran to Juárez. I doubt they will cross the border again."

So, dead. "I wish you wouldn't do this. I wish … if something happens to you…" Nicky brushed fingers over Han's pink cheek. "Children need their mother."

Luna sipped her coffee, her face and shoulders stiff. "You didn't."

Nicky had no answer. It was … complicated.

Han snuggled into the crook of Nicky's arm, his mouth ringed with liquified biscuit, his blinks lengthening. Luna leaned in with a wet wipe to clean his face. He jerked his head and fussed but relaxed into a boneless trust when she finished. His thick dark lashes settled on his cheeks, and his breathing evened out.

Nicky cradled him. She'd saved his life that summer from an acci-dental trailer fire. It connected them, and when he was in her arms, she felt that bond keenly.

"What about the dead man in the closet?" she asked.

"Rémy Tioux? I don't know who killed him or why, but I would like to find out since the crime was attributed to me and mine," Luna said. "You're working on the case?"

"Secondary to the FBI. They have the lead."

"Ah, the FBI. Always in the way. I have some information on your

Mr. Tioux you may want, but this isn't a good place to talk. I'll send a trusted man to your home tonight. Ten o'clock."

"And in exchange?"

"You keep me informed. There's my ride." The large black SUV hummed to the end of the patio. Luna stood.

Nicky kissed the top of Han's head and negotiated him back into the stroller. He settled in the blankets, his little face peaceful in sleep.

"It was good to see you again, Sergeant Matthews." Luna took a step, stopped, and tilted her head to one side, a tiny frown playing on her lips. "Your new friend Charlotte Fields seems very nice. But then, so do I." She pushed the stroller to the truck.

CHAPTER TEN

THE FBI BUILDING in Albuquerque was large, expansive, and impressive. Special Agent Sylvia Song's office was not. Nicky sat across from her at a nondescript Formica-topped desk in a room decorated with every conceivable shade of greige. Song even wore a gray suit with a beige blouse, her only jewelry a necklace with a tiny silver cross.

"I see the FBI has the same decorator as the morgue," Nicky said.

From behind a computer screen, Agent Song shifted to look at her, a tiny frown drawing her brows together. After a moment, she returned her gaze to whatever was on the screen and read silently. She then focused on a yellow legal pad, writing her notes in a blocky uppercase script.

The lone picture attached to the windowless walls contained Song standing next to a draped American flag along with a proudly smiling older couple.

Nicky tried again. "Your parents?"

"Yes. I was adopted as an infant. Italian-Americans. Catholic. My biological father was Chinese-American."

Her answer was rote. A quick explanation to shut down the curious. She'd said nothing about her mother.

"Your report pretty much matches with what Charlotte Fields told us when we interviewed her." Song spoke in a slightly too loud monotone with a faint East Coast accent—New York? New Jersey? "Is it true she was the one who finally discovered the body in the closet? How long had you and your men been on scene? A couple of hours?"

Nicky ignored the jibe. It was a blocking maneuver, staving off more personal questions. Besides, she herself had gotten in a lick yesterday morning about Song and Headley's coffee-and-pastries detour.

Song continued with her briefing.

"Here's our preliminary information. Charlotte Fields, degree from Arizona State—bachelor's, master's. Enrolled in a doctoral program at UNM. She'd met the guy in the closet earlier that week. Said he came by to talk about plants and, uh, genetics. Ancestry stuff. Says she has no idea who killed him. The maintenance guy, Mike Shiosee, was asleep until called. Alibied by his wife. The guy who runs the museum is Dean Patrick MacElroy, PhD, anthropology. Ex-priest." Her eyebrows rose. "Widower, no children. MacElroy said he was in Albuquerque the day before for shopping and was at the Fire-Sky Resort and Casino from about dinnertime until he called the pueblo ride-sharing service. We talked to the driver, Howard Kie. He's confirmed the casino-back-to-the-museum timeline." She swirled the mouse on the desk and clicked. "Turns out the dead guy at the tank was a confidential informant for the Albuquerque police. Explains why the Crybabies cut his throat." Song clicked the mouse again. "We've also received an anonymous tip linking him to a rape in the Heights."

Nicky kept her expression neutral. Luna had said as much that morning.

"Albuquerque Police is handling that lead." Song shifted in her chair. "The other victim is Rémy Tioux, a casino owner-operator out of Biloxi, Mississippi. He is—was—in negotiations to sell his riverboat casino to the Fire-Sky tribe. Been back and forth to New Mexico for the past few years. But here's where it gets interesting. His brother, Perry Tioux, has links to a major drug pipeline and distribution ring in coastal Louisiana and Mississippi."

Nicky rubbed a finger across her lips to hide her surprise. Was this the information Luna's lieutenant would bring tonight? "So Tioux's casino's dirty?" she asked.

"No. You can hardly have a traffic ticket in Mississippi and be associated with a gambling operation. The Gaming Commission in the state is very strict. According to our preliminary investigation, Rémy Tioux's background is squeaky clean. So is the casino's. But you can't choose your family," she said with a shrug. "Assistant SAC Headley's working theory is Chen Cano put out a hit to stop the sale. That the link between the Fire-Sky tribe and the Biloxi casino would open up new territory for Perry Tioux's drug trade. That Cano didn't want the competition." Song sat back, her face a study in neutrality. "Headley believes this was a statement murder. Don't even think about invading my territory or else."

"Rémy Tioux's been traveling to the pueblo for, what, years?" Nicky said. "Why now? Why not a warning first?"

"The deal between Tioux and the pueblo was supposed to be signed yesterday. For some reason, it was delayed. Maybe Cano saw an opportunity and took it."

"Since the Crybabies were offing Angel, might as well make it a two-for-one night?" Nicky didn't even try to keep the sarcasm out of her voice. "Does Agent Headley have an explanation as to why Tioux's body was stuffed in a closet at the museum?"

"We're still going with some kind of initiation," Song said. "His theory involves Rémy Tioux approaching Angel about splitting from the Crybabies and setting up distribution for his brother. When Chen Cano found out, he had them followed and killed. Tioux and Angel would be stealing territory—therefore, the severed hands."

"Why would Tioux approach someone like Angel Benevidez? Besides being a low-level dealer, his autopsy showed he was addicted to meth. There's evidence connecting Tioux and Angel?"

"It's possible Angel's CI handlers have that info."

So, no links yet, but it was early in the investigation. "Why was the riverboat casino deal delayed?" Nicky asked.

"We don't know. We'll be applying for subpoena next week to access the paperwork."

"Next week? Why wait?"

The agent's fingernails tapped a rolling tattoo on the desk. "We don't have any evidence that will stand up in court that Cano murdered Tioux to stop the casino deal."

Nicky parsed Song's statement. Did that mean they had evidence that wouldn't stand up in court? Were Agent Song and Headley keeping information from their law enforcement partners? It wouldn't surprise her. And she could play the game, too.

"Headley and I leave for Biloxi tomorrow. He's convinced interviewing the casino's board and family members will turn up some type of advanced threat or warning from Cano to Tioux." She shrugged. "We're accompanying Rémy Tioux's body."

Nicky straightened in her chair. "This is a murder investigation. You're not keeping the body here as evidence?"

"Turns out Tioux's Indigenous. Natchez Nation. The FBI wants to show it's accommodating to Native American religious practices."

"Tioux's tribe has similar burial customs?" In the pueblo tradition, burials occurred within forty-eight hours of death. New Mexico even passed a law to mandate release of bodies from state or federal custody.

"I don't know. They asked, so we signed the paperwork. It might help future cooperation with other Indigenous sovereign people. Doesn't New Mexico have twenty-three federally recognized tribes? Nineteen Pueblos, three Apache, and…" She pressed her lips together and dropped her gaze to the yellow pad.

"And the Navajo Nation," Nicky finished. "You've done your homework, Agent Song."

In Nicky's experience, most agents passing through Indian Country on field rotations didn't care to learn about the people, traditions, or culture. They'd bully their way through the rotation or maintain their distance. Then they left.

The agent made a noncommittal sound. "While SAC Headley and I are in Biloxi, we'd like you and your partner to do interviews at the

Fire-Sky casino on Tioux's whereabouts the day he was killed. I'll send you his cell phone records and cell tower pings as soon as they drop. Your partner's Ryan Bernal, correct?"

"I don't have a partner," Nicky said. "Most of the time we're too shorthanded on the pueblo to be paired up."

Song smiled, but it didn't reach her eyes. "Headley called your chief of police and detailed what we need from your department. You're to maintain your secondary role in our investigation, especially now that there are national implications. This could turn out to be a very important case, Sergeant Matthews. The FBI has the resources and expertise. We don't need your people." She stopped abruptly.

Aw. And here she was beginning to like Sylvia Song. "Messing things up?" Nicky said. "Even though one of the bodies was found on Fire-Sky sovereign land?"

"You got your training where, Sergeant Matthews? In Artesia, New Mexico, right?" Song tipped her head to the side and pinned Nicky with a faintly patronizing look. "I heard a little bit about you from one of our agents. He worked undercover on your reservation earlier this year and said you have an unnerving tendency to act first and think later."

The Blood Quantum murders. Fire-Sky tribe members chosen by the killer because of their genetic makeup. There'd been two undercover agents on the pueblo for that case. One from the FBI—she'd bet he was the blabbermouth—and one from the DEA: Franco Martinez. Franco had betrayed her trust then, too, by getting her suspended. His superiors had ordered it, so she'd forgiven him. But two months ago, after she and Franco had solved the Stone Fetish murders, he'd betrayed her trust all on his own.

Luckily, she was over it.

Nicky sat back and purposefully relaxed her body. "Act first and think later. Not true. It turns out I can act and think at the same time. It's something we learned to do in Artesia, New Mexico. Don't they teach that at Quantico, Virginia?"

Song blinked at Nicky's mocking tone but quickly hid her response under a completely neutral expression. "Tioux's movements in New

Mexico are where we need you to focus while Agent Headley and I are gone. Put together a timeline. Preliminary info says he had a rental car from the casino concierge service. It's still unaccounted for. We have an APB out for it, and LoJack's been activated, but so far nothing. I'll email you the plate number and description. Anything else?"

"Charlotte Fields was a witness, in the museum, when the bad guys broke in. Does Headley have a theory as to why she wasn't murdered, too?"

"Who knows how these gangbangers think?" Song stood. "Thank you for your time, Sergeant Matthews. We'll keep in touch."

CHAPTER ELEVEN

"It all happened so fast."

Nicky sat with Charlotte Fields in the museum café. Picture windows framed the deserted courtyard, and a misty rain fell, dark clouds filtering the feeble sunlight. The museum was closed until Monday. It would be cleansed and blessed in ceremonies that weekend.

"What were your impressions on the size and age of your assailants?"

Charlotte nibbled her lip and pulled the edge of her sleeves halfway over her hands. She was dressed in the same heavy tunic-length sweater—a deep purple that brought out the green of her eyes —and the thick leggings Nicky had seen her in that morning. But she'd pulled back her hair in a low ponytail.

"Those FBI agents asked me the same thing, so I've been thinking about it, but I really didn't see them. It was late. I thought a door slammed and maybe it was Dean. I came downstairs, and they hit me." Charlotte rubbed shaking fingers between her brows and looked ready to cry. "Like I said, the voices I heard sounded male, but I could be wrong. I think I was barely conscious. I'm sorry."

Nicky softened her features. "Don't be sorry for being a victim. None of this was your fault. I only have a few more questions."

Charlotte nodded and took a deep breath.

"Do you ever use the door the assailants came through? The one to the horno ovens?"

"Yes. Sometimes. But not yesterday."

Mike Shiosee had already given Nicky a list of the access code usage the day of the break-in. The last time any door was opened was at 8:04 P.M., the time Charlotte said she'd gone back to the museum to work. CSU hadn't found fingerprints on the ingress door, inside or out, or the supply closet where the body was found. The doors appeared to have been thoroughly wiped down with cleaner. Nor were prints found on the outside of the janitor's closet where Charlotte had been locked. It could have been attributed to housekeeping, but the rest of the cultural center was a morass of fingerprints from hundreds if not thousands of tourists. FBI was handling identification, but the results would take weeks.

It was just odd the perps would take the time to clean, unless they hadn't been wearing gloves. Nicky tucked that anomaly to one side of her brain.

"What were you working on when you heard the noise and went to investigate?" Nicky asked.

"The fertility and wedding vase exhibition. We're so far behind, and now with all this…" Charlotte's mouth pinched with worry.

"Did you receive any calls Tuesday night?"

"Not on the museum phone. On my personal cell phone, yes. Two. From my brother."

"What's his name?"

"Daniel Fields. He's between jobs right now. He wanted to borrow some money." She shrugged; her smile was embarrassed. "Siblings."

"What time did your brother call?"

Charlotte pulled out her phone. "Ten forty-nine and twelve-fifteen. The second call lasted less than a minute. I told him what he could do with his request and hung up. He always expects me to solve his problems." Charlotte's blush was accompanied with eyes that flashed with anger before she blinked it away.

"What does your brother do for a living?"

"Heavy equipment operator, lumberyards, construction, stuff like that. The last place he lived was Oregon."

"About the deceased," Nicky said. "You told the FBI you'd spoken to him before?"

"Yes. I didn't recognize him because of the … damage." Charlotte's face had paled. "And I didn't really *know* him. He came to the museum looking for someone to identify some native plants. Brought them in zipper bags. My master's was in ethnobotany of the southwestern United States and northern Mexico, so I was able to identify most of what he had."

Which could explain the baggie in Rémy Tioux's pocket. Julie had said she didn't think it was marijuana.

"How many times did he come by?"

"A couple of times in the last week. I think Dean saw him once— last Friday? I couldn't identify one of the herbs. Dean did. I saw him again on Monday, the day before … before…" Charlotte swallowed and stared at her knotted fingers. "We didn't talk that day or anything."

"Did he say where he got these plants he needed identified?"

"No. I assumed from around the reservation or maybe a farmer's market or herbal pharmacy."

"What were they?" Nicky asked.

"Medicinal plants, mostly." Charlotte's brow knit. "The first time, he had a baggie with blue cohosh. *Caulophyllum thalictroides*. Dean identified that one. It's why we thought he'd been visiting herbal pharmacies. It only grows in the eastern United States. The other bag contained oshá root. *Ligusticum porteri*. It smells like very strong celery, so that was an easy one. People used it in love potions." Charlotte smiled. "Perfect for weddings—it's supposed to increase the likelihood of pregnancy. Supposedly it contains oxytocin, but studies have debunked that. The second time he came by, he brought in valerian root. *Valerian arizonica* or *edulis*. It was hard to tell which one. When they're dry, they're ... pungent." She wrinkled her nose. "Like blue cheese and dirty socks. Isovaleric acid. It's used in teas to decrease stress and increase fertility. Basically, he brought in herbs used in Fire-Sky fertility medicines. In fact, part of the exhibition we're setting up is about the usage of medicinal plants for fertility. But you'd know that, right? Because of your mother's research."

Nicky should've expected a woman who'd trained in ethnobotany would know who her mother was. It wasn't like her mom's publications were a secret. She looked down at her notes, avoiding Charlotte's scrutiny. "Did Mr. Tioux give you the reason he wanted this information?"

"No. But, he seemed really sad and frustrated."

Nicky raised her eyes. "Why do you say that?"

Charlotte shrugged. "Just a feeling."

"Did he say anything else?"

"He asked if I knew anything about ancestry or DNA." She dropped her gaze to her knotted her fingers. "I don't."

"Did he say why he needed that kind of information?"

Charlotte shook her head.

"At Starbucks this morning," Nicky said, "you said you and Dean would do a thorough search today to see if the perps took anything. Did you find anything?"

"At first, we didn't think those monsters"—she swallowed—"had taken anything. I mean, to break in and leave a ... a *body*. It must've been some kind of warning or—or message, right?" She leaned toward Nicky. "But *Dean* thinks..." Charlotte bit her lip. "Let me go get him. He can explain."

With this cryptic comment, Charlotte hurried from the café into the empty hallway. Nicky followed more slowly, tamping down unnamed emotions that always invaded whenever her mother came up. She'd known this might happen—not under the circumstances of a murder but since the summer. When Dean had announced the wedding and fertility exhibition. She should've confronted him about it. Instead, like a child, she'd avoided it, hoping it would go away. But the murder had taken away her ability to avoid the connection. She was literally a captive audience because her job, no, her *career* demanded it. A career her mother had vehemently disapproved of.

She blew out a sigh and leaned over the banco set under a series of windows frosted with abstract Native American design elements: clouds slanting stylized rain, stepped pyramids representing mesas, spirals denoting wind or water.

Firm, hurried footsteps sounded at the end of the hall, and the lean form of Dean MacElroy approached, arms outstretched, Charlotte behind him. Nicky stepped close and embraced him tightly, breathing in the mint and sage that always seemed to grace his person—an imprint scent she remembered fondly from her childhood.

"Oh, Nicky, this is just so horrible. If only your mother—" Dean stopped.

Nicky stared at him, brows puckered. If only her mother—what? She stilled at Charlotte's expression. The woman's face was tight, her eyes unfocused, as if she were looking right through Dean's back. Then Charlotte blinked and caught Nicky's arrested gaze, blushing, the softness returning to her cheeks.

Dean straightened and held Nicky at arm's length.

"I am *so* sorry you were assigned to such a terrible murder, my dear, but at the same time, there's no one I trust more to solve it." White hair haloed his face, his beard merging into his sideburns that then blended into an arch of hair high on his forehead. Lack of a mustache gave him an old-fashioned professorial appearance that only complemented his reputation as one of the finest curators in the nation of Puebloan culture. The Tsiba'ashi D'yini Tribal Council had been ecstatic when he'd accepted the position at the Isgaawa Cultural Center and Museum two decades ago.

"I'm only ancillary to the FBI, Dean," Nicky said. "They make the final decisions."

"I still feel much better going forward with you here." Dean turned. "Lottie, you must be exhausted. You can go home now."

Nicky frowned. "But—"

Dean caught her eye, his hand tightening on her arm. She bit off her words.

"You have my card," Nicky said, smiling to soften Dean's dismissal. "Please call me if you remember anything else."

Charlotte's gaze traveled back and forth between the two of them before she nodded and faded out of the hallway.

Dean waited for the sound of a door closing before he said, "Follow me." His voice was hushed even though they were the only two people in the museum.

Dean led her down the series of hallways and through the heavy wooden double doors into the Siow-Carr Gallery—double doors completely open now. Nicky squared her shoulders and followed him inside the huge high-ceilinged room, absorbing the details she'd missed the night of the murder.

Walls painted a rich blue gray contrasted with the browns, tans, and deep reds of the display cases, made to look like the stacked adobe of ancient dwellings. A ladder sat underneath canister lights waiting for adjustment. Against the far wall, a large, stretched canvas showing an ancient joining ceremony stood half finished, a utility cart beside it filled with plastic bottles of acrylic paint and brushes. Wedding and fertility vases were already displayed in a full-sized diorama or singly in blocky glass-covered plinths. Dean led Nicky past a canted table with a display of dried herbs and bright photos of the plants in situ, legends in both English and Keres written underneath.

With a curl of unease, Nicky's gaze slid toward the back corner of the room and the birthing-niche display, the melodious drops of water trickling into the stone basin.

"A preliminary inventory of the room—of the whole museum—told us nothing had been taken, even though some of these pots are literally priceless because of their age and provenance. But"—Dean gestured at a glass box with a double-spouted vase—"this pot was moved. The murderers came to this room."

"Moved? By the murderers? How can you tell?" Nicky asked.

"The lighting. A shift in the shadows and the design motifs." Dean's lips flickered in a smile, but the skin around his eyes was taut. "Lottie noticed the change right away. We thought at first some of the pots had been stolen and replaced by fakes, but all of these are the original pieces."

"There were a lot of people going in and out after the break-in was reported. You don't think the changes in the pots' positions were because of the CSU team?"

"No. I was allowed to supervise."

"But you didn't notice it at that time?"

Dean shook his head.

"There should be crime-scene pictures, so we can compare to your photos, just to make sure."

"Nicky. I am sure."

The grave tone of his voice arrested her.

He gestured toward a clay wedding vase, its two spouts—one representing the husband, one the wife—joined by a double twist of red clay. A spiral painted on the bowl was faded with age.

"Middle Gila polychrome. We believe the black paint is *Cleome serrulata* and hematite, the red is a clay slip, as well as the cream. Normally, these vases were held for weeks by a medicine man, who'd bless and pray over them. They'd be filled with sweet grasses, sacred plants, herbs. Sometimes mixtures were brewed and poured into the interior, only to be boiled off again or dried. The interior was left imbued with residues believed to contribute to longevity within the marriage. A love potion if you will. More tea would be added during the actual ceremony, and the couple would drink. The same, of course, was done with fertility vases. But you know this"—he gave her a quick apologetic smile—"because some of the ancient contents were identified by pioneering work using scrapings from the inside of these pots."

Nicky's throat dried. "Dean."

"The composition of these teas was scientifically analyzed to determine if they contained organic substances that could be tested for modern medicinal uses. After all, it was known for centuries that brewing willow bark calmed headaches because it contained an ingredient similar to that found in aspirin. What else might we find? A cancer treatment? Natural antibiotics? A cure for the common cold? Of course, this all occurred before the tribe put a stop to what they considered a desecration of their culture and traditions." He fixed her with a look. "But not before your mother did the analysis on this pot and about half a dozen other pieces in the exhibit."

Bands seemed to tighten around her chest. "Dean. No."

"The interior of the pots your mother sampled were carefully scraped, dust and chips collected. The sampling was recorded in their descriptions. For instance, this vessel has three scrapes from her work."

He slipped on gloves he'd pulled from a pocket and lifted the glass box surrounding the vase. Gingerly, he picked up the pot, tipping it toward her. "Look inside."

Nicky switched on her flashlight.

The pot was empty of material, but along the curved bottom, her light picked up three shallow scratches, all running in the same direction. Her mother's samples were taken from the residue.

But lying across those scratches were two horizontal slashes, jagged and fresh.

"The people who broke into the museum and left the body, they did that. They took another sample from this pot, from all the pots your mother analyzed years ago. I checked. I don't know why, but there is one person who could shed light on what is going on here."

Nicky met his eyes, lips pinched. "Stop." But it came out as a whisper.

"For whatever reason, your mother's work is linked to the break-in and to a murdered man who was asking about fertility herbs." Dean's expression was fraught with worry. "I don't like this, Nicky. And I don't think you should tell your superiors or the FBI about it until we can get more information. I think we should call—"

"*No*. I'm *not* calling my mother for help. I can handle this. Alone."

Nicky looked away from him, angry at the burn behind her eyes. She would not cry. She'd wasted too many tears as a kid. "Besides, I don't even know where she is."

CHAPTER TWELVE

NICKY PULLED her unit into the open carport beside her home and cut the engine and headlights. An overcast moon threw scant shadows only incrementally blacker than the night, but she could still make out the sharp edges of the old corral fence and the blurred winter skeletons of fruit trees in her backyard. A few leaves still clung to the branches, shivering in a quiet wind. The rain had stopped for now.

In the darkness, she laid her forehead against hands clasped on the steering wheel. Normally the drive home was a personal debrief, a chance to relax and unwind. But tonight, with the murders, the odd pot scrapings, and even odder connection to her mother, meaning she'd need to review her mother's publications on the pot scrapings … Her hands tightened on the wheel.

The motion detector lights hadn't switched on.

Nicky lifted her head, alert. Power outage? Her neighbor's sodium porchlight glowed yellow. Only her house was out? Not likely. Taking in a shaky breath, she pressed the release on her holster, sliding her Glock out with a scratch of sound, and opened the car door. Sticking to the shadows, Nicky skirted her truck and tried the door to her home. Locked. She crept to the back of the carport and scanned the backyard.

The acrid smell of cigarette smoke tainted the air.

"Luna sent me," a voice rasped. "You're late."

The tip of the cigarette glowed in the darkness, placing the man at the edge of her patio.

"Forgot to mark it on my calendar," she said evenly, willing her heartbeat to slow. "I'll let you in the back. Anything you want to keep, leave outside."

She unlocked the side door, stepped inside, and turned the dead-bolt behind her. The light in the utility room worked. That meant this SOB had tampered with her security lights.

A quick search of her home showed it to be free of intruders. She strode back into the utility room and unlocked the door to the back-yard. When she pulled it halfway open, a strong draught of cigarette smoke snaked inside.

Nicky backed away, gun in hand, finger over the trigger guard. She slipped behind the entrance to the kitchen, body shielded, gaze steady on the figure outside. "Keep your hands where I can see them," she said. "No smoking in my house."

The red glow fell to the cement and winked out under a boot. He shouldered the door wider, bumping it against the dryer, and sidled through, one hand palm up, fingers spread. The other clasped a manila file folder.

"Turn around," Nicky ordered. "You know the drill."

He shuffled backward into the open kitchen-den. She holstered her sidearm and patted him down. No weapons. She plucked the file from his fingers, tossed it on her kitchen table, and cuffed him.

"Not necessary," he said.

She grasped him by one elbow and marched him to a chair at the kitchen table.

"Sit. Don't move." Nicky pivoted to the kitchen and turned on the fluorescent light over the sink.

"Too bright." Face screwed up, he squinted his eyes.

"Scatters the cockroaches," she said. "Usually."

Nicky studied the man. Black jeans and sweatshirt, lean, slightly more than medium height with medium skin. Dark hair cut stubble short, smooth cheeks, lips thin but sculpted. Good-looking in a cruel sort of way.

"Javier, right?" Nicky said. "You were with your boss at Starbucks this morning. And earlier this year when she broke into my house to introduce herself." She left the first place she'd seen him unsaid.

He inclined his head, his sharp gaze never leaving her face. Her eyes clashed with his. Even cuffed and disarmed, he fought to take control. She remained silent, feet spread, arms folded, and let the tension build.

Then she broke it. "Would you like a cup of coffee?"

He blinked. Opened his mouth. Closed it on a sneer. "What is it with cops and coffee?"

She raised her eyebrows. "Do you want some or not?"

"Three sugars. And that hazelnut-cream stuff unless you have pumpkin spice." He swiveled on the chair and looked around. "This place looks different. Better. You painted?"

He sat at a small table with two chairs that divided the large rectangular room. Across the Saltillo tile floor from the kitchen was a comfortable denim-upholstered sofa, matching loveseat, and carved wooden coffee and side table, all new. Same with the kitchen appliances, but she hadn't touched the scarred red countertops or white-painted cupboards. They held too many memories of her grandmother.

The airy hiss of the coffee maker signaled the pot was full, the rich scent of dark roast wiping out the lingering stench of cigarettes. After she doctored her mug with sweetener, Nicky fixed Javier's.

She placed his mug on the table and unlocked the cuffs before she went back into the kitchen and leaned against the edge of the sink.

"Talk," she said.

"The folder contains the information we have on the dead guy at the museum, Rémy Tioux. Luna again wants to assure you she did not mandate his death," he said in a soft, ominous monotone. He took a sip of his pumpkin-spice-flavored coffee. "'S good."

Nicky acknowledged the compliment with a dip of her chin.

"Tioux is out of Mississippi." Javier opened the file and spread the papers inside, extracting one. "He owns a Biloxi riverboat casino. That's why he was here. To meet the Fire-Sky Tribal Council and CEO of economic development. A reciprocal visit, it appears. Three of the council members, the CEO, and their wives went to Biloxi a few months ago, ostensibly for a vacation."

Ostensibly? Nicky wondered if he noticed he'd changed his tone and speech pattern. She ambled back to the kitchen table and sat down across from Javier, cradling her coffee.

"I know all this," she said.

He tugged out another page. "Tioux's clean. His brother, Perry, is not. Drugs, prostitution, money laundering. Easy to do in a casino."

"But Rémy Tioux kept him out. Old news, Javier." She brushed the paper to one side, not even looking at it.

The man smiled. A third page pulled. "The pretty FBI agent told you they are leaving on a jet plane tomorrow. Interviews with the Biloxi casino's board and Rémy Tioux's family. But did Agent Song brief you on Perry Tioux's call to Chen Cano yesterday morning?"

Nicky stiffened, then kicked herself for the tell when Javier's smile widened.

"Secretive bastards. Wanting all the credit for themselves. In this call, Perry Tioux was *very* upset about his brother's death because he'd heard the Crybabies murdered Rémy as a warning to him. It was an extremely unfortunate conversation. French, Mandarin, Spanish— insults and threats thrown around in *such* dramatic fashion." His eyes, brown and sharp, watched her closely.

Nicky thunked her mug down on the table. "It was staged. Why?"

"To get the FBI out of New Mexico and out of your way. Chen— Luna—wishes to be absolved of the crime. She trusts you to find out who did this killing." He took a sip of coffee.

"Then they must've talked before they set up the fake call. Did Perry Tioux give Luna any information I can use?"

"He was worried about his brother's mental state. That lately he'd been distracted and sad."

Nicky breathed an internal sigh of relief. Nothing about her mother or the pot scrapings.

"That's it? Rémy Tioux was sad? What am I supposed to do with that?" she asked. But Charlotte Fields had said something similar.

"You're the cop. You figure it out." He slouched in his chair, gang persona back in place. "Because if you don't, Perry Tioux has associates who will come to your reservation and figure out who murdered his brother. Then Luna would have to step in and protect her territory. It will get very messy if she has to deal with this her way."

Nicky's jaw tightened at the threat.

Javier pulled out another page and laid it in front of her. On it was a New Mexico license plate number. "This car was seen near the tank where Angel … died. Two people inside. The one driving very large, the one beside him much smaller. Too dark to see faces."

"Did you help kill Angel Benevidez?" she asked, voice hard.

"No. I would have dumped that pinche culero at the nearest police station. Alive, so he could be prosecuted. The family of the old lady he raped and killed deserved that. But Luna has her own idea of justice, and she's the boss. Now it's my turn to ask a question." He held her gaze steady. "Very few know about Luna. They still see the mythical Chen Cano as the head of the Crybabies. Having a queenpin"—his expression softened—"as a friend would not bode well for a cop if someone found out. I can't make sense of it. And you are nothing but a danger to her. Why haven't you ratted her out?"

"I have my reasons."

"Give me one." He tapped a finger on the table. "Reassure me, Police Sergeant Nicky Matthews."

She offered him the easiest lie. "Luna owes me a life debt for saving her son. That's too valuable to trade or destroy."

The sneer was back. "Just like a cop. Out for what you can get." He drained his coffee and stood.

Nicky followed him as he slipped out through the utility room door. She crossed her arms and leaned against the threshold. Enough light filtered around her to showcase an array of weapons on the small wrought-iron patio table. Javier tucked them away one by one.

He'd tell Luna what she'd said, and it would hurt her friend. She didn't want that.

"You know the real reason I haven't turned her in?" Nicky asked. Javier stilled for a moment. "To give her time to figure out what's important in her life."

He swept up the last of his weapons. Nicky thought she heard him sigh.

"Just like a cop. Trying to save the world from itself." But he sounded strained, even sad. "If Luna finds out anything more, I'll be back." He stepped off the porch and into the darkness.

"Hey," she called. "Next time, leave my motion lights alone."

"Hey," he said, his voice mocking. "I didn't touch your lights."

NICKY GRABBED a package of replacement lights and gloves from a box in her bathroom so she could take the old bulbs to test for fingerprints. Carefully positioning her stepladder, she gathered and bagged the old lights—each one had been loosened from their sockets—and screwed in new ones, averting her face when they popped on.

There were a couple of easy explanations for the tampering: teenage prank, burglars scared off by a passing car or Javier's arrival. The third possibility wasn't so easy. She'd been attacked in her home twice—six years ago and six months ago—by the wife of an ex-lover because the woman thought her husband and Nicky had resumed their relationship. But those attacks had been impulsive. This felt different. Premeditated. Which led to the unsettling conclusion that the perpetrator's motive was unknown.

It had started to rain again, and the shoulders and back of her shirt were getting damp. Nicky bagged the final bulb and stowed the stepladder. Shivering, she headed inside, locking the door behind her. But instead of changing into something dry, she sat at her kitchen table and tugged out her phone.

Compelled by a need to share with someone—from boiling black shadows in the museum and earthen tanks, threats of revenge by regional drug lords, to why her mother might be at the center of a murder investigation—she scrolled through her contact list, pausing at the *M*'s. Franco Martinez's name was absent. He'd blocked her calls and texts after their last major case together. In a fit of anger and hurt, she'd retaliated and deleted Franco from her phone and her life.

Then, yesterday, Ryan had insisted she try to reach out to Franco again. Yesterday, Franco had saved her from being pulled into the water. Yesterday, something had changed, and a tiny flare of hope had ignited.

It didn't matter that she'd deleted his information. His number was etched in her brain. But should she call him?

Nicky twisted her lips into a self-mocking smile. Who was she kidding? He probably wouldn't answer, and if he did, he'd be cold and professional like he'd been whenever they'd coordinated on a case in the past months. Like he'd been yesterday, before and after their fall.

She scrolled to another name, touched it. Chest tight, she stared at her mother's contact information on the screen. They rarely spoke as it was, and with her mother's most recent betrayal—

Before she could talk herself out of it, she touched the icon and pressed the cold glass of her cell against her ear.

It rang ten times before it switched to voicemail. The box was full.

Which was fine. She didn't need her mother or Franco.

Nicky washed Javier's cup, filled her own again, and sat down, this time to dust the security bulbs for fingerprints. Nothing. Not even her old prints. They'd been wiped clean.

She sighed. One more task to complete that evening: rereading her mother's research papers to see if they held any information that could help explain the break-in and murder at the museum.

After cleaning up, she headed down the hallway to her grandmother's old room. Even though she'd hosted no one for years, she kept it as a guest room. Simply furnished, it held a full-sized bed in a metal frame, its coverlet a Native American blanket made of a cotton-wool mix, and a wooden cross hanging on the wall above the pillows. She sat her coffee cup on top of the tall chest of drawers next to her favorite picture, one of her grandmother and herself at seven years old, sitting bareback on a brown horse, both beaming at the camera.

Nicky opened the closet. Boxes, photo albums, and folders full of mementoes her grandmother had felt were too precious to throw away were packed precariously on the shelf above the hanging rod. Nicky had also saved reprints of her mother's scientific publications in one of the folders, at one point hoping to add her own to the substantial stack. That certainly hadn't panned out.

She tugged at the folder containing the papers, dislodged a disintegrating scrapbook, and barely saved it from crashing to the floor by juggling it onto the bed, where it spilled flotsam from her childhood: a third-grade report card, a ribbon from a high school swim meet, a sweet-sixteen birthday card. Nicky gathered up the papers and sat. The familiar creak of bedsprings, something she'd heard every night when her grandmother went to bed, had comforted her growing up. Reassured her that she wasn't alone in the house.

Now, the sound made her want to cry.

Stop stalling. She shuffled the loose material between pages and had stood to jam the scrapbook back in the closet when she noticed a missed piece of paper at her feet. With an exasperated sigh, Nicky bent and picked it up.

And stilled. A rushing of sound—wind or fast-moving water—filled her head.

She didn't remember coloring the picture; she must have been very young, her name written in careful cursive letters at the bottom. A pot with a spiral decoration lay on a yellow floor inside a room with cross-hatched lines that made up its wall—bricks, except the uneven rectangles were tan and brown like the stacked rock walls of an ancient pueblo. A thick scribbled layer of gray crayon formed a ragged opening in the wall. A doorway or ... portal. One she'd seen, she knew.

It had hung over the pool of water at the base of the birthing niche during her walk-through of the museum the night of the murders, had seethed underwater at the earthen tank before she'd retrieved the severed hand.

There was one difference, though. Inside the drawing's doorway stood the black shadow of a little girl, her needle-sharp teeth bared in a bone-chilling smile.

CHAPTER THIRTEEN

NICKY SAT at her desk in the busy police department squad room, staring at her written notes, trying without much success to ignore the raucous laughter coming from the break room. Her plans to visit the Fire-Sky resort and interview the concierge attendants about Tioux's rental car had been derailed by the interim police chief's text at six that morning. She was to report at nine o'clock with an update on the investigation. To prep, she'd come into work early, reread autopsy reports, FBI files, reviewed collected evidence, and attempted to assemble the scant information in a direction other than a potential war between the Crybabies and an avenging flock of Mississippi gangbangers descending on New Mexico—SAC Headley's crap theory.

Then, of course, there was information she hadn't yet added to the file—the pot scrapings. Nicky dropped her head and pressed balled fists against her temples.

Dean's discovery contributed to her niggling headache because the scraping didn't fit. No. That was a lie. They made too much sense: Tioux with his questions and baggies of medicinal plants must be connected to the fertility and wedding vases her mother had analyzed thirty years ago. But how were those clues linked to two brutal murders?

Another rumble of voices followed by another eruption of laughter. Heads swiveled toward the noise, work interrupted.

Enough. Nicky stood, jaw set, and marched to the break room. She stared at the clot of uniformed personnel. Styrofoam cups of coffee and donuts in hand, they stood or sat in a semicircle around an officer who held a tablet. Nicky's glare wiped away grins as officers hurried past her and out of the room until only two men remained. Manny Valentine and Franco Martinez.

Valentine flipped the tablet screen down on the table and settled back in his chair, his expression one of challenge. He'd been a thorn in her side almost from his first day on the job, part of a good-old-boys' network dubbed the "Captain's Crew." Their actions toward those outside their group crossed the line of disrespect too many times for it to go unnoticed, but the captain had pulled their asses from the fire more than once. Valentine was the worst of the lot.

Nicky bared her teeth in a smile. "We've played this game before, Valentine. You always lose."

He grinned, his thick brown mustache curving over his upper lip. "Really, Matthews?" His chair scraped as he stood. Valentine clapped a hand on the shoulder of the man still seated at the table, his eyes boring into Nicky. "Whaddya say, Franco? Beers tonight with me and the guys. Seven-thirty. My place. I'll text you the address."

Franco stood. "Sure."

Triumphant, Valentine winked at Nicky as he left.

Not bothering to hide her disappointment, she met Franco's gaze. "It absolutely amazes me that you've become a part of Valentine's cohort of misogynistic jack-holes." She hadn't voluntarily said a word to him for weeks, not even thanking him for saving her from a soaking at the tank.

Franco strode around the table. Silver threads stood out starkly in the dark brown hair of his temples. A khaki shirt outlined bulky shoulders, and olive-green cargo pants molded muscular thighs, the uniform of the pueblo's Conservation Department. A broad utility belt wrapped around a trim waist and flat stomach, his Glock strapped on his right and a flashlight, Taser, gloves, cuffs, and pouches with extra magazines attached all around.

He stepped in close as he poured himself a cup of coffee, the scent of his woodsy aftershave tickling her nose. She refused to budge.

His gaze dropped to her lips for a long second before he met her eyes again. Could he hear her heart hammering under the buzz of the fluorescent lights? He leaned toward her.

"You know what, Matthews? Maybe you never really knew me at all."

Nicky's smoldering emotions blazed. She took a half step forward, crowding in on him, the heat of her anger burning around them.

"And maybe—just maybe—you should have given me an ounce of trust, should have let me explain what happened instead of jumping to all the wrong conclusions," she hissed. "Dax *never*—"

"*Bullshit*." He squared into her, teeth clenched. "It's always been Dax Stone, hasn't it? Room for no one else. You don't even see how much he still has you hooked. How much your career still depends on his … patronage."

Her breath caught, hurt crashing over her. She stepped away from him. "You have been spending too much time with Captain's Crew if you buy into their garbage." She swallowed the ache in her throat. "Dax and I were over a long time ago. But that's nobody's business."

Heavy silence pressed down on them. She knew she should leave, knew that getting through to him was futile, but waited anyway. Franco frowned into his coffee before meeting her eyes. He took a breath.

"Nicky?" Savannah Analla's voice shattered the tension. "Chief's ready for you now."

Savannah was the director of public safety's executive assistant, acting secretary for the interim chief, and Nicky's best friend since she'd started at the Fire-Sky police force, and Nicky wanted to scream at her to leave.

"Franco? Did you get my text about tomorrow night?" Savannah took a tentative step into the break room, her hesitant smile in her pretty round face exposing the gap between her front teeth. The room's fluorescent lights gleamed off her asymmetric bob of straight dark hair and glinted in her round wire-rimmed glasses. "Maybe one of our last get-togethers before Jinni has her baby. Nicky? You're welcome to come. I've—we ... all of us, have missed you lately. Right, Franco?"

Nicky swung her attention back to Franco. A slight frown knit his brow, the coldness gone from his eyes. He searched her face, looking for what, she couldn't even begin to imagine. She straightened her spine, tilting her chin up.

"Thanks, Savannah, but I have a date."

She brushed past her friend and strode back to her desk to grab her files.

NICKY PAUSED outside the interim chief of police's office. After her disaster of a relationship with Dax Stone—who also happened to be the chief of the New Mexico State Police—ended half a dozen years ago, she'd developed a firm, hard rule: no dating within the confines of law enforcement. With Franco Martinez, she'd almost broken that rule.

It was so much easier to be alone.

Taking a deep breath, she rapped at the door. A brusque "Enter" and she stepped inside. The previous chief had recently retired after receiving a career-ending gunshot wound through her wrist. Still, her bravery would go a long way to get her elected as the first woman in the history of the Fire-Sky People to sit on tribal council.

The tribe had promoted Philip Richards to interim chief. Richards, who'd been captain of the Fire-Sky police for the past two years, had been the head of Captain's Crew and the bane of Nicky's existence. But something had changed radically since his promotion. Maybe someone had warned him that his hostile attitude toward some of his personnel would hinder his ability to be hired permanently as chief. Maybe his increase in professionalism toward her was a ruse. Maybe he'd found Jesus. Whatever it was, in the last few months, Nicky and

Richards's professional relationship had smoothed to one of grudging respect.

"Sergeant Matthews." He smiled, teeth flashing under his narrow bristling mustache, and waved a hand toward a chair. Richards, a short, trim figure in his dark blue uniform, his graying blond hair cut tight over his ears, closed the file cabinet drawer, and marched around his desk. He dropped a heavy folder on one side of his desk before he sat. Behind him was his power wall: photos of him with the governors of the pueblo and the state of New Mexico, local and state dignitaries, even a past US president. On a polished wooden shelf in the center of the photos sat his yellow brick, the one he'd earned at the FBI National Academy after he'd been appointed interim chief. The display mirrored the man's ambition.

"You brought the paperwork and photos on the recent homicides?" Richards asked.

"Yes, sir." She handed a stack of files across his desk, noting the absence of a computer screen and keyboard.

A whiteboard stood to one side of the room, RHYERSON TANK written in red dry-erase marker across the top right of the board, MUSEUM written to its left, and a double arrow linking them. The rest of the board was blank.

Chief laid the files precisely in the middle of a rectangular blotter and opened the top one. "I still like the heft of paper and the visual of the whiteboard. Just a dinosaur, I guess. Don't know that I'll ever be able to change. Now, let's have your summary, Sergeant. Who are our victims? Start with the body at Rhyerson Tank." He spread out a handful of photos.

"Durwin Angel Benevidez." Nicky ran through the details of the homicide, Chief shooting her detailed, intelligent questions. She was impressed.

Richards grunted as he slowly perused the crime-scene glossies. "Scum off the street. Maybe we should give the Crybabies a prize instead of trying to arrest them. I just wish they'd dump their bodies someplace other than my reservation."

His reservation. Nicky masked her surprise at that statement. He'd never been so possessive when he was police captain. In fact, he'd bordered on indifferent, even uncaring.

"Any further leads on the machete?"

"No, sir. OMI believes it was the weapon used to kill Benevidez but not Mr. Tioux. That weapon, possibly an ax, hasn't been found, even after the tank was drained. FBI's traced the machete to a Mexican manufacturer, but they sell thousands a year. They believe it's a dead end."

Richards picked up a sheaf of printed papers. Nicky stayed silent as he read them.

"This second fellow, Rémy Tioux. He's more of a problem for us, isn't he? I've already fielded a couple of calls from tribal council."

"Tioux was staying at the Fire-Sky resort at the invitation of the council," Nicky said. "The tribe was in negotiations to buy his Biloxi riverboat casino. The FBI left this morning for Mississippi and Mr. Tioux's funeral."

"I spoke to Ass-SAC Headley"—Richards smirked—"about the theory he's pushing. That Chen Cano put out a hit because of Tioux's brother. Horseshit, unless they're withholding evidence, and I wouldn't put it past them. Territorial bastards. And tribal council's been pretty cagey about Tioux's visit," Chief said. "What have you heard?"

"Nothing official, sir. Only that Tioux flew in from Mississippi a week before he was murdered to finalize the casino sale with Peter Santibanez." Nicky and Peter Santibanez, the CEO of Fire-Sky Tribal Industries, had a less-than-cordial history. It didn't help that Nicky had been indirectly involved in the death of his son earlier that year.

Chief stared hard at her before he nodded and pulled the third file.

"You'll interview Mr. Santibanez as part of your investigation?"

"Yes, sir. He and his wife are in Biloxi for the funeral, too. FBI will do a primary, and I'll do a follow-up once he's returned to New Mexico."

"Santibanez's wife, too?"

"Yes, sir."

"I trust you'll treat Peter Santibanez with more respect than the last time you interviewed him?"

Nicky's teeth set. "He was a viable suspect in a *series* of tribe-member murders."

"I know, I know." Chief smiled in understanding. "A difficult case. One where you made the Fire-Sky Police Department proud, Sergeant. But right now, we need whatever information Santibanez has without antagonizing him. Understand?"

"Yes, sir." His compliment diffused her anger.

"Now," Richards said mildly. "Explain to me about these pot scrapings and why they aren't included in your report."

Nicky's jaw almost dropped. *Who told Chief Richards?* Not Dean. He'd been insistent about keeping quiet until they found a connection. Charlotte Fields? But surely Dean *told* her—

She cleared her throat, an attempt to recover. "I-I didn't include them because I only found out about them last night. I haven't had time."

Richards waved her to a stop, his smile almost benevolent. "I understand, Sergeant. Things are moving fast."

Nicky shifted on the chair. This was a side of Richards she hadn't been exposed to before. She wasn't completely sure she trusted it. "It's the only link the museum director could find to the break-in. Nothing else of value was taken."

Light green eyes met hers. He held a close-up of the inside of one of the pots, three heavily scored lines like fresh wounds in the clay.

"Is this of value?"

"Possibly." Nicky searched for the best way to explain. "Clay is porous. The pots absorb traces of whatever was placed inside: food, medicinal plants, traditional teas, or potions. The samples from these scratches could be analyzed for historic or cultural knowledge. Or for medicinally useful compounds."

"Like ... bioprospecting." His eyes glinted under the fluorescent lights.

Nicky looked down at her threaded fingers, again to hide her surprise. The microorganism that had infected her had the potential to make the tribe and their economic partners millions. That kind of money attracted speculators, prospectors, and trespassers hoping to strike it rich off the pueblo's biodiverse natural resources.

"Rémy Tioux had baggies filled with medicinal herbs he took to the museum for identification," Chief continued. "But you report these plants are very common. No value there."

He opened the file folder he'd dropped on his desk when Nicky had arrived. Paper hissed over wood as Chief slid a printed abstract toward her. Her pulse quickened as she read the title: *Upscaling organic residue analyses of archaeological ceramics.* When he was captain, Richards had never shown this much insight on cases. She'd chalked that up to a man who'd reached his position not by merit but by brownnosing his superiors. Nicky quickly adjusted her perceptions.

"I don't pretend to understand the science," he said, "but if someone resorted to murder, there must have been something very valuable inside that clay."

Nicky tensed. How much did he know about her mother's research?

"Those pots—the ones with the fresh scrapings—had already been analyzed," she said. "I don't believe anything of value was found."

Richards sat back in his chair. He stared at her through narrowed eyes.

"It's a line of enquiry I'd like you to pursue, Sergeant. We'll bring in experts if necessary." He pursed his lips as he tucked crime-scene photos back in the folder. "One more thing. Conservation has informed me some of the sacred sites on the pueblo have been disturbed recently. Not the hunting shrines. That stopped with the warehouse fire. These sites are areas where the tribal caciques and war chiefs harvest traditional plants for their ceremonies and medicines. Conservation's kept it under wraps by assigning non-Natives to the investigation. You know how quickly gossip spreads around the pueblo."

"Yes, sir."

Richards gave her a faint smile. "These sites are being systemati- cally dug up—the vegetation and soil carried away. Stolen. I can't help but think the theft of traditional plants in situ might be related to the theft of traditional, er, *organic residue* scraped from the bottom of these old pots. Which means the desecrations of the garden sites could also be related to Rémy Tioux's murder. An interesting line of inquiry I want kept ten thirty-five, Sergeant. Confidential. See if we can get ahead of the FBI." He pressed a button on the intercom on his desk. "Savannah? Send in Conservation Agent Martinez."

Nicky's breath caught. She swiveled in her chair to stare at the office door. The knob turned, and Franco walked into the room. Their eyes met, his veiled.

"Agent Martinez has all the details on the site desecrations. We'll put out the story that the police are borrowing Martinez for his DEA background and the possible drug angle, because of Crybaby gang involvement in the murders. I've spoken to Ted Brighton over at Conservation, and we agree there might be a link between the two cases. You two will work together as partners until further notice."

Nicky swung around to stare at Chief Richards. She had the distinct impression his eyes glittered with malice.

CHAPTER FOURTEEN

NICKY LINGERED beside her unit in the chill predawn shadows veiling the Fire-Sky Police Department's parking lot, sipping coffee, and eating a dry breakfast burrito. The eastern edges of clouds began to turn pink from a sun still tucked behind the mountains.

Across the expanse of blacktop, Franco jiggled the shovel and high-lift jack that were locked into racks on the back window of his extra-cab pickup truck, its tailpipe puffing moisture-laden exhaust. He checked the tires before he loaded a bulky nylon pack and rifle case.

When he finished stowing his gear, he jogged back inside the building that housed both the Conservation and Fire Department. Nicky took a last hasty bite of burrito before she opened the door of her unit and shouldered her backpack. Her hand hovered over a second cup of coffee in the console, an impulse she'd regretted even as she'd ordered. She and Franco used to do that for each other in the past, sometimes even *accidentally* meeting at the Bernalillo Starbucks. She closed her fist, leaving his coffee in place—medium roast, extra cream. Instead, she locked her unit and hurried across the blacktop. Nostalgia must've made her weak.

Nicky stripped off her jacket before she climbed into the passenger seat of the idling vehicle. Heated air poured from the vents, quickly cutting the chill that lingered in the folds of her clothes. The mingled scent of coffee, red clay crumbled on floor mats, and something else she couldn't name mixed pungent and familiar. Her throat tightened, but she dismissed it with a mouthful of coffee. She rolled her jacket and tucked it along her left side like a barrier. The truck faced east, giving her an unobstructed view of the sunrise over the distant, hulking gray of the Ortiz Mountains.

The sky had transitioned through an intense gold and settled into pastels when the driver's side door opened.

His "Mornin'," was terse. Nicky hummed in reply. He held two cups of Starbucks coffee, which he slotted into the console.

Heat spiked around her as Franco's bulk filled the cab. She adjusted the hot air vent, tucked stray hair into her bun. Buckled up.

Refused to look at him.

"I brought you coffee," Franco said.

She raised her cup in mock salute, but, against her will, warmth kindled inside her.

They sat in the truck.

"I see you got my text," he said.

"'Seven A.M. Meet at Conservation for a tour of the disturbed medicine gardens. Bring a lunch.'" She nudged the backpack at her feet. The clock on the dash read 7:03.

"You didn't reply," he said.

She pressed her expression into a grimacing smile and shrugged.

He exhaled a harsh breath. "Look, we have to spend the whole day together. Why don't you stop being—"

Her gaze clashed with his. He clamped his mouth shut, jaw flexing.

"What? Childish, Franco? Really?" She twisted her torso and leaned in, so close she could pick out the umber flecks in his eyes. "Do you know why I didn't reply? Because for the past two months, you've treated me like I don't exist. You blocked my texts, my calls, my emails. I tried to explain, apologize, wanted to—" Nicky swallowed. The rush of words made her throat ache. She tore her gaze from his and took a sip of coffee. He'd masked his expression. He was good at that.

Franco shifted the truck in gear. She braced her feet and body as he launched out of the parking lot and onto the main road running through the pueblo.

Nicky ground her shoulders into the seat and turned her head to the side to watch the scenery flash by: an old trailer, satellite dish lashed to the roof with silver duct tape, roofless rock houses huddled on steps of land above brittle cornfields, a herd of skinny feral horses, coats dusty, heads down, trudging single file in a snaking washout. Her mind jumped with all the things she wanted to say but wouldn't.

She purposefully closed that door in her head and opened another. Inside lay the evidence of the museum break-in and murder. She studied each piece, shuffling them for a better fit. The truck ate up the miles, the only sounds the periodic crackle of the radio as Dispatch doled out calls to on-duty cops.

Clouds, undersides gray and heavy, dotted the sky. A wave of dark green forest splotched with golden-leafed aspen climbed the mountains in front of the truck. To her right, snow frosted the crest of Scalding Peak, the dormant volcano so much a part of the Fire-Sky culture and religion. Nicky absorbed her surroundings, the beauty of this place a balm.

She didn't know when the silence between them loosened. It just did. She shifted and studied Franco. The tension had left his shoulders, his expression was softer, and his hands had relaxed on the steering wheel.

"What can you tell me about the looted sites?" she asked.

Franco negotiated a turn onto a narrow, paved road running across a juniper-and-bunchgrass-dotted mesa before he answered.

"The first notice we received was in late summer, the end of August. I got a call to go up to the Broken Bowl airstrip. Someone had reported the nearby medicine garden shrine had been torn up. Most of these sites are only supposed to be known to Fire-Sky tribal members, but there's a bunkhouse in the area for Hotshots during fire season with corrals and a water tank. The tribe also uses it for guided hunts, mostly for non-Natives, so this medicine garden wasn't hidden."

He'd slowed to a normal speed, but Nicky had never been worried. Franco was about the only person she trusted as a driver.

"I got out of the truck," he continued. "One second, I was alone, the next, this guy appeared between a couple of piñons. Sixties, salt-and-pepper hair braided down his back, deep-set eyes, six feet, lanky, square face. He looked tired—like he'd lived hard—but fit. Told me he was the one who reported the damage but wasn't from Fire-Sky. Said tribal council gives him special permission to harvest plants from pueblo land. Called himself the Jemez Medicine Man."

Nicky automatically corrected his pronunciation. "*Hay*-mus. It's a small pueblo about fifty miles north of Albuquerque, almost directly west of Fire-Sky."

"I know, and he pronounced it—" Franco's lips pressed thin, and he slanted her a look. "Forget it. You know this guy?"

"Never met him. People call him for blessings and cleansings, but he's always good about sending someone to the clinic if they're really sick."

"Why doesn't Fire-Sky use their own medicine men?" Franco asked.

"Don't think they have any, at least not right now. They use war chiefs and Catholic priests for blessings, and caciques for certain medicines. What's this guy's real name?"

"Introduced himself as Jimmy Che'chi, but he didn't have ID, or at least that's what he told me. When I ran him, I couldn't find anything. He led me to the site."

Franco bumped the truck down a puddled dirt lane. Clods of mud thrown up by the tires thudded an uneven beat on the undercarriage. The track wound upward through a bedraggled meadow rimmed with frost and into a wall of tall, straight pines, furry cedars, and feathery blue spruce. As they drove, light and shadow dappled the truck and played over his face.

"These medicine gardens are usually built near a seep or spring," Nicky said. "Could someone have dug it up to plant marijuana?"

Franco flashed her a quick frown. "How did you know about the water source?"

She shrugged. "Something I read." In her mother's research articles, but she was keeping *that* confidential for now.

"Timeline's wrong for pot. Even transplanted, there wouldn't be time for the plants to mature. They'd need about two and a half months of growth for a cutting. Besides, the second garden was desecrated in September. The one we're heading to, a few days ago."

"How'd you find out about the second and third site?"

"The Jemez Medicine Man. Again." He pronounced Jemez correctly this time. "I asked him to notify me if any of the other gardens he harvests from were vandalized."

"Some of these medicine gardens have shrines. They're sacred places, and you're not supposed to know the locations." Her tone wasn't judgmental. The Native cops and conservation officers usually handled culturally sensitive calls and issues. That was just the way it worked on the pueblo.

"I told him that, but he wanted me to know. He trusted me." Franco shot her a hard glance.

Nicky's neck burned hot. She turned away from him to stare unseeingly into the trees. The truck dropped into another pothole.

"Nicky, I'm..." His voice deepened. "I'm sor—"

She didn't want to hear it. "Maybe whoever is doing this will come back in the spring and plant pot then."

He exhaled a long breath. "Then why take the plants and soil away from the site? No. These desecrations are harvests. Whoever is doing this is looking for something. That's when I made the connection." His pause was heavy. "With you."

She didn't care for his tone. "What do you mean?"

"Bioprospecting. After the *Albuquerque Journal* ran the article about your generous settlement for the discovery of the bioremediation organism, this is exactly what I expected. A bunch of jack-holes scouting the rez, looking for their pot of gold at the expense of the tribe."

Like you did. It was unsaid, but the words rang clearly.

But it hadn't been like that, and she refused to feel guilty about it.

"It could also explain the pot scrapings," she said evenly. "I assume

Chief told you about those? Do you think Tioux was involved in the medicine garden desecrations?"

"I don't know. We'll need to timeline his visits to the pueblo." Franco stopped the truck in a large circular clearing bounded by towering pines. He stared at her for a long moment, gaze sharp as glass. "You're not going to say anything else about it, are you? About what happened? About your payout?"

Lips sealed, she undid her safety belt and leaned over to grab her backpack.

"Fine." He slammed out of the truck, snatched his gear from the backseat, and strode into the surrounding forest.

Nicky opened the truck door and slid outside, tucking her pack on the seat to grab her jacket. She shrugged it on and stood and breathed in the chill, clean air, staring after Franco.

Had Tioux been visiting the medicine garden sites to harvest plants? Had he discovered something valuable and been murdered for it? Nicky didn't think so, and murder seemed a little extreme. Besides, most of the medicinal herbs and roots used by caciques had already been investigated by scientists like her mother. That was true of the pot-scraping samples, too. Sure, some of the compounds had pharmaceutical value, but it took years and years of study and millions of dollars to bring a potential drug to market. Most never made it out of the lab.

She didn't believe that was Tioux's purpose. He was too open about it, too ignorant. His murder had to be for some other reason.

Nicky pulled her pack out of the truck, closed the door ... and stilled.

Hair prickled on her neck. The feeling of eyes boring into her was strong. Sliding her hand to her sidearm, she glanced casually around the clearing. Franco had said one moment there'd been nothing, the next, the Jemez Medicine Man had appeared. If it was him now, surely he would recognize Franco. No reason to hide.

On edge, Nicky waited. The caw of a raven echoed in the distance. A gusty breeze swept through the trees, shaking loose moisture and pine needles that lightly thudded to earth. Dark clouds scuttled over the sun.

The sensation of being watched faded. It was probably nothing. An overactive imagination brought on by the events of the past few days. With a final scan of the clearing, Nicky shouldered her pack, picked out the trail to the medicine garden and shrine, and headed into the trees.

NICKY LACED her fingers in her lap as Richards tapped through the photos she'd downloaded to his laptop. He'd squared the computer precisely on his desk blotter. A pad of yellow legal paper, the top page half filled with slashing black writing, and a pen to one side of it were aligned in perfect parallel. The rest of the desk was clean. Nothing else cluttered it, not even a coffee cup.

She itched to reach over and knock everything askew.

Franco sat in a second office chair, dwarfing it. It creaked ominously when he moved. His boots were as dirty as hers, as were his cargos and khaki shirt. The hike to and from the disturbed site had been challenging. It had been a long day already and wouldn't end anytime soon—her double date with Julie and Brian was that evening.

Richards gestured at the computer screen. "Whoever did this carried out all this dirt as well as the plants?"

"No, sir," Nicky said. "Just the plants. If I may?" Richards turned the computer, and she leaned forward and tapped the keyboard until she found a close-up of stones strewn to one side of the plot. "They dug up the plot and screened it."

"They?" Richards said.

Nicky shrugged.

"We're not sure how many because they're very good at covering their tracks," Franco said. "No footprints, no trash. Nothing. They were very careful at the site."

Nicky leaned back in her chair. "But careless when they left. The thieves shed some of the plants they'd taken along the trail out—leaves, stems, roots."

Almost like they'd been dropped on purpose. Something tickled in the back of her mind.

"You collected what you found? Get a cursory ID on the plants, Matthews. See if they're valuable," Chief said. "Back to the dirt. You said it was screened?"

"Yes, sir," Nicky replied.

"Like they were looking for something underground," Franco added.

Chief pursed his lips and nodded slowly. He snapped his laptop closed. "What about usage of these gardens to grow psychoactive plants? Peyote or mushrooms? *Salvia?*" Richards raised his eyebrows, his lips twitching.

Nicky's face heated, and she clenched her teeth. An accidental intoxication by salvia smoke had thrust her into the Stone Fetish murder case that summer, a case she and Franco had solved together. That the chief brought it up now—

"A joke, Sergeant," Chief said jovially. "Only a joke."

Franco cleared his throat. "I asked the reporting witness who harvests from these gardens if they contained anything like that. He said no, although he could be lying."

The chief picked up the pen and twiddled it between his fingers. He nodded to the whiteboard, now half filled with names, pictures, dates, and leads.

"Any more thoughts on how Rémy Tioux's murder could be linked to this case?"

"No, sir," Franco answered. "In fact, the more we look into it, the more I'm coming to believe the garden desecrations are just bioprospecting. That there's no relationship to the murder."

Richards's eyebrows rose. He laid down the pen. "That's surprising, Martinez, considering how hard you pressed for this assignment after you brought me the pot-scraping information. Both your captain and I thought your theory connecting the medicine gardens and the murder was very compelling."

Nicky shot him a sharp look. *Franco* had been the one to link the two cases together? He'd been the one who suggested they partner up?

Wait. "*You* told Chief about the pot scrapings?"

Franco's face turned the color of bricks.

"Let's not give up on that link yet." Chief pulled the yellow pad forward. The pen rolled to one side. He realigned it. "I put in a call to Peter Santibanez while you two were out. He and his wife will be back from Tioux's funeral in the morning, and Santibanez said you could stop by their apartment after lunch tomorrow for their interview. FBI's already talked to him but for some reason didn't speak to his wife. You've worked with Headley before, right, Sergeant? Agent Martinez?"

"No, sir," Franco said. "But I've worked with the FBI in the past."

"That's right. Your little undercover operation on the pueblo earlier this summer. Then you know that once the FBI have made up their mind, only a smoking gun will make any impact." His tone dripped sarcasm. "Let's see what we can find out, maybe show them up a little, eh, Matthews? We still haven't found Tioux's rental car." Chief slid a file across the desk with the make, model, license, and VIN. "Stop by the casino concierge and question anyone who might remember anything about where Tioux went on the pueblo. We need a timeline of his final day." He nodded toward the whiteboard. "Martinez, I didn't see a comprehensive interview with Jimmy Che'chi, that medicine man who reported the site desecrations. Find out if he ever saw Tioux at a medicine garden. Oh, and Matthews. Give Martinez half of those plants you collected on the trail today. He also has a source who can help with identification." A slow grin spread over Chief's face. He winked. "Don't you, Martinez?"

Nicky furrowed her brows and glanced at Franco, this time catching guilt in his gaze. The burn of color on his cheeks had only intensified before a mask slipped over his face once again.

CHAPTER FIFTEEN

MEETING OVER, Nicky expected Franco to follow her back into the squad room and retrieve half of the plants they'd collected as evidence. Instead, he bolted.

Nicky darted out the door of the Fire-Sky Admin complex and into the parking lot after him.

"Martinez!"

Franco was halfway to the Conservation building when she caught up. She grabbed his arm. He pivoted toward her, both of them jerking away from the contact. Palm tingling, Nicky shoved her hand into her pocket.

"I dumped the plant samples in one of the interview rooms. We need to divide them," she said. "It won't take long."

Franco stood stiff and unmoving. He wasn't going to come.

"I, um, also have some information from a source about the murders," she offered.

His eyes went flat. "Dax Stone?"

The last case they'd worked on together as partners had started with information given to her by her ex-lover, something she'd held back from Franco at the time.

"Not this time," she said.

A hesitation, a curt nod, and he fell into step beside her. They trudged up the cement stairs to Admin.

"This information," he said.

"Needs to wait till we're behind a closed door."

They skirted the glass-encased center garden, cut through the break room and into the central hub of the police station.

Officers were scattered through the large open area. Fluorescent lights glared down, their buzz adding to the hum of voices. Nicky headed to the interview room that doubled as a resource library and pushed inside, Franco behind her. Limp stems, leaves, and roots with clinging dirt lay spread out across the laminate tabletop on paper towels to dry.

She picked up a stem with a few crumpled gray-brown leaves attached, determined to be professional.

"I identified a few when I picked them up. Doveweed. Concoctions are used for a sick stomach." She twirled the stem in her fingers and nodded to large ruffle-edged leaves on the table. "Yellow dock—an invasive species. Powdered and added to poultices to treat skin sores. This one—globe mallow—is a shampoo ingredient, among other things. I'm not confident about anything else, though. We'll need to bring in experts."

"Plants used in wedding and fertility ceremonies?" Franco asked.

"Not the ones I was able to identify. Let's get everything divided. I don't want you to be late to Savannah's." She laid down the stem and grabbed a stack of plastic evidence baggies.

"We're behind closed doors," Franco said.

Nicky paused and nodded. She pulled out the scrap of paper Javier had given her with the license plate number.

"Someone saw this vehicle near the Rhyerson tank on the night of the murders. Based on the info Chief gave us, it's Rémy Tioux's rental car. My source said there were two people inside—driver and passenger, one large, one small—but it was too dark to see faces."

"Near the tank?"

"Near enough."

"Whoever was in this car could've killed both men?"

Nicky filled out a label, not meeting his eyes. "My sources also say the Crybabies didn't kill Tioux. That it was some kind of copycat."

"*Nicky.*" He leaned toward her, his eyes wide, expression tight with worry.

For her. Warmth crept into her chest.

"Who told you the Crybabies were behind Angel Benevidez's murder?" he said.

"I'm not burning my sources." She tucked a few stems and leaves into the labeled evidence bag. "I need to trust you won't go to anyone with this information until we have more definitive proof. Even to the chief," Nicky said. "Please. I have my reasons."

He searched her face, then nodded curtly.

Nicky almost slumped in relief. They worked silently for a few minutes, sorting the plants until Franco held a clutch of small plastic baggies.

"Who's your taxonomy source? Someone at the DEA?" Nicky asked as she turned out the light and closed the door to the interview room.

"Uh … no. I'm using somebody living on the pueblo."

"Ryan's dad?" He was a Fire-Sky cacique, well versed in tribal medicines. Nicky nodded. "I thought about him, but I've got a friend in the Plant Science department down at New Mexico State."

Franco opened the door to the parking lot. She checked her phone. Only a little after five. She was supposed to meet Judy, Brian, and her date at seven-thirty. Timing would be tight. She tucked her hands deeper in the pockets of her heavy black jacket, and, side by side, they jogged down the cement steps toward her truck.

"You won't use Dean MacElroy?" Franco asked.

"He's a witness in Tioux's murder case, and I don't want anyone to accuse us of tainting or compromising evidence." She pressed the key fob to start her unit and stopped by the driver's side door. Franco walked past her, head down. "When do you want to prep for the Santibanez interview?"

Franco paused but didn't turn around. "Why don't you come to dinner tonight at Savannah's? We can talk there."

"I already told you, I—"

"Have a date. Right. Tomorrow morning. Early. How about seven? I'll meet you here." He started toward the Conservation building again.

"And we have to interview your Jemez Medicine Man," she called after him. "If he was harvesting from this garden, he'd know if the plants dropped on the path were grown there or—" A piece of the puzzle suddenly clicked into place.

Franco stopped again. This time he pivoted to look at her. "Or what?"

"Or whether what we found was a carefully placed trail of bread-crumbs to lead us in a specific direction."

Just like the planted trail of blood from the earthen tank to the murder site.

CHAPTER SIXTEEN

NICKY PARKED at the end of the narrow road lined with cars and trucks tinged yellow by the glow of sodium streetlamps. Cold wrapped her bare legs as she walked to Savannah's house, her two-inch heels clicking on the cement. More vehicles had been pulled into sandy front yards, and the loud thump of music directly across the street indicated a party in progress. Nicky checked the time on her phone. After nine o'clock. Noise ordinance was eleven on the weekends.

She shoved her phone back into the ridiculously tiny purse. Maybe she should just relax and enjoy herself without having her job color every moment of her life. Except …

Except her excuse for showing up at Savannah's after she'd told everyone she had a date was because of work—to give Franco new information about the interview tomorrow.

Or was it so she could break through the barriers she'd built against him and her friends, because she was lonely? Seeing Julie tonight with her fiancé had only emphasized that point.

Nicky picked up her pace, marking Franco's truck with a small jump of her pulse. Ryan's was still tucked under the carport at his house down the road. He and Jinni lived too close to drive. Howard's huge Suburban with its mismatched tires and cracked front windshield sat in the driveway next to Savannah's compact.

When she arrived at the front door, Nicky stood, steadying her breathing before she tried the knob—locked—and knocked.

Wind lifted her hair off her neck and fluttered the edges of her short skirt. Nicky shivered and knocked again, louder. She should have worn her coat. She pivoted to stare at the house across the street as a raucous roar echoed from deep inside. Someone fumbled with the lock, and the door behind her opened. Air, warm and fragrant with the scent of grilled food and something baked and cheesy, spilled out and surrounded her, dissipating her chill.

Savannah stood in the threshold. Astonishment quickly replaced a flash of chagrin.

"The door was locked, and, um, my key isn't on the key chain for my mother's car." Nicky's explanation petered out as Savannah continued to stare. She shifted, suddenly uncomfortable. "I know I said I couldn't come over, but I saw Franco's truck out front, and I need to speak to him about interviews we're doing together tomorrow, and…" Her voice sounded fast and nervous to her own ears. "And I thought I'd stop by."

Savannah grabbed her arm and tugged her inside, her mouth stretching into a huge grin. But it was forced, her eyes in a panic. Howard—who'd been sitting on the sofa next to a half-empty bowl of bright red candy—goggled at her.

She didn't appreciate the shock on his face. So what if she had on a skirt and the sleeves and yolk of her blouse were see-through? Get over—

"Oh. My. God. Are you wearing makeup? Since when do you own makeup? Mascara? Eye shadow?" Savannah reached up and swiped at Nicky's lower lip.

"Hey!" Nicky jerked back and frowned.

Savannah considered the smear of color on her finger. "You have on lipstick. Ryan? Ryan!" Savannah's grip on Nicky's arm as she pulled her across the living room toward the hall bordered on painful.

The guest bedroom door opened, and Ryan stepped out.

"Look. Nicky's here. Where's your phone? I need a picture." Savannah held Nicky in place.

Ryan stilled for a moment, and Nicky went on alert.

"Jinni okay?" she asked.

"Yeah. She's out back with Franco." Ryan ambled down the hall, half in shadow. As he approached, the light from the table lamps behind her warmed his face, revealing an almost rueful smile. He tucked the can he held behind a framed picture on a side table. "First time I've ever seen you in a skirt. You should get dressed up more often, Nicky. You look really nice. I don't have my phone. I left it in the kitchen, I think. Bad habit, especially with Jinni due any day now." He leaned to one side and called, "Jinni? Hon? Can you bring me my phone? It's on the counter by the coffee maker. I guess I have to take a picture. I'm sorry, Nicky."

She stared at the regret in his face. Why did his apology sound deeper than one for just a picture?

"I thought you had a date," Savannah said, her voice too bright, too high. "Are you on your way there?"

"We had dinner. The guy was nice and all." Nicky shrugged.

"So, you drove up from Albuquerque, all dressed up because...?"

Nicky's gaze bounced back and forth between Ryan and Savannah. "Pie?" She couldn't keep the sharp edge out of her voice. "Look, I know I've been distant, and I apologize for it. But what the heck is going o—"

"Ryan? I can't find it." Jinni, Ryan's wife, waddled through the doorway between the kitchen and living room, her hand rubbing circles on her huge pregnant belly. Straight brown, almost black hair slipped around her shoulders, her plain face made pretty with rosy-apple cheeks. "Are you sure you left it in the ki—" She halted in her tracks and stared at Nicky, wide-eyed, mouth open. Even her hand stopped moving.

"Hi." Jinni flashed a desperate glance at Ryan. "I wanted to tell you I have a doctor's appointment next week. Can I stop by your place afterwards again? It's such a long drive into Albuquerque. I have the key you gave me."

"Sure. You know you don't need to ask." No one would meet Nicky's gaze. "What's going on?"

The screen door in the den slid open on a squeal, and Franco's voice called out, "Hey, where'd everybody go?"

Nicky flashed hot and straightened, brushing down the front of her silky top, her gaze on the entryway into the kitchen.

Franco stepped through the opening, head tipped down and smiling, attention on the woman clinging to his arm and beaming up at him. Her expression glowed, slight body shimmering as she giggled. She stretched up on tiptoes to whisper in his ear, and he laughed.

Nicky's heart plummeted straight to the floor, pain and disappointment filling the empty spot in her chest.

Franco looked up, still chuckling. His eyes swept the room, past Nicky to Ryan, then swung back abruptly. So many emotions flickered over his face, she would have been hard-pressed to name them all. Shock, anger, embarrassment, then … nothing.

The woman by his side followed his gaze. Her smile widened.

Charlotte Fields, the intern from the Isgaawa museum.

"Sergeant Matthews? Franco didn't tell me you were coming." Charlotte squeezed his arm, pressing her breasts into Franco's biceps before tugging him along behind her as she navigated between bodies standing still and awkward. She held out her hand. Nicky automatically grasped it. "Any more breakthroughs on the museum case? I know Franco isn't supposed to say anything, but he's been keeping me up-to-date on your progress." She threw a sweet, shy smile over her shoulder.

Nicky realized she was still holding Charlotte's hand and let go.

"No."

"Well, I'm sure your interview with the head of the casino tomorrow—"

Nicky's head whipped up, and her gaze stabbed Franco. Charlotte placed a hand over her mouth and looked back and forth between them.

"I wasn't supposed to say anything about that. I'm *so* sorry."

Jinni gasped and pressed two hands against her swollen belly.

"Oh, my gosh. It's like the baby's doing backflips. Lottie, Savannah. Everyone. Come feel."

The inertia gripping the room broke. Savannah and Charlotte hurried to Jinni, Savannah's gaze catching Nicky's in fleeting apology.

Nicky didn't remember approaching Franco or him her, but they were suddenly close.

"You had a date," he said accusingly.

"Seems I wasn't the only one."

"Why are you here?"

"Rémy Tioux's wife came back to Fire-Sky with the Santibanezes. I wanted you to know."

"You could have texted, called. You didn't have to come."

That hurt. Nicky lashed back. "Oh. Sorry. I'm so used to being blocked on your phone I thought—" She swallowed, eyes suddenly burning. "Forget it. I'll leave so you can get back to your date."

"You don't have—I don't want—*dammit*, Nicky. Don't go."

Silence pulsed between them. Background chatter faded.

Nicky stared up at him, breath broken and shallow. His gaze dropped to her mouth. The brown of his irises blackened.

"Please," she whispered, not sure what she was begging for. "We need to talk."

He leaned closer.

Or had she?

"Franco! You have to come feel this," Charlotte said. "Oh, my gosh! The baby feels like it's fighting to get out."

"Not 'it,'" Jinni said firmly. "She."

Franco straightened, retreating a step. With one last flickering glance, his expression morphed into a pleasant smile. He shoved his hands into his pockets. Knees shaky, Nicky rested against the back of the sofa. He'd masked his emotions like he was switching off a light.

"I'm good. Ryan has rules about strange men feeling up his wife and daughter."

Laughter lightened the air.

Charlotte darted across the room with quick, light steps, her body almost vibrating, her expression coy and playful. She tugged at Franco's wrist and looped his arm over her shoulder, snuggling in close. "I'm tired. How about one piece of pie, then you take me home. Maybe stay for a little while and watch TV?" She nuzzled his arm, pulling it tighter, all fluttery eyelashes. "Or something."

Nicky gritted her teeth against the sting behind her eyes. She pivoted on her heel and scooped up her tiny handbag. "Tomorrow morning at seven, Martinez."

Howard opened the door for her. She strode outside. The bracing cold suited her mood.

Savannah ran after her. "Didn't you want pie?"

"Some other time."

A breeze bit into the skin of her cheeks and wrapped around her bare neck. But the burning in her chest had evaporated the momentary weakness of tears.

CHAPTER SEVENTEEN

NICKY ARRIVED at the Fire-Sky Police Department an hour before sunrise after a quick run, shower, and no good reasons to sit at home except to brood.

A flood of light from the Conservation and FER building allowed her to make out Franco's blue-gray truck among scattered vehicles. Her sense of relief was pathetic. She tried to destroy it by telling herself she didn't know what had happened between Franco and Charlotte last night, no matter how early he'd arrived for their meeting. She snuggled her bare neck deeper in the collar of her jacket and walked briskly into the police station.

Sipping break room coffee doctored with sweetener, Nicky powered up her desktop computer and opened her email. Agent Song had kept her promise to send Rémy Tioux's phone records. She'd also attached a sketchy timeline of Tioux's final days in New Mexico based on interviews with Peter and Marica Santibanez. Nicky printed it out as she scanned the rest of Song's message. The two agents would remain in Biloxi, following up leads for the foreseeable future, and the FBI had decided to give State and Albuquerque PD point on the Angel Benevidez murder because of the Crybaby link.

Good luck with that. Luna Guerra was too smart to let her gang members get caught. After all, nothing had ever come of the human trafficking case from earlier that summer. Now the police and traffickers were back to a cheetah-and-gazelle evolution. Whenever the authorities figured out a route or pushed an illicit shadow into the sun, the gang changed tactics, and everyone started fresh.

Nicky clicked open the phone records and scrolled; a dozen were from his wife's number in Biloxi, with a single call back from him his final day, and double that were business-related phone numbers with Mississippi area codes, brief notes attached. Another half dozen to a law firm in Santa Fe, and one or two to ride-sharing services with a request from Song to find and interview the drivers. Nicky jotted Howard Kie's name on a notepad before she continued down the list of numbers. Howard had told her the night of the murders he'd driven Tioux around the pueblo. That guy always had more information than anyone ever thought he should and was always overlooked.

Her hand stilled on the mouse, and she read Song's next notation: *Need you to follow up*. Rémy Tioux had made a single call to a medical clinic—Santa Fe Fertility Solutions. Nicky brought up her search engine and typed in the clinic's name.

Pastel pinks and blues burst onto the page with photos of a myriad of happy couples and smiling doctors pressing fetal stethoscopes to hugely pregnant bellies. She clicked a page on the menu entitled "Success is a Bundle of Joy!" and ran through an endless slideshow of infants and selected quotes from obviously ecstatic parents: *"SFFS was our last hope. They answered our prayers," "The doctors and nurses* really *care. SFFS made the whole process stress-free."* Nicky's eyes narrowed as she read, *"We appreciated the herbal medicines and the purity of their products and practices—because pregnancy* should *be natural!"*

"It's seven o'clock." Franco's voice.

Mind still far away, her eyes stroked over him. The plains of his face were browned from the sun, his square jaw freshly shaven, silver threads peppering his sideburns. Her gaze continued over a starched white button-down, badge clipped to a worn leather belt, soft faded

Levi's, and black cowboy boots. He set a cup of Starbucks coffee on her desk, next to the fawn Stetson he'd rested on her inbox, grabbed a nearby chair, and, for God's sake, all she could think about was how huge his hands were. Her neck heated with raw attraction, along with other parts of her body. She tore her eyes away and stared at the computer screen, teeth clamped.

"Planning on getting pregnant?" Franco said. He nodded at the screen, one eyebrow and side of his mouth ticking up. "It's not as fun that way." He picked up her Styrofoam cup and transferred it to the desk behind him before he settled and cleared his throat. "Brought you coffee. You look nice."

She grabbed the fresh cup and took a sip to unstick her tongue from the roof of her mouth. Had he noticed she'd applied light makeup or that her blouse and hip-hugging black trousers were a little more form-fitting than usual? It's not like she'd worn them for him.

"A peace offering." His voice was gruff. "So you won't light into me about Lottie Fields."

Nicky nearly choked. "I don't care who you date." She pushed the coffee away.

"I'm not—"

"Oh, please."

"That's not why…" Lips thinned, he folded his arms, all business. "What you got?"

Better. She knew how to deal with this Franco.

"Rémy Tioux called a fertility clinic in Santa Fe the last day he was seen alive."

"He already has a baby."

"Yeah, but it doesn't mean he and his wife didn't need help conceiving. And look at this. Santa Fe Fertility Solutions offer medicinal plant infusions and herbal teas that"—she clicked to the home page and read aloud—"*sooth anxieties and facilitate natural conception.*"

"Do you think Tioux was trying to figure out what this clinic uses and replicate it? Or maybe he consulted them about the herbs he'd picked, too."

"I don't know, but I think we need to ascertain whether Tioux and his wife had medical help getting pregnant and whether it involved plants used in fertility medicines," she said. "Song asked us to follow up even though they've pretty much dismissed Tioux's connection to the museum exhibition as coincidence. We still have to deal with the pot scrapings, though."

Nicky dropped her gaze to study her tightly laced fingers and gather her thoughts. She'd wanted to talk to someone—him—but now she was having a hard time finding the words linking her mother to the damaged pots and murder.

"Franco?" she said. "The scrapings?"

"Who knows when those were made?" His tone was dismissive, but he wouldn't look at her.

"They were made the night of the murders. Wait." Nicky stared at him, struck. "Charlotte told you about the pot scrapings, didn't she? That's how you made the connection between the murders and the medicine garden desecrations."

His gaze flickered up. "Yeah," he admitted.

"Your girlfriend was also the one who noticed a pot had been moved the night of the murder. She's the one who told Dean."

"She's not my—" Franco's jaw bunched. "That's not what she said to me."

"Dean said the pot that changed position had fresh scrape marks. When he checked, he found the others."

"Not about that. Lottie said she can't be sure the second set of scratches weren't already there when she was setting up the exhibit. She said maybe she didn't check them as carefully as she should've. They were so behind that she was under a lot of pressure to get things finished." He shrugged one shoulder and bent to wipe a smudge of dust off his boot.

"Great. Who am I supposed to believe?" Nicky asked sarcastically. "Oh, yeah. *Dean.* Charlotte's just trying to cover her ass."

"Why? It's to her benefit to claim the scrapes were fresh, not that she was careless and missed them." Franco leaned forward, eyes narrowing. "Dean checked the first pot because it had been moved. You searched the gallery. What if you bumped into that pedestal? What if the scrapes he found had nothing to do with the murder?"

Nicky rubbed a finger between her brows. The whispers, the laughing and crying she thought she'd heard had unnerved her. When she'd backed away—

"I could've, I guess. But isn't it a huge coincidence if I bumped into the *exact* pedestal that started our investigation?"

"Lottie said—"

"I don't like coincidences, and I don't want to hear anything else Charlotte said. Have you read the medical report on her for that night? One of the med-techs who examined her at the scene said he didn't believe her story. That the blow to her head might have been staged."

"Come on, Nicky," Franco said, scoffing. "Lottie Fields is no more a suspect in these murders than we are. When she learned about the garden desecrations, she wanted to help, that's all."

"The desecrations are supposed to be kept under wraps. Who told her?"

Franco met her gaze defiantly even as his face reddened. "I'm using her for plant identification."

Nicky gaped at him. "Dammit, Franco. Talk about a conflict of interest. How long have you two been seeing each other?"

"Last night at Savannah's was the only time—" He paused and grimaced. "We may have met for coffee before work a few times, but accidentally."

His answer seared her. How many times had she and Franco met accidentally while getting coffee at the Bernalillo Starbucks? She cut off the thought, but another crept in. Charlotte had approached her at the Starbucks, too. Had she met Franco there earlier? Because then Luna Guerra's cryptic message about Charlotte would make sense.

"If Charlotte's involved, she could be cultivating you for information." Nicky said.

"No." But a perturbed expression crossed his face. "Maybe. I don't know. You sure know how to deflate a guy's ego."

Nicky averted her eyes from his rueful look, not ready to forgive him. "Yeah. It's a class women take at puberty. Let's go over the information we have on the Santibanezes. If possible, I also want to talk to Rémy Tioux's wife since she's staying with them. We can drive up to Santa Fe and visit that fertility clinic Monday. See if the baby was helpfully produced by the herbal medicines offered as part of their treatment. And if Tioux talked to anyone there before his murder."

When they left, Nicky didn't take her coffee.

CHAPTER EIGHTEEN

THE PRIVATE ELEVATOR ride to Peter and Marica Santibanez's apartment at the top of the Fire-Sky Resort and Casino hotel was swift, smooth, and deafeningly quiet. Nicky stared at the burnished, silvery doors, desperately trying to get her head into interview mode. Franco shifted, planting his feet wider, or at least that was how his vague, ghostly reflection moved in front of her. She couldn't make out his features in the cold swirls of aluminum, but she sure as hell wasn't going to look at him. She had to get over her attitude, retreat to a professionalism that was more than the sorry facade she was putting up now.

The elevator opened onto a reception room with a multicolored slate floor and walls tiled in uneven, striated sandstone blocks stacked to a vaulted, turquoise-painted ceiling. Desert grasses and plants sprang up from niches in the floor and wall, their herby scents subtle in the cool air. Tinkling water drew Nicky to a ragged opening in the floor, about a yard in diameter, surrounded by petals of polished black rocks laid out in an irregular flower pattern. Water welled up from the center of spirals carved in the rocks and trickled down the stones to drop like tears into a recessed pool below the floor. She stared down into the rippling surface, her reflection dark and distorted.

"A symbolic depiction of the Place of Emergence," Nicky said.

Franco stepped beside her. "I've heard of it. Don't know much about it."

"Tsiba'ashi D'yini creation stories speak of twin girls emerging from the womb of the earth into the world. From a sipapu of sorts. But Fire-Sky history says they were birthed from sacred waters. Scholars interpret it as a cenote or sinkhole."

"There are sinkholes around here? I know about the Blue Hole in Santa Rosa, but that's a couple hundred miles east of the pueblo."

"Many believe the lakes under Scalding Peak drain into underground rivers. I've heard some tribe members think those rivers lead to caves in the Chiricahua Wilderness." She flashed him a glance. "Like the one where you found Maryellen K'aishuni's body."

It had been the first case they'd partnered on, one where he'd been placed undercover by the DEA. She hadn't known who he was until someone fed her inside information.

Franco was very good at hiding behind his fake identities. Nicky hated it when he used them on her.

"Where's this Place of Emergence supposed to be?" he asked.

"The mountains towards the Jemez Caldera, but I think it's mythical."

He nodded. "Twin girls, huh? I've heard about them. One was the mother of the sister or something."

"'*The mother of one was the sister of the other.*'" Ryan had said that once.

"No men came out of the earth? How did they, um, procreate?" Franco grinned crookedly, his eyebrows waggling. His jovial jack-hole persona shrouded him like a persistent odor. Nicky tamped down welling irritation.

"In the Pacific Northwest Tsimshian culture," she said, "the chief's daughter swallowed a cedar seed and became pregnant."

"Like I said before, not nearly as fun." He winked broadly.

She turned on him and exploded. "*God*, Franco, I'm not a perp in one of your undercover ops, so will you stop—"

Nicky bit off her words. His face had registered shock—eyes wide, jaw dropped—before he'd recovered and put back on a damned mask. She pivoted away to stare into the black pool.

A gentle throat-clearing made her look up.

A woman stood in the open door to the apartment. Short, round-cheeked, plump, and with smooth copper skin. Nicky put her age closer to fifty than forty. Her tan smock and scrub pants pulled a little across her chest and stomach. The name tag on her pocket read, ANNETTE. Nicky schooled her features, but her cheeks were hot.

When Annette finally spoke, her voice was soft with the distinct accent of a native Keresan speaker.

"Sergeant Matthews and Agent Martinez, Mr. Peter and Mrs. Marica will see you now."

NICKY FOLLOWED Annette into a beautifully decorated room. High ceilings and warm southwestern colors predominated. Ganado Red rugs anchored soft leather sofas and chairs on a hardwood floor. The art on the walls included a Tony Abeyta landscape and Shannon Carr-Stevens black-and-white photograph. A large shadow box was filled with more personal items: a photo of young Marica accepting her Miss Indian World crown, a fan of colorfully dyed feathers set over a tiered skirt, a tarnished silver trophy—second place, winged sprint cars, Póncio racing—and half a dozen elaborate ribbon prizes from racing or pageants. A handcrafted dining table sat parallel to a bank of windows with a spectacular view of Scalding Peak, the dormant volcano at the center of Tsiba'ashi D'yini traditional culture.

She stared at its jagged slopes before glancing at Franco. He, too, focused on the view. Earlier that summer, they'd barely escaped death in sacred caves on the mountain as they'd closed in on a serial murderer. But Marica Santibanez's son, PJ, had died, his body never found. Marica blamed them. But in the subsequent investigation, neither she nor Franco—or Ryan—had admitted to killing PJ. They'd been cleared, and the secret of who was responsible for PJ's death was never spoken between them. Franco's gaze slid to hers, silent acknowledgement this interview wouldn't be easy.

Peter and Marica Santibanez stood together at the mouth of a hallway that led to the private part of the apartment. Peter Santibanez eyed them narrowly, long salt-and-pepper hair pulled back into a braid, his handsome square face forbidding. His tenure as CEO of Fire-Sky Tribal Industries led people to swear he held more control over the tribe than the council and governor of the pueblo. Fire-Sky casinos and resorts could compete with the most successful tribal gambling industries in the country.

"Annette, dear? Could you prepare coffee for our guests?"

Marica Santibanez's gentle request contrasted sharply with the coldness of her striking features. Glossy blue-black hair flowed like a silky cape over her shoulders, and winged brows framed cinnamon-brown eyes. Her age showed only in the lengthening of her upper lip and the softening of her jawline and neck. Back in her teens, she'd been Fire-Sky's only Miss Indian World and was still highly involved in the pageant.

Marica flowed into the room and around the front of the sofa. She waved a beringed hand glinting with onyx and turquoise—stones of the elemental Earth and Sky Clans—to straight-backed wooden chairs across from a coffee table. A shirred silver bracelet encircled her wrist, set with a large onyx cabochon. She didn't do anything so plebeian as sit on the sofa as much as arrange herself on it, the soft chamois of her ankle-length skirt puddling in graceful folds over manicured, sandaled feet. Her husband stood behind her and placed a doting hand on her shoulder. Nicky would have bought the implied affection if she hadn't seen the brief stiffening of Marica's features.

Nicky sat, Franco beside her. They'd agreed she'd start. "Thank you for speaking to us," she said, only to be interrupted by a frowning Peter Santibanez.

"We've already been interviewed by the FBI." He snapped his fingers a few times as he pulled up names. "Song and Headley. In Biloxi, after the funeral."

"Yes, sir. Just a follow-up for our files," Nicky replied steadily.

"Mrs. Santibanez? You didn't see Mr. Tioux at all the day he was killed. Wasn't he staying here with you and your husband?"

"No. He requested a private suite this time," Marica said. Except for a hint of distaste in her eyes, the woman maintained a composed, if cold, expression.

"This time? He'd stayed with you in this apartment before?" At her nod, Nicky asked, "What changed?"

"Those earlier trips were less formal," Marica replied. She smoothed nonexistent creases from her skirt. "This trip was business."

"Mr. Santibanez?" Nicky shifted her focus. "Why did the Fire-Sky tribe want to buy an out-of-state casino? Why this casino?"

"A business decision, Sergeant Matthews. Expand the tribe's holdings, diversify. When Rémy originally approached me about selling, the terms were very … reasonable."

An undercurrent colored his answer. Nicky tried to tease it out.

"Mr. Tioux's terms changed? Became … unreasonable?"

Santibanez hesitated. "No."

"Why was he selling?" she asked. "Was this casino tribal owned?"

"It was family owned." His lips twisted. "He said he was selling because he wanted to spend more time with his wife and daughter."

Marica murmured, "Family is—was—extremely important to him."

"You told the FBI you saw Mr. Tioux the morning of the day he was killed," Nicky continued. "He then drove to Santa Fe to meet with the law firm representing Fire-Sky. He never returned to the hotel?"

"Correct," he said irritably. "Are we going to rehash the whole interview, Sergeant Matthews?"

"No, sir, but I find it odd you didn't go with him to the meeting."

Santibanez sighed impatiently. "I had a full schedule that day. I informed Rémy I could video conference if they needed me. They didn't. I told the FBI that, too."

"This meeting with the owner of the casino the tribe was purchasing wasn't important?" Nicky pressed. "Or weren't you important to the meeting?"

Santibanez's cheeks reddened. "I'd seen Rémy's counteroffer. It wasn't in the tribe's best interest, and I advised the council to turn it down."

"Fire-Sky decided not to purchase the Biloxi casino?" This was new information. "Did you apprise Agents Song and Headley of this?"

Santibanez hesitated. "No. Council was still debating the possibility of submitting another offer. After Rémy's death, they ultimately decided not to, or at least not until they could deal with his heirs."

Nicky jotted, *Tioux heirs?* down on her paper.

"We'd be able to verify this with the law firm?" she asked.

"I'm sure an official letter summarizing the meeting will be sent to SAC Headley soon." Santibanez's gaze roamed the room.

Nicky made an indecipherable note, gathering her thoughts. Franco shifted beside her, and they exchanged a glance. Something was off about the Santa Fe meeting.

"How long have you known Mr. Tioux?" she asked.

"About five years," Santibanez answered. "We met at the National Indian Gaming Association convention. He'd just purchased the Biloxi Star Casino." He sighed and once again placed his hand on Marica's shoulder. "He *was* part of the association."

"So along with business, you were friends," Nicky clarified. Santibanez nodded curtly. "You called him"—she looked down at her notes—"three times the day he died. The first two were short. He was on other calls, and you left no messages. But you seem to have connected the third time at seven twenty-five P.M. What was that call about?"

"I asked him to meet us for late supper—nine o'clock—to ease things over. I didn't want the pueblo's decision to interfere with our friendship," Santibanez said. "He never showed. I thought he was upset about the deal falling through and needed time alone, so I didn't check on him. Now I wish I had."

"He was upset?" Nicky asked.

"Of course. He'd put a lot of time and energy into this deal."

"Did he tell you he was going anywhere else before supper?" Nicky asked.

"No," Santibanez answered. "I assumed he was coming straight to the hotel after I spoke to him."

"Did you tell him before the Santa Fe meeting there would be no deal?"

Santibanez stared at her, and she could almost see his mind working. Beside her, Franco pressed his knee briefly against hers.

"I did," Santibanez said. "At breakfast. We were friends. It was the least I could do."

An easy answer that took too long in coming.

"Here?" Nicky indicated the dining table beside the window.

Santibanez's hand pressed into Marica's shoulder. She reached up to squeeze it. "I went to his suite," he said.

"Why did he need to go to Santa Fe if he knew Fire-Sky was turning down his offer?" Nicky asked.

"The deal had progressed further than a handshake, Sergeant," Santibanez said. "There was paperwork he had to sign. This has nothing to do with his murder. It's a dead end, and you know it."

His agitation was growing. Time to switch it up. She pressed her foot against the side of Franco's boot.

"Mr. Tioux was driving one of the hotel's vehicles when he left for Santa Fe?" Franco asked.

"Yes. Has it been found?" Santibanez asked.

"Not yet. Did he ask about medicine gardens and shrines on the pueblo?"

"Yes. Rémy was an Indigenous man. Natchez Trace," Marica answered. "He visited a number of shrines and gardens over the years he and his wife stayed with us. May I pour you some coffee, Sergeant Matthews? Agent Martinez?"

A large Nambé serving tray sat on the side table at Marica Santibanez's elbow: insulated coffeepot, cups, saucers, cream. With a quick turn of her head, Nicky caught Annette's back disappearing through a door to her left. She'd been in and out so quietly, Nicky hadn't even noticed.

"Yes, cream, please. Do you know if he ever met anyone at the gardens?" Franco's profile gentled as he focused on Marica, his gaze lingering on her face when she passed him a cup and saucer.

"Not that he said," Marica replied. Her cheeks had pinkened.

"We believe he was visiting these sites during this trip," Franco explained. "In fact, Sergeant Matthews and I would like a location map of pueblo medicine gardens and shrines, and request access—"

"No. These sites are sacred and off-limits to non-Natives, Agent Martinez. Neither you nor"—Santibanez thrust his chin at Nicky—"are allowed at these places."

"What about Native officers?" Nicky asked. Under some circumstances, like an unattended death, Native officers were sent into homes beforehand to close off rooms containing sacred objects. There should be no difference with sacred places.

Santibanez's frown deepened. "Tribal council and war chiefs would need to be approached for permission."

Franco nodded. "Of course. Was Mr. Tioux involved with drugs?"

"The FBI asked us about drugs," Santibanez said. "I never saw that type of behavior from him."

"You also told the FBI he and his wife came to stay at the Fire-Sky resort a number of times over the years," Nicky said. She and Franco fell into an ingrained rhythm.

"Yes," Marica said. A smile gilded her face. "Rémy's wife Kristina and I knew each other from the pageant circuit. Over the last few years, she's become like a daughter to me."

A perfect opening to ask if Tioux's wife would talk to them. Nicky pulled in a breath....

"No, ma'am," Franco said. "More like sisters. No way anyone could think you have grown children."

Both Santibanez's and Marica's gazes snapped to Franco, scowls now marring their features. *Dammit.* Nicky skewed Franco a glare. They'd agreed not to mention Marica's son, even obliquely. He'd just blown the rest of the interview.

Franco had the grace to turn red as he leaned forward and earnestly gabbled, "I am so sorry, I ... Please forgive me. I just wish we could have saved him from the influence of such an evil man. You know, PJ trained me. Your son? I saw the good in him."

The *good*? Nicky's jaw almost dropped. Peter Santibanez's did.

But Marica's face ... softened.

"Thank you," Marica said. "Not many people even tried to see the hurt deep in my son's soul."

Franco oozed compassion. He gave Marica a puppy-eyed look. "Ma'am, we've accounted for most of Mr. Tioux's time the day he was murdered except ... Can you help us understand his visit to the fertility clinic in Santa Fe?"

His visit? All they had was a phone call.

"He has a child. So why would he...?" Franco trailed off, but the whole of his focus was on Marica.

She plucked at her skirt. "It's not my place to tell you about Rémy and Kristina's journey."

"Their *journey*?" Santibanez blurted. "What the hell are you talking about?"

Marica twisted stiffly to stare up at him. "Sometimes you can be so blind."

"Infertility is hard for men to discuss," Franco said, "especially when it's"—honest to God, he blushed—"the man's problem."

Santibanez goggled, then he blustered. "I don't have a ... a problem."

Marica set her teeth. "Yes, Peter. I *know*."

Nicky jumped in before the conversation veered out of control. She hardened her tone. "Mrs. Santibanez, if you have any information that could help our investigation, you need to tell us, or—"

And Good Cop stepped right up. As much as she hated to admit it, they made a great team.

"Sergeant Matthews, please. Let's respect any confidences exchanged between friends." Franco's gaze never left Marica's face. "Mrs. Tioux is on the pueblo right now. Would you ask her if she'd speak to us?"

The faint mewling cry of a baby came from the darkened hallway, prickling the hair on the back of Nicky's neck.

A plump woman holding a blanket-swaddled child stepped into the room.

"I don't mind answering their questions. I want to find who did this to my husband." Kristina Tioux's voice wobbled. "More than anyone."

———

NICKY AND FRANCO rose to their feet as Peter Santibanez strode to Kristina Tioux, Marica following in a swirl of her skirt. The three held a whispered conversation before Kristina shifted the child into Marica's arms. The little girl peeked over her shoulder, chubby cheeks, unblinking button-black eyes, and a halo of soft black curls.

Santibanez's voice rose, and Nicky made out, "Without a lawyer, I don't recommend—" before Marica hissed something at him. He pivoted and stalked toward Nicky and Franco, his jaw tight and working.

"Kristina will speak to you."

After quick introductions, Marica excused herself and, bouncing the baby in her arms, swept through a swinging door opposite to the hallway.

"Are we done here?" Santibanez asked.

Nicky had developed at least a dozen more questions for the Santibanezes, but this opportunity was too good to pass up. Kristina Tioux hadn't yet been interviewed, even by the FBI.

"Just one more question," Nicky said. "Are Mrs. Tioux and her child Rémy Tioux's heirs?"

Santibanez narrowed his eyes as her words sank in. "What are you implying, Sergeant?"

"Just a question, sir."

"Then ask her because I don't know." His back rigid, Santibanez turned, walked into the hallway, and disappeared. Nicky raised her brows and looked at Franco.

Kristina Tioux perched on the edge of the sofa, hands clasped tightly in her lap. Her blouse of dark blue velour draped over a black skirt belted with delicate silver conchos. She and her daughter looked alike, with the same round cheeks, hair falling in loose curls, and dark eyes, except Kristina's drooped with a mixture of exhaustion and grief. Nicky put her age at around thirty-five.

"Please accept our condolences, Mrs. Tioux," Nicky said. "We'll make this brief."

"Thank you. I'm not sure what I can contribute since I was in Mississippi when Rémy—" A sheen formed in her eyes. Franco grabbed a box of tissues from a side table, placing them before her. She sent him a sad smile and dabbed her cheeks.

"Do you have any idea who might have killed your husband?" Franco asked.

"No. Rémy was well-liked. He did a lot for our community. It—it seems so random." She looked back and forth between them, her expression shattered. "When can I get back his—his—"

"Effects? Soon." Nicky pulled out her phone and brought up the picture of the ring from Tioux's case file. "Is his wedding band an heirloom?"

Kristina took the phone, eyes flashing with relief. "He didn't take it off?"

"Why would he have taken it off?" Nicky asked.

Kristina didn't answer. She was staring at the photo on the phone, hand pressed against her mouth.

"Everything okay?" Nicky asked. She exchanged a glance with Franco, who shrugged.

Kristina thrust the cell back into Nicky's hand. "Yes. Of course. Everything's fine. It's just a bit upsetting t-to see..." She tipped up her chin, jaw firm. "And he wouldn't take it off. The people who did this to him might have taken it off. S-stole it."

"Your husband called you that last day," Nicky said. "Did he say anything to you that might shed light on his death?"

Kristina's gaze dropped to where her fingers were shredding the tissue. "It was a personal call. About how much he missed me and Raven. And—and I texted him. All the time." She looked up, anxious.

"Our daughter. He hated to be away from her. From us. He loves us so much. We have—had—a wonderful marriage."

"Of course." Except Tioux's cell phone records showed he'd made only one five-minute call all week *to* the wife and daughter he'd loved so much. The rest had been made by Kristina and were very short, including a couple of video calls. But maybe he'd used the phone in his hotel room. "Did he say anything about the casino deal?"

"He didn't speak to me much about business. Do you think it may have played a part in…?" Eyes welling, she waved the tissue.

"We're pursuing every angle," Nicky replied. "We have a preliminary outline of your husband's whereabouts, but there's a gap—an hour and a half unaccounted for on the final day. The FBI confirmed he left a meeting with his lawyers in Santa Fe and drove out of the secured parking lot at three-fifty P.M. The next confirmation of his timeline was his call to you at five twenty-seven P.M. Did he say anything about where he'd gone?"

"No." Kristina dropped her gaze again. "There are tribal casinos outside of Santa Fe. Maybe—"

"Tesuque Casino, Pojoaque Cities of Gold, and Buffalo Thunder were all contacted," Nicky said. "They have no record of his visit."

"Then I don't know." Pieces of the tissue fluttered to the floor at Kristina's feet.

"Did your husband use illegal drugs?" Franco asked.

"What?" Her eyes widened. "Of course not. The Gaming Commission in Mississippi is very strict. They have moral turpitude clauses. Even felony arrests, much less convictions, disqualify anyone from owning a casino. If Rémy ever tested positive for drugs or—or had a DWI or—or *anything*, he couldn't operate the casino. The Gaming Commission could even force a sale."

"Why did he want to sell the casino?" Nicky asked.

"He wanted to spend more time with us. After Raven was born, he realized how much of her life, her milestones, he was missing because of late nights and business travel. He loved us so much."

Second time Kristina used that phrase. Who was she trying to convince?

"You and your husband visited the Santibanezes over the last few years," Nicky continued.

"For the Gathering of Nations Powwow in Albuquerque. Marica and I are involved in the Miss Indian World contest."

"The Santibanezes mentioned two or three trips per year," Franco said. "One about a year and a half ago that lasted for two months."

The baby began to cry, muffled by the kitchen door. Kristina knotted her hands around the tissue's remains, her eyes fixed on her fidgeting fingers.

"How long have you been married?" Nicky asked.

"Raven was born in January, on our tenth anniversary." Kristina's voice dropped to a hoarse whisper. "Our miracle baby."

"Marica Santibanez said you and your husband went through a journey," Nicky said. "Did that journey have anything to do with your visits to New Mexico?"

The child's cries increased in volume, piercing the wood panel. Kristina's face paled. "I need to—" She half rose.

Nicky bent forward and instilled her voice with urgency. "Please, Mrs. Tioux. We need to understand. Your husband was searching for medicinal herbs on the pueblo the last week of his life. Asking about traditional medicines used for fertility. Did it have to do with your miracle pregnancy?"

Anxiety filled Kristina's eyes. Or was it fear?

"We came to New Mexico because he didn't want anyone to know about his—our issues. I-I'm sure he only visited the Santa Fe clinic to drop off pictures of Raven, to—to thank them. My daughter—*please*. He—we don't want this to become public knowledge." She stood and gestured weakly. "It has nothing to do with his death."

"Who are your husband's heirs?" Nicky asked.

The crying intensified. Kristina edged away.

"I-I need to…" She hurried to the door and disappeared behind it. The baby's wails fell to hiccupping sobs.

"What are you thinking?" Franco asked.

Nicky met his gaze. They were close, shoulders brushing, her leg pressed along his.

She tipped her head toward the door, eyebrows raised. "That maybe what you said about a man's sensitivity to his, um, virility is true."

"Damn straight." His lips curved into a wicked smile.

Nicky's heart seemed to halt, then beat faster. This Franco next to her was the real man, not one of his undercover characters. The one she'd fallen—

The door to the kitchen opened, and Annette walked to the front door and stared at them.

"I think we're done here." Franco stood, drained his cup, and placed it on the tray. Nicky picked up her cold coffee, skirted the low table, and set it next to his.

A movement in the hallway caught her eye. Peter Santibanez looked back at her for a long moment before he turned and walked away.

CHAPTER NINETEEN

NICKY ENDED her phone call to Agent Song and tucked her phone into her pocket. She strode toward Franco, who leaned against the marble-topped front desk of the hotel, flirting mildly with the receptionist, Jazmine Juanito.

"Hey, Jazzy," Nicky said. "Whenever you want to give all this up and come back to the glitz of Dispatch, just give me a call." She gestured to an abstract arrangement of bare branches twined with native foliage, which graced a circular table in the vaulted foyer. The herbaceous scent of high meadows tinged the air. "I'll see if Lieutenant Pinkett will spring for flowers so you'll feel right at home."

Jazzy laughed. "One of us dealing with death and disaster is enough. I get earfuls of that from Milo." Her husband was one of the paramedics who'd worked the museum murder. Jazzy's smile dropped. "I bet you two are here about that poor man you found at the museum. Such a nice man, but he was upset the whole week he was here."

Nicky exchanged a glance with Franco.

"About what?" she asked.

"Oh, he didn't talk to me, but I could tell. Always frowning or staring off into space while he waited for his car. May the Creator bless his spirit." Jazzy crossed herself, then gestured to the branch-filled vase. "Only time he spoke to me that last day was about that. Said he recognized some of them from the land around here. Wanted to know who gathered them."

"Who did?" Franco asked.

A group of laughing young women glided through the automatic glass doors fronting the hotel, one of them wearing a plastic princess crown with a short white veil.

"Mrs. Santibanez does the flower arrangements for the hotel. She'd know where the plants came from. I told the man that. Gotta go. Bridal shower tonight." She scurried off to greet the women.

Franco ushered Nicky into an open elevator and pressed the button to underground parking.

"We really need to get a map of the pueblo's medicine gardens," he said.

The door dinged and opened into a low concrete space, its ceiling riddled with black girders. The rumble of engines and smell of exhaust greeted Nicky as she stepped onto the cement, Franco at her shoulder.

"Concierge office is at the back," Franco said. "What did FBI say about surveillance video from the casino?"

"They put in a preservation order for the week of Tioux's stay, but legal wrangling over sovereignty issues has delayed release. Song said she'll get them to us as soon as they drop. I also asked her about a call log from the phone in Tioux's hotel room. Maybe he used that phone to call his wife because *he loves her so much*. He certainly didn't use his cell."

"No kidding. Did Song say how their investigation is going?"

"They have a hot lead on a guy who may have followed Tioux here from Mississippi. Trying to track him down now." Nicky grimaced. "Song wasn't impressed by our new information on the fertility clinic, but she said they'll look into Rémy and Kristina's marriage, see whether it was as close and loving as Kristina swears."

They wove between parked cars as they approached the casino side of the garage. Elevator doors opened, disgorging guests and the scent of cigarette smoke and heavy perfume.

As the waiting throng of people streamed inside, Nicky gave them a quick glance, then did a double take. One woman's pregnant silhouette looked familiar. Nicky craned her neck, but the woman was swallowed by the crowd and closing elevator doors.

Nicky and Franco skirted the concrete barriers blocking off a back corner of the garage. Overhead lighting bounced off gleaming luxury cars, sports cars, and off-road vehicles—loaners or rentals for the high-roller guests. A second exit, exclusive to the concierge area, climbed to a booth, barrier arm gates securing both in and out driveways.

Franco gave a low whistle and veered toward a four-wheel-drive pickup truck decked out in chrome, a heavy winch on its front bumper. He pressed his nose to the passenger's side window as he tried the door handle.

"Hey. *Hey*! You're not authorized—*aww*. You messed it up." A bearded man, mid-twenties, brown hair, and in a casino-logoed polo and jeans, hurried toward the truck. In one nitrile-gloved hand, he waved a red rag, in the other, a spray bottle filled with blue liquid. He squirted the window with Franco's noseprint and fingerprints on it and wiped it down before doing the same with the truck door handle. Underneath the ammonia smell of the cleaner, he carried the earthy scent of horses and leather.

Done, he squared off with them, scowling from under impressive brow ridges. Nicky hung back, measuring him against Franco's bulk. The guy was huge. He had at least thirty pounds on Franco and a couple of inches.

"This is a restricted area. You need to leave." He took a step forward, crowding Franco, who held his ground, stance relaxed, face half smiling.

"Just admiring the truck."

Nicky crossed her arms, her movement triggering the guy to glance her way. And blink warily. He inched back, but not before giving her a sliding up-and-down look. Franco's smile dropped.

"You're a cop," the guy said. "Then he's…"

"A cop, too." Nicky pulled her shield. "We're looking for Breedan

Halloran and Jacob Jacob. Is that right?"

"Middle name's Jacob, too. Nice parents, huh? I'm Halloran. Hey, Jacob!" he yelled over his shoulder before he turned back and asked, "This about the dead guy's car again? We told the FBI what we knew. Activated LoJack and everything. Found it yet?"

Two men approached, one just under medium height, wiry, light hair, dark red beard, and sharp features. Eyes sky blue where Halloran's were a muddy green. He was a shadow compared to Halloran. The other man was older, mid-seventies, with bowed legs, a paunch, and wire-rimmed glasses. He wore an onyx bolo around his neck and jingled car keys in his hand. He stiffened as he met Nicky's gaze, then his lips torqued into a sneer. *Great.*

"Mr. Póncio. I didn't expect..." Nicky glanced at Franco. "Mr. Póncio runs the rental-concierge service for the casino. He's also on tribal council and is, ah, Marica Santibanez's father."

Póncio's hostile gaze raked Franco. "I won't shake the hand of people who killed my grandson. You found that car yet? Can't file a claim and get my money back until you do."

"We have a few questions for Mr. Halloran and Mr. Jacob," Nicky said. The man smelled of alcohol. "Mr. Póncio, how much have you had to drink today?"

"Couple of beers at lunch." He pocketed his keys.

"If you drive impaired, I'll have to arrest you. You don't want your tribal driver's license revoked."

Póncio chuckled humorlessly, exposing worn teeth. "For an outsider, you sure are overzealous in enforcing our laws. I have very powerful friends."

Nicky raised an eyebrow but said nothing. Franco edged closer.

"Let me call PonyXpres for you, Mr. Póncio," Jacob Jacob said. "Why don't you wait in the office? Excuse me a minute, officers."

Póncio turned and swayed as they walked away, Jacob steadying him before pulling his phone out and pressing it to his ear.

"Mr. Halloran, did Mr. Tioux take out a car every day during his stay here?" Nicky asked.

"I already told the FBI. He'd take a car in the morning, sometimes switching it out for a four-wheel-drive vehicle in the afternoon."

"Did he ever mention where he went in the four-wheel?"

"No. Just figured it was off-road 'cause his vehicles came back real dirty." Halloran clutched his spray bottle and rag to his chest, a note of outrage in his voice. "Even the insides. Took forever to clean."

"Did he ever stay out after dark on these off-road trips?" Franco asked.

"He was usually back by the time I left—around seven."

"How long have you worked at the casino?" Nicky asked.

"End of July. Me and Jacob started at the same time."

"Did you know each other before?"

Halloran blushed. "Came down from Idaho together. He was following a girlfriend, but it didn't work out. Been with him for two exes now. Thought about heading out to Lovington—oil fields. Both of us have welder's licenses, but this pays pretty good here, and it's not so rough on the body."

"Mr. Halloran, where were you Monday night after work?" Franco asked.

The man's blush deepened, and he dropped his gaze. "Our apartment. We live in Corrales. Me and Jacob were binge-watching shows on his computer."

"Thank you, Mr. Halloran. Want to head to the office?" Franco asked Nicky.

Halloran tagged along behind them.

Franco turned. "I'm sure you have something to do."

Halloran stopped. "Sure. Sure." His gaze darted back and forth between them as he backed away.

Franco leaned down. "I think Halloran has the hots for Jacob."

"You think?"

"I'm kinda psychic that way." Franco widened his eyes and tapped the side of his head. "I have a *fifth sense* for stuff like that."

Nicky stared at him for a beat before she pressed her lips together to hold back a grin. She'd missed this Franco. "Do you have ESPN, too?"

"Sure, sure."

The barrier arm of the concierge driveway rose, and a compact car zipped down. It stopped by the open office door. PonyXpres rideshare. Jacob hurried out to hold the back door of the car open for Mr. Póncio. As the car accelerated back up the ramp, something niggled in the back of Nicky's mind, something she had to do. Jacob stood, hands tucked in his pockets.

"Halloran should've figured out by now whether Jacob's interested," she said.

Franco smiled down at her. "You'd be surprised how long a guy will hang around, even when all hope is gone. Maybe Halloran's afraid to show Jacob who he really is. That it would chase him away."

Though her heart thumped, Nicky raised her eyebrows.

Franco's smile morphed into a chuckle. "Not gonna bite, huh? Your source said two people were in the car they turned away from the earthen tank the night of the murders. One big, one small."

"Yeah." Over her shoulder, Nicky glanced from Jacob to Halloran, who watched them as he cleaned a windshield. "We really need to find that car."

CHAPTER TWENTY

THE SECURITY LIGHT flashed on in her carport as Nicky opened the side door to her house, shivering at the chill in the air. She locked the door behind her and skipped down the two concrete steps. Skirting her unit, she strode onto the driveway gravel. A second light popped on, glimmering over the rain-slick cement of her walled court-yard. Cold drizzle misted her exposed skin, raising gooseflesh.

She adjusted the .40-caliber Glock 27 in her bellyband—a personal weapon, small and easier to carry concealed—and pulled her pink fleece headband over her ears. With a chest-expanding inhalation, Nicky headed down the street at a steady jog.

Sunday morning quiet reigned, the only sounds her breathing and the slap of shoes on wet blacktop. Her body settled into the activity and warmed, blood pumping, cheeks stinging with the cold. Periodi-cally, headlights cut hollows through the darkness as a car rolled by, tires crackling on wet pavement.

Real estate agents labeled her neighborhood as *established and picturesque*, which really meant an area populated with 1940s-era cement-stuccoed adobes, driveways stacked with cars on blocks, and fences held up by tangles of saplings, vines, and force of will. Narrow access lanes demarcated puzzle-piece properties, a maze unless you knew the territory. She did. She'd lived there almost all her life. Her run took her past Mr. Gonzalez's house, well-kept with a yellow ball of porch light above his front door; the Chavez sisters—Sally and Juana, never married—kitchen light glowing, which meant they were making enchiladas for an after-church gathering; and a rental trailer whose tenants she was pretty sure sold drugs. Nicky sped up and braced. Two burly dogs hit the fence with a terrific clang before they let loose snarls and deep-throated barks. They raced Nicky along the fence line before she cut across the road and onto the hard-packed earth lining a weed-filled acequia, her blood pounding a little faster from the punch of adrenaline scared up by those dogs.

She rewound the interviews yesterday to pull out relevant information and form new questions to pursue: Jacob Jacob, Breedan Halloran, and muddy rental cars had confirmed Tioux had roamed the reservation; Marica Santibanez's animosity had softened under Franco's charm enough to link Tioux's visits to medicine gardens and the fertility clinic; and Kristina Tioux had seemed defiant and frightened about her husband's murder. Or was her demeanor linked to the conception of her baby girl? Also, had Peter Santibanez eavesdropped in the hall during Kristina's interview? Why? And how did any of this link to the pot scrapings at the museum?

Clouds silvered on the horizon with the sunrise, brightening the landscape to an unrelieved gray. The end of the path along the acequia diverged into a wooded area between fields. Nicky dove into the trees —her favorite part of the run—keeping to a narrow trail hemmed in by brambles and weeds that scratched at her fabric-covered arms and legs. She dodged or jumped piles of branches and leaves. The path would dump her out on a two-lane road a mile from her house. She sped up, sprinting toward a fallen tree across the path, leaped to clear it—

Her body slammed face-first into the ground.

Nicky lay stunned. She gasped in a breath, rolled dazedly to her back. Something circled her ankle. *Snared.*

With a flare of panic, she jerked her leg. The circle tightened, and the heavy cottonwood branch above her shivered, leaves and rainwater showering down. Panting, Nicky planted her feet and shoved off the downed tree trunk.

A crack, loud as a gunshot, wrenched her attention upward. The overhanging branch swung toward the ground. Her eyes widened. Toward *her*. She yanked into a ball, knees to chin, head wrapped in her arms.

The limb hit the dirt with a vibrating thump.

Everything stilled.

Nicky cracked an eyelid, the thud of her pulse deafening. She lay nestled in a wedge of space next to the tree trunk, cocooned above by a spider web of branches and dead leaves. Her cheek stung. She felt the tiny pokes of twigs through her clothes, the bite around her ankle. With a quick search, she found the wire snaring her leg. She ran her finger over the metal thread, followed it to the loop around the broken branch. Her brow pinched in confusion, then building anger.

Deadfall trap. A stupid prank that could've really hurt someone. Her momentum, then panic, had pulled the limb down.

A twig snapped. Nicky froze. Footsteps crunched, slowed. Paused. Her heart rate spiked again. Slowly, she craned her neck. Visible through the leaves, someone stood down the path, dressed in black, head hooded, face hidden. She opened her mouth to call for help but bit off her words, her scalp prickling. Gaze intent on the stranger, Nicky quietly slipped off the wire loop.

The individual moved closer, another step, gathered speed. One gloved hand raised a baseball bat.

Nicky pulled her sidearm.

"I have a gun."

The person stopped. In the time it took for Nicky to draw her next breath, the figure turned and bolted, melting into trees.

She slithered from under the tangle of branches, muscles bunched and ready for pursuit. Her first step out of the deadfall collapsed her to her knees, her legs like rubber. Unmoving, she stared intently down the narrow path. The man or woman—she hadn't been able to tell—didn't reappear. Gun clutched, she brushed wet leaves and dirt from her face. Blood stained the side of her hand.

Nicky pushed to her feet, feeling for balance. With one eye on the path, she studied the fallen branch. It could have crushed her. She shuddered and swiveled to survey the splintered end of the deadfall branch.

The chill of the rain cut straight to her core. Fresh hatchet marks scored the bark.

Someone had just tried to kill her.

CHAPTER TWENTY-ONE

NICKY SLID her gun into the pouch pocket of her muddy jacket, hand tight around its butt, and limped home. Savannah's compact car sat in front of her house. Rain fell steadily now.

Nicky unlatched the front gate and rolled it open. She slipped through, on edge, jaw clenched, and headed toward the house, cold, stiff, tiny nicks and cuts burning. Savannah, wrapped in a soft wooly scarf and thick coat, huddled by the carport door.

"Hurry up. It's freezing," Savannah said.

Nicky scanned the yard, the walled front patio, and the covered area around her mother's car. They knew where she lived. Tampering with her motion lights might have been a first attempt.

A shadow moved in her garage. Nicky pulled her gun.

"Stay where you are," she ordered. "Savannah, get behind me."

Eyes wide, mouth open, Savannah scuttled out of the carport.

"It's only Howard, Nicky. Oh, my God. Your face is bleeding." Savannah's gloved hand reached out. Nicky sidestepped away, tracking the figure sidling out from behind the car, his eyes owlish behind his thick, black-rimmed glasses. A dark sweatshirt bulked his thin torso, and jeans covered skinny legs.

Nicky exhaled the breath she'd been holding. She lowered her gun. Pain twinging one knee, she unlocked the door.

"Inside," she said.

The familiar scent of her home greeted her as she herded her friends up the steps. She bolted the door and stilled, waiting for the much-needed comfort of her sanctuary to envelop her. It never came.

Savannah and Howard stood, feet rooted to the kitchen floor, staring at her with rounded eyes. Nicky walked past them.

"What the heck was that all about?" Savannah's tone was sharp. "You're limping."

"Make some coffee," Nicky said. "I need a shower."

She turned down the narrow hall to duck into her bedroom, pulled thick sweats from her dresser drawer, and stepped into the bathroom to turn on the water. Her fingers were still wrapped around the butt of her gun. Reluctant to let go, she braced one arm against the edge of the sink and took deep, calming breaths. Her steam-fogged reflection showed a cut on her cheek—not bad but bruising—hair snagged from the tangle of branches, and mud smearing her chin. Hollow brown eyes stared back.

Who was trying to get her attention? And why?

NICKY PADDED SILENTLY DOWN the hallway to the large opening that framed the kitchen and living area, tiles cool on her bare feet. Savannah, back to her, poked at bacon in a sizzling skillet. A carton of eggs stood open beside her friend. She heard a clatter in the utility room.

"Howard? Quit snooping," Savannah called. "Nicky?"

"Eyes in the back of your head. You'll make a great mom someday, Savannah." Nicky shuffled to a cabinet and pulled out a first aid kit. She sat down at the kitchen table and rummaged around for the antibacterial ointment. "Why are you here?"

Savannah stilled for a moment. Then she put the fork down on a spoon rest.

"Over easy?" she asked.

"Yeah." Nicky dabbed her cut. She leaned down to roll up the legs of her sweats, the gun in her shoulder holster digging into her side. She spread ointment over the scrapes on her knees then the heels of both hands as Savannah scooped the bacon onto a paper-towel-draped plate and cracked two eggs into the grease.

"I needed to talk to someone," Savannah finally answered. "A friend."

Nicky scooped up the first aid kit and limped to the cupboard to put it away. She poured herself a cup of coffee, doctored it with artificial sweetener, and tucked her hip against the counter. "Ryan tells me Jinni's your friend now."

Savannah didn't look at her. The sizzle and pop of frying eggs filled the tense silence.

"Maybe I need to talk about Jinni. And Ryan. Plates."

Nicky handed her two plates. Savannah turned off the burner, and they both sat and started to eat.

"What happened, Nicky?" Savannah asked.

With a grimace, Nicky touched her cheek. She also needed someone to talk to.

"You have to promise not to tell. I don't want Ryan or … anyone to know about this. They'll just blow it out of proportion."

Savannah gave a bitter little laugh. "Don't worry. I'm a great secret keeper."

"On my run, I … I triggered a deadfall trap. A branch from an old cottonwood fell on top of me. Someone was there, watching. I couldn't see their face. I think this person was waiting for me. They had a bat." Her throat dried, and she sipped her coffee.

"You think you were the target?" Savannah's brows knitted. "But how did they know where you'd run?"

"Routine, I guess. I should know better, especially since…" Nicky breathed in and out. "Since someone tampered with my security lights a few days ago. I think I'm being watched. Around Bernalillo, Albuquerque, even the pueblo. Last Friday, when I was at a potential crime scene, there may have been someone there, in the trees."

"You need to file a report," Savannah said.

"I've got no evidence that what happened today was anything more than a stupid prank. They'd just tell me to be more careful."

"Then talk to Franco. Nicky, you two are good together. You see connections others don't."

"I can handle this. Besides, he wouldn't care." Nicky probed an egg with her fork. She hadn't meant to sound so petulant.

"Because he brought Lottie Fields to my house for Friday dinner?" Savannah searched Nicky's face. "It's more than that, isn't it? He walked away from you after the Stone Fetish case."

"He should've trusted me. Instead, he just drove off and left." Like her mother, her father, Dax... Nicky forked a bite of egg and chewed, wincing internally at the depths of self-pity. She really needed to get over herself.

"Do you know how hard it is to be friends with Jinni sometimes? How hard it is to hide how I feel?" Savannah sighed. "Don't do what I did. Don't throw away your chance."

Nicky could think of no reply. Savannah had loved Ryan for years but held him at arm's length because he wasn't Fire-Sky. When she'd finally realized how little that mattered, she found she'd waited too long. He'd lost hope and married someone else.

She and Savannah ate, the tink of silverware on ceramic loud in the quiet.

"What did you need to talk about?" Nicky asked.

Savannah laid her fork down. Nicky noticed most of the food was still on her plate. Her friend had been pushing it around instead of eating.

"Ryan's drinking again."

"I saw." Instead of his usual Pellegrino, he'd tucked a beer behind some knickknacks Friday night at Savannah's. "Do you know why?"

"Money. Stress. Jinni's baby's due soon. He's working more overtime shifts, making more jewelry to sell, but all that takes time away from Jinni." Savannah stared down at her congealed eggs. "She's not happy about it."

"She told you this?" Nicky propped her elbows on the table and laced her fingers. "How do you do it? How can you be friends with her?"

Savannah narrowed her eyes. "How are you friends with that rat Dax Stone? Jinni didn't do anything wrong. That's all on me. I can't blame her or Ryan because I didn't get my happy ending."

And that was Savannah to the core. A font of forgiveness Nicky wished she could tap into because there were people in her life she couldn't forgive. Wouldn't forgive.

"There are programs on the pueblo to help people in situations like this," Nicky said.

But Savannah was shaking her head. "They don't qualify. She's not Fire-Sky. Technically, neither is Ryan, even though he was adopted by his stepfather. Nicky, they might have to move away—move to her or his People or off rez."

Savannah stood abruptly. She stacked their dirty plates and marched to the sink to turn on the water. Nicky followed more slowly with the silverware. Her friend pressed her hands on the counter's edge and stared out the small kitchen window.

"What if the real father can help?" Savannah said. "What if he has money and resources?" She turned her head to stare at Nicky. "What if he's Tsiba'ashi D'yini?"

"I thought Jinni said he was dead."

"Everyone knows she's lying."

"Then he should help out. He's the baby's father."

"You don't get it, do you? Ryan and Jinni can't take a Tsiba'ashi D'yini baby and *leave*. It's happened too many times in the past. Tribal council would never agree." Savannah gripped the edge of the sink, knuckles white. "If this is a Fire-Sky child, maybe they shouldn't be raising it. Maybe it should be taken by the real father."

Nicky's breath caught. "Are you serious?"

"It's not Ryan's baby. He married Jinni because he felt sorry for her, not because he loves her."

"Savannah, he won't leave Jinni. That's not who Ryan is. You understand, right?"

Savannah spun toward her, eyes shimmering. She jabbed a finger at Nicky's chest. *"You don't know that."*

"Did Jinni tell you who the baby's father is?"

Savannah hesitated, her expression becoming even more distraught. "What if she did?"

A door slammed, and a sound like marbles ticking on tile snapped their heads toward the laundry room. Howard, bent at the waist, chased Hot Tamale candies across the floor.

"Howard." Savannah straightened, blinking away her tears. "What did I tell you about eating candy before breakfast?"

He stood, sweatshirt shoulders wet, the lenses of his glasses fogged, and stared back and forth between Nicky and Savannah.

"Some went under your washer," he said.

Nicky had forgotten he was there.

CHAPTER TWENTY-TWO

HER GUN WAS next to her cell phone, both on her nightstand and within easy reach. In the dark, Nicky stared up at the spinning ceiling fan, her thoughts swirling between the murder investigation, the attempts on her life, Savannah's visit, and the image of Howard Kie standing in the doorway to her utility room. It halted on Howard.

"People don't much take me into account," he'd once told her.

She'd been guilty of that. Had almost forgotten he was at the museum the morning of the murder.

Howard was on her and Franco's interview list. He drove for PonyX-pres, said he'd taken Rémy Tioux around the pueblo. He was pure blood quantum Fire-Sky. Would he know the locations of the medicine gardens?

She grabbed her phone, flipped her legs over the side of her bed, and scrolled to find Howard's contact info. He picked up after three rings.

"Howard? This is Sergeant Matthews—Nicky. You said at the museum you recognized Mr. Tioux because you'd driven him. Did you ever take him to any medicine gardens?"

"Maybe. Is this an interrogation?" Howard's voice, rusty with sleep, perked up.

"No," she reassured him. "Just questions I need to ask."

"Oh." Silence.

"What is it, Howard?"

"I wanted to be hauled to the station and interrogated in one of your little rooms."

He'd been watching too much TV again.

"What did you mean by 'maybe'?" she asked.

There was a pause. "They are secret places. Sacred places. Medagaana are not allowed. This man was Natchez Nation. He was allowed on some. He said he needed to pray and give offerings."

Not wanted—needed. "You took him to a medicine garden?"

"More than one." Howard paused again. "You sound too nice. Not like a cop."

Nicky rubbed her forehead. He wanted playacting. Hardening her voice, she said, "Mr. Kie, if you help me find Mr. Tioux's rental car, I'll haul you down to the station for a statement."

"Really?" He sounded much happier.

"I'll be at your trailer within the hour, Mr. Kie. I want you to take me to the places you took Mr. Tioux. Be ready." Nicky lowered her voice to a growl. "Or else."

"Better," he said, "but you need to work on your performance." Howard hung up.

Nicky stared at the phone, lips twitching. God, she'd missed Howard Kie.

She dressed in jeans, a long-sleeved base layer, and a waffled olive Henley and strapped on her shoulder holster before she grabbed her black rain jacket. She picked up her keys, hesitated, and hurried to the bathroom to pull out eyeshadow and mascara from a drawer and stopped. She'd hammered Franco for hiding behind his undercover personas—for *playacting*. But what was she doing? Shoving her makeup away, she dialed Franco.

He picked up immediately. "Nicky."

"Meet me behind the FEMA trailer at Howard Kie's. Call me once you're on your way, and I'll explain."

She was out the door and on the road within a minute, her unit's windshield wipers beating away the driving rain.

They found Rémy Tioux's car at the second site Howard took them to.

CHAPTER TWENTY-THREE

NICKY SLAMMED the passenger's side door of Franco's unit, the chill morning air watering her eyes. Although blue sky vied with the clouds, the sides of the cliffs surrounding the Isgaawa museum complex were crisp and dark with receding rain showers.

"We're outta here the second CSU releases the crime scene," Nicky said acidly. "This is all SAC Headley. Still in Mississippi, banishing us like we're interfering in this investigation instead of giving us credit for finding Tioux's rental car and the actual murder location."

Franco matched her steps. "We have some time to burn, and this could be important."

Nicky shot him a sour glance. "Charlotte Field could have *emailed* you her list of plant identifications."

"We'd need to pick up the evidence at some point. Might as well be now. And Lottie said she'd be extra busy with Dean pushing for the original exhibition start date. Look, I'll go talk to Lottie, you can chat with Dean—"

"No way. There's enough conflict of interest already because you two have dated." Nicky stalked to the museum's entrance. "A neutral third party needs to be present."

Franco shot around her to open one of the huge wooden doors. "I consider that a nonissue, Matthews. After all"—his eyes glinted—"we've dated, too."

He was enjoying this. Nicky yanked open the second door and stepped inside the museum's foyer. Soothing flute music warbled through the ceiling sound system. It scraped against her nerves.

Nicky asked at the front for Dean and Charlotte and was directed to the archives room. She threaded her way through a chattering yellow-T-shirted group of schoolchildren, Franco trailing her. A faux wall of stacked adobe bricks created a short hallway to the room, its STAFF ONLY sign displayed above the glass door.

Dean stood behind the flat-topped cabinet that served as the checkout desk, a huge grin gracing his bewhiskered face. On the countertop in front of him, a large book was opened to a delicately drawn and colored lithograph of a plant Nicky didn't recognize.

"Nicky! And Franco. Lottie is so excited you used her to help identify plants. She's even talked about enrolling in a few criminal justice courses. Wasn't that your undergraduate degree, Nicky? After you opted out of chemistry? Lottie?" Dean called. "She even knows your old principal investigator from NMSU. What was his name?"

"John Byers. He's not at State anymore," Nicky said. "He moved to—"

"Arizona. He was the principal investigator for my master's degree." Charlotte stepped out from between two racks of shelved materials, a plant press in her hands. She was dressed in brightly colored running shoes, tight athletic leggings patterned in black-and-white swirls, and a heavy black tunic. Soft red-brown curls floated in a cloud around her head, green eyes clear and bright. *She'd* put on makeup. "Dr. Byers said you were one of his most gifted undergrads. He even let me read a paper you'd authored. *Authored.* As a sophomore. Amazing. Hi, Franco." Charlotte ducked her head coyly. "I missed you this morning for coffee."

Franco met Nicky's flat stare with a sheepish shrug. "Sorry, Lottie. Had to get to work early."

Charlotte sucked in an excited breath as she put the press on the counter between them. "I heard you found the missing car and murder site. And another desecrated medicine garden."

Nicky ground her teeth. *Damn pueblo gossip.* None of that information was supposed to be released.

"We don't know if Mr. Tioux was killed there yet," Franco said.

"Oh." Charlotte's brows knit, and she shot a glance at Dean.

"Why don't we see what Lottie has for you," Dean said, his grin widening.

Charlotte opened the plant press. "Nothing I identified could be considered uncommon or rare, but someone's been experimenting with what would grow in this garden. This first plant is normally found in eastern woodlands. *Caulophyllum thalictroides.* Blue cohosh. Roots and rhizomes relieve women of the pains of childbirth. Next"— she flipped the page—"is *Rubus idaeus*—raspberry. Raspberry-leaf tea is thought to prevent miscarriage. It grows in New Mexico, but this is probably another transplant to this garden. Finally, *Trillium erectum* or birthroot. Enough said, right?" She grinned. "Again, not indigenous to the state. It likes temperate climates. If this is what they stole, I'd say your bioprospectors are going to be disappointed once they realize what they have, especially when they compare it to, um, *previous work* on the pot scrapings. Right, Sergeant Matthews?"

Dean placed his hand on a thick manila folder next to the open lithographs. "Charlotte scoured the internet, looking for your mother's publications and abstracts, Nicky."

Crap. "Dean," Nicky said in a low voice, "I haven't—" She tipped her head toward Franco.

"Don't let him fool you," Charlotte said and tapped Dean playfully on the hand. "He already had quite a few in his files. None of the compounds mentioned in your mother's publications are in the plants Franco gave me."

"What does this have to do with Nicky's mother?" Franco looked back and forth between Dean and Charlotte.

Nicky caught Charlotte's gaze. She didn't like the underlying triumphant gleam in the younger woman's eyes.

"You haven't told your partner about your mother's link to the pot scrapings?" Charlotte asked.

"That hasn't been confirmed," Nicky said through tight lips.

"*Surely* it was relevant that the murderer selected those pots," Charlotte said. "After all, the *only* pottery sampled were ones *your mother* had analyzed." She leaned toward Nicky, a single eyebrow raised.

"That wasn't what you told Agent Martinez, was it, Ms. Fields?" Nicky bent forward until she and Charlotte were practically nose-to-nose. "Didn't you tell him you couldn't be sure when the second scrapings were taken because you were careless when you assessed the pots for the exhibit?"

Charlotte pulled back abruptly and flashed a panicked glance at Dean.

"Lottie! You didn't update the descriptions?" Dean groaned. "You know how important that is for insurance purposes. What if something gets broken or damaged during the exhibition?"

Charlotte wrapped her arms around her middle and suddenly looked close to tears. "Dean, I-I … y-you said…"

Dean rubbed a hand over his face before he straightened and sighed. "This is my fault. We were so behind, and I pushed you to get things done quickly."

"I'm so sorry. I let you down." Charlotte pressed a hand against her forehead and swayed, face crumpling.

Nicky rolled her eyes. Like anyone would believe such drama—

Franco hurried around the counter. "Hey. Are you okay?"

"Some water would be great." Charlotte blinked up at him and smiled tremulously. "Would you come with me?"

"Of course."

They retreated between the bookshelves and disappeared.

"My, my," Dean said. "That young woman certainly is determined."

"She's obsessed with him," Nicky said through clenched teeth.

"No, my dear," he said gravely. "If anything, she's obsessed with *you*."

Nicky made a scoffing noise.

"You don't see it? There are many parallels. She did her graduate degree with your old PI, and her publications are on analytical analysis of natural products in museum artifacts—your original focus. Now she wants to take criminal justice classes, and she has a job near you on the pueblo. She's trying to date your man, cultivate your friends."

"Not counting the CJ stuff, her career trajectory is closer to Mom's," Nicky said. "And he's not my man."

"She'll be too busy with final touches to the fertility exhibition to be much of a worry. And I didn't realize until recently that her brother and one of his friends are staying with her. That's taken up even more of her time." Dean shook his head. "None of my business, but this is." He opened the file folder containing her mother's publications and extracted a single page, the top corner torn as if it had once been stapled. "I don't think you've seen this."

The print was faded with age. "What is it?" Nicky asked.

"I'm guessing abstracts from a meeting, although there's no indication what the meeting was about or where it was held. Second one down from the left. Look who wrote it."

"My parents?" Nicky's brows knit. "Mom never uses her married name on publications. And Dad always published under his middle name, not his first."

"Because he hated the name Hemis growing up. Too Greek for a boy from Lowell, Massachusetts. Look when it was written." Dean pressed a finger under the date. "Right after they were married. Maureen and I attended their wedding, you know. They were so in love. They must have done the work while your mother was a graduate student in your father's lab—a true collaboration."

"Yeah, well, Dad collaborated with a lot of his female students."

"Yes. Poor Helena. His affairs devastated her. You're a lot alike that way."

Nicky sputtered. "I am not like my mother."

Dean sent her a pitying look before he said, "Read the title."

"'Traces of an extinct southwestern orchid *ssp.* found in ancient Puebloan fertility pottery contains potent mammalian parthenogenic compounds.' Oh, come on. Mammals giving birth to their own genetic clones? That's ridiculous." She pushed the page away.

"I know. Outrageous. Lottie had this when she was hired. I'd never even seen it. Read the abstract, Nicky. The work was done on pottery found here. On the Tsiba'ashi D'yini Pueblo. The compounds were extracted—possibly—from one of the pots sampled during the break-in. I say possibly because there are no further publications on this topic. But..." Dean turned to her, eyes bright. "It must be what the bioprospectors are searching for. Think of it, Nicky. *Mammalian parthenogenesis.*"

"It's an abstract, Dean. Nothing more," Nicky countered. "And it says the plant's extinct."

"Have you ever heard of *Rhizanthella gardneri*? Or *Thismia neptunis?*"

Dean pulled the book of lithographs over so she could see the plate. The burnt-orange flower depicted was alien: a tear-shaped cup topped with three needle-slim trident-like protrusions sitting atop a curved white stalk.

"*Thismia neptunis* lives underground in Malaysia. It contains no chlorophyll, so it doesn't need sunlight, and only emerges when it flowers. And it's only been seen twice in the last one hundred and fifty years."

"Why haven't seeds been collected and planted in other places?"

"This orchid is absolutely dependent on a specialized mycorrhizal soil fungi, and no one knows how to grow it. Artificial propagation has failed. The same is true of this orchid."

He flipped to another page. The flower was less alien—waxy pink petals cupping smaller blossoms the shape and color of pomegranate seeds.

"*Rhizanthella gardneri*, found in Australia. It flowers below ground, never emerging from the soil. Both of these orchids are critically endangered, extremely rare. You said these gardens are excavated, as if the bioprospectors are harvesting roots. What if *this* is what they're looking for? A subterranean plant everyone else thinks is extinct? But I don't think it's extinct, and neither do the people searching the medicine gardens. Your mother and father worked on this together."

Dean laid a hand over hers. "Nicky. What if your mother knows where the plant can be found? What if your mother is the key to the murder of Rémy Tioux?"

AS SOON AS they stepped out of the museum's front door, Franco turned on Nicky.

"You should have told me about your mother," he said, voice accusing.

"I'm sure Charlotte filled you in." Nicky's gaze traced the rim of the canyon. Clouds now dominated the blue sky, their undersides heavy with rain. A chill breeze kicked up, and she tugged her jacket closer. She felt sick.

"Hey. Are you okay?"

Same thing he'd said to Charlotte. Franco hesitated before he placed a hand on her shoulder. Nicky closed her eyes, chest tight, wanting nothing more than to lean into him.

"Nicky, what's going on?"

She breathed deeply of the clean, damp air. "Dean's convinced that whoever is digging up these gardens is looking for roots or tubers. Something that grows underground." She wasn't ready to discuss the rest of Dean's suppositions about Charlotte, her mother, the murder... She needed time to think.

"We'd pretty much figured that out." Franco dropped his hand, and they both walked to his unit. After a few steps he said, "A first author paper as an undergrad. Even I know that's impressive."

Nicky increased her pace down the sidewalk and to the truck. "It wasn't published. In fact, it was soundly rejected as derivative. Unoriginal in idea and scope. The push I needed to quit science and switch to law. That didn't work out, either, so I became a cop. Charlotte was okay?" She hadn't meant to ask.

"A ploy to get me alone," he admitted.

She wondered if they'd made another date.

"Pretty drastic to quit your degree because of a rejection." Franco beeped open his unit, and Nicky climbed in the passenger's side. She burrowed deeper into her jacket. Franco started the truck but turned his torso toward her and laid his arm across the steering wheel. "There's more to it?"

Nicky stared out the front windshield. The yellow-shirted schoolchildren now bundled with hoodies and sweatshirts were streaming out of the museum, holding hands, two by two.

"I chose the same field as my mother. Dr. Helena Galini. She never used my father's last name on publications." Except for that abstract. "She's a pioneer in analytical analysis of organic residue on ancient pottery and tools. She was a graduate student in my dad's lab when they got married. It didn't work out. After that, she wasn't around a lot. She traveled to digs all over the world. Her work was—is—important. She's important. I was determined to follow in her footsteps, and I was so proud of my paper I sent her a copy the same day I submitted it for peer review." Scudding clouds covered the sun and covered the whole Isgaawa complex in shadow. Still, Nicky slotted on her sunglasses. "My mother spearheaded its rejection."

Franco studied her, his expression grave. "Why?"

"If you ever meet her, ask," Nicky said. "I'd like to know, too."

CHAPTER TWENTY-FOUR

FRANCO'S FINGERS flexed on the steering wheel as he guided his unit over muddy ridges hardened to cement by the freeze last night. Nicky rocked and swayed in the passenger seat of the truck, anticipating the jarring drops, and bracing for bumps. CSU had released Tioux's murder site that morning, and since Song and Headley wouldn't be back from Mississippi until later that evening, this was the perfect opportunity to review the location before the FBI interfered.

When she'd climbed into the cab for the two-hour drive to the site, Nicky braced for pointed questions about her mother and her connection to the case, but Franco had only said, "Coffee's in the console." It would have been churlish to refuse his offering, especially since, other than a few desultory remarks, he'd stayed quiet and let her think.

Franco negotiated the truck around a stand of fir and continued the climb up the side of the mesa. The link between the murder of Tioux, the pot scrapings at the museum, and her mother chilled Nicky. But how was any of that connected to her disabled security lights and the deadfall trap on her Sunday morning run? Was someone trying to knock her off the Tioux case? Or were the attacks completely unrelated, only a coincidence? She shot a glance at Franco. Maybe she should speak to him about the attacks like Savannah had suggested. Maybe she should call her mother, talk to her about a link. Dean thought her mother could help. He had her most recent contact information, but Nicky didn't want … what? Didn't want her mother interfering? Didn't want her exposed to danger? Or didn't want to deal with the turmoil that boiled up between them whenever they spent more than a minute of time together? She shook her head, impatient with her internal debate.

The truck lunged over the mesa top and crept along two bare furrows snaking through a meadow, its bunch grass crusted with frost. The track continued into a thick stand of ponderosa and wound between trees for another mile before Franco pulled his unit into a clearing, edged on one side by an eroded dirt bank, and turned off the truck. Cocooned in the cab, Nicky studied the scene, absorbing the peaceful isolation and stark beauty defiled by fluttering crime-scene tape tied around a trunk. At the start of the faint path worn between two towering pines, a discarded plastic water bottle rocked back and forth in a shallow depression.

Franco leaned his arms over the steering wheel. "Rain and snow wiped out tire tracks, so no way to trace the perps' vehicle, but the understory protected the scuffs in the pine needles. That puts the attack not ten feet from Tioux's car. CSU thinks his killers were waiting for him. Caught him as he walked up the path."

A gust of wind buffeted the truck. Cold seeped into the cab, replacing the lingering warmth.

"Waiting for him," Nicky murmured. "But how did his killers know he was coming? After his meeting about the casino deal, he only made two calls—one to the Santa Fe fertility clinic and one to his wife in Mississippi. The only phone call he received was from Peter Santibanez, who invited him to dinner. Neither Kristina nor Santibanez said Tioux told them he was going to a shrine. Unless one or both of them lied."

Franco grunted, face grim. "Based on your source, there were at least two bad guys in Tioux's car. After they dropped the body off at the museum and the hands into the tank, they had to come back here to pick up their vehicle. Why didn't they drive both cars out of here and ditch Tioux's car somewhere else?"

"Maybe they wanted us to find it?" Nicky chewed the inside of her lip.

Franco leaned into the back seat and grabbed their jackets. "Ready?"

In answer, Nicky slipped a maroon fleece headband over her ears and opened her door.

Freezing wind bit into exposed skin. She pulled on her heavy black jacket, snuggling into the faux-fur collar before she tugged gloves from her jacket pocket. A thin haze of crystals veiled the sky, seeming to absorb and magnify the sunlight.

Franco walked to the trailhead, a black fleece band covering his ears but his hands bare. Nicky followed him into the dark understory of pines, the furry green boughs blocking all but scant patches of light. He stopped and swept his arm to the right.

"Prelim report says Tioux was taken here. Pep Katina's description of the garden and shrine puts both about a mile to a mile and a half away."

Ice-frosted gashes disturbed the accumulated pine needles, and pink crime-scene flags protruded from the ground. Nicky slipped off her gloves and took pictures, recreating the abduction in her mind. Had Tioux passed his killers, thinking they were there for the same purpose—to visit a sacred place, pray, and give offerings?

Nicky frowned. "Why did CSU think Tioux was taken before he visited the shrine?"

"No evidence he went any farther than these trees."

"Howard told me Rémy Tioux came to these shrines with offerings, but there weren't any on the body. What happened to his offerings?"

"Killers stole them? Stuff like stone fetishes and pottery can be worth big money. His wallet wasn't found either," Franco said.

She raised her hand, waggling her ring finger. "Then why didn't they steal Tioux's wedding band? What if CSU was wrong and Tioux was attacked after he visited the shrine?" Nicky sheathed her hands back in her gloves. "Glad I wore my hiking boots."

THE PATH WENDED UPWARD through winter-brittle grass, patches of tall straight trees, and slippery shale. Wind shirred and tattled between bare branches and whistled through the dark green puffs of pine needles, at times drowning out the crunch of Nicky's boots. Crusts of early snow lay banked in shadowed areas. Ahead of her, Franco topped a steep rise and disappeared. She trudged up after him, ducking her face to blink eyes stinging from the cold.

He waited for her, arms crossed, surveying a scraped circle of earth, the hand-sized rocks that bordered the spokes jumbled throughout. Another desecrated medicine garden.

"This wasn't in CSU's preliminary report." He pulled out his phone.

"Looks pretty fresh. Might have happened after Tioux's murder."

"Do you want to keep going or recall CSU?" Franco asked.

She hesitated. "Keep going. We'll be in trouble for going this far. Might as well make it worth our while. Where's the shrine?"

"According to Pep, just over the hill. I'll catch up in a minute." He took a picture, skirted the edge of disturbed earth, and took another.

Nicky followed the trail through the brown grass up the slope—this one bare and slick—to another flat expanse, much larger than the one that held the garden. She looked back at Franco, who'd knelt down for a close-up of the garden. The land terraced downward. Natural or man-made? She got her answer as she moved to the middle of her terrace and found a large hole, over a dozen feet in diameter and at least eight feet deep. An extinct geyser. At some point, heated water had boiled from the geyser and flowed down, gathering in flat pools on each level. Time and vegetation had eroded much of the geology.

She sidled to the hole and peered inside. Its edges lipped around a depression in the earth, reminding her of a kiva without a roof. In the middle of the sandy floor stood a pyramid, two or three feet high, of stacked rocks on a flat stone base. Wedged between the rocks were prayer sticks of all lengths. Shrine offerings.

A weathered aluminum ladder was propped against the rim.

Nicky knew she should call in a traditional officer to make sure nothing was so sacred it couldn't be photographed, but the shrine was potentially part of a crime scene. She needed to check if Tioux had been there. At least, that's what she told herself as she placed her boot on the top rung.

The sandy floor was soft and deep. Nicky crept to the rock shrine and sat on her heels to catalog the offerings. Mostly prayer sticks, leather thongs or strings tied to feathers of all sizes, painted designs on the shafts faded and peeling. One stick seemed fresher than the others, bluebird feathers bright in the cold afternoon light. A bracelet lay at the base of the stick, its elastic band broken, a dozen square pink beads scattered. She tugged off a glove and, using her fingernail, turned one over and read the inscribed black letter—*V*. Carefully, she flipped the rest of the beads, finding letters on a total of five. She sorted them into a name: *R-A-V-E-N*.

Rémy Tioux's little girl. He'd been here.

Nicky dropped her head in her hand, mind racing. Why had he broken his daughter's bracelet and left it here? A glint of gold caught her eye. She swept her fingers over the sand by the toe of her boot. A ring. Nicky picked it up by its edges. A man's wedding band by the size. There was an inscription. As she read it, shock almost toppled her backward.

Rémy and Kristina Forever

But Rémy Tioux's severed left hand wore a wedding ring.

That ring had an inscription, too.

HMXHM Till death do us part

HM. Nicky's breath came faster. The abstract Dean had showed her, the one Charlotte had dug up. Her mother's married name and her father's hated given name. Helena Matthews. Hemis Matthews. HM by HM. Legs suddenly boneless, she plopped to her rear in the sand.

The ring at the shrine was Rémy Tioux's, one he'd abandoned.

But the ring on Tioux's hand was Hemis Matthews's. Nicky's father.

Kaleidoscope memories whipped through her head. Sitting warm and sheltered on her father's lap, chubby hands tugging at the shiny circlet on his finger. Her dad laughing and slipping the ring over her thumb, crooning, *"You want this, figlia mia numera una?"*

"Hey. What'd you find?" Franco's voice shocked Nicky into standing on wobbly knees. Unobtrusively, she slid the ring into the pocket of her cargos.

"A bracelet Tioux left. CSU was wrong. He was attacked as he was returning to his car." She gestured to the beads with a hand that shook only slightly.

The ring seemed to burn against her leg.

"PETROGLYPHS." Franco jogged to a large boulder at the far end of the shrine terrace.

Nicky stepped off the ladder and trotted after him.

A bone-white spiral had been picked out on the weathered face of the gray rock. Next to it was a round-headed stick figure, arms and legs turning ninety degrees up at the elbows and down at the knees. From between its legs, a meandering tail extended and connected to an egg-shaped oval the size of the stick figure's head, with two small dots chipped out at one end.

"Is that a lizard?" Franco asked.

Nicky shrugged and touched the spiral. "This represents wind or water." She tugged out her phone. "Hey. I have a couple of bars. The path keeps going. There must be something else up there. Why don't you go on ahead? I'll see if I can call in. I'll follow in a minute."

"I have a sat phone in the truck if you want to head back."

"No. Let's keep going."

Franco tipped his head, brows puckered. "You okay?"

"Fine."

"I'll wait while you call."

"Franco. I have to pee." Nicky pointed up the path. "Go."

His cheeks reddened, and he laughed uncomfortably. Without another word, he turned and powered up the slope.

Nicky hurried to the edge of the terrace and stepped into the trees. She unclasped the chain around her neck holding her Spirit's Heart pendant, dug into her pocket for the ring, and threaded it through the necklace. Holding the circle of gold at eye level, she read the inscription again before tucking everything down her top. She ran an agitated hand over her headband and hair, fingers tangling in the bun at her nape, and paced.

Her father's wedding ring on Rémy Tioux's hand. That's why it had looked so familiar to her at the autopsy. First, the exhibition pots her mother had sampled, now a relic from her dead father—both connected to a dead man. A murdered man.

Nothing makes sense.

Franco would come looking for her if she stayed much longer. She dialed Dispatch. After a few seconds, the phone beeped three times. No signal. Of course not since she'd lied about that to get away. She shoved her phone in her pocket and stepped toward the light.

A branch snapped in the woods. Hardly breathing, Nicky slipped behind a tree. Ears pricked, senses alert, she searched the thick brush under the canopy of boughs.

Nothing but the gentle drop of dead pine needles.

She backed out of the woods, pivoted, and strode to the petroglyphs and path, craning her head over her shoulder twice. She climbed the steep bank, boots digging furrows in soft soil, and found herself on a gradual incline upward, the trees atop it spaced unnaturally distant. She cut across the bottom of the slope, counting at least a dozen stumps, flat as tables and silvered with age. Logs cut into sections lay stacked and left to rot. A logging operation too close to a sacred site, shut down more than a decade ago.

"Down the slot and round the cliff," Franco called.

She hurried to his voice, slipping a little on silvery scree that lined the inclined path. Earth rose above her head on both sides, creating a narrow, confined passageway. But as she curved around the mountain, the passage walls fell away and the path led to a flat, semicircular ledge or shelf, maybe fifteen feet wide and thirty feet long. A short cliff banked one side of the shelf, the land above it cleared of trees, brushy and rolling up to the top of the mountain. On the shelf's other side, boulders embedded in the ground lined the top of a crumbling shale slide that dropped off into space and a breathtaking view of the surrounding mountains. A few scraggly pines grew near the bottom edge.

"Didn't realize we were up so high." Franco stared over the expanse, headband around his neck like a loose collar, his face peaceful. He patted a boulder, which came up to the top of his legs. "These must've acted like an ancient guardrail, otherwise one wrong step and you're on a slip 'n' slide to oblivion." He gestured to the opposite end of the ledge. "The path keeps going and drops down onto an old logging road. A second access Pep didn't tell me about. He didn't say anything about this place, either. Look at this."

Franco led Nicky to a concealed opening in the cliff lining the ledge. It hid a stacked rock wall sheltering a small natural basin of water, the stones directly above it stained dark and slick with moisture that trickled out of the earth. Petroglyphs chipped into the rocks mixed with black-painted pictographs. More spirals, hands, a dragonfly.

Nicky froze. An image crept from the depths of her memory. It was all she could do to catch her breath.

"A birthing niche." Her voice was raw and harsh. Hands balled to fists in her pockets to keep them from shaking. "That image. It wasn't a lizard. It was a woman giving birth. The tail was the umbilical. The oval, a baby in the amniotic sac."

"No kidding. I've never seen..." Franco's voice faded as Nicky's vision tunneled.

She stood in a cave, a room of stacked rock in front of her, a painted oval pot listing on its side in the doorway. Water dripped into a small round pool, its surface a purple-black mirror in the thin light from a crack in the rocks behind her, the crack she'd crawled through.

Six years old and she'd been left alone in the slot canyon. Her mother was leading people to dig some rock houses, trusting her father to watch her. Her father told her to play with her toys for a few minutes as he and one of his students slipped away, whispering and touching.

Her Matchbox car bit into the skin of one hand as she reached for the pot with the other, childish fingers ghostly white in the darkness. Her mother liked old pots. She'd take it for her mother. But when she touched it, the walls began to whisper. When she picked it up, the whispers grew louder, became words she didn't understand. And from the water rose the black shadow of a little girl, eyes dots of glowing red light, drifting toward her, hands reaching, fingers long and thin, narrowing to sharp tips, touching her hair, running through her hair, snagging and tearing.

A hand fell on her shoulder.

"Nicky?"

She jerked away, gulping air, stumbled on shaky legs toward the barrier of stones. She tore off her gloves and ripped off the headband, fingers unsteady as she ran them over her hair, checking, smoothing. The cold slapped her skin, but her head swam dizzily. She staggered to the rocks, pitched, fell—

A strong arm banded her waist. She was yanked back into the heat of Franco's chest. He forcefully bent her forward, murmuring in her ear, "Breathe. Hands on your knees, head down. Breathe."

Nicky couldn't do anything else. The black spots swirling behind her eyelids receded as the primitive fear blanketing her seeped away. Her fingers dug painfully into her knees as they steadied. Tears stung. She straightened, and Franco turned her, pulling her tightly against him. Over his shoulder, her blurry gaze searched out the niche.

Franco disentangled his arms and took a step back, pressing his hands into the top of her shoulders. She pulled her eyes away from the cliff wall and met his searching gaze. His face was bleached white, cheeks gray, brown eyes glittering.

"*Dammit*, Nicky. Do you know how close—" His voice choked. "You would have—I almost lost—" Trembling fingers cupped her cheek. His thumb brushed gently over the healing cut on her cheek, and his face dipped forward, breath mingling with hers. Residual fear evaporated, replaced by heat swirling in her belly. Her eyelids fluttered closed. Parted lips brushed softy against Franco's—

A violent *thwack* echoed down the slope above them. Nicky jerked away, twisting toward the birthing niche. The air rumbled. Vibrations beneath her feet transformed into sharp waves of sound. She caught movement from the slope above. Her eyes widened, and she grabbed Franco's arm. A tree trunk, dirt and rocks shooting around it like a dusty halo, barreled and bounced off hillocks of earth with lethal acceleration. Under her hand, Franco's muscles tightened to rock as the log sailed in an arc off the edge of the birthing niche, spinning in the air directly toward them.

CHAPTER TWENTY-FIVE

NICKY AND FRANCO dove behind the stones, the scant ground they took refuge on only as wide as a body before it crumbled away. Nicky tucked herself along the ledge, Franco pulling her head and shoulders under his, pressing her face into prickling grass and pebbles. The spinning trunk slammed with a reverberating *crack* into the top of the rocks shielding them. A shower of wood splinters rained down as the tree trunk careened over them. She turned her head and peered out from under Franco's arm, tracking the log's path as it bounced and rumbled down the slope, crushing bushes and snapping the trunks of the scraggly pines before it disappeared over the edge in a clatter of sliding shale. Its violent progress continued unseen, echoing sounds finally fading to a silence marred only by the thundering of her heart.

Franco collapsed with a single exhale. Her own tensed muscles melted in relief. He levered off her head and shoulders, pushing to his feet. Nicky tucked her knees under her to waver upright. Franco grasped her elbow.

"Interesting." His voice wasn't steady. "And extremely convenient."

Nicky nodded, swallowed, meeting his grave dark eyes. "I think..." She licked her lips, tasting dust and grit, and shuddered in a breath. "I think there was someone in the woods when I—"

The ground collapsed beneath her. Franco grabbed at her arm, but it unbalanced her more. She slammed hard onto her stomach, leaving his fingers clutching dead air. Feet first, she slid with frightening acceleration down toward the edge of nothing.

Without hesitation, Franco dove after her.

"Spread-eagle, Nicky!"

She widened her legs, dug her booted toes into the scree, but it was like the rocks were greased. Her eyes held his determined face like a lifeline as he bodysurfed toward her, arms extended, hands open. Her jacket and shirt rode up under her, shoulder holster jarring over stones as she skidded. Elbows and knees furrowed into disintegrating ground but didn't slow her. She couldn't scream, couldn't cry out. She closed her eyes, unable, unwilling to see her own death. Tears of fear and regret burned like acid.

A hard vise of fingers circled her wrist. Her eyes sprang open.

"Grab my arm!" Franco angled his torso and legs to the right, rocks skeining behind him.

Nicky clutched his wrist convulsively in relief then horror when, with a flash of clarity, she realized she'd pull him over the edge with her. She loosened her grip.

"Dammit, Nicky, now!"

She clamped her fingers tight as her legs hit empty air.

Her body flew off the slope. Nicky cried out as her momentum and shoulder wrenched to a stop. With a rebounding pull, she bounced against the face of the cliff. Panting in terror of the dizzying drop under her swinging legs, she twisted her face upward. Franco, teeth gritted, cinched her wrist with both hands. The top of his shoulders hovered over the edge.

"Give me your other—"

Nicky reached up. He released her arm with one hand, and he grabbed her other wrist in a second bruising crush. "Push with your feet."

Toes scrabbled, dug into rock, found purchase. The pull on her arms lessened slightly as she thrust upward, praying with all her might the protrusions she'd found wouldn't crumble. Face red, Franco roared and retracted his body, muscles bunched, his neck sinewed. He dragged her torso up and over the ledge.

Nicky locked her gaze on his. "Don't let go, please, don't let go," she whispered, her voice a thread of sound. The strain on her arms was intense, muscles and tendons stretched painfully. Rocks jabbed her chest and stomach, only to disintegrate under the pressure. Hips over the top, she began to wiggle, to snake up the ground, Franco her anchor. He'd stopped moving, pulling her up only with his arms. She raised her head, her gaze searching behind him. One of his booted feet was hooked around a tree trunk that had been snapped by the rolling log. His knee torqued in a V, leg shaking with effort. The brute strength of it spun Nicky's head.

"That's as far ... bend my leg. Climb over," he said. His eyes were bloodshot with the strain. "Back of my belt. Knife. Use it as a stake," he rasped. "Knife's against regs. Don't tell ... on me."

Nicky absorbed his face, his eyes, his forced half smile. The welcome familiarity of it gave her hope they wouldn't die. She scooched closer, clutching handfuls of his jacket, pulling up and through his arms, until her lips were at his ear. She pressed her dirty cheek to his, then dropped her forehead into his shoulder, tears of relief scalding.

"Against regs?" she whispered, her throat so dry. "I'll have to weigh your indiscretion against saving my ass, Martinez."

He tightened his arms around her. "What if I told you," he said, breath warm on her skin, "I'm sorry?"

She turned her head so she could stare into his eyes.

The clink and skitter of cascading rocks made them both tense. Franco's head turned toward the noise. Nicky carefully lifted hers. Astonishment stopped her mid-breath.

A red nylon rope snaked down the slope until a looped end hung a foot away from Franco's shoulders.

"Hold me steady," she said. Franco tightened his arms around her waist as she craned her neck to follow the rope upward. It was tied around one of the embedded boulders lining the shelf.

When they climbed to the top of the incline, whoever had sent the rope down to them was gone.

CHAPTER TWENTY-SIX

FRANCO HIT the police station's double doors and stalked inside, Nicky, hunched and scowling, right behind him. Ryan followed her. The doors slammed on the bitter wind that had kicked up during the cloudless sunset. But the cold outside was nothing to Franco's frigid attitude.

Nicky glared at Ryan.

"Dammit, that was not your call to make." She jerked her chin at Franco's back. "He was already pissed because I forgot to mention someone might have been in the woods watching us."

Nicky strained to maintain her confrontational attitude—keep Franco and Ryan off-balance. Stop them from asking hard questions while her emotions and thoughts rushed in frantic circles. Somehow, her mother and father were mixed up in whatever was going on —*mixed up in murder*. Her father was dead, but her mother...

Whoever was behind the murders, the garden desecrations, and the attempts on her life wanted her mother, was trying to lure her back to New Mexico. It was the only thing that made sense.

Dean had offered Nicky her mother's most recent contact information. She kicked herself for not taking it. She needed to call, to warn her. But first—

She touched her shirt and felt Rémy Tioux's wedding ring underneath.

"You have to stop this go-it-alone attitude, Nicky," Ryan said from behind her. "It's dangerous." He'd been part of the Fire-Sky Emergency Rescue team sent to evaluate their injuries at the medicine shrine site. CSU had followed shortly, with Agents Song and Headley.

"You blabbed *everything* while I was in X-ray. I'm surprised they didn't find a knife in my back, too," she said, her tone acid.

In front of her, Franco stomped down the hall. Bracketed by the two men, it felt like a frickin' perp walk, and she'd done nothing wrong.

She hadn't realized she'd spoken out loud until Franco turned on her, bloodshot eyes like ice.

"*Bullshit.*" His shirt was torn, his jacket and cargos streaked with dirt, arm in a white sling just like hers. "I'm your partner. You should have told me you suspected someone was in the woods at Tioux's murder site and at the first garden we visited. You should have told me someone's been stalking you since the museum murders. You lied to me about the cut on your cheek, that you'd been attacked on Sunday. You should have trusted—" He stopped, his lips clamping shut.

Too late. He'd given her an opening big enough to drive a tank through. "Right. I should've talked to you. Asked for your forgiveness, explained what happened. Trusted you because you've given me so much of your trust. Oh, yeah. I remember now. I tried that. And got it thrown back in my face."

"Not again." Ryan walked past. "You both need a purging ceremony."

"Don't start, Ryan." Nicky stabbed a finger after him. "You and Savannah are already on my shit list. She had no business telling you anything, and you shouldn't have repeated it to him."

"Pointing's disrespectful. And Savannah's worried about you," Ryan said. "I'm going to see if she's still here and if she has something to eat." He disappeared around a corner.

Franco pivoted to follow, but Nicky grabbed his arm. She swallowed as his cold gaze settled on her.

"Don't say anything to the chief or FBI about my stalker. Please."

Fluorescent lights buzzing above them deepened the lines on his face. Dirt streaked his forehead and powdered his hair. God, did she look as wrecked as he did?

Franco lowered his face until they were nose-to-nose. "I want to know why as soon as we're done here."

Relief flowed through her aching body. Mentally crossing her fingers, she said, "I promise."

His shoulders relaxed. He nodded.

"I'm going to wash my face," Nicky said. "I'll meet you in Chief's office."

She headed in the direction of the restroom but darted toward the evidence room when Franco was out of sight. There were rules about accessing evidence. She was about to break them and, right now, she didn't care.

When Nicky headed into her debrief with Song and Headley, her father's wedding ring was threaded onto her necklace next to Tioux's and hidden under her shirt.

"YOU DIDN'T SEE or hear anything before the log dislodged?" Headley shifted delicately in Chief's creaking chair. Agent Song tapped her pen against her notepad. She'd been doing it on and off the whole interview, and Nicky was ready to snatch it out of her hand and hurl it across the room.

"For the third time, we heard the sound of an ax before the log came down on us." Patience in shreds, Nicky pressed the flat of her palm on her chair arm and leaned forward in emphasis. She grimaced and jerked, grabbing at her upper arm.

Franco twisted toward her. "Dammit, Matthews. Your shoulder—"

Headley interrupted. "There was absolutely no evidence someone was up there waiting for you. None. Our CSU team scoured the whole area."

"After we called them back to the shrine," Nicky said. "Because they completely missed evidence the first time they processed the scene."

"We're perfectly capable of investigating a crime scene, Sergeant Matthews," Headley said. "While you are perfectly capable of crapping one up. You should've backed out and called for forensics as soon as it became clear—"

"Someone tried to kill us," Franco said, his voice a suppressed roar.

"Who? This phantom in the woods? Some nonexistent person with the ax? Or the guy who lowered the rope and disappeared." Headley flicked open both hands. "Poof."

"The log was a trap. And Julie Knutson at OMI said an ax was used to sever Tioux's hands," Franco said flatly. He stood.

Now Song twiddled her pen between two fingers. "That area was logged in the past. There are tree trunks and stumps scattered all over. Why is it so hard to believe this wasn't an act of the Creator?"

"Because—" Nicky swallowed the rest of her words. She was done with this senseless interrogation. She stared at Song, who looked back impassively, then slid her glance to Headley. He'd touched the screen of his smart watch and frowned. Franco hovered next to her, still scowling.

It'd be easy to slip away from him like she had earlier.

As if he could read her mind, Franco slid his hand into his pocket. When he pulled it out, he displayed her keys in his open palm before he slotted them away again.

Dammit.

"What plant is so valuable that someone would kill for it?" Headley asked. "Even if they found a chemical that could cure cancer, it would take years before it was profitable, if ever. People rarely strike gold like you did, Sergeant." Expression smug, he leaned back and laced his fingers over his abdomen, stretching his thin storky legs out in front of him. "This bioprospecting angle of the investigation is a dead end, officers. Evidence we gathered in Biloxi has confirmed our initial hypothesis. Rémy Tioux's brother is behind his murder, and we'll be preparing an indictment for the US attorney's office. I can't give you all the details yet..."

Headley droned on. Nicky stopped listening. He was wrong. All the scattered pieces had come together when she'd found the ring at the shrine. She wasn't the true target. She was being used as bait. No matter how strained their relationship was, if Nicky was injured—or dead—her mother would come back home. Whoever was behind this wanted Professor Helena Galini, and they were willing to do anything to get her. Even commit murder.

Add in Tioux's search for medicinal plants, the medicine garden desecrations, and the fresh gouges on the pots her mother had analyzed. Were Dean's speculations correct? Was this really about an extinct plant?

Silence filled the room. Headley had stopped talking and was looking at Nicky expectantly.

"You're right." Nicky pressed her lips in an apologetic smile, pressing up slowly from her chair, playing up her stiffness with an accompanying groan. "Must have been an accident. It was a close call, almost going over that cliff." She shuddered dramatically. "We over-reacted."

Headley's face relaxed. Song placed her pen on the table. They were done.

"The clinic doctor mandated a week of sick leave." Nicky rubbed a hand over her right shoulder, massaged it, grimaced. "If you have any more questions, you have my cell number." She pivoted quickly and exited Chief's office, heading for her desk. There was an extra set of house and car keys in the top drawer.

A knot of people stood on the far side of the squad room. Savannah was there with Howard Kie. And Ryan. Chief Richards and her lieutenant, Gavin Pinkett, blocked her view of a black-clad woman.

The woman stepped from behind Chief.

Nicky stumbled to a halt, Franco so close behind he bumped her forward. "Oh, no. No, no, no, no, no."

It was like using an aging app that added twenty-five years to a person's face. Straight brows over dark eyes stared back at Nicky, strong jaw, determined chin, softer with age, and strong, high cheekbones. Her face had more wrinkles and was faintly freckled by the sun, the creases at the corners of her eyes fanned with lighter skin. She hadn't been wearing sunglasses again. A scarf or veil or whatever it was called covered her hair, so Nicky couldn't see whether it had grayed. Probably not. It was genetic. Hair that stayed black into their seventies and eighties.

What had it been? Six years? No, seven. She'd last come a week after her mother's funeral, her excuse that she'd been on a remote dig and hadn't received the news until she'd returned to Rome. She'd only stayed a few days. In fact, Nicky could count the number of times they'd seen each other in the past ten years on one hand. They'd argue bitterly and she'd leave, Nicky believing that was the end of it, that she'd never see her again.

Brown eyes the same shape and color of Nicky's own touched on each rip of Nicky's clothes, the white sling cradling her arm, the healing cut on her cheek. A flicker of worry—fear?—shone on her face before she masked her expression.

"Nicky. I've heard you've had some … problems … the last couple of weeks. I flew in from Thessaloniki to see if I could help." A hesitation. "You remember the dig near the ruins of Galerius's palace—"

"Mom," Nicky said. "Stop."

Shocked silence as eyes bugged and jaws dropped.

"Your mother's a nun?" Franco said.

Nicky clenched her teeth.

"Oh, my God. That explains so much." He doubled over in laughter.

It was contagious. The chief broke down in giggles. Pinkett snorted, his torso shaking. Savannah covered her mouth with a hand, and a grin spread over Ryan's tired features. Only Howard stood placidly, munching Hot Tamales.

Nicky had put the pieces together too late to call and warn her mother to stay away. Now she was here, just where whoever had murdered Tioux wanted her.

And everyone was laughing.

Her frustration and dread boiled over. A single pungent word slipped from her lips.

"*Fuck.*"

CHAPTER TWENTY-SEVEN

NICKY'S deep satisfaction at the shocked faces and gasps of her audience was swept away by her mother's and Franco's disappointed stares.

"Sergeant Matthews. You will apologize for your inappropriate language to Sister, uh … Mother…" Chief's expression was comically embarrassed and confused.

Her mother patted his arm. "Dr. Galini will be just fine, Chief Richards. You said my daughter had some time off because of her injury? I'll take her home. I have to admit, I'm exhausted myself."

Nicky pivoted to Franco and held out her hand, palm up.

He bared his teeth in a smile. "I'll drive. We still have a few things to talk about."

"Liability, officers, means no driving," said Lieutenant Pinkett. "Since your injuries occurred on the job, that includes any pueblo-owned vehicles until you're out of those slings. Matthews, Savannah has volunteered to take you and your mother home. Ryan Bernal said he'll drive you, Agent Martinez. Agent Katina will follow in your personal truck. He should be here shortly."

"While you're recovering, Pinkett and I will liaise with the FBI on the Tioux investigation," Chief said. "But I want both of your reports by tomorrow afternoon. Type them up from home. Headley and Song still in my office?"

At Nicky's nod, Richards and Pinkett wished Nicky's mother good-night and left.

Franco handed Nicky her keys. His expression was masked again, but frustration and something else she couldn't name seemed to vibrate from within him.

"My car's in the admin lot," Savannah said. "G'night, Ryan, Fran-co." She beckoned Nicky and her mother to follow. Howard fell in behind them. Nicky could feel Franco's gaze boring into her back.

"How did you get to the police station?" Nicky asked her mother. "You didn't rent a car?"

"Of course not. I have a perfectly good car parked at your house. I called you a couple of times, but since you didn't answer, I took a shuttle from the airport to the CampFire Casino."

Nicky's phone chimed with a text. She slipped it out of her pocket. There were two missed calls from an unknown number at about the same time she and Franco had arrived at the clinic. The text was from Franco.

We need to talk.

She turned off her phone.

"I called the station and heard you'd been injured. The hotel desk clerk was kind enough to request a rideshare for me, and Howard"— her mother turned her head to smile beatifically at him—"drove me here. My bags are in his vehicle." She leaned in and said in a low voice, "He's a very nice young man, but no way on God's green earth should he have a driver's license."

Nicky slowed her pace to match her mother's. The light scent of vanilla wafers, familiar since childhood, drifted on the air. Nicky's eyes stung. She hadn't even gotten a hug in greeting.

While Howard transferred the luggage to Savannah's trunk, Nicky retrieved her rifle case from her unit. She tucked it next to her moth-er's single bag and old-fashioned briefcase with dial locks. Savannah started her compact.

Her mother beckoned Nicky to the passenger's side of the car.

Nicky halted about a yard away. The distance might as well have been a mile.

"I know you're spoiling for a fight," her mother said. "Let's wait until we don't have an audience." She opened the car door then stopped, her head turned away. "I'm glad you're okay." Her voice was thick. She slid into her seat and closed the door.

Throat tight, Nicky used the back of her hand to rub her eyes dry and climbed in next to Howard.

***

NICKY STOOD with Savannah in the utility room. Howard and her mother were in the kitchen, putting away what was left of the enchiladas Savannah had whipped up while Nicky was in the shower.

"Howard? Let's go," Savannah called. She leaned in to hug Nicky, careful of her shoulder. "I'm not sorry I told Ryan about the attacks, and I'm not sorry he told Franco. Something weird is going on, and you seem to be in the middle of it. Again. The only thing that surprises me is that you haven't had any visions attached."

Nicky dropped her gaze.

"Oh, my God, Nicky, seriously? You didn't tell us?"

"Visions. I see you haven't outgrown this attention-seeking behavior, Nicky," her mother said. She stood behind them, wiping her hands on a dish towel, mouth tight.

"She does see these things. I know." Howard nodded sagely, the ceiling light in the kitchen catching on the thick lenses of his glasses. "You know, too, Doctor. And you know why."

Dead silence.

"Well," Savannah said brightly. "Goodnight, Dr. Galini." She placed a hand on Nicky's arm. "Call me if you need anything, and put your sling back on."

"I told you. I was faking."

Savannah rolled her eyes.

Nicky waited in the carport until Savannah backed out of the driveway, then walked her property, searching for signs she was being watched. When she finished, her security lights created a brilliant bubble around her home. She locked the side door behind her.

Her mother stood by her kitchen table, arms folded. She hadn't changed clothes, but she had uncovered her hair. It fell to her shoulders, straight and black with only a few gray threads.

Nicky thrust out her jaw and mirrored her mother's stance. "Why are you dressed like that? You're not a nun yet."

"I'm not training to be a nun. That would mean giving up..." Her mother paused. "It would mean entering a convent for a life of prayer and seclusion. I'm training to be a sister so I can stay in this world and continue to contribute. And I'm still in the formation process. What's this about your visions?" Her mother tipped her chin at the holster tucked in Nicky's waistband. "Why are you wearing your gun? And what happened to your grandmother's furniture?"

Deflection. Nice try. "You told me you were in training when you came after Grandmother's funeral." Nicky gestured at her mother's severe black outfit. "How long does it take?"

Her mother's mouth compressed. The tiny lines around her lips caused a pang in Nicky's chest. Her mother would turn sixty that year. Time moved so fast.

"Until I'm ready."

"Just another way to abandon your obligations and ignore your failures."

Her mother's face hardened even further. "This is the most difficult decision I've ever had to make. Why does it have to be about you?"

Nicky blinked, staggered.

"It's not about me. It's never been about me. Not when you left your seven-year-old child to be raised by her grandmother." Nicky's voice was sharp with sarcasm. "I'm the only thing you had to give up. Not your digs or your travels. That's what constitutes your continued contribution to the world, isn't it?"

"I came back to New Mexico annually. After you finished middle school, I flew you to digs during the summer—"

"Where I was treated like every other student." Nicky lifted her chin, masking her hurt. "I don't see why it's a difficult decision. You gave up your worldly ties a long time ago."

"Nicky, I had to leave. I had no choice."

"You *chose* to leave without me."

Her mother's expression turned pleading. "Don't you understand? Your father would have *used* you to get me back, and I couldn't ... I had to make it look—"

"Like you didn't care?" Nicky said. "Great job, Mom. I was convinced."

"When I got pregnant, he promised he wouldn't cheat on me ever again." Her mother sat down on a kitchen chair like her knees had given out. "Then my career took off, and suddenly it was me giving keynotes and getting funding." She clasped her hands on her lap. "His infidelities started again. Worse, because he didn't try to hide it anymore. He even put you in danger on our last dig together. Left you alone and went off with one of his graduate students. I was devastated."

"So, you dumped me with Grandmother and never looked back."

"Don't be dramatic."

"It's the truth."

Her mother dropped her gaze to her knotted fingers. "I loved your father more than anything. After I left, I couldn't function. I wasn't fit to be your mother. But I knew you were safe here. For years, that's about the only thing that sustained me."

"Oh, please." Nicky marched down the hall and into her grandmother's old room. Her mother's suitcase was tucked in a corner, the briefcase on the bed. She took down her box of mementos from the closet, grabbed the folder full of reprints, and strode back into the kitchen to drop it on the table.

"What's this?" her mother asked.

"Your publications. Research articles, reviews, chapters, white papers. Your books are in my office. While you were so devastated you couldn't function, you certainly could work."

A clenched fist hit the folder. "It took me *years* to get over your father. It's the way we love in this family."

"Not again. That's stupid romantic bullshit, and you know it."

"Is it? Your grandfather passed when your grandmother was in her forties. She never remarried and wore her wedding ring until the day she died. And you. Dax Stone broke up with you while you were in law school, and you completely changed your life and career." She studied Nicky, her expression faintly smug. "He's still in your life, isn't he?"

"Only because we're both in law enforcement," Nicky said defensively. "We have to meet because of our jobs."

"How convenient." She could hear her sarcasm reflected back in her mother's words.

"I didn't become a cop because of Dax." She hadn't.

Had she?

Nicky sat down at the table. Her mother's hand covered hers. She held still, even though all she wanted to do was clasp it and hold on tightly. Keep her safe from whoever had lured her back.

"You asked why I haven't taken my vows." Her mother sighed and squeezed Nicky's fingers. "I realized—as did my Mother Superior—I might have chosen this vocation to escape the memory of your father. But time has healed that wound. Michael doesn't haunt me anymore. He's in the past. And I'm ready to move forward—finally."

Without me. Again. Nicky pulled her hand away.

"I would argue the past is still a problem." Nicky was about to blow up the bridge to her mother's "new" life. She tried to suppress her odd eagerness without much success. She unclasped her necklace, slid off the ring from the shrine, and placed it on the table. "That wedding ring belongs to a recent homicide victim. I found it at a medicine garden shrine he'd visited the day of his murder, which is very interesting considering this."

She slipped her father's wedding band from the necklace and held it out. Her mother's face paled.

Guilt swept over her for treating her mother differently—worse—than other victims or witnesses she'd encounter in the course of an investigation. But this was how it was with her mother. Highs and lows that wrung out her emotions. She needed to get a grip.

"I found this on a dead man's severed hand. It's inscribed. 'Till death do us part. *HMXHM.*' Helena Matthews and Hemis Matthews."

The front door slammed. In one smooth motion, Nicky spilled the ring from her fingers, swiveled up, drew her gun—

And dropped the muzzle. Franco stood in the hallway, arms crossed, a black gym bag on the floor by his feet.

CHAPTER TWENTY-EIGHT

NICKY TUCKED her weapon back into her holster. "I locked that door."

Franco jangled her extra set of keys from a finger, his smile all teeth. He'd showered and changed. A shoulder holster peeked out from under his heavy coat.

Her mother's chair scraped against the tiled floor. "You're Nicky's partner," she said. "I'm Helena Galini."

Franco's visage melted into a charming smile. He pocketed the keys and strode forward, hand extended.

"Francisco Martinez, ma'am. Please, call me Franco. I'd like to apologize for earlier today. My words and actions were unforgivable. In my defense, your daughter can be pretty frustrating to work with at times."

Both Franco and her mother sent her a pinch-mouthed look. Her mother, still a little pale, nodded. "Very trying."

"Yes, ma'am. Your daughter and I have also dated."

Her mother straightened and fixed Franco with a speculative gaze.

"I may have screwed up there, too," he admitted.

His smile was dizzying.

"Why are you here?" Nicky said.

Franco brushed by her and picked up his duffle. "Because someone tried to kill us today. Until we find out the who and why, I'm not leaving your side. *Partner.*" He nodded to the sofa. "I can sleep there."

"No, you can't," Nicky said. "And I'm perfectly capable of taking care of myself."

"Well, she's right about one of those things." Her mother bustled across the room to open a door off the front hallway. "Last time I was here, the office had a daybed. Ah. It still does." Franco followed and peered in the room. With surprising suddenness, her mother clasped Franco in a hug. "Thank you for saving my daughter's life today." She pulled back and searched his face, clenched fists pressing into his arms. "Please call me Helena."

Nicky dropped her head and sighed. *Great.*

Red-faced and with an awkward bob of his head, Franco disappeared through the doorway. When he came back out, he'd removed his jacket. The brown leather of his holster looped over his shoulders and attached on both sides to his belt. His long-sleeved black T-shirt outlined the thick muscles of his chest and arms. He picked up her mother's hand and led her back to the table. Gently, he pried open her fist. The gold in her palm gleamed in the fluorescent light.

"I haven't seen this ring for over twenty-five years. God bless his soul, it was on a man's severed hand?" Helena made the sign of the cross.

"I'm afraid so." Nicky scooped up the second ring from the table. The pressure from Franco's gaze was intense. "This is Tioux's actual wedding band. He left it at a shrine, along with his daughter's baby bracelet."

"And you put your career, hell, your future in jeopardy when you took it," Franco said. "It's evidence in a murder investigation."

"I did it to protect my mother. She's in danger."

Her mother jerked to stare at Nicky, a frown on her face.

"For whatever reason, these rings link her to the museum break-in, the assault on Charlotte, the murders," Nicky said. "And I'm going to find out what's going on. Don't give me that look, Franco. You would've done the same thing."

Franco folded her mother's fingers around the ring again.

"This is not just about your mother, Nicky. Whoever is behind the ring on Tioux's finger is targeting you, too. There've been too many attempts on your life to ignore."

Nicky scoffed. "They were only to get my mom to come back home. And, ta-da. It worked."

"Attempts?" Her mother looked back and forth between them.

"And she's being stalked," Franco said.

Her mother dropped into a chair again.

"Franco. Stop." Nicky grabbed a bottle of water out of the fridge, opened it, and went down on her haunches at her mother's side. "Drink. When did you last eat?"

Helena waved Nicky away. "I want to understand what's going on. Who is this man who had Michael's ring?"

"Rémy Tioux," Franco said. "A Native American casino owner from Mississippi."

"Natchez Nation," Nicky added.

Her mother shook her head. "I've never heard of him."

"He's visited the pueblo for a number of years." Franco pulled an armchair from the den to the table and sat down. Nicky took the second kitchen chair. "This last visit, the day he was murdered, he was supposed to sign papers selling his casino in Biloxi to the Tsiba'ashi D'yini Pueblo."

Nicky picked up the thread. "But Fire-Sky withdrew their offer. Instead, Tioux went to the medicine shrine, where he left his wedding ring and a bracelet with his daughter's name. Evidence shows he was probably kidnapped or killed as he was leaving. His body was left in the closet of the Isgaawa museum, his hands severed and dropped into an earthen tank."

"Why?" her mother asked.

"We're not completely sure, but he'd been searching the pueblo and harvesting medicinal plants," Nicky said. "He brought the plants to the museum for identification. He even had some on him when his body was discovered. All of them were associated with fertility or pregnancy medicines."

"Like the ones I identified from the pot scrapings after Michael and I were first married." Brows knitted, her mother slipped the wedding band on and off her index finger.

"We think the night Tioux was killed, the bad guys took more scapings from the same pots you'd analyzed before. Dean thinks that's the key, Mom," Nicky said. "Those pot scrapings ... and you."

"It's been so long, and everything back then was so entwined with your father." Her mother shrugged, gaze still focused on the ring.

"Before the murder, medicine garden shrines on the pueblo were being dug up, desecrated by an unknown person or persons. Because of a case earlier this summer"—Franco slid a glance at Nicky—"we think bioprospectors are searching for valuable plants or something. For unknown reasons, they graduated to murder."

"Valuable like the organism that infected Nicky? Dean told me about it in an email." Her mother looked up from her hands. "Why was this man Rémy gathering fertility herbs?"

"Apparently, he and his wife needed the help of specialists to get pregnant, so they used a fertility clinic up in Santa Fe. Part of the treatment was Native American herbal teas. Maybe Tioux was trying to recreate the mixtures. We're not sure." Nicky shifted. "His wife admitted she and Tioux traveled to New Mexico so they could hide their infertility."

"That's not uncommon," Helena said. "There's a lot of internal shame when everyone around you is pregnant and your body won't cooperate."

"On their website, the clinic had a tab on herbal medications they use in the process," Nicky said. "We speculate that's gotta be the link."

"But this couple did get pregnant and have a child?" her mother asked.

"Yes. Raven," Franco said. "Cute kid. Less than a year old."

"Then why did this man Tioux abandon his wedding ring and the baby's bracelet at the shrine?" Helena asked.

"Again, we don't know. His wife's interview was odd, too," Franco said. "She kept insisting that Tioux loved her and the baby. Trying to convince us."

"Maybe trying to convince herself." Nicky stood and wandered to the cupboard. She grabbed a Tupperware full of chocolate-chip cookies and brought them to the table. "Tioux visited the clinic the day he was murdered, but Kristina said that was to deliver thanks and pictures of Raven to share on their baby wall." She popped open the lid, her hand bumping Franco's as they reached for the cookies.

Franco took a bite. "Savannah?"

"Mine. I can cook. I just don't like to." Nicky munched for a few moments, fingers quietly drumming on the table. "We were planning to visit the fertility clinic this week. Of course, we can't go in any official capacity until we've been cleared for duty. But the clinic does have an online appointment schedule that includes walk-ins. I checked." Nicky smiled and raised her brows, cursing the stupid heat warming her cheeks. "Franco? Would you like to have a baby with me?"

Franco's eyes widened before a grin stretched across his face.

"Great idea," her mother said. "I'll drive."

CHAPTER TWENTY-NINE

When Nicky and Franco arrived for their appointment at Santa Fe Fertility Solutions, they were greeted on the threshold by name and graciously invited to hang their damp outerwear by the door. Nicky smoothed her sweater over her bellyband holster and surreptitiously studied the cool spa-like waiting room. Cream and aqua, its mahogany furniture sculpted in waves and curves, very upscale, very soothing. Two other couples occupied the room: one, whispering and smiling, the woman obviously pregnant; the other, hands knotted together, sending envious yet hopeful glances at the first woman's rounded abdomen.

In a hushed voice, the twenty-something receptionist handed Franco a tablet and asked them to fill out a digital form. Then they were led down a hallway to a second room, where the receptionist ushered them inside with a murmured "The doctor will be with you in a moment," before he left, pulling the door closed behind him with a discrete snick.

A few minutes later, a second, internal door opened, and a slight woman, eyes a faded blue behind rimless glasses and chin-length blond-gray hair framing a softly wrinkled face, stepped inside. She wore a perfectly pressed white coat, her stethoscope looping out of the large patch pocket at her hip.

Painted in soothing grays and tans, the walls were lined with glossy black-and-white photos of parents and singles staring with awe and joy at tiny babies. Nicky gazed longingly at the pictures, then, brows puckered, mouth taut with nervousness, caught and held Franco's gaze. He extended his hand to her. Undercover persona firmly in place, she took it and held on like he was her lifeline before she turned her attention to the woman.

"Welcome, Monique and Frank. I'm Dr. Summerweaver, and I'm so happy you've accomplished this first difficult step. Talking with someone can help with your journey. Please, take a seat."

Journey. Marica Santibanez had used that same language, probably heard from Kristina Tioux.

Two chairs faced one that held a black tablet facedown on its seat; no table or desk created a barrier between them. Nicky and Franco settled into theirs, hands still linked.

"Difficult step?" Nicky tightened her expression. "I thought it would solve our difficulties."

"This is just the beginning." The doctor smiled, her attention on Nicky. "This bond—between you as a couple and our practitioners and associates—will become, in so many ways, a partnership. And because we believe in truth and openness at our clinic, you need to know your quest for a child may not be successful, no matter which path you decide to take." She paused, a note of warning in her voice. "And it will test your relationship."

"We're not worried about us," Franco said. He lifted their clasped hands and brushed Nicky's skin with his lips, brown eyes melting into hers. A surge of attraction and trust beat through her. Damn, he was good.

"Infertility treatment puts a high level of stress on couples. It makes some stronger, but, statistically, one in five will ultimately break apart. There are no guarantees a full-term pregnancy and birth will occur, although our clinic's full-term success rate is a little higher than the average of sixty-five percent. You've seen the photos of our successes all around you. Going forward, that will be our focus."

Dr. Summerweaver picked up the tablet and tapped the screen a few times. She settled into her chair, knees only inches away. "So, Monique and Frank. If you feel comfortable, please tell me your story."

Franco sat back. After claiming over coffee that morning he was the better liar, Nicky agreed he should fill in the specifics of their past "life" together. She braced, ready to absorb the details.

"We've been together since college. I played football; Mona played sousaphone in the marching band. One day before a game, I accidentally threw a football into her bell, and it got stuck. Had a hell of a time pulling it out. Finally had to deflate it. After that, I figured the least I could do was buy her dinner."

She was going to kill him.

"I joined the army, but my absences only made our love grow stronger. After I got out, we eloped. Got married at the Elvis Chapel in Vegas eight years ago. Actually, we both still work in the casino business, although Mona's quit stripping. Aged out." He sat forward, sincere and focused on Dr. Summerweaver. "That's how we found out about your clinic. Friends of ours who own a casino in Mississippi had a baby because of you. A little girl named Raven."

Dr. Summerweaver's eyes flared before she shuttered them.

Nicky jumped in. "Kristina—Kristina Tioux? She told me one reason they chose your clinic was because you use natural herbs and medicinal teas to stimulate fertility and maintain healthy pregnancies," she said as if she'd memorized the line word for word. "I am *very* into alternative treatments."

"It's one path you can choose," Summerweaver replied. "We retain an herbalist who blends her teas to each patient's specifications and needs. All of our products are organic, and some are wild harvested on Indigenous Nation lands, although sustainability is important to us."

"These plants are grown on New Mexico pueblos and reservations?" Nicky asked.

"Some of them in medicine gardens. And while many of the recipes we use have their roots in Indigenous cultures, we supplement our knowledge with primary scientific literature."

"We love science," Nicky gushed. "Could we have the same herbalist who worked with our friends, Kristina and Rémy?"

Dr. Summerweaver hesitated. "I'm afraid I can't discuss patients."

"And we completely understand, but the stuff worked," Nicky said. "We've been trying to get pregnant for eight years."

"*Diligently* trying. All times of the month, exotic positions, two or three times a day." Franco rubbed his fingers back and forth over his thigh as he spoke, his forehead pinched with sincerity.

Nicky pressed her hand over his, stopping the movement. She sent him an adoring smile. "Thank goodness for pharmaceutical help, especially after Frank's 'slowdown.'" She air-quoted the word. "His online pharmacist assured him it's a natural part of the aging process."

Dr. Summerweaver's eyes narrowed. She looked back and forth between them, mouth pinched. *Crap.* They'd pushed too far. Nicky reached for Franco's hand again. He clasped it tightly.

"Hm. I see stress is already apparent. This type of passive-aggressive behavior is not uncommon. Luckily, all of our fertility packages come with counseling."

Nicky inwardly sighed in relief.

"And the herbalist?" she asked. "Kristina told us such wonderful things about her."

Dr. Summerweaver stiffened, her lips pressing into a thin line.

Nicky's heart rate ticked up. "We can come back if she isn't in today."

The doctor stood and stepped behind her chair, expression hard. She clutched the iPad against her chest like a shield. "Who sent you?"

Nicky exchanged a glance with Franco.

"This isn't the first time a fake couple has tried to infiltrate our clinic," Summerweaver continued. "You tell Mr. Tioux's lawyers that his wife's treatments were done by a strict protocol and were well-documented. His complaint against us was completely unfounded."

"Rémy Tioux is dead, murdered," Nicky said, then added, "What complaint?"

"His heirs' lawyers, then." The doctor strode to the door and opened it, the lenses of her glasses glinting like ice. "You need to leave. Now."

Nicky reached into her purse, fingers closing on her badge, but Franco grabbed her arm. He shook his head. She dropped her badge and walked through the door, Franco's hand on her lower back.

He paused at the threshold. "What gave us away? The Elvis Chapel?"

"Please. This is Santa Fe. That doesn't even make my top fifty of weird. You slipped up. The herbalist who treated Kristina Tioux was a man."

A man who harvested fertility herbs from pueblo medicine gardens. Before Nicky could blurt out a name, Franco said, "Jimmy Che'chi."

"*Him.*" Summerweaver's mouth screwed up like she'd tasted something bad. "The so-called Jemez Medicine Man."

CHAPTER THIRTY

Nicky and Franco huddled under an overhanging portico supported by whitewashed wooden columns carved in spiraling twists. She scanned the narrow street lined with blocky flat-roofed adobes capped with sharp red bricks rising to three stories. Cold drizzle darkened the rough brown stucco. A car rolled by, the sticky noise of its tires loud on wet blacktop.

"Where's your mom?" Franco slid his hand off Nicky's back, leaving a lingering warmth.

Across and down the street, Nicky's mother poked her head out of a door and waved at them, her pale oval face surrounded by the black of her veil.

"Over there," Nicky said and waved back. "At that café."

"I could use some lunch," Franco said. He grabbed Nicky's hand.

Startled, she faltered to a stop, their clasped hands bridging the distance between them. Her heartbeat kicked up a notch.

"Aren't we still playacting?" He winked at her.

"Are we?" Deciding to humor him, Nicky tightened her hold. "You really love the undercover part, don't you?"

"It's fun with the right partner. I'm nothing special on my own."

Franco tugged her into the misty rain, and they ran across the street before she had time to digest his statement.

Her mother's brown eyes sparkled, and her smile took twenty years off her face. More than once since she'd come home, the thought that they looked more like sisters than mother and daughter filtered through Nicky's head.

Franco shepherded Nicky under the heavy overhang, still holding her hand.

"Helena." He drew the name out playfully. "What have you been up to?"

She leaned in, grinning back at him. "Wielding Catholic guilt like a terrible, swift sword, God forgive me. How did you do?"

"With a little manipulation, we were able to verify the name of the herbalist who worked with Rémy and Kristina Tioux," Franco answered. "He's well-known on Fire-Sky but AWOL."

"I hope he's all right. What if the killers got to him?" Her mother clapped a hand over her mouth, eyes wide. "Or what if he's the killer?"

Nicky and Franco exchanged glances.

"That has crossed our minds," Nicky said.

"Well, I think I've discovered another possible motive for Mr. Tioux's murder. I decided to reconnoiter the building after you two went inside. A young woman they use to tidy up the exam rooms was smoking out one of the windows when I peeked in. She immediately apologized and begged forgiveness, then asked if her grandmother had sent me. Let's just say I took advantage." She chuckled and laid a hand on Nicky's arm. "Do you remember when you were in middle school and you and Rebecca Vaio stole that pack of cigarettes from Mrs. Baca? Your grandmother caught you and made you smoke the rest of the pack?"

"Best aversion therapy ever. I was sick for a week." Nicky eyed her mother. "But you weren't there. How did you—"

"I know a lot more than you think." Her mother's smile turned gentle.

Nicky drew in a soft breath, touched by the admission.

"I offered to buy the clinic maid—Maria Anita—lunch." Helena placed a hand on the café's door. "We've already ordered, but I've taken a vow of poverty and don't carry cash, so you'll have to pay."

Nicky cleared a constricted throat. "Typical." Realizing how tightly she held Franco's hand, she released it and followed her mother through the door.

The café was quirky and warm and smelled of carne adovada and blue-corn muffins. A chalkboard menu attached to the wall behind the counter listed its fare as New Mexican cuisine and included calabacitas, stuffed sopapillas, green chile stew, and menudo served on Sundays. Mismatched tables and painted chairs lined the narrow dining area. Nicky quickly spotted a slight young woman in aqua scrubs, face screwed up with worry. Behind her, a trompe l'oeil mural depicted a dusty road leading into an old Spanish pueblo.

Nicky and Franco ordered and sat.

"Sister said you were police?" Maria Anita chewed her lip. Her eyes were a pretty hazel brown, and her features held a mixture of cultures so common in New Mexico: Anglo, Hispanic, Native American. "I won't get in trouble if I talk to you, will I?" Her chapped hands fidgeted with a battered cell phone.

"You'd be helping in a murder investigation." Franco leaned his forearms on the table. He'd dressed for the appointment in a dark blue plaid button-down and pressed blue jeans over oiled brown cowboy boots. Strength and reassurance emanated from him. Maria Anita's gaze traced the width of his shoulders and breadth of his chest before settling on his face with a wistful expression.

"Do you remember Rémy and Kristina Tioux?" Nicky asked.

"Oh, yeah." Maria Anita nodded vigorously, eyes wide. "*He* came in last week. Monday, right when the clinic was closing. And he was totally pis—*ticked* off." She grimaced. "Sorry, Sister. The docs ordered Guillermo—the front-desk guy—and techs and nurses to leave. But they always forget about me. I mean, that's what they want, someone invisible, you know? Dr. Meyers told me that when I first started. Did you meet him? He's the big doctor." She deepened her voice. "'*Don't ever bother the clients, Maria. Act like they can't see you, and they won't.*' I mean, it's not like I sneak around or anything, and the people who come in have their own worries. Imagine, not being able to have babies. I mean, I have two." She hung her head. "Which is why I shouldn't smoke, because it's a waste of money. Las chicas buenas no fuman ni beben. Good girls don't smoke or drink."

Nicky's mother smiled and nodded serenely, but laughter danced in her eyes. Nicky only just managed to keep her expression neutral.

Their food came, and Nicky prompted her to continue.

"This guy? Tioux?" Maria Anita continued. "He was ranting about his wife and kid, telling them he was going to sue the clinic out of existence for what they'd done. Said he had proof and would make sure they never practiced medicine again."

Nicky bumped shoulders with Franco. "You heard all this?"

"I *saw*. I was *in the room*. They didn't even look. I mean, there's this little closet where they have their fancy coffee machine, and I was restocking. But still. Dr. Balderamos—he's the little one—and Dr. Summerweaver were trying to calm this guy down. He was so upset. He had a folder and kept slapping down papers. I mean, I thought these docs were shady—teas and massages and couples' trips to spas. D'you know how much they *charge*?" She rolled her eyes and slathered a sopapilla with honey before she sobered and met Franco's then Nicky's gaze. "And you know why this guy was mad? Because he did a paternity test on his daughter—Raven's her name. Isn't that pretty? I mean, he was almost crying because, you know what? It turns out, she's not his kid."

Shaking her head, she broke off a piece of her fried dough, golden threads of honey drizzling down, and popped it in her mouth.

CHAPTER THIRTY-ONE

EVEN THOUGH IT was cold and drizzling, Nicky's mother insisted their trip to Santa Fe include stops at Loretto Chapel to see the Miraculous Staircase, the Saint Francis Cathedral, and the San Miguel Chapel on the Old Santa Fe Trail. Nicky itched to talk about what they'd found out, how it integrated into the case, and plan a new interview and confrontation of Kristina Tioux, but her mother insisted on silence.

"You always did like to think out loud. There's time enough to talk back at your house tonight. Enjoy the silence. It's renewing." Her mother slid into a hand-carved pew at San Miguel and knelt in prayer. Franco sat in a different area of the church, his expression pensive, before he, too, bowed his head.

The rain, cold, and season had decreased tourist traffic to a minimum, which layered the sacred spaces with peacefulness. Nicky's churning impatience melted a little more at each stop. With no one to talk to, she absorbed details: the graceful curve of the staircase, the black granite baptismal font and pool, brilliant stained-glass windows, or humble wood-carved Stations of the Cross. Plastered adobe walls ascended to high ceilings braced with enormous, peeled logs, and a statue of Saint Michael, dating from the 1700s, was centered in the elaborate reredos behind the altar.

Her gaze slid to her mother, whose hand cradled her forehead. At each church, Helena's eyes lit up as she entered. At each sanctuary, she prayed. At each church, Nicky saw something in her mother's devotion that made her heart ache while at the same time brought a creeping understanding and maybe a tiny bit of forgiveness. She wasn't sure yet.

The drive home continued in silence, interrupted only by the tinkling of Franco's phone for an incoming text. He turned it off without looking at the screen.

They arrived back at the house at dusk, rainclouds adding to the gloom. Jinni's empty car was parked against the curb out front, windshield beaded with rain. She had a key and must've already been inside the house. Once Nicky opened the driveway gate, her mother slid the Mazda into the carport.

Ryan opened the side door, Jinni peeking over his shoulder.

"Hey, Nicky. See you finally moved in, Franco. 'Bout time." He smiled, but his hazel eyes were dark. Something was off. "Jinni insisted we bring food to make up for the imposition."

They tromped inside and made introductions. Her mother exclaimed over Jinni and drew her to sit down at the table, pleading exhaustion. Jinni waddled over with a laugh and lowered herself onto a chair. Two large pizza boxes lay stacked on the counter, next to a simple fresh salad in a ceramic bowl.

"You two relax, and we'll serve," Ryan said. He beckoned Nicky and Franco into the kitchen.

"I forgot to give you the gate control last night for Jinni," Nicky said. "Didn't expect you to come with her to her doctor's appointment. Thought you'd be working." She leaned her hip against the counter. Franco's bulk warmed her back.

"Glad I did." Ryan unstuck paper plates and laid them out. "When I walked around to the back of your property to find an easy way in for Jinni, I found cigarette butts, one still burning." He lowered his voice. "Someone's watching your house."

Both she and Franco started toward the door, Nicky's fingers sliding to the gun in her bellyband.

Ryan stopped them with a quick "Later. I don't want to upset Jinni. Besides, I scared off whoever was there." He turned his head to the table. "Jinni, hon? Cheese or pepperoni and green chile?"

Ryan's face transformed to a fierce protectiveness that left Nicky stunned.

He loved Jinni. Did Savannah know?

Did *he*?

"Very funny, Oyemshi. See, Nicky? I'm teaching him Zuni." Jinni rubbed her belly, a smile making her plain features glow. "Our maga may want pizza, but n'aaya can only stomach salad."

"And he's teaching you Keres." Nicky brought Jinni's food and a second plate with a slice of pizza and salad for her mother. Franco followed with glasses of iced tea.

"I've managed to convince Ryan to take me to the exhibition opening at the museum Friday night." Jinni patted her stomach. "Probably our last night out together for a long time. I even bought a tent—I mean dress—to wear. Are you going?"

Nicky's "No," landed on top of her mother's "Of course," and Franco's "Yes."

"I want to see the exact pots those people sampled," Helena said, "and, besides, don't criminals always return to the scene of their crime?"

Jinni's eyes sparkled with excitement. "Sometimes I wish I hadn't quit the police force."

"Not sure how many people will show up, even though Fire-Sky caciques and the priest at the mission blessed the building," Ryan said. "That should decrease the possibility of harmful spirits." He eyed Nicky. "Speaking of spirits, Savannah said you've seen something."

"Savannah has a big mouth." Nicky took a bite of pizza. People in the room stared at her with a mix of expressions, from fascination to humor to ire. Franco had gone stone-faced, his mask donned. "It was nothing."

"And always has been," her mother said firmly.

"You don't believe your daughter has visions?" Ryan asked.

"As the only child of busy parents, Nicky had a rich fantasy life."

"*Absent* parents," Nicky corrected.

"You saw ghosts and spirits as a child? You told me your awakening happened when you started working on the rez," Ryan said.

"It was only one time, when I was about six." Nicky peeled off a pepperoni slice and popped it in her mouth. "What's weird is—" She hitched up a shoulder. "It's the same one I'm experiencing now."

"The birthing niche," Franco said. "Is that what scared you?" He stood, feet planted, arms crossed, his square jaw hard.

"Yes. Whatever this thing is." Against an odd swelling fear, Nicky donned a wry smile and asked Jinni, "You remember earlier this year? When the Roybals had the priest bless their house?"

Jinni spread her hand protectively over her stomach. "That ghost cloud in the closet of their daughter's room."

"She told me it was her friend and to leave it alone."

Jinni looked up at Ryan. "It disappeared only after the Jemez Medicine Man smudged and blessed the room."

"Before we found Rémy Tioux's body, I did a sweep of the museum." Nicky toyed with her fork. "And this same ... *thing* was in the exhibition room at the mock birthing niche. Later, when we were casting nets for evidence at the earthen tank—"

"The boiling water," Franco said. "Something black, underneath."

"You saw that. I wasn't sure. Then, at the birthing niche up on the cliff, everything came back to me. With a vengeance." She rubbed the gooseflesh on her arms, her laugh humorless.

"Tell us," Ryan said.

Nicky met his gaze. It reassured her she would be believed. "It's black. And small—child-sized, even. Not solid—more like emptiness. Sometimes, two red eyes look out at me. Sometimes, it smiles." Chills ran up her neck. "But the smile..." Eyes widening, she sucked in a breath. "The petroglyph, by the shrine. That thing tethered to the mother. That's it."

"A baby?" Franco said.

"Yes," Jinni said slowly. Her eyes were wide with something like fear. "But not really."

"What is it?" Nicky asked.

"I don't know its name, but I've heard many explanations. Some say it's the soul of a child waiting to be born. Others say it's one who didn't survive coming into this world and is waiting to come back, to be reborn." Jinni reached up a hand to Ryan, who clasped it tightly. "And some say it's the pain. Grief and sadness felt by the mother and father, the family and clan when a child passes at birth. Maybe it's all of that." She leaned forward and captured Nicky's gaze with hers. "You lost your mother at a young age, and now again because she's joining the church, right?"

"Am I the villain in this tale?" Nicky's mother asked the room.

"And after the warehouse fire this summer, Franco abandoned you," Jinni continued. "You chose to be alone instead of fixing yourself. It would attach to you then. And now."

"But all of this has happened in the last couple of weeks," Nicky said. "What's changed?"

Jinni sat back. She slid her hand from Ryan's and laid it on her belly. "I don't know."

"How does she get rid of it?" Franco asked.

Nicky shot him a glance.

"The Jemez Medicine Man, I guess," Ryan said. "He got rid of it in the village."

"Franco? Did you ever ask Dean or Charlotte if he came to the museum?" Nicky asked.

"Who is this medicine man? And who is Charlotte?" Her mother again.

"I didn't think to," Franco replied. "I can call—"

"No. We'll go to the exhibition opening. Get Charlotte and Dean alone."

Her mother stood, face tight, bumping the table and knocking over the glasses of tea. Jinni, who couldn't move fast enough, got drenched.

"I'm so sorry." Helena grabbed dish towels from the kitchen and handed Nicky one. Nicky dropped to her knees and blotted a puddle on the floor.

"You need a bigger table," Franco said.

"She had one, inherited along with many other valuable family heirlooms. All gone." Helena scooped up sliding ice cubes and marched them to the sink.

Nicky's face burned at the judgment in her mother's tone. She'd had to sell off her inheritance for a mortgage balloon payment or lose her home. Hurt and anger replaced the inkling of forgiveness that had crept into her heart that afternoon.

With a long, dramatic exhalation, Helena stepped to Nicky's side. "I'm sorry. As a postulant, I know better than to judge."

"How about as a mother?" Nicky snapped and stood, banging her head against the bottom of the table. Ignoring the pain, she dropped the towel in the sink. Her fingers bit into the edge of the basin as she struggled to regain control of her emotions.

"'*Only for a short while have you loaned us to each other,'*" Jinni said into the silence. "That's part of a prayer. Jesuit. It comes to my head when I think about holding my daughter for the first time."

Ryan placed his hands on her shoulders. He kissed the top of her head. "Who knew I'd married such a wise woman?"

"I don't know about wise, but tired and wet." Jinni sighed. "Maybe we should go."

Outside security lights popped on.

A dark shape, head covered, passed by the kitchen window, too fast to see clearly. The doorbell rang. Nicky swiveled and exchanged a glance with Franco. He held his hand up for quiet. In tandem, they drew their weapons and strode toward the front hall.

The diamond-patterned grip of her gun bit into her palm. Finger across the trigger guard, Nicky sidled to the door.

"Who is it?"

"Lottie. I-I need to talk to Franco. I know he's here. His truck's out front." Her voice was shrill.

Nicky shot a glare at Franco. She slid her Glock back into the holster, flipped on the hall light, and unlocked the door. Charlotte, head covered in the hood of her black jacket, stood wet and bedraggled on the threshold, her face tight with anger.

Nicky backed into the kitchen to stand next to her mother. Jinni, wide-eyed, was still at the table, Ryan behind her. Franco appeared to be glued to the floor beneath the threshold to the kitchen.

Charlotte scraped back the hood as she marched up to Franco, eyes shimmering. "I thought—I thought you and—and me—"

"I," Nicky's mother said, correcting grammar under her breath.

"I thought *we*—" Charlotte, her welling eyes never leaving Franco, leveled a finger at Nicky. "Are you sleeping with her?" It came out as a wail.

Nicky's mother tucked her hands into the wide bell sleeves of her habit and stepped into the hall. "Not yet," she answered dryly.

Eyes rolling white, Franco barked out a nervous laugh. He retreated fast.

Charlotte stared at Nicky's mother, expression morphing from stormy to confused to dumbstruck when her gaze dropped to the wedding band strung around Helena's neck. She grabbed at her own neckline, fingers scrabbling. Finding nothing, her hand tightened into a fist, knuckles tight.

Disquieting calm replaced her wild emotion. "Dr. Galini. I-I didn't think you'd come. Dean's going to be shocked."

"Do I know you?" Helena crossed her arms.

Charlotte smiled, but it was forced. "I've attended a couple of your conference presentations, but we haven't been formally introduced." She held out her hand, fingers shaking. "I'm Charlotte Fields. And I'm very happy to finally meet you."

CHAPTER THIRTY-TWO

NICKY SNUGGLED DEEPER into her heavy jacket in the passenger seat of Franco's parked truck—his personal vehicle so they wouldn't attract attention. She sipped her coffee, her gaze scanning the circular driveway and portico of the Fire-Sky Resort and Casino hotel. Both she and Franco had a direct view of the valet podium, a lucky break finding an open slot so close and strategic.

Stacked rock columns and rough vigas decorated the hotel's adobe facade, and geometric designs and huge images of ancient petroglyphs ran up its sides. Its tans and browns transitioned to a fawn blue that blended into the sky as it rose to its fifteen-story height. It was as if the structure disappeared into thin air.

The hotel profits were on par with Indian casinos on the East Coast. No wonder there was money enough to purchase the Biloxi riverboat resort from Rémy Tioux.

Nicky's cell phone chirped with a text message.

"It's Jazzy at the front desk," she said. "The Santibanezes are in the lobby waiting for Marica's car. His is the white Tundra, heavy on the chrome. Hers is a silver—*wow*."

Franco gave a whistle.

A sleek, low-slung coupe purred into the drive. Peter and Marica stepped out of the hotel, deep in conversation. As Marica broke from her husband, he grasped her arm and pulled her into an awkward kiss. Valets opened the doors of their respective vehicles, one loading a small suitcase into the back seat of the truck. The truck pulled out, the coupe following, both turning toward the freeway.

"Does the tribe pay for their transportation as well as their condo?" Franco craned his neck to peer up to the top floor of the hotel.

"I think so, but Marica has family money. Her father owns a string of car lots and garages all over northern New Mexico. They were wealthy enough that she and a couple of her brothers raced."

"Really? NASCAR, rally, Formula 1?"

"I don't know. Cars." Nicky climbed out of the truck. "Jazzy said Santibanez is headed to Santa Fe and Marica to Albuquerque. He's gone till tomorrow evening but plans to attend the opening at the museum tomorrow night. She's out until after lunch. That means Kristina's alone with Raven."

Jazzy didn't look up from her computer as they passed the front desk. Nicky casually swept up the key card lying on the granite top and strolled to the bank of elevators, Franco at her heels. The doors to one of the elevators opened, and Nicky nodded as a hotel guest stepped out. In the empty car, she flashed the card against the panel and punched the button to the penthouse.

"I didn't sleep with Lottie," Franco said.

Nicky deliberately focused on the swirl-etched aluminum doors, refusing to look at Franco or acknowledge the swoop in her gut.

"Sure, I kissed her—I was pretty pissed at you at the time—but it was weird. Like I was kissing my sister or something."

If she pounded her head against the doors, she'd probably leave a mark on the shiny surface.

"When I kiss *you*—"

"Why are you doing this right now?" She couldn't keep the desperate edge from her voice.

He was slow to answer. She shot him a sideways glance, and his look made her whole body burn.

He grinned. "Captive audience."

The elevator opened, and Nicky shot out and into the Place of Emergence foyer, where the low throb of drums from the unobtrusive sound system blended with the tinkle of water from the fountain. She pressed the doorbell.

Franco's whispered, "Running away again," and followed her.

The Santibanezes's maid, Annette, opened the doors to the apartment and stepped out, her face impassive. With her tan scrubs, she blended into the background of the room.

"We'd like to speak to Kristina Tioux." The words came out fast and high. Nicky took a calming breath. "Tell her it has to do with her husband's wedding ring."

Annette nodded and slipped through the door, closing it behind her. The vibration of drums echoed in the still room.

Nicky dashed another look at Franco. She had a minute, maybe less. Knotting her hands together, she said, "Did you know I never gave Dax Stone a key to my house?"

Captive audience, confession time, whatever. Maybe it was time Franco was confronted with a few of *her* truths.

"I think that ate at him," Nicky continued. "During the White-Hawk case, he even changed the locks at my house without my permission. Said mine were too easy to jimmy. And the table you complained about last night? He bought it and put it in my house, also without asking permission."

Franco had gone rigid. "Does he still have a key to the new locks?"

She released a sigh of disappointment. "Not my point. Whether he has a key is irrelevant because I didn't give it to him. He took it. He didn't care that I didn't give him permission."

"He's why you became a cop."

Her mother had said the same thing. Maybe they were right. But maybe it's where she'd needed to be all along.

Was that how her mother felt? That the church had initially shielded her against the grief of her husband's infidelity, their divorce, and his death? Was it only later that she'd realized she had found her true calling? That what had pushed her into her vocation no longer played any role in her path forward?

The drumbeat faded, and the sound of muffled voices came from the apartment.

"Nicky?" Franco shoved his hands deep into the pockets of his jeans, keys clinking under fidgeting fingers. She met his eyes and once again saw the real Franco. "Do you still love him?"

The doors opened. Her answer to Franco's question would have to wait.

Kristina Tioux stood in the threshold, eyes blinking back moisture, expression tense. "You have Rémy's wedding ring?"

"I do," Nicky said.

With obvious reluctance, Kristina invited them inside. The jingle of bells and excited cooing drew them to the large carved dining table. On the floor at one end, Raven lay on a play mat, arms and legs waving and kicking at toys dangling from a zoo-themed baby gym.

The baby didn't spare them a look, her dark eyes too focused on the brightly colored animals.

Kristina motioned to the table and sat where she could watch her daughter. Nicky and Franco slid into chairs across from her. This time when Annette brought out a tray of coffee, Nicky noticed. The woman flicked her a cold look before she disappeared behind the swinging door to the kitchen.

"The ring. Can I see it?" Kristina asked.

Nicky tugged out a small zipper bag. She opened it and placed the gold circle on the table.

"We found it at a shrine in the mountains associated with a medicine wheel garden and birthing niche," Nicky said. "Along with a broken bracelet with Raven's name. Why did your husband leave those things?"

Kristina shook her head mutely.

"You lied about the first ring we showed you. Why?" Franco's voice was deep and stern.

"Because I thought ... I thought—" Her mouth worked. Then she blurted, "I didn't cheat on him. I don't care what he said, what the

DNA tests say. Raven is Rémy's daughter. That he could accuse me of
… of…" Kristina's face crumpled.

"Why didn't he believe Raven was his daughter?" Nicky asked.

A rattle shirred from the gym. Raven kicked excitedly.

"Because of a stupid blood test. My husband made a lot of money,
had access to more. We're at risk for kidnappings, and we didn't want
to take a chance with our child. We did identity kits through a doctor
friend of Rémy's. Fingerprints, DNA—he swabbed our cheeks. It stays
good for something like seven years in the freezer. And our blood type.
Raven didn't even cry when he poked her heel. She was so good."
Kristina rubbed a thumb over the side of her coffee cup. "But there
was a problem. Rémy's friend told us that probably Raven's kit was
bad and laughed it off. He asked Rémy to bring her back the next day,
and he'd have a fresh kit. I knew something was wrong, but I never
suspected it would be about Raven's paternity." She looked up at
them. "According to the blood tests, Raven and I are both O negative.
Rémy's AB negative. That means…" Kristina faltered.

"Raven should have either an A-negative or a B-negative blood
type." Nicky said. She'd read quite a lot about genetics and genes for a
case involving illegal organ harvests and transplants.

"Rémy had another paternity test done—not through his friend.
He said he was too humiliated and embarrassed. That test proved I
was Raven's mother, but he wasn't the father. He was furious. He
accused me of *cheating* on him, but it's not true! There must have been
a mix-up at the fertility clinic. Something *they* did, not me."

No one had found any indication of DNA tests in Rémy Tioux's
digital correspondence, on his computer, or in his hotel room and
rental car. But he must have confronted Dr. Summerweaver with one
at the Santa Fe fertility clinic and threatened to sue. She'd practically
confirmed it when they'd met with her, and Maria Anita had told them
Tioux had thrown a handful of papers in the doctors' faces.

"Did you get pregnant by in vitro fertilization?" Nicky asked.
Dozens of cases had come to light where donor eggs had been accidentally fertilized with the wrong sperm, or corrupt clinic doctors
knowingly substituted their own.

"We did two rounds. Nothing. But there were ... changes in my treatment before the third round. It turned out we didn't need in vitro. I got pregnant naturally." She shrugged and averted her eyes.

"Changes?" Franco asked.

"The herbal teas. That's all. I told Rémy."

"Is that why your husband was searching the gardens on the pueblo? Why he questioned experts about medicinal herbs?" Nicky paused. "Do you know what he was looking for?"

"Not just what but who," Franco said. "Your herbalist was Jimmy Che'chi. If you didn't cheat—"

"I didn't. I swear."

"Then how could herbal teas cause you to get pregnant with a child that isn't your husband's?" Franco asked.

Kristina tilted her chin up, defiance in her eyes. "You don't believe me, but I don't care. Jimmy told me to expect a miracle. I got one, and that's all that matters."

A miracle? What compounds in medicinal herbs could cause an infertile couple to conceive?

"Do you know where Jimmy Che'chi is now?" Franco asked.

Kristina shook her head.

"Why did you identify the wrong ring as your husband's?" Nicky asked.

"Because he told me he was going to take it off. That if he couldn't find answers, he would divorce me, tell his family—my family—everything. When you said his ring was still on his finger, I was so relieved. Then it wasn't his, and I was afraid if I said anything ... I didn't want any more questions about Raven's paternity. And Peter is helping me do a new DNA test that will prove—"

"Peter Santibanez? Why does he care?" Franco asked.

Kristina pinched her lips together and dropped her gaze to her laced fingers.

"Is it because he wants to renegotiate the riverboat casino deal with Rémy's heirs?" Nicky asked. "But if Raven's not your husband's child—"

Kristina lifted blazing eyes. "She *is* his child. It's not *fair* that Raven won't inherit her father's money and business. The DNA tests *must* be wrong."

"If he believed you cheated, then both of you could be disinherited," Nicky said. "Is that why your husband visited lawyers the day he died? To make changes to his will?"

"No. At least ... no." Kristina looked sullen. "The Mississippi Gaming Commission refused to approve Fire-Sky's purchase of the riverboat casino. Rémy had to sign paperwork claiming the deposit. All that money, and because of a stupid DNA test, I—*Raven* gets nothing."

Nicky caught Franco's eyes before she turned back to Kristina. "We were told that Fire-Sky turned down the deal," Franco said.

"Does it matter?"

"What do you know about the other ring? The one you originally identified as your husband's?" Nicky asked.

"Nothing." Kristina stood. The baby had fallen asleep on the floor, one little fist curled loosely above her head, long lashes brushing the tops of plump cheeks. "I don't want to answer any more questions."

Nicky pressed. "This help from Peter Santibanez. Why—?"

"Please leave or I'll call security."

FRANCO PRESSED the button to the private elevator, but Nicky hung back, hoping the serenity of the foyer would cool her churning thoughts.

"We need to talk to the FBI," Franco said. "If Raven isn't Tioux's biological daughter, and no one in Mississippi knew, Kristina had a strong motive for her husband's murder."

"So do the doctors at the Santa Fe fertility clinic," Nicky said. "Remember how Maria Anita described them? The big one and the little one—just like the guys seen in Tioux's rental car the night of his murder."

"That's an interesting coincidence, isn't it? Because if Raven's DNA test implicated the clinic in negligence, that would bring some pretty terrible publicity, plus possible loss of their licenses and livelihoods."

"Both Kristina and the doctors might want that test to disappear. We need to find it." Nicky stepped closer to the trickling water and stared into the black pool in the floor. "There's just one thing that doesn't fit. Why was my father's wedding ring on Rémy Tioux's finger?"

The elevator dinged, and the doors rolled open. Behind Nicky, the latch clicked. She stiffened, lips compressing.

From inside the elevator, Franco asked, "Coming?"

Nicky stopped just outside the doors. "Wait for me downstairs," she said in a low voice. Although his expression turned curious, he didn't question her, only nodded.

The elevator slid closed, and carved wooden doors to the apartment cracked open. Annette peered through the gap. Her eyes widened when she saw Nicky.

"I bet you hear and see more than your employers realize." Nicky strolled toward her. "You're asked to be invisible, and after a while, no one even notices you're there."

Annette hesitated. Nicky thought she might slam the door shut, but she slipped into the foyer. Contempt flickered over her features. "You and your partner didn't notice me. Neither did the FBI. No one wanted to interview me. People don't much take me into account."

Now where had Nicky heard that before?

"I'm listening."

"The day that man was murdered, he was up here, having breakfast with Mr. Santibanez. They had an argument. That man told Mr. Santibanez his offer for the casino had been turned down. Something about a morals clause in the original agreement between Mississippi Gaming and Tsiba'ashi D'yini. Because tribal pinsibaar-it'itra—councilmen—would be in charge of the casino, Mississippi had to run background checks on them. Council said that violated Fire-Sky sovereignty laws and refused. But I don't think that's the reason. I don't think those men could've passed a background check."

Nicky stepped closer. "So, Mississippi stopped the deal, not Fire-Sky." Santibanez had lied.

"Mr. Santibanez and that man yelled at each other about it. Mr. Santibanez said he'd used the tribe's money to buy agreements so that the background checks wouldn't happen." Annette shook her head. "That man from Mississippi was so angry about the bribes."

Nicky's brow creased. "Bribes?"

"The next day, after that man was gone from this earth, Mr. Santibanez called the governor and said the deal's on hold because of Mr. Tioux's murder. That he's working with *Mrs.* Tioux now to complete the contract or get the tribe's money back, which was a lie."

"The governor and tribal council knew about the bribes Santibanez paid?" A knot grew in Nicky's stomach at the potential illegality.

"Not that money back. The other money. The deposit on the Mississippi casino." Annette paused. "Tribal council doesn't know the deal was turned down by Mississippi that day. They think everything is okay, that they don't have to do the background checks because of the bribes Mr. Santibanez paid. But that man told Mr. Santibanez that Fire-Sky forfeited the money they pledged to purchase the Biloxi casino. That the Tsiba'ashi D'yini People lost twenty-seven million dollars—half the purchase price. Which means once tribal council finds out, Mr. Santibanez will also lose." She looked around the beautiful foyer and shrugged.

Which all added up to a terrific motive for murder.

"That's why Mr. Santibanez is helping Mrs. Tioux and her baby. As that man's heirs, she's told him it's in her power to help him, but not if she can't prove the baby is her husband's."

"A new DNA test."

"Haa'a."

The soothing sounds of a burbling stream now accompanied the rhythm of drums, and howls of wolves piped through the speakers.

"There's more," Annette said. "Before dinner that night, Mr. Santibanez called that man. I couldn't hear what he said, but he left after, very fast, and was gone for a couple of hours. When he came back to the apartment before dinner, his shoes were muddy. He had mud here, too." She bent and touched a knee. "Like he fell. There were broken pine needles in the cuffs of his trousers."

Rémy Tioux's clothes had contained pine needles.

"Did you keep anything?" Nicky asked.

"It was all cleaned."

No evidence. And she couldn't confront Santibanez about it until after he returned from Santa Fe.

Nicky had one more question.

"Why are you telling me this? You could lose your job."

"Because Mrs. Marica deserves better. She's been very good to me, and it's not fair what he's doing to her with Mrs. Tioux. He's *courting* that woman," she said with a curl of her lip. "Mrs. Marica doesn't need to worry about another one."

"Another what?"

Annette shrugged.

NICKY STEPPED out of the elevator and strode over to Franco.

"We need to go to security. The search warrant for the hotel's CCTV the evening of Tioux's murder was approved?"

"On Monday, along with the phone records from Tioux's room. No calls except to concierge, probably to book vehicles," Franco said. "Aguilar reviewed the CCTV, but Tioux didn't come back to the hotel that night."

"What about Peter Santibanez's movements?"

"Only to corroborate his alibi," Franco replied.

"Then he missed something."

Franco fell into step beside her. "Like what?"

"Santibanez's prints were found on Tioux's abandoned rental car. I think I know why."

CHAPTER THIRTY-THREE

NICKY JOINED in the applause when Dr. Dean MacElroy was announced. He sat in a single row of chairs on a stage in the Isgaawa museum's packed auditorium, along with Nicky's mother, Charlotte Fields, two other young curators, and a Native man Nicky didn't recognize. Dean ascended to the podium, a huge smile wreathing his face, while Nicky threaded through the standing-room-only crowd to one side of the rows of chairs and leaned against a wall next to Franco. Savannah, Howard, Ryan, and Jinni sat near the middle of the crowd, Savannah in her grandmother's brain-tanned deerskin skirt and moccasins, Jinni in a red dress with tiny white polka dots. Peter and Marica Santibanez were seated in the front row with other tribal dignitaries, including the governor and members of the tribal council.

Franco leaned in, mouth to Nicky's ear. "I wonder how many people are here because of the exhibition and how many are here because of the murder?" His breath tickled her neck. "God, you smell good."

She ignored the tingles warming her skin.

"I imagine at least half are here out of macabre curiosity," she said. "Kristina Tioux didn't come. No surprise there."

Franco tipped his head toward the stage. "Your mom decided to give a speech?"

"No. But after Dean's visit this morning, she agreed to sit on stage."

Dean had arrived unannounced during breakfast with an apologetic Charlotte in tow. Franco had practically bolted from the house, excusing himself to do yard cleanup. Nicky didn't know where he'd found a chainsaw and clippers, but the tangle of bushes, saplings, and waist-high weeds behind her property had been cleared and piled to burn later. He'd come back inside after their visitors left, dirty and wet with rain and sweat. No good places for a spy or stalker to hide anymore.

On stage, Dean motioned to a painted washing basin displayed on a plinth beside him and launched into a detailed history.

"Did, uh, Lottie explain why she ran out of the house the other night?" Franco rubbed his jaw and swept his gaze over the crowd. Nicky noticed he'd placed himself so the podium hid Charlotte from view.

"She said it was the shock of meeting Dr. Helena Galini, her inspiration and academic idol. Charlotte told us she's diligently following in her career footprints. Did you know Dean thought I was the focus of Charlotte's obsession?"

That got Franco's attention. He stared at Nicky, his brows furrowed.

"Maybe she'll trade her interest in criminal justice for religious studies," Nicky said. "Shh. Dean's introducing Mom."

"And Dr. Helena Galini, a very dear, very old friend."

Nicky's mother, looking very nunlike in a black wool tunic with bell sleeves and a white coif covered by a black veil, stood and smiled at Dean as applause died down.

"How long have we known each other, Helena?" Dean asked.

"Forty years?"

"At least." Dean grinned. "Without Dr. Galini's pioneering work on the analytical analysis of archeological pottery, important cultural contributions of Indigenous Peoples in science and medicine would be lost and forgotten. Because of discoveries from scientists like Dr. Galini, it's no great leap to imagine compounds found inside basins like this could one day be used to cure cancer or treat Alzheimer's."

Franco sighed beside her. "An invitation for every bioprospecting pothunter in the region. Wouldn't that muddy up our investigation."

"I don't think he realizes how it sounds," Nicky whispered back. "He's always been fascinated by Mom and Dad's research."

Dean paused, his smile faltering. "Again, I wish to thank you all for coming to what I hope is an informative and enlightening exhibition. I will end my little speech with an announcement. This will be my last show at the Isgaawa Cultural Center and Museum. I am leaving the position of museum director at the end of the month."

Nicky straightened, shock running through her. Murmured conversations swelled in the room, people shifting on their seats in agitation and surprise.

Except for tribal council in the front row.

"It is my privilege to introduce the new museum director, Dr. Lionel Seymour Hand. He comes to us from the Smithsonian's National Museum of the American Indian in Washington, DC, by way of Acoma and Fire-Sky heritage."

Dr. Hand, a barrel-chested man, stood and gave a single wave to gasps and murmurs and hesitant applause. His broad, lean face was sculpted with high, hollow cheeks, a square jaw, and a wide mouth with a chiseled lower lip. His black hair was parted in the middle and worn in two braids laced with leather thongs. Nicky estimated his age in the early forties. Although he wasn't as tall as Dean, his presence was palpable. Many of the Fire-Sky tribal members in the audience had wary or hard expressions as they stared at the new director. A few abruptly stood and walked out of the room. Savannah scowled, and even Howard frowned.

"What's the crowd saying?" Franco asked Nicky.

"*Muuk'aitra ham'asdi'ini.* Lion's hand or lion's paw."

He snorted. "Not as scary as Sand Spider."

"What?"

"Movie reference. I didn't know Dean was retiring."

"Neither did I," she said. Her mother caught and held Nicky's gaze. She tapped her lips and laid a finger across them, pointing toward Dr. Hand's back. Nicky shook her head, not understanding.

Hand sat down again without speaking, which seemed to take Dean by surprise.

"Well. Nothing is left to say except I invite you all to head to the Siow-Carr Gallery for the exhibition," Dean finished.

As the crowd milled out of the room, the front row of dignitaries rose and stepped toward the stage and offered their welcome to Dr. Hand. Her mother leaned toward Dean and spoke in his ear. Charlotte sidled up behind her and reached out a tentative hand to touch her shoulder, but then her mother pivoted and hurried off the stage, black skirts flapping. Charlotte's fingers curled into a fist as she watched her leave.

"Dean will meet us in the archives when he can get away," her mother said. "This museum is such a maze. You lead."

"Franco and I need to speak to Peter Santibanez," Nicky said.

"That man is too much of a politician to leave early," her mother replied. "Look at him."

Santibanez was all white smiles, head thrown back in laughter as he clapped the governor on his shoulder. He turned to clasp the hand of another council member and met Nicky's eyes. A frown flickered over his features before the toothy smile was again in place. Kristina must have told him about their visit. He'd be prepared for them.

"What was it about Dr. Hand—" Nicky began.

Savannah rushed up, her expression stormy. Howard trailed behind. "Did you see that? I can't believe tribal council hired that … that…" She spat something in Keresan.

Ryan barked a laugh. "That's a word I won't teach you, Jinni."

"Really?" Jinni's eyes danced. "I think we need to chat, Savannah."

"You were all raised on the pueblo?" Helena asked. "I need you to come with us."

Nicky led the group toward the exit. "Did the council force Dean out?"

"Supposedly they told him if he didn't retire, they would fire him," Savannah said. "At least that's the rumor circulating in the crowd."

"Does the rumor say why?" Nicky's worried eyes found Dean on the stage. Why hadn't he told her?

"No. But Dean's replacement is completely unacceptable." Savannah turned to glare at Lionel Hand.

Caught behind the slow-moving crowd funneling through the doors, Nicky stopped, too. Hand was still on stage with Dean and the bevy of junior curators. Charlotte was gone. A few of the council members stood and talked nearby, including Peter and Marica Santibanez. Hand appeared to be listening to Marica's father, Simón Póncio, but his hooded gaze ran over the people around Nicky, lightly touching on her and finally coming to rest on her mother.

"Why is he unacceptable?" Nicky asked.

"He sold out the Fire-Sky and Acoma People by secretly video-taping sacred dances and ceremonies. *And* he's a convicted pothunter, selling our heritage for a few bucks." Savannah had the group's attention now, as well as Lionel Hand's. She lifted her chin, cheeks flushing deep red, and stared defiantly at the new museum director. "Oh, yeah. I almost forgot. He's also a murderer."

That raised Nicky's eyebrows.

"All that happened when he was just a kid. He served his time and obviously made something of himself," Ryan said quietly. "Doesn't he deserve a second chance?"

Left unsaid was the second chance the Fire-Sky tribe had given Ryan after his youthful indiscretions had led to the death of Savannah's brother.

Savannah threw him a narrow-eyed look before she pushed through the crowd and marched toward the hall containing the archives. The fringe around the bottom of her hide skirt flicked in agitated fashion.

"That's not all," Helena said, lowering her voice. "I'm sure he's the L. S. Hand listed as a coauthor on research papers your father published right before he died."

Next to her, Howard tipped a box of Hot Tamales into his palm, spilling out red candies. Nicky plucked one up and popped it into her mouth, cinnamon bursting on her tongue as she contemplated Dr. Lionel Hand.

Associated with her dad, huh? Funny how he'd just happened to show up on the pueblo around the same time her father's wedding ring had been found on a dead man.

CHAPTER THIRTY-FOUR

THE EXHIBITION OPENING had drained most guests away from the other rooms in the museum, and the gallery leading to the archives was deserted. It was one of Nicky's favorites, displaying everything from ancient pottery pieced together from fragments to colorful contemporary vessels to wobbly clay bowls made by schoolchildren in cultural programs that helped link them to their heritage.

Jinni and Savannah talked quietly across the room next to a long display detailing changes in glazes and design on pottery over hundreds of years. Howard, sneaking bites of candy from his box, circled a table filled with seed pots, their tiny openings large enough to push harvested grain through but too small for foraging mice or rats. Franco stood to one side of a spotlighted plinth, chuckling at something Ryan had said. He looked good dressed in black wool trousers—no cargos tonight—black leather loafers, a deep blue dress shirt, and a charcoal sports jacket to hide his shoulder holster.

"For goodness' sakes, stop drooling over Franco and read this."

Nicky jerked her gaze away, neck burning. "Mom, I'm not—"

Her mother rolled her eyes and angled the screen of her phone. "'Organic geochemical and DNA analysis of archaeological medicine pots from northern Chilean domestic ceramics.'" She swiped the author line larger. "Hand's the first author, and H. M. Matthews is the corresponding author. And this"—she tapped to open a second page— "'Matrilineal inheritance in South American natives exhibits mainly four mitochondrial DNA haplogroups,' L. S. Hand. Published five years after Michael's death."

Dean appeared and hurried past Nicky to punch in the key code to the archives room. Lights blinked on automatically as Nicky and her mother followed him in. He slid behind the counter and disappeared between stacks.

Savannah, Franco, Ryan, and Howard crowded into the room after them.

"Where's Jinni?" Nicky asked.

"Some of her friends from the police department are here, so she went back to the exhibit to chat. But she gave me permission to stay." Ryan's eyes crinkled with humor. "One last investigation before the baby's born, then I'm back on the sidelines for a while."

Nicky's phone chimed. A text from Savannah.

That's what Jinni told him. Not sure, but I think the baby daddy is here.

Nicky's stomach plummeted. Her gaze slipped to Ryan. He caught it and mouthed, *What?* She shook her head and shoved her phone into her shoulder bag.

Dean returned and laid two thick folders on the counter. "These are your publications, Helena." He placed a hand on the second folder. "Michael's are in this one."

"Why didn't you tell me about Lionel Hand?" her mother asked. She flipped open the file containing her deceased-husband's publications and began to sort through them.

"And why didn't you tell us you were being forced to retire?" Nicky asked.

Dean rubbed his whiskered chin with agitated fingers. "The council asked me to keep it secret." Bitterness crept into his tone. "They want to increase traffic to the museum, make money on it. One of the council members even suggested those tiresome hands-on, interactive exhibits. This is a serious museum, not some ridiculous playground."

"Dean?" Nicky reached across the counter. "Will you be okay? If you need a place to stay or help financially…" While Dean's position was prestigious, salaries for museum directors were not.

He patted her hand but worry swirled deep in his eyes. "Thank you, my dear. I think I have everything figured out. Almost."

"I didn't know the extent of Michael's association with Lionel Hand." Her mother indicated a pile of sorted articles. "I avoided everything about Michael after we divorced."

"They teamed up for over ten years," Dean said. "Without Michael's mentoring, Hand would never have gotten the Smithsonian position. He's very well-respected."

"Except he's a criminal and traitor to his People," Savannah interjected.

"Yes," Dean said simply. "But that didn't stop the council from hiring him. They said they wanted new blood. Native blood."

"It's their right to promote their own People." Ryan's tone was firm.

"Even when I've dedicated the last twenty years of my life and career to this place? I had other job offers—more important, more lucrative. But my passion was helping *these* people." Dean's voice choked. He blinked rapidly, cleared his throat, then held his arms wide. "I oversaw the building design of this museum, collected and archived their rich history. But because I don't have the right genetics, I'm discarded."

Nicky bent over the desk and sorted through papers. But inside, her heart was tight with sympathy. As much as she loved working on the Fire-Sky Pueblo, even though she put her life on the line to protect their culture and traditions, she was an outsider. It was the right of the Fire-Sky People to promote and nurture their own. That placed her and her job in a precarious position. Nicky was willing to live under those rules, but there might come a time when she would stand in Dean's shoes.

She shook the thoughts from her head. This was not about her. This was about a murder investigation.

"When did the council tell you they wanted someone else as director?" Franco asked.

Nicky stiffened. She recognized Franco's offhand tone. He was onto something.

"After I hired Lottie," Dean said. "The intern she replaced—the one who got hurt—was paid with outside grant money. Council was angry about the added expense of Lottie's salary, but what could I do? Lottie was a last-minute hire, and I needed help."

"She was perfect for the position, considering," Franco said.

"Considering what?" asked Savannah.

"Her background in traditional plants."

Franco's answer seemed incomplete. Nicky waited for him to elaborate. Instead, he smiled lazily and waved a hand at the article she held. "What'd you find?"

"That Lionel Hand has an ethnobotany background, too. Listen to this title: 'Medicinal plants and ethnopharmacology of traditional healers of pueblo cultures in New Mexico.'" She flipped to the end of the article. "Hand and Dad are coauthors on at least ten of the references."

"He had access to pottery from all over North America at the Smithsonian," Helena said, eyebrows raised.

"Was Hand on the rez before he was hired?" Savannah asked Dean.

"For interviews. He's been staying with relatives up on Scalding Peak, waiting until I vacate my home at the end of the month so he can move in." Resentment rose again in his tone.

"I'm so sorry, Dean." Helena touched his arm.

"What I don't understand is how it was kept so quiet. Nothing stays secret for long on the pueblo," Savannah said.

"Some people are good secret keepers," Howard said. The sweet scent of cinnamon drifted in the air.

"Savannah, why did you ask about Dr. Hand being on the pueblo?" Dean's eyes opened wide. "You think he's behind the medicine garden desecrations."

"Yes." Savannah thrust her chin out. "He sold his People out before."

"Leave it alone, Savannah," Ryan said.

Savannah reddened but continued to push her point. "He was raised on Fire-Sky, and he studies medicinal plants. It makes perfect sense. Have the desecrations stopped, Franco?"

"Native officers checking gardens and shrines off-limits to non-Natives have found nothing so far," Franco said. "But the gardens that were dug up are pretty well-known both on and off the pueblo—except for the one where we found Tioux's car."

"That's why I asked you all here," Helena said. "Dean? Could you get that map of the pueblo?"

Dean hurried to the wall and pulled off a large xeroxed map attached by pushpins. He spread it over the countertop before rummaging in a drawer for a marker.

"This doesn't cover the whole pueblo," he said, "but there are shrines and gardens in these mountains. What if Lionel Hand or other bioprospectors—"

"Or Jimmy Che'chi," Nicky added.

Howard choked on a Hot Tamale. Ryan thumped him on the back, hard.

"Howard, put those away," Savannah said. "No eating in the museum. Stop pounding him, Ryan. He's not choking anymore."

"Then stop defending him," Ryan said under his breath.

"You know about the Jemez Medicine Man?" Howard asked, voice clogged with phlegm.

Nicky flashed him a quick glance. He'd mispronounced Jemez, but no one seemed to notice.

"What I'm interested in is why these gardens are targets," Nicky's mother said. What are these thieves—maybe murderers—looking for?" She held out the red Sharpie. "Franco, would you mark the locations of the harvested sites you've found?"

Franco looked at Dean, who nodded, before he placed a red *X* at five points on the map.

"Savannah, do you know of any others, even if they haven't been desecrated?" Helena asked.

"Not gardens. Only shrines, and I'm not comfortable..."

Helena smiled. "I understand. Howard?"

He took the pen and marked four more sites.

"What exactly are you looking for?" Ryan asked.

"Patterns. Think of the roads that guided ancient Peoples to Chaco Canyon," Helena answered. "Linear, pre-Columbian constructions, over mesas, through canyons. Demarcated with *herraduras*—crescent-shaped shrines—earthen mounds, and thousands of sherds. Not whole pots dropped and broken in situ, but fragments of different pots."

"You think the placement of the Fire-Sky shrines might be laid out in some kind of path?" Franco asked. "Leading to what?"

"I don't know. That's what we need to find out." Nicky's mother smiled faintly. "Ryan? Your turn."

Dean blinked at her, his mouth ajar. "A pattern of shrines. I never thought of that."

"I only know of two more." Ryan *X*'ed the map. "The ones we found burned and looted this past summer—during the WhiteHawk investigation."

Nicky stared hard at the red *X's*, a piece of the puzzle snapping into place. "Ryan—"

His phone chimed. He smiled, his face softening. "Jinni." Savannah swallowed and looked away. "She's gonna head home but wants to know if you'll give me a ride, Savannah."

"Of course. Is she okay to drive? I mean she's so … pregnant."

"She drove us to the museum. And you need me here, right?" Ryan looked around the room, eyes almost pleading. "She said she didn't mind if I stay."

Franco elbowed him. "God, you are so whipped."

"Lord's name in vain, Franco," Helena's voice was singsong, her attention on the map.

He straightened. "Yes, ma'am. Sorry, ma'am."

Ryan elbowed him back. "Now who's pathetic, choirboy?"

"You." Franco pushed Ryan, who staggered back. "Because Jinni's got you tight by the—"

Grinning, Ryan grabbed his arm.

"If you two would stop horsing around and focus on the map." This from Dean with a bite.

Like rowdy boys caught out, Franco and Ryan dropped their hands to their sides and gave each other askance looks. They were so entertaining Nicky almost didn't notice her mother slip a publication up one of her wide bell sleeves. Almost.

"I need to get Jinni the keys," Ryan said. "Be right back."

Nicky edged around the group. "I'll go with Ryan and make sure Peter Santibanez is still here."

Franco gave her a quizzical look but bent over the map with the others.

She and Ryan walked briskly through the deserted gallery toward the exhibition.

"The topo map, Ryan. The one I brought to Savannah's house during the WhiteHawk case," she said. "Marked—"

"By the ghost of Geronimo Elk," he finished.

"When I saw him at the station that night, I thought he came back to help his family—to help me." Nicky shivered. "That's why he marked the map with the locations of both the looted and hidden hunting shrines."

"But it wasn't all that useful in the WhiteHawk investigation, was it?"

"No. We solved the case before the other shrines were ever touched." Nicky met Ryan's gaze. "Do you think this is the map's true purpose? To lead us to the people who desecrated the medicine garden shrines and murdered Rémy Tioux? You've had it all this time. Is there a pattern?"

"The markings seem random to me, but I've never really thought about it."

"Can we come by tomorrow morning? I'll bring donuts and coffee."

Ryan smiled. "My kind of breakfast."

She and Ryan reached the open double doors to the Siow-Carr Gallery. Peter and Marica Santibanez stood near the middle of the room, holding court with dignitaries. Nicky caught a glimpse of Jinni sitting in a chair along one wall with a few grandmothers adorned with squash-blossom necklaces and heavy silver earrings stretching their earlobes. Ryan strode to Jinni and tugged her to her feet. She gave him an adoring smile as he placed a hand on her swollen belly. Nicky meandered through the crowd until she faced the birthing niche. The humming noise of conversation masked the tinkle of water. Her eyes traced the carved spiral in the rock slab.

A niggle of awareness refocused her gaze. Charlotte Fields was watching her from across the room but quickly turned away to say something to the man beside her. He stood slightly taller than Charlotte, lean with dark auburn hair. Nicky couldn't make out the color of his eyes, but his face shared Charlotte's fine features. Dean had said her brother was visiting. The guy leaned in to listen, then frowned and nodded. A third man, much larger—dirty blond hair, heavy brows, and hulking shoulders but a delicate chin—stood behind the two. He stared at Nicky, his face expressionless. The hair on her arms prickled. Her own gaze challenged him until he dropped his eyes to Charlotte and the other guy. At least by size, they matched the description of the two individuals seen by Luna Guerra's men the night of the murders. But so did the two guys who ran the concierge service out of the Fire-Sky resort—Jacob and Halloran—and, according to Maria Anita, the two doctors at the Santa Fe fertility clinic—Balderamos and Meyers: small and big.

Ryan stepped in front of her, blocking her view.

"Jinni?" she asked.

"Headed out. Said to tell you goodbye." His expression turned quizzical. "What was up in the archives room? When you gave me that look?"

Nicky forced a smile. "Nothing. Ready to get back?"

When he stepped out of her line of sight and toward the exit, Charlotte and the two men were gone.

CHAPTER THIRTY-FIVE

BACK IN THE ARCHIVES ROOM, Nicky simmered with frustration. None of the lines drawn through the known shrines pointed anywhere specific.

"There must be places we're missing on the other side of this canyon," Dean said. "Your father would've known. One year, he trekked the pueblo for weeks with only a horse and guide, collecting plant samples. Do you have his maps and notes, Helena? Nicky? Did he send you anything? Leave you journals or notes?"

"I got nothing from him," Nicky said flatly. "Ever."

Her mother pressed her lips together. "He sent me something right before he died. A locked briefcase. I haven't opened it."

"Helena! It's been years since he passed." Dean's face was a mask of astonishment. "Where's this case? There could be information inside that would pinpoint the location—"

"Of sacred shrines outsiders have no business knowing?" Savannah stood stiffly, chin raised.

Dean gave her a strained smile. The silence stretched uncomfortably.

Howard stepped forward, clutching his candy box, expression grave. "Savannah, those who wrecked our shrines may have taken a life. We should understand why they did this before they hurt someone else."

"He's right," Ryan said.

Howard blinked at him. A slow smile creased his face.

"Now who's taking his side?" But Savannah's expression softened as she eyed the two men. "Are we done? Can we please go see this special exhibit now?"

"Franco." Nicky touched his arm. "We'd better catch Santibanez before he leaves."

Howard carefully closed the top of his candy, slid it into a pocket, and sidled up to Nicky's mother. He cocked out an awkward elbow and said, "I don't understand why you scraped our ancestors' pots. They're empty, except for ghosts that linger around them and this place. Could I escort you to the exhibition and you tell me your reasons?"

Nicky's mother took Howard's elbow, lips twitching. Howard turned to Nicky, a sweet smile on his face. "Don't worry, auk'iinishi. I'll protect her."

Nicky smiled. "Thanks, friend."

Franco pushed open the archive room's door as Dean said, "But, Helena, this briefcase from Michael. Where is it?"

The door closed, and her mother's reply cut off.

Neither Peter nor Marica Santibanez were in the exhibition hall, but a quick question to a tribal council member directed Nicky and Franco to a gallery at the back of the museum.

Peter Santibanez stood alone in the room, in a hall dedicated to Fire-Sky military veterans. Glass-topped tables and boxes were filled with artifacts from the battlefield: helmets, uniforms, guns, bayonets and knives, letters and diaries.

With raised eyebrows and a twisted smile, he toasted the bank of photos with a plastic cup of ice.

"My grandfather." Santibanez tipped his head toward a photo of a dark-haired, square-jawed young man, frozen in time—khakis, headphones, transistor radio, and microphone. Another young man, bespectacled and blond, knelt next to him, pencil in hand, transcribing. "Did you know the military used other Indian languages and tribes as code talkers? Not just Navajo. It started in the First World War—Choctaw. But I'm sure you're not here for a history lesson."

"You lied to us when we questioned you about Rémy Tioux, Mr. Santibanez." Nicky kept her tone pleasant. "That's obstruction of justice, a felony."

Santibanez turned and opened his arms as wide as his smile, his handsome broad face an echo of his grandfather's features. "Just another crime to add to the Mississippi Gaming Commission's reasons not to sanction the Biloxi casino deal. Poor little Kristina called me after you left my apartment yesterday. She was so *sorry* for what she told you." He dropped his arms, face twisting in disgust. "So sorry she turned out to be the slut Rémy thought she was. The kid's not his."

Nicky bristled at the slur. She exchanged a glance with Franco, who raised a restraining hand and shook his head.

"Aren't you two supposed to be on injury leave? Is this a Fire-Sky-police-sanctioned interview?" Santibanez tipped ice into his mouth and crunched it as he eyed them coldly. "Or are you freelancing?"

Shrugging like it didn't matter, he moved along the line of photos, stopping with his back to them. Nicky's lips thinned.

"In our culture and tradition, the role of a man is to protect and provide," Santibanez said. "The military fulfills that tradition in a world where Indians are stranded on our sovereign islands—or should I say corralled? It's a way to escape, you know? To become the warriors we once were, regarded with the utmost respect in our communities."

"Kristina Tioux," Franco prompted.

"I sent paternity tests to two different companies. Both came back the same. Tioux's not the father of the child. Kristina won't be able to salvage the casino deal. Her daughter doesn't inherit."

"We'll need you to send us the paternity results as soon as possible," Franco said.

"And I'll need to see a warrant before I do," Santibanez replied.

"But you didn't know the DNA results when you confronted Tioux at breakfast that morning." Nicky played her hunch. "Or at the medicine shrine later that evening, did you?"

His shoulders stiffened.

She pressed. "The potential loss of twenty-seven million dollars of tribal money is a great motive for murder."

This time when Santibanez tipped the glass to his mouth, his hand trembled. He turned his head to Franco.

"What was it like? Afghanistan?"

Franco's expression blanked. He tucked his thumbs in his belt. "Hell, sir. With buddies you would die for. War makes you into someone you weren't before."

"A better someone? Or worse?"

Franco hesitated, then shrugged.

Santibanez stared at him, his expression grave, before he said, "When I called Tioux that evening, he told me he was going straight to the shrine. I got there first, confronted him, maybe even laid hands on him. He told me about Kristina and Raven. So, I told him we had more in common than he knew. That my son wasn't my son." His chuckle was without humor. "That he should be happy to figure that out now, when the little girl was young." He paused and met Nicky's eyes. "But I didn't kill him. I was back at the hotel for dinner and drinks at nine o'clock. When Rémy didn't show, I wasn't surprised. He was in mourning for who he thought was his daughter. The deal didn't matter to him anymore."

The hotel's CCTV had confirmed Santibanez's timeline.

"Your prints were found on the door handle of his car," Nicky said.

"Rémy's briefcase was in the back seat. I knew it had all the contracts and documents for the casino sale. I figured if I could see them, they'd give me an edge, so once he disappeared up the path ... I was desperate. But not desperate enough to kill." He smiled, but his eyes were distant. "The door was locked."

"You could have sent someone up to the shrine to murder him," Franco said.

Santibanez's laugh was real this time. "Who? My loyal henchmen? 'Take that man to the museum, cut off his hands, and lock him in a closet so he'll be found in spectacular fashion.' There's a cliff—as you well know—by the birthing shrine. A much more convenient location to dump a body." He tipped his cup up one more time, but he was out of ice. "I've called an emergency tribal council meeting tomorrow to tell them the whole of it. What you don't understand is that I insured the deposit against just such a contingency. The tribe won't get all of its money back, but we'll get a substantial amount. I'll lose face but eventually recover." He sighed and cocked an eyebrow at Nicky. "Sergeant? You may not like me, but my whole life is about protecting and providing for my People."

Clipping footsteps approached. Marica Santibanez swept into the far side of the gallery, bringing with her the scent of outdoors and the tickling smell of cigarettes. Rain droplets sparkled in her hair and on her shawl. She halted in a swirl of velvet.

"There you are. I'm ready to leave." When she caught sight of Nicky and Franco, she clutched at her skirt with white-knuckled hands. "Unless they're here to arrest you?" Was that hope in her voice?

"No, ma'am," Nicky said. "Just to inform your husband he'll need to come to the station on Monday and correct his interview statements. I doubt the FBI will be so forgiving."

Santibanez laughed again. "They won't care. They're off on some wild goose chase over Rémy's drug-kingpin brother in Mississippi. Idiots. It's obvious that whoever is behind this murder knows the pueblo like the back of his hand."

WHEN NICKY GOT BACK to the exhibition hall, she found Savannah eyeing Ryan and fuming. He'd struck up a conversation with Lionel Hand.

"He's doing it on purpose, just to make me mad," Savannah said.

"I think he's enjoying a last night out before the baby's born," Nicky said.

"Where's Franco?"

"In the military gallery. He'd never seen it and wanted a few minutes. I guess his grandfather was a Marine."

Savannah snorted. "And a jack-hole, from what he's said. I don't think Franco will ever admit it, but his grandfather made his life miserable. When he dropped out of college to join the army, he said the old man tore him a new one. Called him weak, always acting on his emotions, always running away."

Nicky stared at her. "I've never heard any of this."

"At Friday-night dinners. He started to open up after you two, for no better word, broke up. I think it's his way of trying to understand why he reacted like he did with you and Dax. If he was running away again. He's also seeing a counselor, although I probably shouldn't have told you that." Savannah waved her hand dismissively and smiled. "Maybe I'm not such a good secret keeper. You didn't arrest Peter Santibanez?"

Running away. Nicky blinked and focused on the conversation. "Um, no. I don't think he's capable of murder, even if he is a ruthless bastard. He loves his—your—People too much to do something that would take him away from them." She pulled her mouth into a wry smile. "Santibanez firmly believes the tribe needs him more than he needs them. I'm not so sure."

Besides, the murderer had to be connected to the ring on Rémy Tioux's finger. Her father's ring.

Savannah nodded toward the birthing niche. "You need to go and rescue your mother from Dean. I'm going to pry Ryan away from *that man* and take him home. See you tomorrow morning? Ryan told me you wanted to meet at his house."

Nicky tipped her head. "Are you okay with us studying the map with the shrines?"

"Not completely. If you *do* find something, you need to take me or Howard along with you. These are sacred places, not open to outsiders —even Ryan." Savannah gave Nicky a searching look. "You understand?"

Nicky nodded. Tribal culture wasn't an easy line to walk some-times, especially while upholding the law, which made it interesting that someone from another pueblo was given access to Fire-Sky sacred places.

They parted, and Nicky headed to where Dean had her mother pinned, his voice rising above the crowd's noise as she got closer.

"—in the briefcase. I'm sure it will solve this puzzle. Let me drive you home, and we can retrieve— Ah, Nicky." Dean turned to greet her, excitement glowing in his eyes. "I know you want to stay a bit longer. I can take Helena back to your house."

"What do you know about the Jemez Medicine Man? Has he ever come to the museum to speak to you?"

Dean blinked, appearing to struggle with the abrupt change in subject. "No."

"Has Charlotte ever said anything about meeting him?"

He frowned. "Not that I know of. Nicky, this briefcase your mother has—"

"I thought I recognized it. It was Dad's?" Nicky asked her mother, but Dean answered.

"Yes, but Nicky, we need to—"

"Ready to go?" Franco stepped to the edge of the group and pulled out his truck keys.

They exited the museum to moonlight painting the rain-swept parking lot a phosphorescent blue. Franco helped Nicky's mother up the high step and into the back seat of his truck. He climbed into the driver's side as Nicky twisted in the passenger seat to buckle on her seatbelt. Her shoulder twinged, and she took a second to massage it.

Franco started the engine and blasted the heater against the chill. "You going to ask her about the paper she slipped up her sleeve?"

"You saw her do it, too?" Nicky asked, surprised.

"Barely. For a sister of the church, she has fast hands."

Her mother shifted in the back seat. "What are you two talking about?"

"You stole one of Dad's papers when we were in the archives," Nicky said. "Why?"

CHAPTER THIRTY-SIX

THE LIGHTS in Nicky's kitchen gave off a cozy glow. Working in tandem with Franco, she spooned hot-chocolate mix into mugs while he poured the hot water. Helena sat at the kitchen table, her hand splayed on the faux-wood side of the unopened briefcase lying on the tabletop. Nicky set a steaming mug next to the piece of paper that had once been crumpled up her mother's sleeve. It contained the odd abstract authored by both her parents, the one Dean had been so interested in.

Franco rotated the paper toward him. "'Potent mammalian parth-en-o-gen-ic compounds.' What does that mean?"

"Parthenogenesis is a reproductive strategy. Females of certain species—some insects, plants, even a few reptiles—develop offspring without the need for sperm," Nicky said.

"In a sense, virgin births, but all progeny are female." With a swift movement, Helena pulled off her wimple and combed fingers through her hair. "Genetic twins of the mother."

"You mean clones? No males necessary?" Lips twisted, Franco pushed the page away. "Yeah. Right."

"Afraid of becoming obsolete?" Nicky taunted. "Mom, do you remember any of this research?"

"Vaguely." Helena busied herself with her mug, stirring, tapping the spoon on the lip, setting it down on the table. "We had some new instrumentation, but it wasn't working the way we needed it to, so I started tinkering with some of Michael's synthesized compounds. Reengineered the equipment *and* my methods. The results were spectacular." Smiling wanly at Franco, she explained, "My undergraduate degrees were in chemical and mechanical engineering. My PhD focus was analytical and organic chemistry of archeologic samples. We patented the techniques I developed."

"I used some of them as an undergrad," Nicky said sourly. "Not that it mattered."

Her mother's cheeks pinkened, but she otherwise ignored the jibe and picked up the abstract page. "'Preliminary feeding experiments on ten virgin BALB/c mice showed three developed spontaneous parthenogenic pregnancies, two of which resulted in the death of the mothers mid-term and one in the birth of stillborn pups.'"

"That's not good," Franco said.

"It certainly didn't work well in mice." Helena's fingernails drummed the table. "If I remember correctly, the compound he fed the animals was constructed using my experiments on the Fire-Sky pottery scrapings. Michael could synthesize almost anything. He had a gift."

"The same pots in the fertility exhibition?" Franco asked.

"Yes," Nicky answered, eyeing her mother. "They have detailed provenances. Mom's maiden name is in the description, and the scraping dates were anywhere from five to two years before the abstract was published. Do you know where he presented this?"

"He? You mean where did your *father* present the abstract?' Helena asked.

Nicky shrugged. She had good childhood memories of her dad, even though he'd been so deliberately and painfully absent from her life before he'd died. Sometimes it was difficult to grapple with her feelings for him.

"Kuala Lumpur. It was a small meeting on the potential of medical compounds developed from rare plants—bioprospecting. Clinical trials on paclitaxel—the chemotherapy agent extracted from yew trees—were ongoing at the time and were looking to be a huge success, so there was an explosion of interest in shamanism and curenderos and traditional cures. I didn't go because I was pregnant with you." She knotted her hands on top of the briefcase, knuckles white.

"Malaysia. That's where one of the orchids Dean told me about is located. *Thismia neptunis*," Nicky said. "He believes the plant containing this parthenogenic compound Mom and Dad found in the pot scrapings may not be extinct. That it might be hidden under-ground. That's why the people digging up the medicine gardens are screening the dirt."

"Dean talked to you about this?" Franco asked her.

"He thinks it's directly related to Rémy Tioux's murder. That Tioux must have surprised the culprits, and they killed him to cover up their activities. Except it doesn't explain the placement of the body or Dad's ring."

"The second set of scrapings in those pots," Helena said, gaze darting to Nicky. "You believe the murderers did this when they left Tioux's body at the museum. How were those scrapings discovered?"

"Charlotte Fields noticed one of the pots had been moved in the exhibit," Nicky said. "She told Dean, and he found the sample marks."

"Did you confirm that the pot was moved?"

"We did a comparison of videos before the electricity was cut and after it was restored." Nicky looked between Franco and her mother. "I thought I might have moved it during the walk-through of the building that night. I was ... startled. I might have bumped into a display. The fresh scrapings prove it wasn't me."

"But what if it *was* you?" Franco said. "Charlotte admitted she didn't check them thoroughly because she was rushed. What if the secondary sampling Dean and Lottie found occurred *before* the murder? It never made sense that the guys who murdered and dumped Tioux's body took the time to find those pots, disassemble the displays, scrape samples, and put everything back together. Why didn't they just take them?"

Pieces of the puzzle that hadn't seemed to fit suddenly snapped into place.

"You're thinking it was an inside job?" Nicky asked him.

"Of course," Helena said slowly. She tapped the pilfered paper. "Because of this."

Franco nodded, his expression smug. "Who's obsolete *now*?"

"Charlotte still could've scraped the pots," Nicky countered. "And Dean said she had this abstract when she started her internship."

Helena raised her eyebrows. "So, Charlotte could be the inside connection?"

"You're both forgetting Lionel Hand," Franco said. "He was on the reservation about the same time. He worked with your father and probably knew about the parthen-whatever research. Who knows what kind of access he was given to the museum by the council? Besides, Lottie told me *Dean* was the one who contacted her about the internship."

"Dean told *me* she called him after the first intern got hurt," Nicky returned, a flare of angry heat climbing her neck.

"You think she might have had something to do with the first intern's injury?" Franco thumped his mug on the counter, his frown closer to a scowl.

He didn't like that implication. Too bad.

"Charlotte's brother and his friend are staying with her in the staff house. I saw them at the exhibition, and they fit the description of the two men seen in Tioux's car the night of the murder. We need to run them."

Franco's eyes narrowed, and Nicky braced for an argument. Instead, he nodded.

"Someone else at the museum could've taken the samples," Helena said. "Another staff member?" She nibbled at her lip. "Nicky? Could Dean be the insider?"

Nicky's mouth dropped open. She shook her head slowly, incredulity pulling her features. "How can you say that? How can you accuse him? After Grandmother, he's been the one constant in my life. You and Dad were absent. Dean wasn't."

Helena slid her gaze away.

But a door in Nicky's mind opened a crack.

No.

She quickly changed the subject. "The briefcase, Mom. Why haven't you opened it? It's been years since Dad died."

Helena set down her mug. "I haven't been ready. Michael's betrayals, his womanizing, his lies, superseded everything. I didn't want to do the hard work of dealing with it all, including you. It wasn't until I converted to Catholicism that I started to question my past actions."

"Why did you reject Nicky's first research paper?" Franco asked.

Nicky turned her head toward him, eyes wide with shock.

"She told you about that?" Helena sighed. "At the time I felt she could do better than be in a second-rate lab conducting derivative work."

"*What?*" Nicky blinked. "But that's how science works. You develop better techniques, retest samples—"

"No." Her mother leveled a finger at her. "Not *my* daughter."

She stared at her mother, a knot of anger tightening in her chest. "So, the rejection of my paper wasn't about me? It was about *you?*" Nicky had never appreciated being raised by her grandmother as much as she did right then.

Helena curled her hands around her mug. "You were so much younger than I was when I published my first paper. Now that I look back, I might have been jealous."

Nicky's mind reeled. Her mother had been *jealous* of her? "You destroyed something I loved. Then I crashed and burned in law school and in wasted relationships, over and over until I became a cop. Even then you didn't approve."

Helena lifted her face. "Nicky—"

"But if you hadn't pissed me off about my research, I wouldn't have ended up where I am now." The knot in Nicky's chest began to loosen. "And I wouldn't have the friends I have and treasure more than anything." Almost involuntarily, she caught Franco's eye.

He held her gaze, his expression soft and a little sad. He mouthed, *Proud of you.*

Warmth filled her chest.

"I have a lot to atone for, I know. Maybe we can start with you forgiving me about your research article." Helena covered Nicky's hand with hers and squeezed. "We can work on repairing our relationship after we figure out what's going on with your investigation."

Her mother trying to avoid dealing with any kind of deep emotion—*again*. But hadn't Nicky been accused of the same thing? Running away? She flicked a quick glance at Franco. Maybe she was more like her mother than she wanted to admit.

Helena let go of Nicky's hand, beckoned Franco toward the table, and briskly swiveled the top of the briefcase toward her. "I've carried this stupid thing with me everywhere for years, like it's been my cross to bear. And I'm tired of it. Let's open her up."

"You remember the combination?" Franco asked.

"The date Michael and I were married." With a twirl of the numbered tumbler and a snap, Helena popped the lid. Inside was a stack of large manila envelopes. Her mother scooped them out. Franco whisked away the empty briefcase, then he and Nicky sat down at the table as her mother dealt the envelopes out like playing cards.

"Let's see what Michael wanted me to know." Helena unsealed the packet on the top of her stack. Nicky and Franco did the same.

"Notebooks filled with data," Nicky's mother said as she riffled through the pages.

"I have letters," Nicky said. "Written to you...." She pressed a hand to her mouth. "And to me." She opened a pink envelope. "'Happy birthday. Love, Daddy.' There's ten dollars inside." At least a dozen cards lay on the table. "Why didn't he mail them?"

"Looks like he did." Franco reached over to tap another envelope. RETURN TO SENDER was stamped on the front.

"Your grandmother may have had something to do with that," Helena murmured. "She was very protective of you."

Franco dumped the contents of his packet on the table and picked up a page. "You will never guess the name of the guide your father used when he explored the Fire-Sky Pueblo."

"Jimmy Che'chi," Nicky said promptly. "Seems obvious now."

"Okay, smart-ass." Franco picked up a yellowed scrap of newspaper. "From the *Talkative Tongue*. It's an obituary. For a tribe member named James Che'chi."

Nicky and Helena stared.

"Then who the hell's running around on the rez?" Nicky asked. "We really need to *find* this guy."

"Language," her mother scolded.

Nicky's phone rang. "It's Savannah." She tapped the green icon. "Hey, you'll *never* guess what we found."

"Nicky?" Savannah's voice was thick. "It's Jinni."

"The baby? Is she in labor?" Nicky said, voice rising with excitement.

"No. There's been an accident."

CHAPTER THIRTY-SEVEN

NICKY RAN inside the doors at the UNM Trauma Center, her mother and Franco behind her. The smell hit her first. Stale, cold, with the underlying tang of disinfectant. Her stomach roiled. She scanned the crowd in the waiting room, recognizing faces: Ryan's mother and father, Howard, a scattering of Fire-Sky Police Department personnel, some still dressed up from the exhibition, some in uniform. Officer Cyrus Aguilar stood with Manny Valentine. Savannah paced near the double doors labeled NO ADMITTANCE. Nicky hurried over to her.

"What's going on? Why wasn't I called in? We heard nothing—"

"Jinni's 911 call was routed to Albuquerque. No one at Fire-Sky knew until they called Ryan."

Nicky's shoulders relaxed, and she sighed in relief. "So, she's conscious."

Savannah's chin wobbled. She shook her head. "They said it was a miracle she could make the call at all."

"Where's Ryan?" Franco asked.

"They took him back because … decisions have to be made about…"

Nicky closed her eyes as blood rushed from her head. Franco's hand steadied her. "What happened?"

"They think her car hydroplaned, spun out, and rolled down the cliff just a few miles from the museum. When we left the exhibition, we drove right past—" Savannah dropped her face into her hands. Nicky's eyes burned with tears. They must have passed the crash site, too, but it had been so dark, and the rain had started again.

"We dropped Howard off, then went to Ryan's house. Jinni's car wasn't there. Ryan was frantic. He called, and her phone went straight to voicemail. We were about to backtrack and look for her when the hospital…" Savannah used a trembling finger to wipe tears from under her glasses. "I called you and Ryan's parents before I drove him here."

Helena, who'd been hovering in the back, said, "Point out Ryan's parents to me, Savannah."

She indicated an older couple holding each other tightly, and Helena headed toward them. More tribal members arrived. Through the glass doors and window, Nicky could see some gathered in small groups outside. For once, she was glad about how fast news spread over the pueblo.

"The baby?" Nicky asked.

Savannah shook her head. "I-I don't know."

They waited. When the walls began to close in on them, they went outside en masse.

Nicky stared into the sky. Dark clouds swirled, low and threatening. Franco brought her and Savannah coffee, but no one spoke, afraid to turn their horrible churning thoughts into words.

It had seemed like forever when a ripple went through the crowd. The automatic doors opened, and Ryan walked outside, a pink-wrapped bundle cradled in his arms. He searched the crowd, his face a gaunt mask, until he found his mother and father and beckoned them. They took tentative steps, still clutching each other. His mother, a tall, spare woman with a sharp profile, her gray hair down around her shoulders, leaned in when Ryan adjusted the blankets. Nicky could see the baby's cheek before Ryan's mother and stepfather pulled him tightly into a hug, their shoulders shaking. After a few moments, they disengaged, and Ryan stepped away. Others moved closer to see the baby, nodding and murmuring in Keres, her native language so she would know who she was and to whom she belonged. A waft of cedar smoke scented the moist air, tradition at the birth of a child.

Ryan spied Nicky and Franco. He stepped with purpose in their direction.

When he came close, the pain in his face pierced Nicky. Tears started and wouldn't stop, blurring the world around her. Behind her Franco sniffed, his breath broken.

Ryan's mouth opened, but no words emerged. He closed his eyes, swallowed hard, and tried again. In Keresan, he said, "I would like you to meet my daughter." He tipped the bundle toward Nicky and Franco.

Through clouds pregnant with rain, the soft light of dawn touched delicate features: a rosebud mouth, warm skin, pink cheeks, and a black tuft of downy hair. She was perfect.

"She will not have her mother … to … guide her." Ryan choked and released a sob. "I would ask you to act as her godmother, Nicky. She will need someone strong and bold and unafraid, like Jinni—" He bowed his head, buried his face in the blanket.

Nicky slipped her arms around Franco's waist and turned into his shoulder, sobbing. He pulled her tightly to him, his own body shaking.

Ryan sucked in a deep, shuddering breath, only to release it steadily. He switched to English. "And she will need a warrior as her godfather, Franco, someone who will fight and protect her always. Would you do this for us? For my daughter's mother and for me?"

Franco straightened. "I would be proud to."

Nicky hardly recognized his voice, so torn up with grief, but it gave her the strength to turn and face Ryan. "So would I."

Ryan nodded and backed away. The crowd gathered around him and the baby. He turned in a circle, holding her out to them, to nods and murmured prayers.

And rain began to fall, and the People cried. No one moved to go inside but turned their faces to the sky, welcoming it.

"Because this life is only the road to our destination," Ryan murmured. In Keresan, he said, "The rain comes to usher Jinni home."

CHAPTER THIRTY-EIGHT

JINNI'S BODY was released late Saturday, tenderly wrapped in a woolen blanket, and buried immediately. Nicky took her turn grave-guarding, relieving Ryan and his father Sunday afternoon. Cyrus Aguilar and Gracie José, officers who'd worked with Jinni when she was on the Fire-Sky police force, joined her. They were relieved by Franco and Howard Kie at midnight, and Nicky headed home to catch a few hours of sleep before her Monday shift. No one had been given leave. Chief Richards had been adamant. They still had a murder to solve.

Exhausted, Nicky sat in Savannah's office at the police station and watched silently as her friend fidgeted at her desk until everything was straightened, right-angled, and stacked. Savannah picked up her coffee, put it down, stood, sat.

"When's Franco coming in?" Savannah asked.

Nicky turned her phone over and glanced at the screen. "Maybe ten minutes. Instead of going home after grave-guarding, he showered and changed at Ryan's. Said my mom made it safely to the Bernals." Ryan and the baby were staying with his parents for the time being. His mother had offered to watch her new granddaughter. Helena had volunteered to help.

"That baby is *not* Deandra's granddaughter." Savannah rubbed her forehead with stiff fingers, her mouth pursed. "Nicky, you have to talk to Ryan, make him take his name off the birth certificate. He's not Bebe's biological father."

Ryan and Jinni had named their daughter Elizabeth Bernal—Bebe for short. Ryan wouldn't announce his daughter's Keresan name until the christening.

Nicky frowned. "What does it matter now? Jinni's family didn't even respond to her death."

Savannah cringed. *Death* was not spoken out loud in Fire-Sky culture because it was believed to bring ghosts. "I just don't think it's fair to the real father. What if she talked to him at the exhibition? He should help, you know. Child support or something." She fussed with her stapler, opening it to load more staples, closing it because she'd filled it five minutes ago. "He must know by now about her passing. He must—"

"Leave it alone, Savannah." Nicky closed her eyes against the burn of fatigue.

Savannah quieted and started typing, but restlessness got the better of her again.

"Chief wants you to go right in when Peter Santibanez leaves," she told Nicky for the third time. Headley and Song were in with the chief, interviewing Santibanez. "It's a wonder the FBI haven't arrested his ass for lying to you about the night Rémy Tioux was murdered." Third time Savannah had said that, too.

"Because he didn't do it," Nicky repeated. Once the FBI was done with Santibanez, she and Franco would brief them on what they'd found out last week. Well, most of it. A cold ball of worry settled in her stomach. She still wasn't sure what she'd do with the issue of her father's ring and how it had ended up on a dead man's hand.

"—should put the biological father's name on the birth certificate. It's not even legal."

Nicky's eyes popped open. The stubborn set to Savannah's jaw made her sit up. "Savannah. Let that secret die with her. Please." Her phone dinged with a text. "Franco just drove up. You want to buzz the chief?"

Nicky stood and headed out into the corridor toward the parking lot door to meet Franco, only to bump into Peter Santibanez.

They faced each other in the quiet hall. Although he held himself with shoulders squared—his red cotton shirt crisp under a heathered-gray sports jacket, his long black-and-white hair in a braid on his neck—he seemed to have aged since the exhibition. Then, astonishingly, he smiled at her, his handsome craggy face lightening.

"I confessed about the riverboat casino deal. The FBI raked me over the coals but won't charge me for obstruction of justice since I'm cooperating fully now."

Nicky nodded. Like word of Jinni's death and birth of Ryan's daughter, that gossip had spread around the pueblo over the weekend.

"I, ah, emailed you and Martinez the results of Raven Tioux's DNA tests. No need for a warrant. I doubt they're admissible as evidence anyway. Kristina Tioux is still in New Mexico. FBI will try to reinterview her in light of the revelation that her daughter is not Rémy's." Santibanez shifted, his gaze sliding to the interior glass walls and garden of the Admin complex. "The woman who passed from this earth in the car crash..." He cleared his throat, eyes skittering away.

Nicky hated that he wouldn't say her name. "Jinni Bernal."

"Yes. Her husband's family is well-respected on the pueblo, even though neither her husband nor this woman was Tsiba'ashi D'yini. The tribe is willing to give them assistance if they need it."

Santibanez looked like he wanted to say more, but the door burst open and Franco strode inside, bringing with him the scent of rain.

THE DOUR EXPRESSIONS on Headley's and Song's faces set the mood for what Nicky was sure would be a hostile briefing. She and Franco arranged their chairs across from the FBI agents, but the few feet that separated them felt like a chasm. Behind his desk, Chief had angled his chair to face the two agents, not so subtly indicating his support for his officers. Clad in a black suit, Headley crossed his arms over his wide chest, his long skinny legs incongruous against the bulk of his upper body. Agent Song, in a conservative navy dress appropriate enough for a funeral, dropped her gaze briefly to the tablet's screen before she pinned Nicky, then Franco, with cold brown eyes.

"We have plenty to tell you about our investigation, but I think we'll save the best for last since you weren't inclined to keep us updated on your end," Song said, mouth twisting. "The actions you took should have been cleared by us, especially since your requests for background checks were a substantial amount of work."

Her tone was biting, and Nicky's fingers curled into fists. She consciously relaxed them, managing to keep her expression neutral. "You and Agent Headley were in Mississippi, pursuing the drug cartel angle or whatever when these leads came up. Agent Martinez and I submitted our reports immediately, and Chief forwarded them to you."

"I gave them permission to request FBI background checks because they were busy honoring a fallen comrade, so cut my officers a break." Surprisingly, Chief Richards's voice was mild. His desk chair creaked as he rocked slightly. "I don't keep my investigators on a leash, Agent Song. Their undercover investigation was a dandy piece of work. What Sergeant Matthews and Agent Martinez found in Santa Fe could go directly to motive in Tioux's murder."

"Except that the doctors—Summerweaver, Balderamos, and Meyers—have alibis," Headley said.

"That doesn't mean they couldn't have hired or directed someone to do the deed," Franco pointed out. "If Tioux went public with his accusations, it would have ruined their business. His murder appears to have solved that potential problem."

"You mean the two men the, ahem, *anonymous witness* saw?" Song's words dripped with derision. "Completely uncorroborated and buried in your report when you could have told me when we met last week? Unless you can bring in your witness, your tip's worthless because we've accounted for all extraneous fingerprints on Tioux's car, including Peter Santibanez's and the concierge workers'. Every other inch of the car was wiped clean."

Nicky's brow wrinkled. *Wiped clean....*

Headley tapped his device and rotated it toward Franco and Nicky, displaying an old black-and-white photo from a newspaper clipping. It was the same man in the obituary they'd found in Helena's briefcase Friday night. "Dr. Summerweaver told us a man who called himself Jimmy Che'chi was the Tiouxs's traditional herbalist. But it seems Che'chi died about fifteen years ago and was not the same person who worked for the clinic. This is the real Jimmy Che'chi. Do you recognize him?"

Nicky and Franco shook their heads.

"The clinic didn't have an ID or social security number on file?" Franco asked.

Headley scowled. "New Mexico has no requirement to use E-Verify for employment. Nor do they have anything on file, adhering to this man's traditional wishes. We subpoenaed their CCTV, but they're arguing doctor-patient confidentiality because patients are in the videos. It could take weeks to get anything."

"Agent Martinez has met the man, Che'chi. He's the one who originally reported the garden desecrations," Chief said, flipping open a file on his desk. "It's in Martinez's reports, as you well know."

"We've sent agents to the Jemez Reservation for info into this Jimmy Che'chi." Headley incorrectly pronounced it as *Gem*-ez, adding to the variety of ways non-locals tended to butcher the name. "Unless anyone has something to add? Nothing? We still have quite a list to cover, including..." He angled his tablet and scrolled. "Kristina Tioux and her child, enquiries into the first museum intern, the museum's new director, visitors staying with the current intern, Charlotte Fields—"

"What about your gang-hit angle? Tioux's brother, the Crybabies." Chief propped his elbows on his desk, his voice clipped and strong. "You've spent an enormous amount of time on it but now seem to be shifting back into *our* territory, co-opting my people's investigation."

Nicky held back a smirk, appreciating the chief's territoriality like she never had in the past.

"We're a team here, Richards," Headley said heavily.

"Sure, Headley. Especially when *your* track runs you into a dead end." Chief smiled, showing his teeth.

"Our leads temporarily kept us from the Fire-Sky connection," Song said, "but we're remedying that now."

Which was too bad. Luna's plan to keep the FBI agents out of the way had worked for a while, but now there were even more questions to answer. How did the fake Jimmy Che'chi fit in? He was a link to her father, the medicine gardens, and to Rémy, Kristina, and Raven Tioux through the fertility clinic. Was he also a link to the murder?

"Agent Song is saying that your investigation is now merging with ours," Headley interjected. "Our leads have brought us back to Kristina Tioux and her allegedly illegitimate daughter." He fixed Nicky and Franco with a gimlet eye. "But neither the clinic nor Kristina Tioux is cooperating. Therefore, we're in the process of obtaining a subpoena to do the DNA testing."

Franco frowned. "We have—"

Nicky kicked him in the process of shifting in her chair. "You said you have background info on Dr. Hand and Charlotte Fields?" she asked Headley.

"Lionel Hand was hired by the council after they asked Dean MacElroy to step down at the end of the year over differences in..." Headley slid a finger over his screen. "The future direction of the museum. There's no evidence Hand knew Tioux or that his hiring is in any way related to Tioux's murder. We also did financials on Dr. MacElroy and Dr. Hand. I have to tell you, I'm glad I didn't go into, um, museology. For that much schooling, they get paid crap." He smirked, enjoying his own joke. Song was the only person who responded, her smile more of a grimace.

"Now, about Dr. MacElroy's original fall-semester hire. Nothing nefarious occurred. The kid tore his Achilles's tendon in a flag football game a week before his internship," Headley said. "Which leads us to Charlotte Fields, his replacement. Our preliminary background check after the museum break-in didn't turn up anything, but once her DNA was processed, we got a hit from a crime scene about ten years ago—attempted murder."

Franco leaned forward and stabbed a finger at Headley. "She had nothing to do with that, and you know it. She was a witness, that's all. Her mother assaulted Lottie's stepfather. They took her DNA to rule her out. Lottie wouldn't hurt a fly."

Nicky's jaw dropped. "You knew about this?"

"Lottie told me," he said gruffly.

"What the hell, Franco? She's a potential suspect in Tioux's murder!"

"She didn't kill Tioux. She was attacked, a victim."

"Not according to your partner." Headley raised an eyebrow. "In her report, Sergeant Matthews indicated that Charlotte Fields could be involved via her brother and his friend, *and* that the paramedic at the scene who treated her injury thought she'd faked it."

Franco swiveled in his chair, eyes hot. "What the hell, Nicky?"

"Calm down, Martinez," Chief ordered. "And, Agent Headley, I've had about enough of you trying to divide my investigative team. Let's hear the whole story."

"Charlotte Fields's mother, Sheila Fields, maiden name, Wilson, took a baseball bat to her husband's head—one Alberto Fields," Headley said. "She didn't kill him but was convicted of felony assault. She died in prison a few years ago. Cancer."

"Alberto found out Charlotte wasn't his biological daughter," Song added. "That, apparently, was what started the fight."

"That still doesn't rule her out as a suspect in Tioux's murder. What about her brother and the friend?" Nicky asked.

"Their background checks turned up something that might interest you and Agent Martinez." Headley looked smug—again. Nicky braced. "They're members of the AOL—Associated Oregon Lumberjacks—a union representing the, uh, 'harvest and sustainable management of forests.'"

"So, it's possible that someone did tamper with that log that almost killed you," Agent Song said, one eyebrow winging up. "As I said, best for last."

Teeth clenched, Nicky levered out of her chair. When she looked to Franco, he was on his feet, his face pale.

"So maybe Charlotte would hurt a fly," Nicky said flatly. "We'd better go ask her."

Franco set his jaw and nodded. He beat her to the office door, reached to open it—

"I already sent my men to the museum," Headley said. "Charlotte and Dan Fields and their friend, Evan Bright, are missing. It seems they packed up and left in the middle of the night. We've got an APB out for them."

Headley slid his hand down his tie to hold it against the front of his dress shirt and stood, white teeth flashing in his dark face as he smiled coldly. "And, Chief Richards, since your investigators don't seem to play well with others, I'm ordering Fire-Sky police to officially back off this case. The FBI is taking over."

CHAPTER THIRTY-NINE

NICKY PULLED into her empty carport, windshield wipers sweeping away the last of a misting rain. Franco's truck sat across the street, and the light from the kitchen window glowed.

Nicky crossed her arms over the steering wheel, staring into the wet shadows of the backyard. She and Franco hadn't had time to talk after the meeting with Headley and Song. She'd been called to direct traffic around a jackknifed semi on the off-ramp of the CampFire Casino, and he'd been sent to an elk-car collision near Scalding Peak. She'd been glad for the break to calm down and think, not that a solution had become apparent in the Tioux case.

But no way was she giving up the investigation, so screw the FBI. Her mother and father were somehow caught up in this case, and her mother could still be in danger. She needed to find and talk to whoever was passing himself off as Jimmy Che'chi before the FBI got to him. And it was only a matter of time until Headley and Song found out the wedding ring in evidence was not the same one found on Rémy Tioux's finger. It would be smart to return her dad's ring as soon as possible—which would only open up a new can of worms when Headley and Song made the connection to her mother and father.

Her thoughts flying in different directions, Nicky headed inside her house. The savory scent of red chile embraced her. She hung her heavy jacket on a hook by the door and unbuckled her duty belt as she strode into the brightness of the kitchen-den area. And stopped short.

A wooden table, large enough for the four chairs positioned around it, sat in place of the smaller table. Franco's laptop lay open on its surface.

Nicky hung her duty belt over the back of a chair and propped her hands on her hips. "Are you serious?"

Franco, dressed in jeans and a black T-shirt, pulled glasses from a cabinet, his face expressionless as he filled them with ice. "You needed a bigger table."

"No, I didn't. Mom will leave soon. You'll leave even sooner." And she'd be alone again. Nicky swept her hand across the smooth circle of dark brown wood. The legs' graceful curves were held together by a black wrought-iron ring. It fit, both the space and with her new furniture. "Where's the old table?"

"Out by the curb unless someone's already taken it." His face in profile, Franco laid out placemats. He paused. "If you don't like it…"

She shoved her hands in her pockets. "There's no reason to be jealous of Dax Stone."

He tilted his chin. "Good. There's no reason for you to be jealous of Charlotte Fields."

"I'm not—" At his raised eyebrows, she clamped her lips shut, then shrugged. "Good. Where's Mom?"

"On her way home from the Bernals. Ryan called me when she left."

"I'm just making sure she's—"

"Safe. I know." His expression softened. He gestured toward the laptop. "I thought we could look over the paternity tests from Santibanez while we wait for dinner to heat up."

"If we continue investigating this case, we go against FBI orders."

He chuckled. "Since when has that ever bothered you? We're in this together, Nicky. Until we solve it."

She nodded, warmth expanding in her chest. "Did you really make dinner?"

"No." He quirked a smile. "Ryan and his parents have been inundated with food. This was just *one* of Savannah's casserole contributions. Deandra didn't have any more room in the freezer, so she gave it to me to bring home."

Home. Nicky's stomach flipped. Did he realize what he'd said?

She pulled out a chair and sat down. It was cushioned on the seat and back. Comfortable. "Speaking of Savannah, she will not shut up about Ryan's name on Bebe's birth certificate."

"Ryan's devoted to that little girl. I'm sure he'll make a pretty good father, but time will tell." Franco handed her a glass of iced tea and sat. "Family's a crapshoot." He tapped the computer on and logged in.

"Cynical, Agent Martinez. And you were raised by both biological parents, who are still together and happily married, right?"

"Sure." He took a drink of tea.

"After the age of seven, all I had was a grandmother."

"Who did a pretty good job." He scooted his chair closer and angled the screen. "You were lucky. Not all grandparents are sweetness and light."

Nicky slanted him a glance. Savannah had told her Franco's grandfather was a harsh man. She wanted to ask him about it but mentally bit her tongue. There was so much going on, and things were still too unstable between them. She'd wait for a better time.

Franco laid an arm across the back of her chair and clicked open Santibanez's email. "You kicked me so I wouldn't share this with the FBI. Why?"

"Besides the fact they're jack-holes and they took us off the investigation? Let them jump through hoops and get their own test." She opened the attachment and scanned through the initial declarations. "Kristina said she gave Santibanez the blood cards she and Rémy had done for child ID. Santibanez sent the samples to two different testing facilities. This lab tested twenty-one markers." She scrolled to a table with four columns. "Here's the list of marker loci."

"The loci are genes?"

"Some of them. They're chosen because of high variation in DNA sequence across populations. It makes them especially useful for paternity. The first column are controls to make sure the test was done correctly." She pointed to the second column of paired numbers. "These are Rémy's results. Each number represents an allele for that specific marker. For this locus, Rémy's alleles are twenty-two and fourteen—one inherited from his mother and one from his father. The third column is Kristina's, and her paired alleles are six and eleven—again, one from her father and one from her mother."

"Those markers aren't the same, but Rémy and Kristina share a few, er, alleles at some of the other locations they tested."

"But not a lot. That means they aren't closely related. The more alleles two people share, the more closely they're related. The fourth column has Raven's alleles. If she's Rémy and Kristina's baby, she should have randomly inherited one of Rémy's alleles and one of Kristina's." Nicky frowned in confusion at Raven's results. "This can't be right."

"'Probability of paternity, zero percent,'" Franco read. "'Alleged father is excluded as the biological father.' I guess that solves that."

But it didn't. Raven's alleles were exactly the same as Kristina's.

Nicky pulled up the second test. Different genetic loci were used, but the results were the same: Rémy was excluded as the father, and Kristina and Raven's genetic profiles were identical.

"There's got to be a mistake. They must have accidentally used Kristina's DNA in place of Raven's, because otherwise they're—"

She shook her head, but ice settled in her gut. *It can't be.*

"They're what?"

"If these results are correct, it means..." The ball of ice expanded. "Kristina and Raven are ... clones."

CHAPTER FORTY

A SCREAM PIERCED the air before a car alarm blared. Both came from Nicky's carport. She and Franco bolted from the table toward the sound, Franco throwing open the side door to the carport, Nicky dogging his steps. The car alarm struck her like a wall of sound. Motion lights glared over two sets of grappling bodies. Franco leaped down the stairs, momentum slamming him into the side of her truck before he scrambled to the backyard and rushed two wrestling, black-clad figures. They fell as a mass, grunting and rolling.

Nicky, arms braced, hit the passenger's side door, then ran to her mother, who vigorously defended herself against two more assailants. Veil torn away, sleeves flapping, Helena whapped a clipboard down on a ski-masked head. Nicky darted forward, jabbed at the closest attacker, and felt the nose crunch under the heel of her hand. The figure screamed, cupped hands over their face, and staggered away. Nicky pivoted. The second masked assailant grabbed her mother from behind. A grim-faced Helena threw a vicious elbow to the gut. Her attacker fell back, a hand tangled in Helena's necklace.

"It's mine! He gave it to me." A woman's voice, high, hysterical, screamed to be heard over the shrieking car alarm. She twisted the chain, and the wedding ring twirled along it. Helena staggered back, the chain cutting deep into her skin.

Nicky looped an arm around the woman's neck. "Let go or I swear to God—" She tightened her arm, increased pressure.

"He gave it ... to me," the woman wheezed. *"Michael ... Matth ... ews. Our ... dad."*

The woman dropped the chain and clawed at Nicky's arm. Necklace twined in shaky fingers, Helena dipped her hand in a pocket, and the alarm silenced. Nicky yanked the ski mask off. Charlotte's red-brown hair tumbled out.

Wide-eyed and pale as milk, her mother breathed out a feeble, "Let her go."

But surprise had already loosened Nicky's hold. She dropped arms heavy as lead and stepped back to lean against the side of her truck, glad for the support. Charlotte sank, catching herself on the side-view mirror of Helena's car, hand at her throat. She was in the valley between the Mazda and Tahoe, boxed in between Nicky and Helena.

Nicky spun at the click of handcuffs. A compact figure in black pushed the man with the broken nose against the storage cabinets. Franco stood behind another larger man in the gap between the carport and driveway. Their hoods removed, Nicky recognized both attackers. They'd been with Charlotte at the exhibition: Daniel Fields, blood oozing from his nose to drip from his chin, and Evan Bright, face and hair smeared with mud. They stared at the cement floor.

Javier, Luna's second-in-command, sported the start of a black eye —Franco, a bruise on his chin. Both were dirty and wet and breathing hard.

"Javier. Glad you were here." Nicky tried for normal, but the world around her kept tipping, and her gaze kept flicking to Charlotte. *Sister.*

"Maybe we should get these clowns inside and have a chat," Javier said. His voice held no inflection, the singsong gang patois absent. "They have some explaining to do."

Franco glared at Nicky. "Yeah, Javier. Explaining would be good."

NICKY CRADLED her cup of coffee and studied the seated trio. Charlotte's head bowed over a steaming mug of tea. Both Daniel and Evan hunched in chairs, their wrists now cuffed in the front. The all-black they'd worn for the attack was soggy and dirty and wasn't menacing anymore—just absurd.

Helena, antibiotic cream coating the abrasions on her neck, dabbed the last of the blood off Daniel's face, her hands sheathed in blue nitrile gloves taken from a pouch in Nicky's duty belt. Cotton pledgets were shoved up his nostrils, and two black eyes stared over a hugely swollen nose.

"I like the table, Nicky." Her mother gathered up discarded first aid packaging and bloodied washcloths. "It fits the room much better."

Franco, a baggie of ice pressed against his jaw, raised his eyebrows. "*Much* better."

Javier stood between Nicky and Franco, hands braced on his hips. He'd shed his wet sweatshirt; his shoulder holster—empty—was strapped across his body. Franco had unloaded the weapon, refused to give it back, and taken a switchblade off of him.

"Yeah, I saw these pendejos running through your gate after her car pulled inside." Javier jerked his chin in Helena's direction. "They're lucky I didn't cut them," he continued menacingly, catching Evan Bright's shrinking gaze.

"Knock it off," Nicky said. "You're DEA. I attended a seminar you taught at a BIA conference three years ago."

Startled out of his sinister scowl, Javier grimaced. His stiff posture relaxed. "I thought you recognized me the first time we met."

"I'm DEA," Franco said, waving the ice bag. "Why the hell wasn't I informed? Who is this guy?"

"Not now, Franco." Nicky said. "Mom? May I have Dad's ring?"

Helena unclasped the chain, slipped off the ring, and pressed it into Nicky's hand. Nicky curled her fingers around her mother's and squeezed before she let go. She placed the golden circle on the table. Charlotte's gaze lasered to it.

"You're my half sister," Nicky said. Charlotte nodded. "Daniel?"

"Different dad. My mom was pregnant with me when she got married, but I didn't know that until a package with Dad's ring and a note showed up at our house about ten years ago. Neither did my stepdad. Alberto Fields."

"I know that name," Helena said. "He was a lithics expert. Married Sheila Wilson, one of Michael's protégées. A talented archeological ethnobiologist. You know, you're the image of your mother. And *she* was the final straw." All eyes on her, Helena sighed and tucked her hands into her torn sleeves. "Michael and I were running a dig, cataloging dozens of ruins exposed by a forest fire northwest of Albuquerque. I was supposed to take a group of students to a large complex of stone houses that morning. Michael"—she suddenly looked sad—"was going to keep you with him, Nicky. Instead, he went off with Sheila and left you alone. You were only six."

Nicky frowned. "In a slot canyon, right? I had some toy, a little car. It fell into a crack in the rocks, and I climbed in after it. There was a room. And a pot. And a pool of water." Her frown cleared. "It was a birthing niche." That's where she'd seen the swirling black mass for the first time. "I got scared and ran. You found me and drove to Grandmother's. And you left me," she finished, voice flat.

"But not alone," Franco said softly.

"Was the information about your real father—our father—in your mother's police report?" Nicky asked Charlotte. The FBI couldn't know, or they would have called her out during the briefing that morning.

"I don't think Mom told them. He'd been dead for years anyway."

"If Michael was dead, who sent you the ring?" Helena asked, brows furrowed.

Charlotte shrugged. "I figured it was some lawyer for Dad's estate."

"What happened after your mother was arrested?" Franco asked.

"She pled guilty instead of going to trial." Charlotte ran a finger around the top of her mug. "But she explained her affair to me. That my father never truly loved anyone but Helena—that he refused to give her a divorce, refused to take that ring off his finger. I don't think my mother ever recovered from that." She looked at Helena, expression angry and anguished. "What made you so special that it ended up ruining her life? I had to know. I started studying both you and him—together, separate—trying to figure it out. I read all your papers, attended conferences where you lectured. Waited for the right moment when I could confront you publicly, embarrass you. Make you understand what harm you'd done to my mom and me."

Nicky stared at her sister, realization staggering her. Charlotte had let her anger and obsession dictate her path.

But hadn't she done the same thing?

Charlotte bowed her head. "Then, I began to listen, really listen to what people said about you and my father. Heard how he tried to ... to blackmail you. If you didn't go back to him, he'd ruin your career. After a while, I began to admire how you stood up to him. What you'd accomplished in the face of such pressure."

Silence filled the kitchen.

"I think his pride was hurt more by my leaving than anything," Helena said, but she seemed preoccupied. "Michael always was a sore loser."

"He wasn't all bad. The note had a bank account number on it. Back child support, so Daniel and I were all right financially. I mean, that proves he must have loved me, right? He sent me this. *Me.*" Charlotte picked up the ring. "The note said it was his most prized possession."

Every word hit Nicky like a blow, cracking the barriers she'd built and hidden behind for years.

Her father hadn't willed her anything. All he'd ever done was send her a handful of generic birthday cards with ten dollars inside. Hands clenched to keep from shaking; sick inside, she was six years old again, left alone in that canyon, screaming for someone to find her.

Her heart tightened like a fist.

"You've had the ring ever since?" Nicky asked, posture brittle.

"Yes." Charlotte touched her collar. "I wore it around my neck, too."

"Interesting. Then how did it get on the finger of a murder victim?"

"What?" Charlotte paled, wide, panicked eyes darting to Nicky.

"The break-in at the museum was a setup. Your brother and his friend helped you kill Rémy Tioux and chop off his hands." Nicky circled the table and yanked Charlotte out of her chair. "You knew I was your half sister when you took the job, didn't you? Is that why you put the ring on Tioux's finger? To get my attention? To get back at my mother?" She gave Charlotte a hard shake, snapping the smaller woman's head back.

Heavy arms latched around Nicky and pulled her into the kitchen. Vision tunneling with red, she struggled to get back to Charlotte, but Franco held her fast and turned her around.

"Calm down," he said. "Look at me."

Nicky blinked away burning moisture and stared into his dark brown eyes, traced his features until her gaze fell on the darkening bruise on his jaw. She brushed it lightly with a trembling hand. "Are you taking her side again?"

Franco leaned in, lips to her ear. "No. But play along."

Right. Good cop to her bad—except she hadn't been playing.

"Hey. I told you she's always felt more like a sister to me," he whispered. "Now we know why."

Franco released her and took a breath, his expression morphing before Nicky's eyes. His brow furrowed, his jaw hardened, and eyes that had crinkled with a faint smile turned stern. He took the chair across from Charlotte. Nicky stood behind him, face set.

"Why'd you do this, Lottie? Why'd you attack Dr. Matthews?"

Charlotte's chin wobbled. "Because she took my ring."

"None of you deserve an explanation after what Lottie's been through." Evan Bright thrust his chin out, eyes bulging and red. "We were going to grab the ring and leave. She's a nun, for God's sake. She wasn't supposed to put up a fight."

"It was a stupid idea to begin with," Daniel said, his voice thick and nasal.

"You bought the masks," Evan shouted.

"I was drunk."

Helena brought her hand down hard on the tabletop. "Both of you, zip it."

The two men hunched in their chairs, petulant scowls on their faces.

"'*Wine is a mocker, and beer is a brawler. Whoever is led astray by them is...*' an ... an idiot. With apologies to Proverbs 20:1." Helena tucked her hands back into her torn sleeves. There was still a troubled wrinkle between her eyes, but she appeared less distracted. "Continue, Franco."

"Tell me about the ring, Lottie," he said.

Daniel leaned forward. "We didn't kill anyone. We weren't even in New Mexico."

"Easily checked," Javier said from the kitchen. He was pouring pumpkin-spice creamer into his coffee.

"Then do it," Daniel challenged. "We were still in Oregon."

Helena stared him down like an avenging angel. "What did I say, Daniel?"

He cowed but shot Helena a resentful glance.

Franco continued. "Lottie? Were you wearing the ring the night you were attacked at the museum?"

"No, I swear." She reached her hand across the table, palm up in supplication. "After the murder and ... and us dating—"

Nicky leaned over Franco and scowled. Charlotte shrank in her chair.

"—and working to get the exhibition ready, I thought I'd misplaced it until I saw it around Dr. Matthews's neck. Then I didn't know what to think." Charlotte's luminous green eyes, magnified with tears, looked up at Franco. "Was it really on Mr. Tioux's finger?" At Franco's nod, she shuddered.

"Where was the ring the night you were attacked?" Franco asked.

"At my house—the one by the museum—in a jewelry pouch I keep on the dresser."

"Who had access to your house?"

Charlotte sat back and took a deep breath, brows drawn. "Mike Shiosee because he does maintenance. Dean. He has an extra set of keys for all the buildings. But honestly, I didn't lock the door most days. Anyone could have taken it."

"Did you know the FBI is searching for you?" Franco asked.

Charlotte's mouth dropped open. "Why?"

"Let's start with the fact your brother and his friend tried to kill Franco and me last Tuesday." Nicky crossed her arms, mouth tight. "You released those logs by the cliff that almost killed us, didn't you?"

The two men goggled at her before Daniel sputtered, "Logs? We didn't—no way—are you *insane*?"

"You're lumberjacks."

"Were. For like two days," Evan said, hunching even further in his chair. "That was *way* too much work. And really dangerous. We came to New Mexico looking for easi—*safer* jobs."

"You said Tuesday? We have an alibi," Daniel said eagerly. "Lottie sent us to Albuquerque to get groceries. We ended up at a micro-brewery and might have stayed for a while. I bet they have security cameras."

Charlotte glared at them. "You spent the money I gave you on *beer*? You said you got lost."

Both men looked sheepish.

These two guys were clowns, and the lumberjack thing was just a stupid coincidence.

Franco squatted down in front of Charlotte and took her hand. Nicky set her teeth and looked away.

"Lottie? The FBI is searching for you because you and Daniel and Evan disappeared. It made you look guilty, leaving without telling anyone."

She blinked at him. "But ... but ... Dean *told* us we had to leave. That the tribal council said we had to vacate the house so Dr. Hand could move in. Immediately. We had no place to go, so we stayed at my principal investigator's house in Albuquerque."

"I thought Dr. Hand was moving into Dean's house," Helena said.

"When did you find out about the internship at the Fire-Sky museum?" Nicky asked.

"Everyone knows about it at my department," Charlotte said. "Dean chooses someone from UNM every fall. It's very prestigious."

"No. About the opening this summer?"

"Oh. Right after Robbie Moore got hurt. That's the student who had to drop out. I just started my PhD program, and I'm not really eligible, but Dean arranged everything. He knew I wanted to meet you and thought it would be better if we could become ... friends before I told you. Lessen the shock. Then, when he said he was trying to get Dr. Matthews to come for the exhibition—that was like a cherry on top for me."

Nicky's mind blanked for a moment. "Dean knew you were my half sister?"

"I guess our dad told him. Dean approached me at a conference about five years ago. He even encouraged me to apply to UNM for my PhD. But he said you didn't know about me, so I had to go slow. I'm sorry. I mean, I've known about you since Dad sent me his ring. My mother explained." Charlotte shrugged. "I wanted to meet you, and this was the perfect opportunity. I imagine it was a shock."

Shock was an understatement. Especially Charlotte's connection to Tioux's murder through their father's wedding ring.

"Let's go back to Rémy Tioux." Franco released Charlotte's hand and stood. "You said Tioux never showed you the DNA testing he'd done on his daughter."

"No. He only asked me about DNA and ancestry stuff."

"Do you know if he talked to Dean about it?" Franco asked.

"I think so. I mean, I sent him to Dean."

Franco exchanged a raised-eyebrow glance with Nicky.

"Mom? Can you get Dad's abstract?" Nicky said.

Helena nodded and hurried into Nicky's study. She returned with the paper and laid it on the table in front of Charlotte. "Do you know about this?"

Charlotte bent over it and scanned the page. "Only because Dean showed it to me."

"You didn't bring it with you as part of my mother and our father's publications?" Nicky asked.

"I thought I'd read everything he wrote, but I'd never seen this before," Charlotte said. "I mean, come on. A chemical that can cause mammalian parthenogenesis—virgin births? Clonal offspring? That's ridiculous. If this plant existed and it worked, it would be worth billions to agriculture and pharmaceutical companies. And what if it worked on humans? Can you imagine?"

"Raven Tioux," Franco said under his breath.

"Yeah," Nicky replied, just as softly.

But the plant was extinct. Wasn't it?

The fertility pots.

"Charlotte," Nicky said, "did you take the second scrapings from the pots in the exhibition?"

Her half sister's eyes bulged. "No! I would never desecrate—"

Nicky cut her off. "What did those pots have in common? Besides the samples taken by my mother."

"The same temper composition. And they were dated within a hundred years of each other," Charlotte replied promptly.

"At the time I sampled them," Helena explained, "Michael and I speculated they'd been made by the same artisan, maybe used by the same shaman. They have similar painted designs—spirals, which makes sense. Birth is about renewal, emergence, and the winding journey it sets you on."

"When I ran away from the birthing niche as a kid, you were still in the canyon. Why?" Nicky asked her mother. "You'd left with your group for the ruins."

"One of my students noticed a petroglyph on the canyon wall. There was a second one farther down. We realized they were acting like markers, probably for the birthing niche you found."

"Glyphs. Of what?"

"Spirals." Helena's eyes sparkled, and a smile played on her lips.

"Spirals? Why are they important?" Franco asked.

"In Native American Puebloan culture, they represent either wind or water, or the genesis of a journey beginning from the center and expanding outward," Nicky said slowly.

Perhaps birth acted like a metaphor, representing something bigger. Like the beginning of life on earth. A *Genesis* story.

Pieces of the case fell into place, but Nicky didn't want to speculate on anything just yet.

"I'll call Agent Song and tell her to pick up these three." At Daniel's and Evan's loud protestations, Nicky said, "If what you say is true, they'll release you within twenty-four hours. Maybe less. Agree or I'll leave you cuffed," she warned. They nodded reluctantly. "Charlotte? Make sure you tell them everything—even about Dad's ring." Nicky unclasped her necklace and slipped the ring onto the chain. It would have to go back into evidence.

"I promise," Charlotte said. "I-I know I haven't earned your trust, but I'd like to. You're the only sister I've got."

Helena rolled her eyes and hissed a breath.

Wide-eyed and openmouthed, Charlotte looked back and forth between them. "You mean ... there are *more?*"

"We don't have time," Nicky said dryly. "And about that trust. You can earn some of it now. My house key." She pressed it into Charlotte's cold hands. Nicky cupped them in hers and squeezed gently. "Come back here when the FBI lets you go. We'll talk then. Okay?"

Charlotte searched Nicky's eyes, then gave her a faint smile. "Okay. And for what it's worth ... Nicky, Dr. Galini? I'm sorry. Really."

Helena sent Charlotte a forced smile and stiff nod but quickly focused back on Nicky. Color had returned to her cheeks. "What next?"

"Call Ryan and ask him to meet you at his house. Ask him for the pueblo map marked by Geronimo Elk. See if you can connect the marks on the map in a—"

"Spiral? And see where it leads?" Helena smiled. "Let me change into jeans." She hurried down the hall.

"Javier? You'd better clear out." Nicky pivoted toward the kitchen. His coffee cup was washed and draining by the sink.

"Already gone. I gave him his gun back—unloaded," Franco said. "What about us?"

Nicky grabbed her jacket and car keys. "We're heading to the museum to reinterview Dean. I think he knows more about the parthenogenesis plant and these medicine garden desecrations than he told us."

CHAPTER FORTY-ONE

RAGGED WATERFALLS of mist rolled over the top of the circular canyon walls that wrapped around the Isgaawa Cultural Center and Museum. Nicky's unit skidded to a halt in front of Dean MacElroy's home, its flat-roofed structure blending into the darkened landscape. Bitter cold watered her eyes as she exited the truck. She knocked and rang the doorbell. "Dean! It's Nicky. I need to speak to you." She tamped down worry. He hadn't answered any of her phone calls on the drive up.

She and Franco traipsed around the house and found only one dim light on in the kitchen. All the doors were locked, and the windows secured.

"Mike Shiosee knows we're coming." Franco had called the museum caretaker while Nicky had phoned Dean. "I'll go get him and the key." He sprinted across the parking lot toward the two homes on the other side of the museum.

Thunder rumbled to the west. Pulling deeper inside her heavy jacket, Nicky huffed white breath into the still, cold night. Another storm was rolling in. With the plunge in temperature, it was sure to bring sleet and snow.

The crunch of footsteps on gravel heralded Franco and Mike's arrival, their bulky shadows backlit by the parking lot lights.

Nicky spotlighted the lock with her flashlight, and Mike opened the door. He made to step over the threshold, but Nicky stopped him. His eyes rounded when Nicky and Franco drew their sidearms. He quietly tucked himself into a shadow on the porch, out of the way.

Nicky slipped inside and switched on the light, Franco at her back. The house was tidy and cool, its neatness marred only by half-packed cardboard boxes. Nothing seemed out of place. Nicky ran her hand over books slotted into a crate. She hadn't even had a chance to speak to Dean about where he was going or if he'd found another position.

"Maybe he's at the museum," Franco said.

Mike locked Dean's front door, and Nicky and Franco followed him to the museum, but a search turned up nothing.

"Dean's still not answering his cell." Nicky hit end on her screen and tucked her phone into her pocket. She, Franco, and Mike stood in the vast foyer, lights blazing. "Did you talk to him today, Mike?"

"No. But that's not unusual. I'm pretty busy, especially with all this rain." He gestured to the ceiling. "We've had some roof leaks."

"Did you notice a car or truck at his house today?" Franco asked. "Dean uses PonyXpres, right?"

Mike's broad forehead wrinkled. "Come to think of it, yeah. But not today. Yesterday. A big white SUV—"

Nicky's tension drained. "Howard's truck. Dean must have called for a ride."

She pulled her phone, dialed Howard's number, and pressed the phone to her ear.

"Howard Kie?" Mike said. "No, no. This was a nice SUV. Intact. Howard has a different-colored passenger door and all that duct tape holding up his bumper and window. Besides, there were two guys in the car."

"Two men?" Franco said. "What did they look like?"

"I didn't really see their faces, but one was really big—bigger than you—and the other kinda medium or small."

The ringing stopped, and Howard Kie spoke in a raspy whisper. "How did you know?"

"What?" That greeting was weird, even for Howard.

"They came to the Chishe's house. I'm staying there while he's away with his *n'aaya* and *uwaka*. To watch over it."

Nicky rearranged Howard's words to make sense of them. "You're staying at Ryan's house while he's at his mom's with the baby."

"Haa'a. Then they came."

"Who came?"

"Your mother and the Chishe. They created the path on the spirit map."

"The spiral worked?" She caught Franco's glance and grinned.

"Haa'a. I saw exactly. It's very clever. Then I went to the toilet because I drank a lot of coffee today."

"Why are you whispering?"

"Because those two guys came. I made sure they didn't see me. I'm good at not getting noticed."

"Two guys?" The hair on her arms prickled. "What two guys?"

"The ones who came into the house." He paused. "They had guns and took your mom and Ryan."

"They took my mom?" Nicky went numb, phone sliding from her hand.

Franco grabbed it. He pressed it against his ear.

"Howard, it's Franco." Intense concentration etched his face, and long seconds passed as Howard talked. "We're on our way. And Howard? Be careful, buddy. They've killed before." He turned to Mike. "Do you have the key to the archives room? We need to get a map."

TOO SHAKEN TO DRIVE, Nicky sat in the passenger seat of her unit, arms braced as Franco squealed around a sharp curve in the road leading away from the museum.

"Howard's *where*?" She stared hard at his profile.

"In the horse trailer hitched to the kidnappers' SUV," Franco said.

"He snuck inside when they put Ryan and your mom in the car. Ryan was fighting them. I think he knew Howard needed the cover. Your mom didn't answer her phone?"

"Straight to voicemail. They might have turned it off or got rid of it."

"Call Savannah again. Howard said she can track his phone."

"The kidnappers have horses?" Nicky hit the redial button.

Franco accelerated on a straightaway. "No, but Howard said there were packsaddles and camping gear inside the trailer. That probably means—"

Nicky held up her hand as Savannah picked up. "Hey. What's up? Sorry, I was in the shower."

"Howard says you can track his phone," Nicky said. She enabled the speaker so Franco could hear. "I need you to do that, okay?"

"Did he lose it again? If that guy's head wasn't screwed on—"

"No. Savannah, listen. My mom…" Her voice unexpectedly choked. She breathed deeply, tamping down a surge of trembling. Franco's hand squeezed her shoulder.

"What's going on?" Savannah's voice turned serious.

"Two men—I think the ones who murdered Rémy Tioux—took my mom and Ryan. At gunpoint."

Savannah inhaled sharply.

"Howard saw them," Nicky said. "They drove off in a white SUV. I need you to track his phone. He hid in a horse trailer they were pulling. Franco and I are on our way to your house. We'll pick you up."

"The baby?"

"With Ryan's parents. They only took Ryan and my mom."

"And Dean," Franco added. "Howard said he was in the back seat of the SUV."

"The police?" Savannah asked.

"I'll phone them when I hang up." Her phone vibrated in her hand. Another call. *Dean.* "We're about thirty minutes out, Savannah. Be ready." Nicky stared at the screen. She pressed the end-and-accept icon, then hit speaker again. "Where are you?"

"Don't call the police. Please." Dean's voice strained with panic. "They have someone watching the police department. If you alert the police or—or FBI, they said they'd kill us. They have your mother and Ryan Bernal. They said they'll release us unharmed, but only if you don't involve the pol—"

The phone cut off. Nicky hit redial. It immediately went to voicemail.

Grim-faced, Franco switched on the lights and siren and sped under the freeway and onto the west side of the reservation at over a hundred miles an hour.

Fifteen minutes from Savannah's house, it started to snow.

CHAPTER FORTY-TWO

SAVANNAH PULLED Nicky into a hug as soon as she walked through the front door. Nicky held on hard, absorbing the warmth. She didn't realize how cold she was until then.

She let go, and Savannah moved to Franco, wrapping her arms around him, too.

When she released him, she said, "You went to Ryan's house first?" His home was just down the street.

"Mom's car was parked at the curb," Nicky replied. "The door was unlocked, and I found Mom's cell phone and bag. Ryan's keys, cell, and wallet were on the counter in the kitchen."

"There was a Hot Tamale dissolving in the snow of the driveway." Franco smiled faintly. "We thought it was blood. It must've dropped out of Howard's pocket when he climbed into the trailer."

"What's that?" Savannah indicated the cardboard tube in his hand.

"The map we marked up at the exhibition opening. Dean had it tacked to a corkboard in his office. It looks like they took the one at Ryan's with them."

Savannah led them into the kitchen and the bitter scent of freshly brewed coffee. Mugs were set out next to cream and packets of sweetener. Her laptop sat open on the breakfast bar.

"What about the police?" Savannah asked as she woke it up.

"Dean MacElroy called. They took him, too. He warned Nicky not to contact them or they'd harm her mother." Franco eyed Savannah. "And Ryan. And if they find Howard…"

Savannah stilled, lips compressed, before she nodded and motioned to the computer screen. She scrolled a satellite map until she found a moving dot—the GPS signal on Howard's phone. "It looks like they're headed for the mountains northwest of Scalding Peak."

"Not good. Cell signal is spotty or nonexistent." Franco handed Nicky a cup of coffee.

"You know that area, right? You patrol up there," Nicky said.

"Yes, but there are half a dozen jumping-off places into the tribe's wilderness," he said. "There are no good roads or tracks. If that's where they're headed, they have to go in on foot or horseback."

He didn't have to say how easy it would be to disappear.

"That could explain the packsaddles and gear. They probably have horses stashed somewhere. You said they had the map?" Savannah scrunched up her nose. "The one Geronimo Elk's … spirit marked up?"

"We figured out the pattern," Nicky said. "It's a spiral. I think it leads to—"

"The Place of Emergence." Savannah met Nicky's gaze, her glasses reflecting the satellite map on the screen. "I know."

Nicky blinked. "You do?"

"Don't sound so surprised. I've lived here all my life, heard the stories, visited the shrines—although I draw the line at getting medicined. And since Ryan and the baby, and Howard staying at Ryan's house, and your mother…" She shrugged. "I've been sort of by myself in the evenings, so I started putting together the puzzle pieces because I don't think these bad guys are smarter than us." Her smile was wry. "Anyway, I don't know who the murderers are, just what they want."

"What do they want?" Franco leaned his hip against the counter, expression unreadable.

"A plant from the fertility medicine in those old pots that makes *'the mother of one the sister of the other.'* I don't have any idea what that means, but I bet it grows in the Place of Emergence." Savannah paused. "Or did."

"I think it's still growing there." Nicky explained their suspicions about Kristina and Raven Tioux. "If you know the way, we'll need you as a guide." Stomach churning, she put down her coffee.

Savannah gestured to a stack of winter hiking gear on the sofa. Her hunting backpack and scabbarded rifle was propped by the door.

"I'm ready, but…" She drew in a breath. "I said I knew where the path of the shrines led. I didn't say I knew exactly." Savannah clicked the touchpad to drop another pin on the blinking signal from Howard's phone, stood, and scooped up the computer and her coffee. "Let's look at the map you brought. Dining table, Franco. There's a red Sharpie in the junk drawer."

Nicky followed Franco and Savannah through the kitchen and back into the living and dining room.

Savannah leaned over the map, twiddling the marker. She pulled the cap off with her teeth and marked ten more X's, saying, "Shrine locations," then, "Let's see what we get," and began to draw an arc from the outermost mark, spiraling through every X. She stopped, resting the pen's tip on an area printed with tightly spaced contour lines. "That's it. The Place of Emergence should be right"—Savannah lifted the marker and dotted a circle encompassing a diameter of at least half a kilometer around the point—"here." She blew out a long breath. "Somewhere."

"On a cliff?" Nicky said. The contour lines represented areas of equal elevation. Densely spaced lines meant a steep rise or drop.

"That's more of a slope. Optimistically, about a day's ride from Fry Bacon Ridge. That's one of the jump-off points I was talking about." Franco took the marker and boxed another area next to parallel dotted lines that represented an unimproved road. "There's a barn and corrals here, plus barracks for firefighters and Hotshots."

"Do you think that's where they're going?" Savannah asked. "Because we just lost signal." She dropped a final pin on the computer, but a spiderweb of tracks threaded away from it and over the map.

They could end up anywhere. Nicky's stomach flipped sickly, but she squared her shoulders and caught Franco's eye. He nodded, jaw hard.

"If we can't track them, it means whoever the bad guys have watching over us can't track us, either."

"What if they have a satellite phone?" Savannah said.

"A chance we'll have to take." Franco said. "But I have my doubts about anyone monitoring us. I think all the bad guys are in that truck."

"And because of Howard, we know their general location, and they don't know we're onto them," Nicky added. "Savannah, once we're up there, can you get us to the Place of Emergence?"

"On a good day, maybe. But, with this weather?" She shook her head. "There's a whiteout in the mountains that's not supposed to clear until morning. If we left now, we'd probably get stuck and freeze to death before we got to the first dropped pin. And you said a day's ride, Franco. If we hike it, I guarantee it will take way more time that we might not have."

"The weather means the bad guys can't go anywhere, either. They'll have to hunker down—I hope at Fry Bacon Ridge. Which gives us the rest of the night to prepare." Nicky pulled out her phone. "We're gonna call in the cavalry."

"What? *You* have a *plan* that doesn't involve running headfirst into danger?" Although Savannah's expression was tense, her lips curved faintly, and faux awe edged her voice.

Time was ticking away, and her mother was in danger. When Franco had begun talking strategy in the truck, she'd forced herself to listen. He'd been persuasive, and with the snow, she had to admit—reluctantly—he'd also been right.

Nicky mustered a smile. "There is still an element of running directly into danger, but Franco convinced me not to do it alone this time."

Savannah grinned. "Then screw the cavalry. Call in the Indians. We do kick-ass work."

CHAPTER FORTY-THREE

NICKY'S BREATH sent hard puffs of white into the chill dawn air as she ducked behind a tree. The altitude and cold made each inhalation dig sharply into her lungs. She leaned around the trunk and studied the shadowed open space between her location and the Quonset hut. The horse barn sat farther back, the five-bar pipe-metal corral empty. But the snow was trampled by tracks—human and horse—and the bad guys' truck and two-stall horse trailer were parked underneath tall pines, hidden from anyone who wasn't looking.

"Ghost one in place, front door in sight," she said into the speaker mic pinned to her shoulder.

By the barn, a flash of movement caught the corner of her eye.

"Ghost three checking animal shelter," Officer Cyrus Aguilar said, voice low. "Empty. Checking track and trailer. Empty." A pause. "Ghost three in place."

"Ghost two ready. No lights, no movement," Franco said. He'd snuck around to the back door of the Quonset hut with Officer Brandy Sykes.

"Ghost four ready," Brandy whispered. Nicky couldn't see either of them, but Aguilar's placement had their six.

Waiting for one more. Manny Valentine. Not her first or even last choice, but Franco trusted him. And she trusted Franco.

"Ghost five, front exit in sight," Valentine said. The trajectory of his and Nicky's weapons would be at a forty-five-degree angle if anyone came out the front.

A sparkling burst of pink light lit up the rocky pine-dotted slope above the ridge, streaking lingering cirrus clouds in gold and tangerine. Sunrise.

Nicky gave the signal: "Go." She shouldered her AR-15, stepped out from the trees, and knelt, one knee down on the wet mat of pine needles.

"Door breach," Franco said. "Now."

Insulated walls muffled a metallic thump. Muscles tightened, and Nicky's heart rate kicked as Franco and Brandy entered the building. Slow seconds passed, each one counted in her head. The sunlight rolled down the mountain. Tops of trees glimmered and glowed white. Nicky kept her crosshairs tight.

"Clear," Franco said.

"Ghost four exiting the front of the building," Brandy said.

"Stand down, Ghost five." Nicky dropped her muzzle, still alert. Light swept the line of shadow down the road, catching Valentine as he lowered the muzzle of his AR.

The front door opened, and Brandy stepped out. She held her handgun at the ready and crept into the open space before she crossed the road and disappeared in the trees. Valentine paralleled her.

Nicky's shoulder speaker cued.

"I found tracks," Brandy said. "Horses."

Franco exited the hut, stepping into the rapidly melting slush. The black of his clothes absorbed the sunlight. He keyed his mic. "All clear, Pep. Bring up the truck."

Nicky stood, her AR positioned cross-body, and trotted across the road to Franco. Cyrus Aguilar tramped from in between the hut and corral and joined them.

"Five or six animals in the corral, maybe two or three days," Aguilar said. "They left this morning, except—"

"Sarge." Brandy Sykes jogged toward Nicky, bulky in her black vest. She'd holstered her sidearm. "A bunch of horses went down the side of the ridge across the road from the cabin. I glassed the canyon but didn't see anything."

Aguilar frowned at the interruption but took a half step back and waited.

Valentine joined the circle of black-clad bodies. "And I got more hoofprints coming in at an angle to the tracks Sykes reported."

"From where?" Nicky asked.

He shrugged.

"Find their origin."

Valentine nodded and trotted back into the trees.

Nicky turned back to Aguilar. "Except what, Officer Aguilar?"

"Looks like someone tried to release the horses last night. Found some shell casings at the edge of the clearing and a fresh bullet scar in a tree fifty feet farther. About one hundred feet out, I found this." He opened his hand, a sticky red Hot Tamale in his palm. *Howard.* "Thought it was blood at first. I found hoof and shoe prints, too. I think he got away with at least one of the animals. He might be the second set of tracks."

Nicky clamped her jaw. "That means the bad guys know someone's onto them."

Valentine broke in on the speaker, breathing hard. "Ghost five, over."

"Report," Nicky said. The low thrum of a diesel engine vibrated through the trees.

"You're not gonna ... believe this," he panted. "A camp. Sheltered by overhanging rocks. Three horses. Three people. Campfire's still warm."

Nicky's gaze flashed to Franco's. "More bad guys?"

"Then why didn't they stay in the hut?" Franco dropped his chin and spoke into the mic. "Full investigation of the camp, Valentine." He looked up. "Aguilar and Sykes? Go get the units. Matthews has extra evidence kits in hers. Do a thorough search of the hut and outbuildings. Photos, and bag any evidence you find. As soon as Sergeant

Matthews and I leave with Savannah, contact Chief Richards by satellite phone. He'll call the FBI and brief them on what's going on. You'll have lots of company before the end of the day."

"Don't know about that." Sykes tilted her face to the sky. "Weather's calling for heavy snow."

"We'll contact you on our phone every two hours, if possible, and give you our coordinates," Nicky said, voice rising over the increasing noise of the truck engine.

A huge red dually pickup topped the rise, towing a fully enclosed horse trailer. Even with chains on the tires, it ground and slid through icy mud and snow. As it pulled up beside Nicky and the other officers, the driver's side window hummed down. Pep Katina peered out. Savannah craned her neck from the passenger seat.

"Man, you couldn't pay me to do that again. We almost went over the edge a half a dozen times." But he grinned. "Where do you want the horses?"

"Corral for now," Franco said. "Nicky and I'll change in the Quonset."

"They're not here?" Savannah asked, clutching a second jacket tightly to her chest.

"No, but they were. And without you and Howard, we'd be nowhere. Thank God you microchipped him." Franco smiled at his joke, but his expression was tight. "They should be easy to track with the snow. You sure you want to go with us, Savannah? Pep said he'd—"

"I promised Ryan's parents I'd bring him back safe. If you leave me, I swear I'll just follow on foot." Tears stood in her eyes. "I need to do this."

Savannah had loved Ryan for years, and he her, but... Nicky shifted uneasily. Something else was going on. What that was, Nicky couldn't guess.

"You have the body armor I gave you?" she asked.

Savannah wiped her eyes and nodded.

"You need to follow our orders without questions," Franco said.

Savannah nodded again. She and Pep slid out of the truck and headed to the horse trailer. Nicky opened the back door of the pickup, stowed her AR, and grabbed her bag of gear. Franco opened the door on the other side, slotted his AR-15 next to hers, hefted out a bag, and picked up a scabbarded rifle.

As they trudged side by side toward the Quonset, Nicky caught his eye. "Who the heck are the guys in the camp Valentine found? What the hell is going on?"

CHAPTER FORTY-FOUR

CAREFUL TO MAINTAIN cover behind a clump of piñons, Nicky reined in her bay gelding next to Franco's leggy sorrel. Savannah pulled her chestnut mare up beside Nicky.

"Why are we stopping?" Nicky asked, tone sharp, breath puffing white. She'd led their small group for the first three hours of the ride, her pace fast on a trail churned with hoofprints that made the bad guys easy to follow. But when her impatience had cost them thirty minutes on an ill-advised shortcut, Franco took over. They'd slowed considerably, and her frustration built.

Franco shot her a side-eye but didn't answer. He lifted a monocular rangefinder to glass the valley below.

"I'm glad," Savannah said. "Every cell in my back and butt is screaming at me, and I have to pee."

"You can go back," Nicky snapped.

"Stop it, Nicky. You're not the only one under pressure." Savannah swung her leg over the saddle, kicked her stirrup loose to slowly slide to the ground, and groaned. She looped the reins over a branch, unsheathed her rifle, and marched off into the forest behind them, disappearing between the pines.

Fat white puffs drifted in the air, the snowfall thickening steadily. It transformed the high mesa, plating the dried brown meadows, gray rocks, and deep green pines with silver. Franco swung off his horse and walked it toward the edge of the cliff, studying the ground. The hoofprints they'd been following for five hours were filling with fresh powder. Another thirty minutes and they'd be covered.

Nicky dismounted and tethered her horse. She tugged down her hat, glad the wide brim kept most of the snow off her face. Squaring her shoulders, she strode toward Franco until she stood directly in front of him. He stared into the distance over her head, even though falling snow concealed the mountains on the other side of the valley.

"We shouldn't have brought Savannah," Nicky said.

"She's kept us on track by identifying the shrines."

"Snow's covering the tracks. If we don't hurry, we'll lose them."

Franco pulled in a deep breath. "The horses needed a break. We needed a break."

"They're getting away."

"And if they do, you'll blame me," Franco said, matching her sharpness.

Taken aback by his response, Nicky hesitated. "We had a plan."

"And sometimes, no matter how hard you try, plans fall apart, and everything blows up in your face." He dropped his rangefinder and scrubbed at his jaw with a leather-gloved hand. Finally, he looked her in the eye. "Sometimes, nothing you do is good enough."

"This is my mother, Franco. And Ryan, and Howard. We have to save them."

"And what if we don't? Then what happens? We're too close to this, Nicky, too emotionally involved."

"No. That's what makes us good cops. We have to care. It takes a toll when things don't go as planned, but that should make us stronger. So we do better next time."

Realization hit.

"That's why you hide behind your masks, isn't it? The dumb jock; the loyal, good-humored buddy; the suave, charming cop. You care too much. That's why you run when things get too intense."

His expression bleak, he said, "It's easier."

The Franco she'd fallen in love with abandoned her when he hid behind his masks. She'd had enough of people abandoning her.

"Since when is life easy?" Nicky stared up at the dull gray sky, letting snow land on her face, the tiny stings of cold melting until they dripped down her cheeks. "Why do you think they kidnapped my mom and Ryan? They have the map, and hostages would only slow them down." She inched closer to the edge, where hoof and boot prints funneled through a notch. "Leverage? Do they still need something from them? What?"

"I've upset you," Franco said. He swept off his hat.

Flecks of silver in his sideburns glimmered in the cloud-filtered sunlight. She smiled inside. His hair was almost too short to have hat head. Almost.

"Who else would know about this weird plant? My father or Jimmy Che'chi, but they're both dead. Whoever mixed herbs for the Santa Fe fertility clinic knew because Raven's genetics prove the plant worked. Like Charlotte said, it would be worth a lot of money. Human parthenogenesis. Imagine."

"Nicky," Franco said. "I'm sorry."

Nicky barked a laugh. "A blanket 'I'm sorry'? You might be, but nothing changes. When situations become difficult, you still hide. You still leave." Only a scattering of snow drifted down now. The veil of white lifted from the mountains across the valley.

Franco's footsteps crunched in the snowy silence.

"I know I have problems, but you can't expect me to be perfect, to never slip up and do stupid things."

She looked up at his face, and what she found in his eyes warmed her. She tugged off a glove and laid her fingers over his cold cheek. "No one's perfect. Especially not me. I don't expect that. But I do expect honesty between us."

"I'm trying."

"And I'd never blame you if things go wrong, but you have to trust me enough to realize that."

She pushed up on her toes and pressed a lingering kiss on the corner of his mouth. His hand slid around her waist, tightening.

"Nicky! Franco!"

Nicky broke away and ran toward Savannah's shout. It didn't come from the forest but from the other side of the brush where the horses were tied. Franco darted to his mount and retrieved his rifle.

On her belly, Savannah waved from an outcropping of boulders above them. Franco bounded up, Nicky scrambling behind. She flung herself down on her stomach beside Savannah.

"On the other side, on that slope," Savannah said.

Nicky peered over the valley still veiled by lingering snowfall. "What? I can't..." She glanced at Franco, but he shook his head.

"Because it's hidden." Savannah levered up. "Lie down exactly where I did and align yourself with the arrows."

"Arrows?" Nicky shifted.

Three red arrows formed out of Hot Tamales stained the snow in front of her. They pointed across the vast expanse of air.

Savannah grinned. "Howard left a trail of candy from the shrine. He's brought us to exactly the right place because you can only see it from here." Her grin softened. "Our genesis. Where our histories tell us we began."

A breeze picked up and swept over the outcropping of rocks, tickling Nicky's exposed skin. It strengthened and blew the fading snow into a swirl that seemed to part before her eyes.

And she saw it, folded between trees, in a sloped clearing. Huge slick plates of flat rock in the shape of a flower, snow tucked around them, the center a deeper black. Nicky shifted her head to the right, then to the left. Even a few inches in either direction obscured them.

She elbowed Franco. "Give me your monocular."

He passed it to her, and she held it to her eye, adjusting the focus. At the center of the rocks, darker than the blackest onyx, was a round opening, a puncture in the earth from which tendrils of steam unraveled in the air above.

The opening spiraled dizzily as she stared. A form rose within the steam, creeping up through the dark hole, hunched with effort. It wavered in the mist as it stood, black against black, swallowing the light. Nicky's breath quickened. She zoomed in.

As if it felt her scrutiny, the figure lifted its head and stared at her with eyes burning like fire. She'd seen it before: in the museum and at the birthing niche as a child. It grinned, exposing needle-sharp teeth.

"*Guw'aadzi, sha'au. Key shro'kch.*"

She shouldn't have been able to hear it, but she did.

Hello, sister. I see you.

CHAPTER FORTY-FIVE

A DISTANT RIFLE shot echoed off the canyon walls.

Franco pushed to one knee and pointed to the valley. "Down there."

Nicky scrambled to a crouch and swung the lens away from the black spirit creature. She searched for movement and found it in a large meadow on the valley floor. Two mounted horses, jerking and spinning in panic, churned the snow. A rider leveled a handgun and fired into the trees at the opposite end of the clearing. From across the valley, a rifle barked in reply a split second before one of the horses reared. Its rider fell to the ground, the horse bolting away.

"From the ledge above!" Savannah said.

Nicky swung the eyepiece up, focusing with frantic fingers. A large man tucked between a tumble of boulders, rifle aimed at the group in the meadow, squeezed off a second shot. Nicky could see the puff of gun smoke before the retort rang across the valley.

"Shooter in the rocks," Nicky said.

Another rifle shot cracked from below. The man with the handgun popped off three rounds before he wheeled his horse and bolted into the forest, leaving the downed figure in the snow.

"A second one in the trees at the end of the meadow. Ambush,"

Franco said grimly. He knelt and rested his rifle on the bare branch of a wind-stunted cedar. His was scoped for long-distance accuracy. "Do you see the hostages?"

Nicky searched the opposite slope. Three people mounted on horses, reins held tight by one of them. The third man was swathed in a heavy coat, hat and gaiter mask hiding his face. But nothing hid the silver handgun he pointed at the remaining pair.

"Fifty paces behind the sniper," Nicky said. "Go for the shooter if you have a shot."

Franco fired, the boom of his rifle ringing in Nicky's ears. Stone powdered six inches from the sniper's nose. He ducked and disappeared.

"You got his attention."

He fired again. "The hostages?"

Nicky focused closer and found her mother on one of the horses, one hand extended to a man's—Ryan's—shoulder. His arms were twisted behind his back. The horses tossed their heads, hooves shifting restlessly, but the third bad guy controlled them. She didn't see Dean.

Unless …

"Get to cover. *Please*, get to cover," Savannah whispered. "Oh, God, I think he's—"

Nicky dropped her monocular back to the meadow, widening her field of vision. The rider was still down in the snow.

A mounted mule darted from the trees and slid to a halt next to the unmoving form, its skinny rider jumping to the ground. Nicky's hand tightened on the monocular. "That guy's *Howard*."

A man in a sky-blue jacket stepped from a stand of birch trees, rifle shouldered.

Pulse jumping in her throat, Nicky said, "Bad guy, left side of the clearing!"

"I see that son of a—" Savannah cocked and raised her rifle to her shoulder in one smooth motion. She fired. The man spun and dove back for cover. "Might not hit him without a scope, but I'll make him think twice." She levered out the spent shell and fired again.

Howard hoisted the fallen man up onto the mule while Franco continued shooting at the sniper in the rocks to suppress his fire. The man on the mule drooped over its neck but kicked it into the trees. Howard raised his hands above his head and ran directly toward the bad guy in the birch.

"Stop shooting!" Nicky said. "Dammit. Howard's giving himself up."

"Nicky?" Franco said, his voice urgent.

She read his mind. "Go," she replied, "but be careful. Savannah will cover you."

He pivoted and disappeared behind the rocks. Within seconds, Franco mounted and guided his horse down the trail to retrieve the injured rider.

Savannah shouldered her rifle again, scanning the trees.

Across the valley, the gunman in the blue jacket, now on horseback, maneuvered up the rise, using rocks and trees for cover. Howard, tied by his wrists to a long rope held by the rider, stumbled behind him. When they reached the hostages and their captor, the man pointed to the rocky outcropping where she and Savannah knelt.

Ears still ringing from the gunfire, Nicky watched through her glass as the group of horses, leading her mother and Ryan, Howard still trotting behind, turned up the slope and vanished. No sign of the sniper.

"It's going to get dark soon. What do we do?" Savannah asked.

Nicky dropped the monocular from her eye. "We wait for Franco."

THE CLACKING of hooves on stones heralded Franco's return. Nicky jumped down from the rocks, Savannah at her heels, and darted to the trailhead. Franco ponied a mule, its rider slumped in the saddle. A second horse trailed the mule, this one riderless but packed with gear. Franco hoisted the limp man from the mule's saddle and laid him in a bed of pine needles under the trees. The man's left arm was out of his jacket sleeve and lashed tightly over his chest. He'd lost his hat, but a balaclava hid his face. Savannah knelt beside him with the first aid kit.

"Hit high up in the arm. Bullet broke the bone, I think. He'd field dressed the wound by the time we found each other. Lost some blood, though. Managed to stay conscious up the trail." With careful hands, Franco slipped the woolen hood off the man's head.

Nicky recognized him from the fertility exhibition.

"Lionel Hand." Savannah covered her mouth with gloved fingers.

Hand cracked open dark brown eyes. "Just Lionel. What the hell you bring her for?" He was limp, his voice dry and weak, but at Savannah's outraged gasp, his well-defined lips quirked. "To make coffee?"

Savannah scowled.

"She knows the country. Found the opening to the Place of Emergence for us." Franco slid an arm around his shoulders and lifted him. Lionel groaned and paled. Franco tilted the thermos Nicky had handed him to Lionel's mouth. After a few sips, he turned his head away.

"Bet she just followed Howard Kie's clues. Little Sister'll be dead-weight when you find the bad guys. They mean business."

"You jack-hole, don't call me that. I'm not of your clan. And I saved your ass down in that valley."

Lionel raised his brows. "That was you shooting? Sure you didn't hit me?"

Lips pinched, Savannah glared him. "If I'd aimed to hit you, you'd be dead."

Hand snorted, then gritted his teeth. "Aw, *shit*, that hurts."

"He's right about the danger, Savannah," Nicky said. "Now that we know where the opening is, we need you to stay with Dr. Hand."

Savannah's jaw clenched, but after a few tense seconds, she gave a curt nod.

"What happened while I was gone?" Franco asked Nicky.

"I don't know what happened to the sniper. The bad guy in the valley rode up to the others. He had Howard. They all disappeared—including Mom and Ryan—toward the Place of Emergence. Nothing since then."

Franco stared hard at her, and her pulse accelerated. He'd picked up on what she'd deliberately left out. Dean.

"Even with a map, they didn't know the way, those bad ones," Lionel said. He'd closed his eyes and sagged back. "Would've gotten lost. We couldn't let that happen. Too dangerous for the hostages. We cobbled together a plan to get them to the opening, hoping for backup. I was supposed to lead them in, divide them. They ambushed us instead. That's why Howard gave himself up. To clue in your mother and the fireman. Then take 'em there. Safe, warm inside."

"How do you know so much about this place?" Savannah asked. "Planning to steal from it, too?"

"Savannah, stop," Nicky said. Hand was weak, and they didn't need him expending energy on pointless arguing.

"I don't need defending, Sergeant, especially not from the likes of her." Lionel's gaze was fierce. "From the chamber they're in, what they want can only be accessed down a flume. With the rain and snow, the water will be running fast, and Howard can't swim. They have to send someone strong—the young firefighter and your mother. They think she knows what they need." He groaned and paled even further, his lips the only color in his face. "Won't send one of their own because it would split them up. And they need someone to pull the travelers back to earth. You need to take the climbing gear in my saddle. Convince them to use the harness." His head arched back, neck corded in pain. Crimson seeped through his torn shirt sleeve.

Savannah grabbed a handful of bandages from the first aid kit. She ripped open the packages and stacked them in a thick pad.

"Cut everything away, Franco," Savannah said.

He pulled his knife and sliced at the bullet-shredded fabric, peeling back a folded cloth packed over the wound. Blood oozed from the ugly dark hole.

"Why were you at Fry Bacon Ridge? Who's the third man?" Franco asked.

"Did he get away?" Lionel chuckled weakly. "Give yourselves up. You, Sergeant, volunteer to go with your mother. He'll be a surprise.

Knows a back way into the *tsiba'ashi y'uuni* room. Mother, sister, daughter. They will protect you." He slurred the last words.

"I don't understand," Nicky said.

Savannah pressed the pad onto the wound. Lionel's eyes opened wide, then rolled back as he went limp.

"Sorry," Savannah said. "There's ammonia inhalant—smelling salts—in the kit."

"We've wasted too much time. We've got to get down the trail before dark. Savannah, I'll need your horse. Mine's spent," Franco said. "We'll leave you the satellite phone. Call in backup and tell them to bring a travois for Dr. Hand. I'll get a fire started. The deadfall under the pine trees should be dry enough to keep it going."

Nicky undid the cinch and slid Franco's saddle off his tired horse to switch it out with Savannah's. "Will you be okay, Savannah?"

"My sleeping bag's rated minus twenty. What about him?" She gestured to Hand.

"I'll leave you my bag and some snap warmers," Franco said. "Try to get more hot liquid down him if he wakes up."

Nicky finished with the horses as Franco set up camp. Savannah put through her call to the Fire-Sky Search and Rescue. "The road's so bad, they only made it up to Fry Bacon Ridge an hour ago. They won't be able to come until tomorrow morning. I gave them my coordinates. FBI's pissed, by the way." She tromped to her saddle, unsheathed the rifle, and held it out. "Nicky?"

"Nah. I have my Glock and Franco. You keep it in case of bears or lions."

"I have a lion." Savannah gestured to Hand. "Not that he's worth a damn."

"When he wakes up, get the name of the other man he and Howard were with and why they were out here," Nicky said. She swung up on her horse and settled into the cold leather, muscles protesting. Franco waited for her by the trailhead. "Savannah, what's the *tsiba'ashi y'uuni*? The Fire-Song room?"

"I don't know. Just ... be careful. The ghosts who stay in the Place of Emergence are dangerous."

The swirling black spirit whispered again in Nicky's mind. "You don't believe in ghosts and spirits."

"But you do. According to Ryan and Howard, that makes you a target. Nicky?" Savannah laid a hand on her thigh. "Bring them back safe."

In the deepening dusk, Nicky nodded, turned her horse, and dropped over the edge.

CHAPTER FORTY-SIX

DARKNESS HAD FALLEN by the time Nicky and Franco found the camp where the bad guys had secured their animals. Nicky hunkered down behind a tree to cover Franco as he drew his gun and stole in close. Seconds ticked by before Franco, silent as a cat, returned through patchy snow, gesturing for her to follow him. Together they ducked under snow-dusted pine boughs into a circular clearing sheltered from the wind. Still, the damp chill cut into the bones of her bare hand holding her Glock.

"Left their horses highlined. Otherwise deserted. No gear, only tack. Not sure they're even coming back." Franco flicked on his headlamp. A horse jerked, the whites of its eyes showing. He ran his hand over the withers of a stocky buckskin. "You recognize these animals?"

"From the Fire-Sky hunting remuda." Nicky holstered her sidearm and slid on her glove. The casino resort stables were less than half a mile from the hotel for guests inclined to ride for pleasure, but most of the horses were pack animals used for guided elk hunts in the pueblo's backcountry. "Don't you have to hire someone to take them out?"

"That would explain why the bad guys are equipped for this country and weather. But where's the guide?"

"Paid off? Or he's in on it. He could be the third guy."

Franco played his headlamp over saddles and empty packs tucked under the trees. The light caught on a square of white paper tacked to a trunk. She hurried to it, Franco behind her, and switched on her lamp. The edge of the paper was heavily stained with blood.

"There's blood on this saddle, too," Franco said. "We might have hit one of the bad guys."

"Or one of the hostages is injured." Nicky yanked the note from the tree, breathing shallowly to press back nausea.

"'Sergeant Matthews and whoever else come to the opening unarmed climb down the ladder or your mother will die first that's what they say. Your friend, Howard.'" Body rigid, throat tight, she said, "It's what Lionel Hand told us to do. Surrender to them."

Franco pulled her into his chest, but his warmth and strength couldn't thaw the cold permeating her body. "Or we wait for backup. They're trapped in that hole underground."

"My mom, Franco. I have to…" Her voice broke.

"Not without me, partner," he whispered.

They clutched each other for a long moment, the only sound the muffled crunch of hooves on a blanket of pine needles.

Nicky untangled herself. She breathed in the icy air and straightened her shoulders.

"We'd better go."

Branches rustled at the far end of the trees. Nicky reached up to turn off her headlamp. Franco did the same. With quick steps, she retreated behind the cover of a tree trunk, Franco next to her. She tugged off her glove and drew her Glock, the sliding of cold metal over the leather holster loud in the dense quiet. She waited for her eyes to adjust to the pitch blackness surrounding her.

"Hey," a man's voice said. "I was with Lionel and Howard."

Nicky froze. The voice wasn't loud, but it resonated in her chest. Uninvited imagery and memories exploded. She closed her eyes as waves of recognition engulfed her, weakening her knees.

Dear God. It all makes sense now. Everything.

Almost.

"Officer Martinez?" the man called. "We met. At the first garden desecration. Jimmy Che'chi."

"Che'chi's dead," Franco said. His shadowy bulk stepped from behind the tree.

"We were pretty good friends. Figured he wouldn't mind if I used his name." The shush of nylon fabric through pine boughs filtered toward them until the tall silhouette of a man was outlined darkly against patches of snow. "Lionel?"

"Hit in the arm. We left him with a member of our group and contacted Fire-Sky Rescue. They'll get him to a hospital."

"I didn't want to leave him, but we had to stick to the plan. It's just, I can't pull it off on my own. Would be glad for the help." He took another step forward and pulled his cowboy hat off to run a leather-clad hand over his hair, smoothing it. Nodding, he said, "There's someone there with you."

Nicky stepped out from behind her tree and let out the breath she hadn't realized she'd held. The man's gaze fixed on her shadowed face.

"I'm going to switch my light on," Franco said. "But I'll shoot you if you make one threatening move."

Franco tugged off his headlamp and switched it on, pointing the narrow beam at the man's face. The brightness made him wince and turn away, the silver in his straight black hair glinting.

"This is Sergeant Nicky Matthews from the Fire-Sky police," Franco said. "Nicky, *this* is the Jemez Medicine Man."

She stared into the man's face. Still craggy and square, with a defined brow ridge and high forehead with those three distinct creases. His chin was pointed and lips thin, but the light caught deep-set gray-green eyes—the same color as Charlotte's. Still handsome but much leaner than the last time she'd seen him, even wrapped in a puffy black parka.

"Not *Hay*-mus," Nicky said quietly. "I thought everyone was saying it wrong—but you were right the first time, Franco. Howard, too."

"Howard knew. He's a good secret keeper." The man stepped closer. "Been a long time, sweetheart."

"Since two years before you died."

"Before..." Franco's head swiveled back and forth between them. "What's going on?"

"Franco, meet *Hemis* Michael Matthews, PhD, anthropologist, organic chemist. Cheater, liar, serial philanderer. The man the bad guys really want. My father." Nicky holstered her Glock with a shaking hand. "Only they don't know he's still alive."

CHAPTER FORTY-SEVEN

A DIFFUSE COLUMN of light shot from the opening of the Place of Emergence. The flower formed by five teardrop-shaped rocks surrounding the entrance sat flat against the slanted hillside. Nicky lay prone on one of the lower petals, Franco next to her on another. Steamy waves of air pulsed over them.

"Almost like the cave is breathing," Nicky said softly. Her gloved fingers swept over the spiral petroglyphs chipped into the face of the stone. Just like the rocks in the foyer of Peter and Marica Santibanez's condo.

"How much longer?" She edged closer to the hole and peered inside.

Franco consulted his wristwatch. "Nine minutes, twenty-seven seconds. What's it look like?"

"There's a light hung on a metal pin at the bottom of a ten-foot rock tunnel, same diameter as the entrance. It leads to a ladder." Crudely cut poles stuck out above the edge of the passage. "Maybe fifty feet to the floor. Looks like a big cavern."

Franco groaned and rolled onto his side to face her. "Caves? Why'd it have to be caves?"

Acting again, trying to lighten the moment. But he had a very real fear of enclosed spaces—especially caves. Something she'd learned during the Blood Quantum murder case earlier that summer.

She squeezed his shoulder with a gloved hand. "You gonna be okay?"

"Sure, sure." He inched closer, a large coil of pink-and-turquoise climbing rope slung over his shoulder. "At least we don't have to belay down." He tugged his climbing harness. "Nice to have these anyway if it's as steep as it looks. Ready?"

White wisps of mist rose above them and coalesced into sinuous threads curling into the sky. Nicky's vision wavered. She closed her eyes, swamped by doubt, head and heart pounding. "What if I can't pull it off? If it's my fault I lose my mom?" She suppressed hysterical laughter. "And my dad? Again."

"It wasn't your fault they left."

She knew that, but deep down, a childish kernel of doubt threatened.

Her eyes popped open. Franco was close enough to share her breath. In the glow of light from the cave, she traced the laugh lines fanning from his brown eyes, the nose slightly too big and lips slightly too thin, cheeks and squared chin dark with stubble. She nodded in understanding. "This is why you do it. Why you hide. Become someone detached from the emotion of a tough situation."

His lips quirked in a bitter half smile. "But I don't use it as a tool. I use it to dam stuff up. A shrink back in Afghanistan told me that a long time ago, and I didn't want to believe him. But he was right. I'm ... I'm seeing a therapist about it now." He breathed deeply. "Nicky. Don't hide your fear—use it to convince these guys you have the best plan to get them what they want." He checked his watch. "Your father should be in place."

Use my fear. Nicky nodded and pulled herself back to the edge of the Place of Emergence.

"Hey," her voice croaked. *Use my fear.* She took a fortifying breath. "Hey!" Her call echoed as it bounced around the chamber below. "We disarmed. Now what?"

NICKY LANDED LIGHTLY on the packed earth. Like a pink-and-turquoise snake, the nylon cord lay in a scrambled pile at her feet. She glanced up at Franco, who maneuvered his way down the lattice of peeled logs without the use of the climbing rope.

"You! Big man on the ladder. Stop." The voice was harsh and deep and so full of absolute rage that the hair on Nicky's neck prickled. "You on the ground. Don't turn around. Hands on your head. Step back." She laced her fingers on top of her head and shuffled back. "More. *More, goddammit.* Get away from the *fucking* ladder or I will blow his *fucking brains out.*"

Dragging steps approached Nicky from behind, and rough hands ran over her body in a hard, thorough search. At her ear, a second voice said, "She's wearing body armor. I can't tell if she's armed or not. Turn around."

Nicky pivoted and stared into Jacob Jacob's sky-blue eyes. One of the men who worked at the Fire-Sky Resort and Casino's concierge. Her gaze flitted behind him. Jacob's friend, Breedan Halloran, ground the muzzle of a gun into the top of Ryan's head. Ryan knelt at Halloran's feet, hands behind his back, his handsome face bruised and bloodied, eyes blazing.

Jacob hobbled away. Nicky dropped her gaze to his heavily bandaged thigh.

"Was it you who shot me, bitch?"

"No."

Jacob raised a gun to Franco's back. His finger tightened.

"He didn't, either!" Her voice shook. "We left the person who shot you on the ridge with the man you wounded. I swear."

"What about the guy who rode away?"

Nicky shook her head. "There's only the two of us."

Jacob shoved the muzzle of the gun under her chin. *"Where's the other man?"*

Nicky swallowed, using her fear to make her lie believable. "I don't know! We found the note—my mom—" Acid tears burned down her cheeks.

Jacob lowered his weapon. "Take off your vest."

With shaking hands, Nicky unclipped her harness. Jacob yanked it away. She pulled her heavy sweater and long-sleeved base layer over her head and tossed them to one side, then unfastened the light body armor and pitched it onto her clothes. A dri-fit T-shirt covered her black sports bra. Hands clasped on top of her head, she pivoted slowly, her gaze searching the dark overhangs in the huge cavern. She found her mother and Dean MacElroy half hidden in the shadows. Howard, a dark silhouette, stood alone on a shingle of rock at the edge of a swiftly flowing underground river that seemed to disappear into the curved rock wall of the cave.

"On your knees. Cross your ankles," Jacob ordered. Nicky dropped and complied. "You, on the ladder. Come down slowly." He leaned toward Nicky, face white and hard. "If you move, I'll shoot him. I may do it anyway to prove I'm serious."

The creak of wood and trickles of rocks and dirt ended in a thump of boots behind her.

He motioned to Franco. "Strip, including the vest."

Clothing rustled.

"Hey! Get over here," Jacob said.

With the corner of her eye, Nicky caught Howard scuttling toward her, the light revealing one eye swollen closed.

"Search him, Skinny Man." Jacob once again placed his gun against Nicky's head. "And do a good job."

Sweat beaded Nicky's upper lip and forehead as the warmth and humidity of the cave encased her.

Howard patted Franco down. "He has no weapons."

"Get back to your spot." Howard darted toward the river but tripped over Nicky's pile of clothes and sprawled to the ground. Jacob sneered at Howard's tangled limbs but quickly focused his attention back to Franco. "On your knees," he said. "Breedan. Bring the fireman."

With a vicious yank, Halloran jerked Ryan to his feet and shoved him forward, instructing him to kneel to the left of her. Jacob limped to one side, gun still trained on Nicky, giving Ryan a wide berth. He eased down to sit on a smooth altar-like stone. From his new position, he covered all of them—Ryan, Franco, and Howard, who was back on his shingle.

Ryan turned and dropped to his knees. "Savannah shot that bastard?" he asked. "That's my girl."

"*Shut. Up,*" Jacob said to Ryan. Then he stared down at Franco. "I have a few questions, and if you answer them correctly, I won't kill you. I know why she's here." He gestured to Nicky with his gun. "We've got her mother. Why didn't you run, Big Man? Go get help?"

"Because she's my partner," Franco said.

Jacob smiled. It wasn't nice. "From the gossip I've heard, she's a little more than that. Isn't that right, Uncle Dean?"

Uncle Dean.

Nicky flinched, blood draining from her face. She'd called him that as a child growing up. Thought of him as a father figure. Trusted him. Now, all of her unspoken suspicions were laid bare. Dean MacElroy was the third bad guy.

Dean led her mother out from under the overhang and into the light, hand tight on her arm, a small silver revolver held to her mother's side. Helena gave Nicky a tentative, brave smile and mouthed, *I'm okay,* but her eyes were smudged purple with exhaustion.

Dean's expression was strained. "Nicky, did he speak with you? Is he still here?"

Did Dean know—or suspect—her father was somewhere in the caves? She drew her brows together in mock confusion. "Who?"

"The man called Jimmy Che'chi. He's the one who treated Rémy Tioux's wife with medicine made from the plants. He *must* know where they are. *He must know.*" Dean's voice spiraled.

"*You said the nun would know,*" Halloran roared. "How do we find those damned plants if she doesn't?" He waved his gun, and Dean cringed back. "Plants that turn babies into clones. Plants that are *supposed to make us rich.* That's what you promised, isn't it, *Uncle Dean?*" The rage was back in his voice.

Dean, eyes wide and pinned on Halloran's red visage, asked, "Where are the plants, Helena?"

"I told you, I don't know."

"Make her tell you." Halloran stabbed a finger at Dean. "Do it."

"Dean, please," Nicky begged. "She said she doesn't know."

Halloran whipped his head to Nicky, training his gun on her chest. "*Shut up!*"

"Uncle Dean?" Jacob said calmly, eyes like blue ice.

Dean licked his lips, gaze skittering back to Helena. He pointed his gun at Helena's head. "Where are they?"

"I don't know."

"*Where are they?*"

"I. Don't. Know."

The echo of the words rebounded off the rocky walls.

"If she doesn't know where they are, then there's no reason to keep her alive," Jacob said, staring at his uncle. "Or any of you."

Dean clamped his trembling jaw tight. He pushed the muzzle of his gun into Helena's temple. Her eyes closed, and her lips began to move in silent prayer.

"*No!* I know where they are," Nicky screamed, barely holding on to the ragged edges of her control. "Please, Dean. Don't hurt her. *Please.*" She lifted her face to him and sobbed.

"You see, Uncle Dean?" Jacob smirked. "All we needed was the right leverage."

"Of course." Hand shaking, Dean lowered his gun, a forced smile flickering on his face. "Tell us, Nicky. Tell us everything."

CHAPTER FORTY-EIGHT

NICKY RAISED A SHAKING hand and pointed to the river. "Down the second opening in the rock wall. But—but it's treacherous. To go through the passage successfully, you'll need a harness and someone strong to hold the ropes of anyone traveling down the tunnel to keep them from being swept away."

Dean studied her. "And how do you know this?"

Had she given too much detail? Was he suspicious?

"Dad. In birthday cards when I was a kid. He'd send me ten dollars and weird ramblings about fertility and flumes."

"Birthday cards." He blinked, then a half smile curved his lips, and his eyes softened. "Ten dollars. Sounds like Michael."

He'd bought it. Relief bowed her shoulders. "Let my mom go. Please, Dean."

Jacob shifted, catching his uncle's attention. The younger man raised his eyebrows, and, after a moment, Dean nodded. When he turned back to Nicky, his expression was masked by belligerence, but underneath...

When had Dean realized he'd lost control of this?

"You actually saved those cards? How sentimental." Dean sneered as he pulled Helena to her feet. "All those attempts on your life to get your mother here. But it was *you* who Michael confided in."

"You. Nun," Halloran said. "Pick up that harness. Put it back on her." He used his gun like a finger and pointed it at Nicky. "Let's send her down that tunnel and see if she's telling the truth."

Nicky slumped further as if in defeat, but internally grim triumph took the edge off her fear. Now she needed to convince Halloran and Jacob to send her mother with her to the Fire-Song room.

"Dean, please. You were Michael's best man. You and Maureen were Nicky's godparents. Why are you doing this?" Helena clutched Nicky. Even in the warmth of the cavern, her hands were like ice.

He looked back and forth between Helena and Nicky, and the mask slipped. "You have to understand, after the Fire-Sky council announced I would be replaced by Lionel Hand, I had nowhere to go, no money, no job prospects because of my age." His voice was thin and quavering, his eyes glistening. "The only thing I had was Michael's odd abstract about human parthenogenesis and the pots you sampled. *I* could repeat those experiments; I could find the parthenogenic compound. Find the actual plant. It would be a boon to mankind, and I would never have to worry about money again." He ran an agitated hand through his fringe of hair. "But you wouldn't return my calls or texts, Helena, so I decided I could do this myself. I called my nephew—my sister's boy. You remember Patricia?"

Helena slid the harness over Nicky's shoulders. "I remember her calling her *boy* an opportunistic ne'er-do-well," she said under her breath.

Nicky heard Franco snort. Dean cringed, and Jacob narrowed his eyes.

"H-he was between jobs, and he and his … Breedan agreed to come and help for a cut of the profits. But the labs I sent the scrapings to couldn't replicate your data. So I sent Jacob and Breedan into the pueblo's sacred places, places I would've kept secret for the rest of my life, but my abrupt dismissal made me feel like it was so much misplaced loyalty. After all I've done for this tribe. After all I've sacrificed..." He stared blankly over Nicky's head. "They found nothing. Every path led to a dead end.

"Then Rémy Tioux dropped right in my lap with his little girl's DNA test." He blinked as if waking from a dream, and a slow smile creased his face. "I thought it was a mistake—that the mother's sample had been accidently run twice—but Tioux was adamant that the results were connected to the fertility medicines the clinic in Santa Fe was giving his wife. Charlotte unwittingly solved the puzzle. We were setting up the fertility exhibition, and she asked me what it meant." Dean's eyes seemed to glow with an eerie inner brilliance, an odd contrast to the strain etching his face.

"What meant?" Helena asked.

"'The mother of one is the sister of the other.' Genetic twins. Clones issued forth from the Place of Emergence because of a fertility medicine created and lost by the Fire-Sky People. But it wasn't lost. Raven Tioux's DNA test finally made sense. Someone had found the source and was harvesting and using it."

"I never believed it was Charlotte who took the second scrapings from those pots," Franco said.

"Poor Charlotte. No, that was only a lure, like putting Michael's ring on Rémy Tioux's finger. You used to play with it when you sat in your father's lap as a child, Nicky. Except you didn't recognize the ring, and you refused to call your mother." He swallowed and sent a glance to Jacob. "That's when Jacob and Breedan decided to resort to more ... drastic measures."

"No. That's when you decided, old man," Breedan said. "You were playing your stupid games when I'd already staked out her house and knew her routine." He leaned toward Nicky and held her gaze. "Followed her on early morning runs, ready to grab her—"

"Except all you did was clue her in something was up," Jacob said. He shifted his leg, grimacing. "When you messed with her security lights, she'd already stationed a man in her backyard."

Javier, courtesy of Luna Guerra. He'd probably saved her life that night.

"That stupid deadfall branch was your idea," Breedan shot back.

"We could've shot her from the trees—that would've brought her mother back home. But *no*, you and Dean wanted it to look like an accident. What the fuck did it matter? We'd already killed Tioux."

"This again?" Jacob rolled his eyes. "We murder a cop, and the whole world comes crashing down on our heads."

"Damn straight," Franco said.

"Like a thousand of brick," Ryan added.

Breedan swelled with rage. "*Shut up.*" He turned to his friend, his teeth gritted and eyes glossy with moisture, pleading. "Jacob. She pulled a gun. She could've *killed* you. And now you've been shot."

"You should've called your mother, Nicky. Why didn't you?" Dean said. "*I* was the one leaving messages and texts telling her how worried I was that someone was trying to harm you. Still nothing. One word from you, and she..." He stopped, eyes widening. A slow smile wreathed his face. "You figured it out, didn't you? After the logs at the murder site, *you figured it out*. It was such a gamble, but I knew you were too thorough, too responsible not to investigate. And I was right because I know you, Nicky. I know you very well."

He gave her a gentle, avuncular smile, one she'd seen on his face so many times over the years, and her chest ached. She'd held on to Dean because he was a link in a chain to her parents. But he'd never really understood her or the on-and-off relationship with her mother and depth of her hurt. She pushed her sentiment away.

"How did you know when we'd be there?" Nicky asked.

"An aftermarket tracking device. Póncio has them on all his rentals," Jacob said. "We put one under your vehicle at the casino, did the same thing to follow Tioux."

"That log trap wasn't even necessary. My mother was already on her way."

"Yes, but it gave us something just as valuable. Leverage." Dean gestured to Franco. "This man saved you from going over that cliff, risked his life for you." He licked his lips, eyes once again darting to Breedan and Jacob. "Would you be willing to do the same for him?"

First, they'd threatened her mother, now Franco. What if her father and Franco were wrong? What if she couldn't save anyone? A crashing wave of fear paralyzed Nicky.

Her mother wrapped her arms around Nicky's shoulders.

"Hold up," Ryan called. "I'm totally confused. I thought your leverage over Nicky was her mother. Didn't you, Franco?"

"Yeah. I thought that," Franco answered in his dumb-jock voice. "Why are you switching?"

"I mean, it makes no sense. They haven't even slept together," Ryan said.

"For God's sake, Ryan," Franco hissed. "Nicky's mother's right there."

The clowning interruption broke her paralysis. Nicky threw Franco a glance, catching his wink back at her. She exhaled the breath she'd been holding and straightened her spine. She could do this.

"We're switching because we have the guns, asshole," Jacob replied. His face was the color of parchment, and blood trickled down the side of his leg, puddling next to his foot.

"And since you're all in full-confession mode, could someone explain why you murdered Rémy Tioux?" Ryan asked.

"Uncle Dean wanted to know who supplied the plants to the fertility clinic. We followed Tioux to that shrine to ask nicely, but he wouldn't cooperate. His neck got broke." Jacob shrugged. "I mean, it happened accidently. Uncle Dean panicked. Told us to dump him at that tank. Said it was a prime spot for gang executions, and everyone would think Tioux got crossways with some thugs. Except someone was already there, so we took him to the museum. Uncle Dean came up with the rest to get your mom here—the hand, the ring. He figured she would know where the plant was."

"How'd you end up at Fry Bacon Ridge?" Franco asked. "You only got the map yesterday."

Jacob shot Franco a smug look. "Me and Breedan have been scouting different sites since we've been on the pueblo," he said. "Once we had the map and knew where to start, we put our plans in motion. We'd already bribed a guy at the stable, and—"

"*God almighty*, will you two *shut up*?" Halloran gestured wildly with his gun. "Can't you see they're stalling? We need to get that plant and get Jacob to a doctor or he might *die*." The last word came out on a sob.

"Doctors have to report gunshot wounds to the police," Ryan volunteered.

Halloran's skin mottled red. Teeth bared, he rushed at Ryan and pressed the gun to the middle of his forehead. Ryan's eyes went flat and cold. "One more *fucking* word—"

Helena's "*No*," was accompanied by a tightening of her arms around Nicky and a shuffle of Franco's feet. Nicky tensed, ready to back Franco up—

Dean raised a shaking hand before he remembered to level his gun. He pleaded, "Franco, Nicky, *don't*."

"Breedan! Think for a minute." Jacob jabbed his gun at the river. "The current's too fast because of the storm. With my leg, I'm not gonna be able to pull back anyone who goes into the water. We need that guy."

Halloran pulled the gun away, but he was a ticking time bomb.

Jacob turned to Nicky. "What do you know about the tunnel?"

"It's about a hundred feet long, but it branches. To the left is the *tsiba'ashi y'uuni*. The Fire-Song room. The plant that's used for the fertility medicine is in there."

"And the right side?"

Nicky sniffed and wiped her eyes. "I don't know."

Halloran scowled. "He put this in birthday cards?"

"The Fire-Song room?" Helena interrupted, an arrested expression on her face. "I know that name. Michael talked about it and—and orchids, but that was so long ago." Her brow puckered, then cleared. "Protocorms. The parthenogenic compound is in the protocorms. Michael speculated that it was the interaction between the plant and a specific mycorrhizal fungus that creates the compound. I remember! You have to harvest the protocorm."

Nicky stared at her, openmouthed. Howard. He must've relayed Lionel Hand's plan after he'd given himself up. Did she know her husband was still alive, too? "What's a protocorm?"

"Why can't she just dig up a bunch of plants?" Jacob asked. "We'll put them in dirt and grow them."

"Orchids. I didn't—it's not that simple," Dean said. Bright blue eyes stared hard at Helena.

"No," she said firmly. "They won't be able to grow outside the Fire-Song room."

Nicky swiveled to her mother. "Tell me what to look for."

"That's just it. Protocorms are different for every orchid. I won't know until I see them."

"*You're* not going," Nicky declared loudly. She tightened the harness. "I'll harvest whatever I can find and bring it back. You show me the protocorm, I'll go back—"

"They're stalling again," Halloran said. "We have to get out of here before the cops show up. I say send her and her mother. Together."

Jacob heaved himself up. "If we send them both, they could just as easily stall in the orchid cave."

With narrowed eyes, Halloran shifted his gaze and stared at each of the hostages: Nicky, Helena, Franco, Ryan, and Howard.

"Not if they know we're serious." He raised his gun and fired.

Howard jerked, eyes blinking in shock. He clutched his chest and slowly toppled backward into the river.

CHAPTER FORTY-NINE

"I DON'T SEE Howard's body. What if he got sucked into the flume? What if he—" Nicky's voice caught. She stood on the spit of rock where Howard had been shot. She couldn't stop crying. *Not Howard.* Dark water swirled inches from her feet, mist and steam rising above the roiling black surface.

Franco, eyes red, his face wet with tears, leaned his forehead onto hers briefly before he clipped a carabiner, attached to the pink-and-turquoise rope, onto her climbing harness. "Don't think about it." He glanced over his shoulder. Dean and Halloran stood about twenty feet away, talking in low tones to Jacob. "Ryan and I will be on this end of the rope. Remember, keep to the *right.*"

Lying about the location of the Fire-Song room was only one small way they hoped to gain time to escape.

Ryan finished harnessing Helena and used a rope clamp to attach her carabiner leash ten feet behind Nicky.

"Hey," Jacob said. He held up a waterproof pouch before tossing it to Franco. "There's a walkie-talkie and extra bags for the plants."

"Dean? We'll need something to dig with," Helena said, wiping at her eyes.

The three bad guys put their heads together, Halloran whispering fiercely before Dean pulled out a small pocketknife. His back to Jacob and Halloran, he caught Nicky's gaze. She narrowed her eyes. Was he trying to help them? Her heart lifted with hope, and she gave him an almost imperceptible nod. He tossed the knife in her direction. It skittered over rocks before it came to rest in a muddy puddle. She fished it out. Barely two inches long, but it could be useful in the right hands. Franco opened the waterproof pouch, and Nicky dropped a small rock—which she'd scooped up with the knife—into it instead.

"Put in the wristwatch," Halloran said. "For check-ins."

Franco unstrapped his watch and tucked it in the pouch before zipping it closed and stuffing it into a climbing pack on Nicky's back. He secured her headlamp. Ryan fixed Helena's. Nicky exchanged a glance with her mother, who nodded.

"Okay," Nicky called.

"You get it, right?" Halloran scowled. "If you don't call and tell us what's going on—"

"All we want is the plant, Nicky, Helena," Dean said hurriedly. "After we have it, we'll leave you in this cave—alive. I promise."

"If you try to stall," Jacob continued, ignoring his uncle, "Franco and Ryan will die, and it will be your fault."

A sick choking swamped Nicky. Tears scalded her eyes, and her shoulders shook. Franco wrapped his arms around her. He brought his lips to her ears. "Don't. Getting you and your mom to safety was always part of the plan."

A desperate plan at the probable expense of Franco's and Ryan's lives. They'd already lost Howard. She drew back and stared up at him, his face blurred by her tears. She laid a hand on his cheek. He covered it with his, took Dean's knife from her fingers, and bent his head to kiss her tenderly.

"Be ready," she whispered against his lips, "and don't die. I'll make it worth your while, I promise." She stepped back, holding his gaze with hers. What she saw gave her strength. "Ready, Mom? Ryan?"

Ryan nodded and picked up the rope. Franco grabbed the length behind him and looped it around his back. Nicky switched on her headlamp and took her mother's hand. The men fed out rope from the coil on the ground as she walked into the warm, rushing current, boots filling with water, her mother following. With a measured breath, she wiped her face and squared her shoulders.

Then Nicky stepped into nothing and went under.

NICKY RELEASED her mom's hand, not wanting to pull her down with her, and opened her eyes, her headlamp illuminating surprisingly clear water. She looked down to find the bottom.

That's when she saw them.

Hunched shadows clung to the rock ledges below. Dozens of pairs of glowing red eyes stared back at her from the black depths. One smiled, teeth like daggers, and launched itself toward her, long hair streaming, blackened hands reaching up. Air burst from Nicky's nose and mouth in a scream. She kicked hard, breaking the surface to suck in a huge gasp of air. Something clamped around her ankle and tugged her beneath, but the rope yanked her to the surface again.

"Nicky!" Helena was already at the far wall, standing in waist-deep water, braced in the second channel. She pulled at the rope leashed to Nicky's harness. Nicky kicked the spectral hand away and swam, panic and fear driving her toward the tunnel. The water caught her as it drained into the entrance. She banged into her mother, knocked her off her feet, and they both were swept inside.

The rope tightened again, and Nicky managed to get her feet planted. She grabbed her mother's harness as she slipped by, and held her until Helena, too, got her footing. Nicky wiped water from her eyes, adjusted her headlamp, and peered behind her. She stood about fifteen feet in from the entrance. Water spun past her and rushed down a short drop.

"Are you okay?" she asked.

"I am now. When you went under, it scared the—the *hell* out of me." Her mother's hair was plastered to her cheek.

Nicky smiled. "Mom. Language." She felt a quick, sharp tug on the rope. Franco and Ryan. She cocked an ear, but the sound of the rushing water dampened out voices from the cavern. She tugged back twice, indicating both she and her mother were fine.

"Look." Helena pointed to the smooth wall on their right. About every three feet, hand-sized notches were carved into the rock. "Did your father tell you about those in your birthday cards?"

"I'll explain, but we'd better keep moving," Nicky said. Her head-lamp lit up half a dozen yards of a wormhole flume. She tipped her chin down, sweeping her light over the water, but it only reflected back. If those creatures crawled along the tunnel at their feet, she couldn't see them.

"Dad's not dead." Nicky hooked her fingers in a notch and slid her boots forward on the stone floor. The rope stayed taut behind her, the guys feeding her line with each step. "He's been calling himself Jimmy Che'chi. He's waiting for us in the Fire-Song room."

They inched along, her mother silent. Finally, she asked, "How long have you known?"

"I didn't know for sure until tonight," Nicky said. "Why don't you sound more surprised?"

Her mother hesitated. "His death was always plausible because he was forever mixed up with shady characters and sketchy deals all over the world. But I could never get firsthand confirmation. So I was afraid to open the briefcase, to find out he'd faked his death. I didn't know how I'd feel about it. Didn't want to deal with the repercussions."

"That's why you haven't committed to the church. If he was alive…"

"Technically, Michael and I would still be married in the eyes of the church because it didn't recognize our divorce. A deal-breaker, but not the only reason."

The tug of water on her legs increased. Nicky's light traced the widening tunnel. A wedge of rock divided the flow into two sections.

"Dad said the channel to the left leads to a waterfall into a bottomless pit, so hold on tight." She had to yell over the roar of sound.

"How dramatic. Sounds like Michael."

Once they shuffled past the split, the water slowed, and they quickened their pace.

"How much farther?" her mother asked.

"I don't know." Nicky looked back. "You okay?"

But her mom stared ahead. She'd switched off her headlamp. "Turn your light off."

"Do you see something?" Alarm sharpened her voice. She swiveled the light wildly. Were the creatures back?

"Just do it."

Nicky braced for pitch black and turned off her light. But the blackness didn't come. Instead, an eerie orange glow painted the glistening walls and sheened the water—as if a campfire burned in the distance. She took a step forward, then another, up a gentle rise until the water was only above her knees, then ducked through an opening into a cave smaller than the one from which they'd come...

And gasped.

Dotting the rocky walls and ceiling were flowers, their shape more alien than anything Nicky had ever seen. They weren't large—no bigger than her thumb—with three half-circle petals surrounding a center face with tiny red slits for eyes and a gaping mouth filled with what looked like teeth.

"*Dracula simia.* Monkey-faced orchids," her mother said, voice hushed. "Except..."

"They're bioluminescent," Nicky replied in awe.

Her father stepped from behind a plinth of rock dotted with what appeared to be points of orange flame.

"Hello, Helena. It's been a long time."

The fire orchids flickered, and the room filled with pure golden light.

CHAPTER FIFTY

HER FATHER RUSHED into the water. He and Nicky looped arms around her mother's waist and led her onto a sandy beach, staggering a little at the pull of the rope attachment. It stretched behind them and lay across the top of the sluggishly flowing water, curving upward to the carabiner on Nicky's harness. She gave the rope three hard tugs, the signal they'd made it to the Fire-Song room and received two tugs in acknowledgment. She unclipped her mother's leash, and her mother and father came together in a tight embrace.

"You're too vibrant to live your life in black," Michael said when he pulled away. His hands caressed her shoulders, his gaze roving her features.

"It's a moot point. I don't qualify to be a nun if my husband's alive." Her mother sighed and brushed a lock of hair off his forehead. "You've gotten so thin. You're not taking care of yourself."

"And you've become more beautiful."

The orchids' glow softened as her mother blushed and shook her head. "Always the charmer."

Nicky turned away, more touched than she wanted to be by their reunion. It was a childish dream come true to see them together. In this magical glowing room, the three of them were the fantasy of a family she'd never experienced.

If only there weren't other pressing concerns.

"Mom? The walkie-talkie," Nicky said. "I need to check in with the bad guys. Get out of your harness." The light adjusted to orange again.

Helena hurried to Nicky's backpack and found the pouch. Nicky lashed Franco's watch to her wrist, then pulled out the walkie-talkie.

"Dean? We're in the Fire-Song room," Nicky said. "The orchids ... they're bioluminescent. They change color, like a chameleon. Orange and gold and..." She couldn't keep the wonder from her voice. "It's ... it's amazing. Over."

"The protocorms. Have you found them?" Dean asked.

"Mother's looking now," Nicky lied. "I want to speak to Franco and Ryan." Silence. "Dean? *Dean*." Her emotions flared in fear and anger. The room's glow flashed bright red before the plants settled to a simmering burnt orange. "You promised."

"Don't you trust us?" It was Jacob who answered, a sick smile in his voice. "Say hello, guys."

"I'm fine." Franco's voice sounded distant.

"Me, too," Ryan said.

"We need to unharness, Dean," Nicky said. "The orchids are growing on the walls and ceilings, and I'll have to climb to harvest what we need. Over."

"Nicky, dear?" Dean said. "The clock is ticking. Update us again in ten minutes. If you don't, they'll shoot Franco."

Hands shaking, Nicky switched off the walkie-talkie and quickly slipped out of her harness, fastening it over the rough surface of a rock and tugging on the rope to make sure it was secure.

"Ten minutes isn't enough time. We'll need fifteen, minimum." Michael handed Nicky her Glock. "What's this talk about protocorms?"

"I told Dean it's the only part of the plant with the parthenogenic compound," Helena said.

"No, it's the root—"

"It doesn't matter." Nicky's voice rose, and the flowers' light flared.

"What's going on?" Helena, brows lowered, looked back and forth between Nicky and Michael.

Nicky ignored her. "You two need to get going."

"Two? Nicky, you're coming with us." Michael frowned. "That's what we agreed on."

"Nope. That's what you and Franco agreed on." She faced her father and mother, shoulders squared. "I'm not leaving him or Ryan to die at the hands of those jack-holes." The light from the flowers dimmed, then sharpened to a dayglow pink. "Franco and I tucked the rifle and extra ammo next to the cavern opening, like we agreed. I need you up there when I come back through the tunnel. Franco's waiting for you to fire the first shot before he and Ryan try to take out Halloran and Jacob. Dean's mine."

"No." Michael clutched Helena's hand. "We won't leave our daughter—"

"You're worried about me now?" Nicky laughed. "That's *rich*. How long have you been hiding on the rez, Father? Hiding behind Jimmy Che'chi's name? And yet you never contacted me. Never told me you were alive." White-hot light strobed from the orchids with each word. "And when you died, you didn't send me—your only legitimate child— anything, but you managed to give Charlotte Fields your wedding ring. One inscribed with my"—she hit her chest with a fist, her control at a breaking point—"mother's initials. So, excuse me if I decide to do whatever the *hell* I want. And what in *hell* is going on with these stupid flowers?"

The echo of her voice died away before Michael spoke. "They absorb emotion," he said quietly. "They seem to be especially sensitive to yours. Sweetheart? For what it's worth, I'm sorry."

Everyone was sorry. Her anger drained. She glanced at Franco's watch. "I've got three minutes before I check in. Follow the plan, Dad. Get up to the opening. Franco and I left the guns tucked under the topmost rock petal. I'll stall as long as possible. Please hurry. I'm..." She pulled in a deep breath. "I'm depending on you."

Michael's expression was stark. He nodded.

Helena put a hand on Nicky's shoulder, cupping her cheek with the other. "You got what you wanted. I can't be a nun *or* a sister anymore." The white light shifted to a pale gold.

"You think that's what I wanted?" Nicky pressed her lips tight to keep them from trembling. "We don't have time for this."

"I know," Helena said, brows wrinkled. "And I—we—can't do anything about the past. But if we get out of here safely, maybe we can … I mean, I want to…"

"Well, well. I wasn't expecting this." Dean's voice echoed eerily throughout the Fire-Song room.

The orchids responded with a blood-red glow.

CHAPTER FIFTY-ONE

NICKY SPUN toward Dean's voice, shielding her mother with her body, hiding her gun behind her thigh. Submerged to his waist in swirling waters, Dean stood inside the tunnel entrance, a dark silhouette.

"After your description, I had to see it for myself." Unabashed awe infused his voice. "This room is spectacular. And because Michael—or should I say Jimmy Che'chi?—is here, I assume there's an easier way in."

Her father stepped to Nicky's side. "The only way out is back through the main cavern. I got here before you."

He was so convincing, Nicky almost believed him. But then, her dad had always been a good liar.

"Dean," Michael said, "let my daughter and wife go, and I'll *give* you the fertility medicine formula."

"But now that the orchids have been found, we don't need any of you. This could be my discovery alone." He shifted a step closer.

"Dean, *please*." Helena held out a hand. "Those boys—they've taken over, they've hurt people. That's not who you are."

"It's not who I was. But now…" Regret flavored his voice. "I didn't mean for this to happen. They got impatient, and things got out of hand."

"Out of hand, Dean?" Nicky said. "You murdered a man and covered it up."

"It was an accident," Dean cried. "We never had any intention to harm that man, but—but *you* ... you should have told me Michael was alive. If I'd known, if you'd trusted me, we could have avoided all this. I thought we were close enough for that, that you were practically a daughter—"

"You broke the law, Dean. And now you're trying to—to justify your actions by blaming me?" Jaw clenched, Nicky took a step toward him but was halted by her mother's restraining hand. "This is all just a convenient excuse to convince yourself—"

"*No.*" Like a child confronted by his lies, Dean shook his head violently. "Jacob's right. He's my family. Not you. You're just like the rest of them. Like the council, the pueblo. You've betrayed me, Nicky. I misplaced my loyalty in you."

As Dean spoke, something crawled along the wall above his head, its long stringy hair dangling inches from his shoulder. He didn't appear to notice, but the flowers did. Their light flickered into an eerie bilious green.

Dean moved closer but kept to the shadows. The entities around him emanated a low hissing buzz that prickled at Nicky's nape. "Breedan is itching to put a bullet in Ryan Bernal's brainpan. He has such rage inside him, stoked by my nephew, I'm afraid. He's in love with Jacob...."

Dean kept talking, but Nicky stopped listening. Her breath shuddered as more creatures stole over the rocky lip of the entrance and into the orchid cavern to perch facedown above the threshold.

"Dear God," her father choked out. Two more rose slowly from the water, long bony fingers gliding over the surface.

Nicky reached for his hand. "You see them?"

"All my life." He clutched her fingers in a steely grip.

"I don't want to do this, but there *must* be consequences. Helena? Give me the walkie-talkie. I need to call in this ... this treachery to

Jacob. Nicky? You choose who'll be first to die—Franco or Ryan?" Dean raised the silver handgun from the shadows.

Nicky dropped her father's hand and stepped into her Weaver stance, Glock leveled at Dean. "Drop the gun. Now."

"*Another lie?*" Dean strangled on the words. "You weren't supposed to have any weapons!"

"Hello?" Helena said into the walkie-talkie. "It's our ten-minute check-in. Dean is here, helping us harvest. We'll come back soon." She carefully placed the walkie-talkie on a flat rock, then smashed it with a stone.

"No!" Dean took a jerky step forward.

"They only had two of those," Helena said. "Now he has no way to contact the others except to go back."

"*Why did you do that?* You're forcing my hand." Dean's voice choked.

"Then stay here. Come with us." Nicky met his anguished eyes. She slowly lowered the muzzle of her gun. "*Please.*"

Dean waivered, his face painted half by shadow, half by the red glow of the orchids. The creatures above him crept closer as he drew in a shuddering sigh and slumped.

"It's too late, Nicky," he whispered and disappeared into the blackness of the tunnel.

"*Dammit.* I thought for a moment—" Helena scowled. "Catch him, Nicky. Your father and I will get up to the entrance."

Michael grabbed Nicky's arm. "Come with your mother and me. We can still save Franco and Ryan."

"Not if Dean gets away." Nicky shook him off and switched on her headlamp. She tucked the Glock in her waistband and splashed into the water, grabbed the rope, and pulled herself hand over hand through the deepening pool. The creatures submerged, and the flowers changed colors, the air glowing bright red-pink. She looked up at the forms above the tunnel opening. Red eyes stared back. One opened its slash of a mouth in a silent scream. Like huge black spiders, they scuttled down the wall and into the flume as she plowed after Dean.

The light from the luminescent orchids died away as Nicky

churned up the tunnel. The skittering black specters kept pace along the ceiling and walls. Nicky pointed her headlamp at one, and the light disappeared into its infinite blackness.

Ahead of her, Dean approached the split in the channel. The need to stop him before he reached the cavern powered Nicky forward, her headlamp beam jerking wildly. Dean stopped and flattened himself against the wall. The light glinted off silver—*his gun.* With mind-numbing swiftness, she was yanked under the water's surface, the double tap of Dean's gunshots muffled. One of the entities, its long hair streaming in the current, stared at her. Its mouth opened.

"Guw'aadzi, sha'au."

Hello, sister. The voice echoed in Nicky's head. She swiveled her gaze all around, skin crawling. More and more surrounded her, all staring, all baring rows of razor-sharp teeth. Then they ... smiled?

And she remembered.

The mother of one was the sister of the other.

Sha'au, n'aaya, koo-mahtz'anyi, Nicky replied voicelessly. *Sisters, mothers, help me. This man is bad.*

"Haa'a." We know. Eyes narrowed to slits, and their grins turned malevolent. *"Bau'shru..."*

Be careful... In a flash, they disappeared.

Nicky pushed off the tunnel floor and burst out of the water, Glock in hand, finger on the trigger, but Dean was already out of her headlamp's range. She shoved the gun back into her waistband and pulled herself along the rope. At the split, black water rushed past her, the sound from the left-hand side deafening. The current had strengthened. She heaved herself forward, past the junction, arms straining with effort. Ten steps, twenty, hand over hand.

A high, shrill scream pierced the air, then a *pop, pop, pop* of a gun. Nicky's heart slammed into her ribs. Had Dean reached the cavern? Had he told Jacob and Halloran? Had they already shot Franco and Ryan? More shots echoed down the tunnel. She surged ahead, panting, crying—

The rope went slack. Nicky staggered back, water rolling her along the wall, her fingers scrabbling for the carved protrusions. Another cry, closer. She seized a handhold, halted her backward slide. Her lamp caught Dean, unanchored, flailing, careening toward her, fighting off the clinging, scrabbling creatures.

He slammed against the far wall, eyes white with terror. "Help me!" His arm outstretched, hand open, Nicky grasped it but couldn't hold on. He flashed past, spinning in the current. Nicky threw herself after him. Rushing water swept her off her feet. She crashed against the rocks, breath whooshing out with pain. Black hands then long skinny arms materialized from the rocks around her, and strong fingers plucked her hair and grabbed her clothes. Heads emerged, eyes burning red. The entities hissed and gibbered as she found her footing. Something slithered against her legs. Her headlamp lit up the pink-and-green climbing rope snaking by. She grabbed it and dove back into the flow.

Dean's head, gray curls plastered to his skull, bobbed ahead of her. "Nicky!"

The black entities suddenly released him and sank under the surface. The roar of sound crescendoed, and Nicky's eyes widened. Water curled over an edge. *The falls.*

"Dean! Catch the rope!" Nicky pushed off the bottom and launched herself toward a large rock to the right of the drop-off as she threw the rope. It looped into the air toward Dean's outstretched arms, but the water sucked him away. Nicky hit the rock, clawed her way up, and drew in the slack as fast as she could to re-throw, but Dean slid over the falls.

"Nicky! *Nicky!*"

She scrambled to the edge of the rock. Dean released a piercing scream as, arms wheeling, body twisting, he fell out of her light and into the black void below.

NICKY DROPPED HER HEAD, reliving the terror in Dean's eyes. She still had to get out of here, get back to the cavern. See if … A sob escaped. If Jacob and Halloran had shot Franco and Ryan or if her mother and father had reached the rifle in time. Even then, the odds weren't good.

Spray from the falls mingled with hot tears. She pushed to her knees. Her tired brain attempted to come up with a way to get to at least the Fire-Song room.

"Hey."

Nicky inhaled at the sound of a voice. She looked around wildly, her headlamp bouncing off glimmering wet rocks. Were the creatures back? But they only spoke Keresan.

"Uh, I'm down here."

Nicky crawled to the edge and looked down. Right below her, clinging to the slippery rocks, his feet resting on a small ledge, stood Howard Kie, eyes blinking against the mist. He'd lost his glasses, and his hair stuck up in clumps.

"They shot you. You're dead." It was a stupid thing to say, but she couldn't think of anything else.

"Your bulletproof vest. When I tripped, I picked it up." He gestured with his chin. "Could you throw me that rope? I think I could climb up with some help."

CHAPTER FIFTY-TWO

NICKY AND HOWARD retreated to the Fire-Song room through an increasingly strong rush of water. She was frantic to leave the caves, but her headlamp had died only a few steps down the path to the back entrance, and they had to backtrack.

Howard touched her arm and pointed to a high-water mark on the walls. "This cave has flooded in the past, and the water level is rising. I hope they come to get us soon." He paused and said gently, "Sergeant? Everything will be over by now. You can't change what has already happened." Then he wandered around, periodically touching a blossom flickering with orange-yellow light.

He was right. She was powerless and could do nothing but wait. Exhaustion crashed through her, and tears seeped from the corners of her eyes. She lay down, the sandy shore of the Fire-Song room warm against her back.

What if Franco was already dead? She'd been a fool and a coward, looking for excuses to push him away. What if Ryan's daughter had to grow up without a mother *and* a father? Could Nicky help her navigate that difficult world? What if her own mother and father disappeared from her life again? *What if …*

Light altered around her. The fertility orchids transitioned from orange to gold to a rich cobalt blue, pulsing against the walls and ceiling, wrapping Nicky in their calming glow.

Soothed by the light and sound of water lapping against the sand, cocooned by the warmth of the room, she relaxed, and her thoughts unspooled.

The creatures had crawled back into the Fire-Song room and tucked themselves into dark nooks on the rocky walls, hanks of hair veiling their eyes, watching. Bathed in the blue light, they looked different. It blunted and softened their faces and gave tone to the skin of their arms and legs. Maybe they were the spirits of children lost at birth, waiting to emerge into the outside world. To change from who they were to someone new.

Would this place change her the same way?

She slipped into a restless doze, with dreams and nightmares of being held under water until she stopped fighting.

"Wake up, sweetheart."

Nicky swam from the depths. Her lashes fluttered open, and she blinked up into her father's deep-set eyes. He didn't look anything like the bluff, hearty man she remembered from her childhood. He'd changed, too, but who was he now?

Panic flooded her. She levered up, pulse pounding. "Ryan? Franco?" The light intensified to electric blue. The creatures scuttled like beetles up the wall to halt at the high-water mark.

"Everyone's fine, except the two kidnappers."

A muscle-melting wave of relief hit her so hard her head swam.

"Your friend Savannah and another conservation officer—Pep Katina—got to the opening before your mother and me. Pep winged one of the men—the large one—and somehow Ryan got hold of a small knife. The biggest guy has a bullet wound *and* looks like a pin cushion." He shook his head. "The one shot in the leg threw down his gun and gave himself up. Franco hog-tied them before your mother and Ryan treated their wounds. Ryan said both men would live."

"You let Mom go back down in the cave?"

The light flickered purple as the orchids closest to Nicky turned red. The spirit creatures' eyes burned brighter. Some bared their teeth.

Her father's breath caught as his gaze darted around the room. His voice shook a little when he answered.

"I couldn't stop her. I never could. Besides, her clothes and boots were wet, and it's warm in the cave. She's safe with your friends. She's the one who, uh, ordered us to find you."

"Us?"

"Franco and me. He's waiting at the back entrance with horses and dry clothes. He wanted to come but appears to have a problem with caves. The tunnel to the Fire-Song room is confining in spots."

He rose and extended his hand. She ignored it and pushed to her feet.

"He's close?" Brows puckered, Nicky peered into the darkness of the escape passage.

"Close enough." Her father paused. "I'd like to get to know that young man better, since he appears interested in my daughter. Notwithstanding his claustrophobia, I approve."

"You don't get a vote anymore." But it was funny how his words warmed her. "What about Lionel Hand? Savannah didn't just leave him." The blue light morphed to pink.

"Apparently Pep and another officer rode ahead of the main search party and found them a few hours after you left. Savannah insisted on following you, and Pep insisted on going with her. They left Lionel with the extra officer." He cleared his throat, his gaze darting around the room. "It seems that the orchids respond to you, as do the creatures. I didn't realize there were so many."

"They helped me when I asked, and probably saved my life."

"Because you were here with your mother, I imagine."

Mother, sister, daughter. They will protect you. Lionel Hand's words made sense now.

"They've been more active since the medicine garden desecrations started."

And since the fertility pots had been scraped again. Maybe that's why she'd had her first vision during the museum walk-through the night of the murder.

"They only tolerate me when I've come to harvest," Michael

continued. "I think because the medicine creates more children. That's what they are, you know. All little girls, apparently. Did you know geneticists have determined we all start out as female embryos?" He licked his lips and leaned closer, his voice a whisper. "They hang around birthing niches."

"I know. The first time I saw one was in that arroyo. When you left me and went off with one of your students."

Michael picked up her hand and held it between his palms. "I've regretted that every moment of my life. That day, with my selfish actions, I lost you. No matter what happens, I want you to know that I'm sorry."

She tugged her hand away and eyed him warily. "What do you mean, 'no matter what happens'?"

His gaze held her, but his smile was sad. "You are so much like your mother."

"I seem to have inherited a few things from my father." A warning yellow light bathed the walls, and the listening creatures around them shivered into the deepest black. "You're leaving again, aren't you?"

Her father sighed and looked away. "I'll take you close enough to the exit of the cave so you'll get out safely."

"You mean you'll abandon me like you did before." Any warmth she'd felt earlier dissipated.

"No. This time, you won't be alone. Someone's waiting for you."

She faced him, fists clenched at her side.

"Why are you leaving?"

"Nicky, sweetheart, I'm a wanted man, by multiple governments, some not very nice. I've done things—"

"I don't want to know."

Nicky almost laughed when his face fell. Did he want her to see him as some international outlaw? Want to impress her?

"How did you know about Dean and those two men? How did you know to follow them?"

"I didn't. I was shadowing your mother. Gathering the courage to speak to her, to tell her—" Michael blew out a long breath. "I saw Dean and those men kidnap her and Ryan Bernal. Then Howard climbed in the horse trailer. He must've seen me because he called—"

"How do you even *know* Howard?"

"He hired me to help him get rid of a spirit who lived under his trailer. It, uh, turned out to be a pack of feral dogs." Michael smiled. "When he said he knew you, I may have asked him too many questions, and he guessed. I asked him to keep my identity a secret."

Howard, who'd been standing behind him, nodded. "I knew Michael was watching over your mother, because I was watching over her, too."

"Once Howard explained about the kidnapping, I realized there was no time to waste and contacted Lionel. You see, I've been staying with his family up on Scalding Peak." Her father gestured to Howard. "Before he lost cell signal, Howard told us to meet him with my horses and gear at Fry Bacon Ridge. It was my jump-off point when I came here to harvest. He filled us in when Lionel and I arrived, and we contrived a plan. Lionel was to give himself up and lead them into the Place of Emergence. We'd try to rescue Helena and Ryan once he was inside."

"I tried to run off Dr. MacElroy's horses so they couldn't leave," Howard said from behind him. "But they shot at me. Instead, I took one of their mules, which was good. Michael and Lionel only brought two horses."

"Since the kidnappers knew someone was onto them, they left immediately, even though it was still dark. We followed at a safe distance and tried to flank them in the valley. That's when they ambushed us, and Lionel was shot."

Their story filled in gaps and overlapped with what she knew. But Nicky had so many more questions burning inside her.

"You masqueraded as Jimmy Che'chi for years, and you never let me know you were here," she said.

"I thought about it a lot—telling you I was here, I was alive. But I owed Lionel Hand. I was desperate when he hired me as a curator at the Smithsonian, altered documents so my real identity stayed hidden. Then we devised a way for him to continue our research on traditional medicines by placing me on the pueblo as a-a family member, which meant..."

"Which meant you were pretending to be Native," Nicky said, her voice hard. "How could you *do* that? It's a betrayal of the Fire-Sky People, their culture—"

"It was wrong, I know, but I never claimed to be a member of this tribe, or any tribe. I just let everyone assume I was. The *Hemis* Medicine Man, not Jemez. But, sweetheart, if what Lionel did to help me—to fool the tribe—is ever discovered... He would lose whatever standing he's regained with his People." Michael sighed. "He asked me to keep it a secret from you, and it was easier to hide than to deal with the pain I'd caused. Always has been." He ran a shaking hand over his hair.

"Then Dean hired Charlotte," he continued. "Lionel came back to the pueblo, and the garden desecrations started up. Something didn't feel right. And when your mother showed up out of the blue..." He lifted somber eyes to Nicky. "When I heard the man was murdered at the shrine, I went there. I was in the trees by the garden when you and Franco showed up. I watched you. I was about to leave when I heard the logs—I didn't see anyone else, though. It was me who dropped the climbing rope. I keep a couple in my saddle packs in case I need to gather plants growing in difficult places. I was experimenting with different medicinal plants to see what would grow in the gardens, you see. Plants I needed—" He stopped, lips pressed together like he'd said too much.

"Plants you needed for the medicines you gave those women at the fertility clinic." Nicky's voice rose. "You were experimenting—"

"No. I was helping women at the clinic get pregnant, be happy, have a family, maybe because I've brought so much misery to the women I've loved through the years. Because children bring joy. The medicine works to increase natural fertility if it's used properly, and I needed the money." Face tight, he glanced at the shoreline. "The water's rising fast. We need to leave."

"The ring, Dad. You sent it to Charlotte, not me. Why?"

His lips pursed, and his expression bordered on petulant. "You never asked me for anything, even returned the birthday cards I sent you. You didn't need me. You had your grandmother. Were happy without me. Your mother didn't need me, either. At least, not in the way I wanted. But you need me now." His jaw firmed, and he lifted his chin, but uncertainty lingered in the depths of his gaze.

Nicky blinked at him, seeing her father for what he truly was. *He wants to be the hero.* He'd never accepted Helena's success because it took the spotlight from him. He'd wanted a wife to fit to who *he* was, to prop him up, adapt to *his* wants. Instead, Helena tried to change him, forced him to make promises he couldn't keep. And Nicky had followed in her mother's footsteps. Before Franco came into her life, she'd chosen a charming, handsome narcissist, thinking she could change him, too, and their relationship had been a disaster.

But change couldn't be forced. It had to be voluntary. And loving someone meant accepting who they were and who they might always be.

Nicky stared at her father, understanding him a little better. Forgiveness would take a lot longer.

"You're right," she said simply. "I need you now."

His stiff shoulders melted, and he smiled. "Let's go. Franco's waiting."

Her heart leaped, and the flowers glowed blossom pink.

Michael fitted a headlamp over his head. He handed a second one to Nicky and paused. "Dean?"

She shook her head.

"Could I have a headlight?"

"I'm sorry, Howard, I don't have an extra," her father said. "I didn't expect you."

"No one ever does." He scratched his ear. "I'll stay behind you, Michael, and lead Sergeant Matthews. I owe her my life."

Nicky straightened, alarmed. Saving a person's life had special meaning in the Fire-Sky culture. "No, you don't. I absolve you of that burden."

Howard smiled and shook his head pityingly. "It's not that easy."

Then he breathed deeply and pivoted slowly, staring at the Fire-Song room. "Access will be blocked with the rising water."

"Yes. For a while," Michael replied. He ducked under the overhang of rock and into the back way out of the cave, his light blazing into the passage before him.

Nicky took one last look at the creatures perched above her. "*Dawaa'e, ga'au*," she said, her voice a whisper. *Thank you, sisters.* Light from the fertility orchids intensified to a blinding white that swamped out the spirit creatures' swirling blackness. When it dimmed, they were gone.

She and Howard followed her father out of the orchid cave through a serpentine passage so narrow in places they had to crawl. Spirals carved into the rock acted as markers. Nicky illuminated each one with her headlamp, fingers brushing over them.

Michael stopped at a juncture of two passages, one gray with diffuse light, the other obsidian. He pointed into the darkness.

"This is where we part. I need to get going before it fills with water," he said, his face stark in Nicky's headlamp. "Pep Katina said the FBI was flying in helicopters. They should be here at dawn." He waved a hand toward the light. "Soon."

Nicky stared into the tired, red-rimmed eyes of her father.

"Running from problems in your life can be exhausting," she said.

He chuckled. "I don't need a lecture from my daughter. If I could've changed, I would have a long time ago."

She didn't believe him for an instant.

His expression softened. "If nothing else, I wish I could've been the father you needed."

Nicky didn't reply.

"Well. I guess I should go." He hesitated, nodded, then turned to leave.

"Daddy?"

He turned back, and Nicky threw her arms around him. When she let go, his eyes were wet, and she blinked away tears of her own.

"If you need anything..." She choked.

"You'll hear from me. Howard?" Michael extended his hand, and the two men grasped and held each other's wrists. "Thank you." He strode down the dark passage. Nicky and Howard waited until the light from his headlamp faded to complete darkness.

"You should've told me, Howard."

"About your father? It was not my secret to tell." Howard sniffed. "Besides, sometimes you learn more when secrets are kept."

"That doesn't even make sense. Come on. Let's find Franco and some dry clothes."

"It's a new day," he said portentously and followed her toward the light.

"Do you know where my dad's going?"

"Yes. But it's a secret between me and your father. What did you see in the tsiba'ashi y'uuni room? Were there spirits?"

"Sorry. Can't tell you. It's a secret between me and my sisters."

"You have only one sister."

Nicky smiled and hurried down the tunnel.

THE BACK ENTRANCE was well hidden under a rocky overhang guarded by a thick copse of bushy pines. Two horses and Howard's mule were strung on a highline, their packs unloaded and piled in a dry section of the cave, a thermos nestled on top.

Franco paced outside the entrance. His head snapped up and found her, and he rushed to her and swept her into a strong embrace. Her arms twined around his waist and held him for a long moment.

Still holding her, he leaned back and grinned. Then his face softened incrementally until all she could see was his soul, golden light shining from inside him.

"You found Howard," he said.

"Yep." Her throat was tight. "Long story."

"Later, then." He looked around. "You know, we've got to stop meeting like this."

"Yeah. My fault for wanting you to change when I know how much you hate caves." Nicky captured his gaze. "I've pushed too hard, and I'm sorry."

"Stuff I needed to hear." He smoothed his thumb over her cheek. "Besides, I wouldn't have hung around unless I was willing to try."

A distant throbbing announced the arrival of the rescue helicopter.

Nicky cupped Franco's face. "If you're willing, that's all I can ask."

He leaned down and kissed her.

CHAPTER FIFTY-THREE

"ARE WE DONE?" Nicky shifted in an uncomfortable chair she was sure Agent Song had brought in specifically for this interview. Her third one in the last seven days.

Song, who'd been typing on her computer for the last five minutes, looked up, a single eyebrow raised. "I have a few more questions," she said and continued typing.

Nicky knew she was being punished for cutting the FBI out of the loop in the kidnapping, even though Chief Richards had justified the action to the Feds. They'd had to move fast and with stealth because of the threats against the hostages. Adding an extra layer of law enforcement would have bogged them down.

She hunched in her chair, her thoughts souring. Franco. Running from her. Again.

As if Song could read her mind, she asked, "When will Agent Martinez return from leave?"

Like Song didn't know.

"Not sure," Nicky said.

She, her mother, and Howard had climbed into the helicopter while Franco, Ryan, and Pep had volunteered to bring back the horses. Initially, with the chaos of crime-scene cleanup, Franco's absence hadn't worried her. Then she'd gotten a text from him saying he was going to Arizona for a family visit. Then, nothing. That had been a week ago with no reply to her tentative messages. After her third unanswered text, she'd stopped trying. It hadn't helped that rumors flying around the department speculated he was about to tender his resignation because he'd been recruited back to the DEA at a much higher pay grade. She swallowed against a tightness in her throat that wouldn't go away.

"Let's talk about your father," Song said.

Nicky straightened in the chair, wincing at a twinge in her shoulder. She'd reinjured it trying to save Dean.

"We tracked him to the border."

"Which one?" Nicky asked.

"Mexico. We know he has contacts and friends in South America." She pushed a picture of a tall, thin man in a baseball cap toward Nicky.

Nicky picked up the photo. It certainly did look like her father. A lot. But it wasn't.

Notwithstanding his dramatic farewell down the tunnel, Michael had shown up at her door the first night Nicky and her mother had been back at home, hat in hand, needing a place to lie low. Nicky had called in a favor. Luna Guerra—aka Chen Cano—had assured Nicky and her mother she could hide Michael in plain sight. For all Nicky knew, he was working as a janitor for the FBI somewhere in this building. What was more surprising was how well her mother, the almost-nun, and Luna, the ruthless leader of an international drug cartel, got along. Helena had even babysat Luna's son and niece one evening at Nicky's house. Nicky, fully armed and on alert, had assisted.

But her mother was leaving to go back to Rome after the christening of Ryan's daughter that coming weekend.

"If you have any idea where he is, Sergeant Matthews—"

"I don't, and I've told you I didn't even know he was in the area until the operation at the Place of Emergence."

Song attacked from a different direction. "We still need to find Dr.

MacElroy's body."

"And I've explained a dozen times that's impossible."

"Why won't the Fire-Sky Tribal Council let us inside that place?"

Nicky sighed. She'd explained that a dozen times, too. "It's sacred for them. It's something all non-Native officers have to understand when they work on the rez—some places are off-limits. It's why the tribe tries very hard to train and hire its own People."

Song dropped her gaze. Her fingers smoothed over the manila file folder that held the bogus pictures of Nicky's father. "What if it's someone who's ... First Nation? What if it was someone who was born on the Diné Reservation to a Diné mother?"

The hum of the fluorescent lights filled the silence.

"You know it's not that simple, especially if this person wasn't raised in the culture," Nicky said. She glanced at the picture of Song with her adoptive parents. "Why hasn't this ... someone ... informed the FBI of their heritage?"

"Because it would place her in a diversity box and stir up resentment among the rank and file. It's difficult enough being a woman in law enforcement."

Nicky nodded in assent. She'd been accused of sleeping with a powerful man to get to her rank so quickly and had to work twice as hard to prove her worth. "It might also get her promoted."

"Because of her genetics?" Song's lips twisted. "She'd rather move up by merit. Besides, a promotion would come with a transfer. This someone's decided to stick around the area. Maybe one day she'll have the courage to visit her mother's family in Shiprock." She sighed and squared the folders on her desk. "The DNA finally came back on the rope that tied Rémy Tioux's wrists. Positive for both Jacob and Halloran. More evidence against them."

"I heard they've been transferred to a federal facility, and that they're making noises about suing the tribe for excessive force." Nicky smiled. "Good luck with that. Tribal council has to give permission for any lawsuits against them, and I don't think that will happen." She stood. "You were adopted, right? I was raised by my grandmother after my mom and dad left. Maybe we can have coffee sometime—and talk, especially since my parents have recently come back into my life."

Song sat back in the chair. "Why?"

Nicky shrugged on her jacket. "Maybe because my parents' return helped me understand that what I resented for so many years—their leaving—might have been the best thing they did for me. Even if I'm still not quite there yet." She handed Song a business card. "My personal cell's on the back."

Song flipped it over and rubbed her thumb over the handwritten number. "Agent Martinez will be back Friday night. He mentioned the christening on Sunday of Ryan Bernal's little girl."

Nicky shoved her hands into her pockets and nodded. Without another word, she pivoted and headed down the corridor, desperate to get outside and breathe fresh air.

CHAPTER FIFTY-FOUR

NICKY PARKED her mother's car in the dusty parking lot outside the old adobe church in Ruby Crest. Next to her, Helena gathered up her bag and the covered casserole dish of green chile lasagna. Cars and trucks brimming with tribe members continued to stream in behind them, all come to celebrate the Catholic baptism and Fire-Sky naming ceremony for Ryan's daughter. As Nicky exited, she lifted her hand to a family who lived next to Ryan in the Mount St. Helens neighborhood. The two young boys, hair slicked flat, swam in pristine black trousers at least one size too big and narrow white dress shirts buttoned to their chins—Sunday best. Their mother carried a covered tray of home-cooked food for the gathering afterward.

Nicky walked around the car to stand by her mother. They both looked out at the vista of fluffy white clouds topping stacked red-and-yellow rock mesas. Chill air warmed in the bright sun, and the sweeping valleys below wore the faded fawns and browns of winter grasses.

"Well?" Nicky asked Helena. "Will you?"

"I'll come back to New Mexico for Christmas, but the rest ... I need to untangle the mess with my marriage and the church, then write a grant to work on the parthenogenic compounds in the *Dracula tsiba'ashi* orchids." She gave a small laugh. "I'm a little surprised tribal council wants to pursue it."

"Dad said there's nothing wrong with the medicine if it's used correctly, which Kristina Tioux finally confessed she didn't—off the record, of course. Agent Song said Kristina isn't cooperating. She's still afraid Raven will have to forfeit her inheritance if the baby's genetics are made public." She'd met Sylvia Song for coffee yesterday morning. Neither had been ready to talk about their childhoods, so they'd discussed the Tioux murder case instead. "That's good for the tribe. They want to suppress any information until your research is up and running. And Savannah told me tribal lawyers have already approached Dr. Summerweaver with a nondisclosure agreement," Nicky said. "She'll sign because she doesn't want to lose her license and clinic."

"I'm glad the tribe trusted me—although I'm sure Lionel Hand had something to do with that. He's home from the hospital?"

"Recovering." The bullet he'd caught had snapped his humerus. "The FBI's pressuring him about Dad and what he knows about his disappearance. Song said he's not talking, either."

Helena shot Nicky a glance. "Did your father ever tell you why he supplied the medicine?"

"He said children bring joy."

Her mother snorted.

"And he needed the money." Nicky gave a resigned shrug before smoothing her blouse. "I, uh, I'm glad Charlotte decided to stay at UNM and finish her PhD. Lionel invited her to continue her internship at the museum." She lifted her gaze to catch her mother's. "Make this your home base. Stay with me when you're in between assignments."

"I'll think about it. I promise." She squeezed Nicky's hand. "You're sure you don't know where your father is? Luna won't tell me."

"I honestly don't." But that didn't mean she expected him to have disappeared forever.

Her mother checked the time on her phone.

"That's too bad. He and I still have a few things we need to settle.

Where's Franco? He should be here already." Franco, Deandra Bernal, and Helena had arranged the dessert, punch, and coffee for after the ceremony and potluck. Helena headed toward the adobe bingo hall, her bright calico broom skirt swishing with each quick step. She'd thrown off her habits for new clothes since she'd been rescued from the Place of Emergence.

"Savannah said he went to Albuquerque to get the cake." He hadn't called Nicky when he'd gotten back to New Mexico. But he'd called Savannah and Ryan. They'd relayed to her and her mother that he'd returned and would see her at the ceremony, but he'd be "busy" on Saturday. She'd shrugged with a feigned nonchalance that had elicited an eye roll from Savannah. "He's a good Catholic choirboy." Sarcasm edged Nicky's tone. "He'll be here."

Helena *tsk*ed. "Don't be ugly. He probably had a very good reason to leave for Arizona after all that happened."

Maybe he did, but not knowing left her feeling like she teetered on the edge of that cliff again, ready to plunge into an abyss. She shook her head in disgust. The chief had offered her time off after the investigation had been turned over to the Feds, and she'd gladly taken it. Why was she upset with Franco because he'd done the same? Maybe because she'd expected him to spend that time with her. Had been sure he would.

And now she wasn't sure of anything.

Helena hurried onto the wide cement sidewalk running alongside the bingo hall and ducked into one of the open double doors. Nicky followed. Two elderly ladies in flowered dresses, their earlobes stretched with heavy silver-and-turquoise earrings, bustled along a white-draped table filled with coffee urns, a crystal-cut plastic bowl brimming with crimson punch, Styrofoam cups, and paper napkins. One end of table was half filled with plates of food brought by guests: a slow-cooker pot full of posole, stacks of fry bread draped in flour-sack towels, and casserole dishes of green enchiladas and husk-wrapped tamales. A large area in the center of the table had been left open.

Nicky's mother gave the lasagna to one of the ladies and ran her gaze over the table. She gave a small, satisfied nod. "All we need is the cake."

"And it's here," Franco said.

Nicky whirled. Her heart froze, then pounded so hard it was all she could hear.

He strode in, a huge cake box perched across his forearms, and gently set it on the table. With deft hands, the two elder ladies opened the box to expose a lavishly decorated cake. They cooed and beamed as they slid it out and arranged napkins, forks, and plates around it.

The two little boys, one with already-mussed hair, the other with mud-spattered trousers, ran inside the hall to press against the table. A sneaky finger extended for a swipe of frosting. Their father rushed in and tugged at their arms, scolding them in Keres as they left.

Franco stood, straight and tense, staring into Nicky's eyes. His charcoal-gray suit hugged his broad shoulders, and tailored slacks covered the muscles of his thighs like a second skin. He'd brushed back his silver-peppered dark hair, his square jaw clean-shaven. A leather-braided bolo tie, cinched with an inch-diameter coral petit-point clasp, bisected a blindingly white shirt. Nicky stared at the ornament. With a trembling finger, she touched her Spirit's Heart pendant at her throat.

Her stomach flipped, shocked at the sudden welling of possessiveness she felt toward him.

"What do you think?" he asked, then cleared his throat.

Her mind scrambled.

"The cake." His eyes were tight, his mouth drawn. "Is it okay?"

Pink and lavender frosting roses piled high and spilled down each corner of the huge white sheet cake. A cherubic plastic baby with pink bows lay, hands folded under her cheek, in a plastic bassinet, and *Bebe's Baptism* was written across the top in dark pink icing.

"It tells me our goddaughter is in for some serious future spoiling."

"That's a given." He stepped toward her, palms up. "Nicky, I'm sorry I left the way I did."

"You're back now." Suddenly, his absence didn't seem so important. Nicky closed the distance between them. She leaned toward him and took a breath. "You smell like cookies."

He gave her a slight smile, and his rigid posture softened. She touched the coral bolo clasp.

"We match," he said, his voice vibrating through her. "I thought since we're the godparents ... Do you like it?"

"Yeah. I like it." She searched his dark brown eyes. "We need to talk."

"I know. After." He leaned closer. Her hand flattened on his chest, and she measured the thump of his heart. As cliché as it sounded, time stood still.

"The ceremony's about to start." Her mother's voice broke their spell.

Franco grabbed Nicky's hand and clasped it tightly. She stared down at their entwined fingers, then turned her face up to his. Her chest swelled with a contented sigh. It felt ... right. The whole world felt right.

"We met for the first time in this same room," he said.

She smiled. "Yeah."

Together, they walked toward the sanctuary, hand in hand, shoulders touching. As Nicky passed her mother, Helena whispered, "Sure you want me to live with you between assignments?" And winked.

CHAPTER FIFTY-FIVE

SAN MIGUEL ARCHANGEL church at the center of Ruby Crest was a stolid yellow-beige structure, the core of its stuccoed walls built with adobe blocks baked in the harsh New Mexico sun over three hundred years ago. It reminded Nicky of the San Esteban del Rey Mission in Acoma Pueblo's Sky City, only miniaturized, with the same blocky bell towers bookending the square, flat face of the entrance. Both of the carved wooden doors were open.

Following Ryan, who held a sleeping Bebe, Nicky and Franco stepped over the threshold onto the dirt floor and into the cool shadow of the vestibule. A steep flight of stairs ran up one side, and a short, closed door was embedded in the wall on the right. A stoup with holy water hung over a table holding a guest book and tourist postcards. Franco dipped his fingers in the water and blessed himself.

The cramped vestibule opened into a nave scented with dust and incense. Enormous hand-hewn beams burnished to a gleaming red brown spanned the high ceiling above. Narrow wooden pews sat perpendicular to whitewashed walls painted with Native American designs in browns, yellows, and reds and hung with the Stations of the Cross. Three square windows, south facing and high, let sunlight inside.

Robed in white with a golden stole, the priest stood at the end of the aisle of pews, hands clasped and smiling. As Ryan passed, attendees stood. Those on the aisle murmured blessings in Keres and touched the baby's soft pink swaddling or Ryan's dress shirt. Ryan's parents waited for their son and granddaughter in the front pew, Helena behind them with Savannah and Howard Kie. Ryan's stepfather, a respected tribal elder, had dressed in traditional garb: soft brown leather leggings over calf-high moccasins, and a cream-colored tunic, his waist elaborately wrapped by a narrow stole woven in the traditional colors of his Antelope Clan. Ryan stopped next to him and his mother. He tucked Bebe close and flung an arm around his mother's shoulders, pulling her in tightly. They stood, enfolded together in silence only broken by tearful sniffs of the congregation. Franco's hand tightened around Nicky's, and her eyes filled, but she blinked back her tears, determined to be strong for her friend.

When Ryan and Bebe continued toward the priest, the only man Ryan had ever known as his father walked proudly beside him. The carved reredos covered the whole back of the church, many of its elements hundreds of years old. A huge pottery bowl filled with water rested on a broad pillar before the altar. The priest caught Nicky's eyes and motioned with his chin for her and Franco to step up. Ryan's father moved to face the congregation, mirroring the priest on the other side of the baptismal font.

With everyone in their place, the priest raised his hands.

"What name do you give your child?" he asked.

"Elizabeth Jinni Bernal," Ryan replied.

The priest nodded to Ryan's father, who, in Keres, said, "What name shall this daughter of the Antelope Clan be called?"

Nicky held her breath. This would be the first time the baby's traditional name would be spoken and announced to her People.

"She will be called Kaacha Magə," Ryan said.

Raining Girl. Beautiful and perfect.

"What do you ask of God's church for Elizabeth?" the priest asked.

"Baptism."

"By asking to have your child baptized, you are accepting responsibility to train her in the practice of the faith, to bring her up to keep God's commandments as Christ taught us, by loving God and our neighbors. Do you understand what you are undertaking?"

"I do," Ryan said.

Ryan's father echoed the words in Keres. "This purification by the sacred waters of our land means you will bring Raining Girl to know the Creator and to love her People. She will be one with her People. Do you understand this undertaking?"

"Haa'a," Ryan replied.

"And to all those gathered to celebrate Raining Girl, will you do the same?"

The congregation's voices lifted and filled the space. "Haa'a."

The priest, gray eyes weighed by the heavy folds of his eyelids, turned to Nicky and Franco.

"Are you ready to help the parent in his duty to this child?"

"We are," she and Franco replied in unison.

"Elizabeth—Bebe. The Christian community welcomes you with great joy. In its name I claim you for Christ our Savior by the sign of his cross." He dabbled his fingers in the water of the bowl. Ryan tugged back the blankets, exposing Bebe's face. With a gentle touch, the priest traced a cross on her forehead. He stepped back, and Ryan's father moved forward to dip his hand in the bowl.

He pressed his cupped palm over her silky dark hair and was opening his mouth to speak when the light in the church changed. A hum of voices started in the pews, breaking the sacredness of the moment, and the whole congregation pivoted in a slow wave to stare down the aisle. Nicky followed their gaze. She exchanged a glance with Franco. He was frowning, just as confused as she was.

Marica Santibanez, her husband Peter trailing behind her, strode toward them with firm steps on the dirt floor of the church. Behind her were Chief Richards, Lieutenant Pinkett, and the social worker Nicky had met during the WhiteHawk case.

"Please stop this ceremony," the social worker said as she sidled to the front of the group. "The father of this child is claiming custody."

Ryan's face went white. "I'm the father—"

"The biological father," the woman said sharply. "Chief Richards?"

Richards stepped forward, face tight, his thin mustache twitching. "I'm sorry, Lieutenant Bernal, I truly am. The birth certificate was challenged. There's a, um, paternity test, and it shows you aren't…"

"That information was taken to an emergency meeting of the Fire-Sky Tribal Council." Marica Santibanez's voice rang out strong. "They have ordered the immediate removal of this baby to her rightful father."

The hum of voices turned into a buzz. Some congregation members looked angrily at the intruders, others sent confused or dark glances at Ryan. Nicky's gaze shot to Savannah. Her best friend's expression was haunted. She stared at Peter Santibanez as if mesmerized.

"Who is the biological father?" The question burst from Nicky's lips.

Marica grabbed her husband's arm and tugged him forward.

"I am," Santibanez said. His eyes slid from one person to another, never resting on anyone. "I would take my daughter."

He stepped toward Ryan, but Franco blocked him, arm raised.

"*No.*"

"Agent Martinez, please." Pinkett extended his hand in a restraining gesture, the dark skin of his shaved head beading with sweat. "I don't want to have to arrest you."

The priest hurried to stand between Franco and Santibanez. "I will not have the sanctity of the church interfered with in such a way. This ceremony is sacred—"

"Except Ryan Bernal sinned," Marica said calmly. "He falsified documents to claim he was the father of this child." She turned to address the congregation, shoulders back, her chin held high. "That man, who is not of our blood, would have claimed—taken—a child of our People like so many others—the church, the state, this country—have done in our past. Can we allow this to happen again? If we do, when will it ever stop?"

Then Marica pivoted to stare straight into Savannah's gray face.

"Thank you, Savannah, for telling me the truth of this child's paternity. If you hadn't, a great wrong would have been committed against our People."

Wide-eyed horror stamped Savannah's expression. "No. You're lying. I-I *didn't*—"

Marica wove her way to Ryan and gently disentangled the baby from his arms. He blinked, as if coming out of a trance, but didn't protest as he let his daughter go, his arms falling slack to his side.

As Marica turned, Nicky stepped in front of her. "Why are you doing this now?" She was surprised at the calm in her voice.

Marica leaned in, and the subtle floral of her perfume mixed with the delicate scent of the sleeping baby.

"There's never a good time to lose a child. Like I lost my son when Ryan Bernal murdered him in that cave." Malice flitted over Marica's expression. "An eye for an eye, Sergeant Matthews. Move out of my way. I'm taking my husband's daughter home."

CHAPTER FIFTY-SIX

NICKY CURSED UNDER HER BREATH. Ryan's red pickup sat haphazardly skewed near the handicap parking spots at the Fire-Sky resort hotel, her mother's silver Mazda parked behind it. She pulled her unit next to Officer Cyrus Aguilar's and cued her mic.

"Two-one-three, Dispatch, arrived resort casino."

She secured her vehicle and strode under the portico that covered the wide circular drive to the hotel, passing behind an elegant burnt-orange Porsche Cayenne parked prominently along the curve. She dodged the regular hustle of guests trailing luggage and bellhops maneuvering baggage carts and stepped through the automatic entrance into the foyer. Her gaze slid to the elevator that had taken her and Franco up to the Santibanez apartment almost four weeks earlier. It seemed a lifetime ago.

Jazzy Juanito waited for her, wringing her hands. "Security has him in the back. He wanted Franco Martinez, but when I called him, the phone went to voice mail."

Franco had been tied up with the FBI for the last two days. He'd been staying with Ryan at night. She and Franco hadn't yet talked about his absence. They'd both agreed Ryan and his catastrophe came first.

"I had to call someone," Jazzy continued. "He was yelling and pounding on the elevators and staggering around." She leaned in to whisper, eyes rolling with worry. "Drunk as a skunk. Sister Helena—I mean, your mom—tried to get him back outside and into her car. He kept breaking away and yelling that poor baby's name." She tipped her face up and fake called, "'*Bebe, Bebe.*' So sad. He fell and knocked over the table by the levitators, uh, elevators. Cyrus is with him, and your mom."

With a quick glance to make sure she wasn't needed at the desk, Jazzy beckoned Nicky to follow and scurried through an opening into a narrow corridor housing security, CCTV computers and monitors, and hotel operations. A gray-blue metal door at the end of the hall led into a monitoring anteroom. Nicky found her mother and Officer Cyrus Aguilar inside with Val Temper, lead security officer at the resort. Through a one-way glass window into a small interview room, Nicky could see Ryan. He sat, his arms, head, and chest sprawled over a tabletop, his bright golden-brown hair unkempt. He looked like he was sleeping.

"Hey, Sergeant." Temper stuck his hand out to shake Nicky's. "You guys gotta keep your boy here away from the Santibanezes. They are this close to filing an order of protection." He ran his hand agitatedly back and forth over his buzz cut, pulling his ill-fitting polyester suit jacket askew, his weapon holster playing peekaboo underneath.

She glanced inquiringly at her mother. Helena had spent most of the last few days with either the Bernals or Ryan for support. Ryan's devastating loss of both his wife and daughter had triggered her to stay in New Mexico until the end of the week.

"He was fine this morning—rational, helping me." Helena stopped, lips pressed tight.

"With what?" Nicky asked.

"We bagged the last of Jinni's clothes for donations. But he refused to give Bebe's away. That's probably what triggered this."

"Where's he getting the alcohol?" Nicky walked to the window. "Aguilar, after you take him home, search again. We must have missed something." They'd found two caches the first time he'd showed up drunk at the hotel.

Cyrus nodded, his face stamped with sympathy as he stared at Ryan.

"Val, mind if I talk to him?" Nicky asked.

"Be my guest." Val put his hand on the door out to the hallway. "Next time, Sergeant, I'll have to report him to council—I'm actually surprised Peter Santibanez hasn't. It'll be the end of his job, and you know what that means." He opened the door and left.

Without his job, Ryan couldn't live on the pueblo because he wasn't a tribal member. He'd have to leave. It would be his second banishment, and one Nicky wasn't sure her friend would survive. She sighed and entered the little room.

A spiderweb of hair covered Ryan's slack face.

"Ryan."

His chest heaved. "I wanted to make sure she's okay. She's so little, so helpless." He picked his head up off the table and cradled it in trembling hands. "Didn't believe in love at first sight. Wrong about that. Loved her from the second I saw her. All I had was a few days. She'll forget me, but I won't ever…" He let out a ragged sob.

Nicky stepped around the table and knelt beside him, sick at heart.

"You're her godparent," he said, eyes pleading. "Do something. Get her back. Please."

She brushed away the hair tangled in the wetness on his face and cupped his cheeks.

"Ryan, the DNA…"

He pulled back from her. "Why did Savannah do this? Why does she hate me?"

"She doesn't hate you. She—" But Nicky had no excuses to give. Savannah had been absent from work, and the couple of times Nicky had called had gone to voicemail. Her actions seemed to cement her guilt.

"'S'cause I married Jinni." He nodded sagely, bloodshot eyes rolling. "You know, at first I did it to get back at Savannah. That's why this happened, you know? Punishment."

Ryan's face hardened, and his lips twisted cruelly. Alarm shivered up Nicky's back. He stood, and she scrambled to her feet. He stabbed a finger into her chest.

"*You*. Get Bebe back, out of the hands of those—" He spat out filthy words in *Abáachi mizaa*. "If you don't, I'll—"

"*Ryan*."

His hands bit into her shoulders. In the same instance, Nicky brought her arms up and knocked his away. She grabbed his wrist and twisted, slamming him facedown on the table. The door burst open. Cyrus rushed in to assist, but Ryan's body had melted. All Nicky heard besides her and Cyrus's panting breaths was, "*So sorry, so sorry, so sorry...*"

CHAPTER FIFTY-SEVEN

NICKY STOOD next to the open driver's side window of her mother's car and watched as Cyrus Aguilar drove away, Ryan slumped against the back passenger's side window.

"My flight's tomorrow." Helena started the car. "But Ryan still needs help."

"We'll figure something out. Why don't you head home and pack? I've asked Cyrus to stay with him until Franco gets there." Nicky leaned into the car to kiss her mother's cheek. "I'll see you tonight. Love you, Mom." She stepped back as her mother drove off.

"Nicky!" Jazzy called. She beckoned from just inside the hotel's foyer.

Nicky shook herself mentally and slotted her churning thoughts to one side.

"Did Cyrus go?" Jazzy asked. "He left his jacket."

She followed a darting Jazzy to the marble counter. The Fire-Sky-issue jacket lay on top.

"Will Ryan be all—" The elevator dinged, and Jazzy's eyes opened wider than her mouth. "No one's seen that baby since they came back from the christening," she hissed.

Nicky spun. Coming toward her was Marica Santibanez, Bebe cradled in her arms. Annette forged in front of her, pushing a high-end baby carriage. She flicked a panicked look at Nicky and surged toward the automatic doors.

Stomach in knots, Nicky stepped into Marica Santibanez's path. "I want to see Bebe. Her father needs to know she's okay."

The woman came to an abrupt halt.

Marica could step around her, and Nicky could do nothing. But as she stared into Marica's eyes, a shadow passed over them, and Marica dropped her gaze. She tugged down the blanket to expose the little girl. "That's not her name anymore."

Nicky touched the baby's petal-soft cheek. Unfocused gray-brown eyes blinked up at her.

"Let Ryan see her, be a part of her life." It was a futile request, but Nicky had to try.

"Let a murderer around my daughter?"

"He didn't kill PJ. I did."

The woman smiled. It didn't reach her eyes. "Franco Martinez already tried that a few days ago. I didn't believe him, either, although you all had a hand in my son's death. Now, move out of my way, or I'll call security."

Nicky stayed in place for a long moment and stared impassively into Marica's face. When she finally stepped to one side, Marica tightened her hold on the baby and marched away. Annette stood beside the burnt-orange Porsche SUV while Marica buckled the baby into a rear-facing car seat. They both rounded to the driver's side, Marica getting behind the wheel and Annette in the back next to Bebe.

"You know, I used to feel sorry for her. Mrs. Santibanez?" Jazzy said, her mouth tight and arms crossed. "Because of how much her husband fooled around. Of course, I didn't know about the baby's mother." She slanted Nicky a glance, her eyes eager for gossip, but Nicky refused to indulge.

The Porsche started up and pulled out of the drive. It turned onto a back road east, toward the interstate.

"I thought Marica drove a silver Audi," Nicky mused. "How many cars do the Santibanezes own?"

Jazzy *hmph*ed. "It's from the hotel's luxury concierge. She wrecked hers. Yeah. Coming back from that pot exhibit at the museum a few weeks ago. Mr. Santibanez had a little too much to drink, so Mrs. Santibanez drove and smashed into a pole in the garage. Messed up the front something awful." Jazzy ducked behind the front desk. "It shocked us all because she's an amazing driver. She used to race, you know? A lot better than her brothers. There's an awards case over by the coffeepot with her medals and such. Grab a coffee. It's free. Gotta go. Customers." Jazzy turned to smile and greet an elderly couple.

Nicky stirred Sweet'N Low into her coffee, hoping its heat would erase the chill that had settled into her after her confrontation with Marica. She wandered over to the trophy case. Along with awards garnered by the resort and hotel, Marica Santibanez's race trophies and ribbons were on display. She'd done all kinds of racing—stock cars, rally cars, dirt track, oval track, even demolition derby. In one photo, a beaming Marica sat in the open window of a dented car, hand raised in a wave. It was a young face, with joy shining from the eyes. It reminded her of Jinni Bernal's expression when she'd spread her fingers over her pregnant belly and looked at Ryan.

Nicky's hand tightened on her cup, mouth suddenly dry. Jinni's accident report indicated her car had hydroplaned on the wet asphalt and she'd lost control. There'd been no evidence at the scene to say otherwise, and, in their grief, no one had questioned the report's conclusions because of the treacherous road and rainy weather.

She questioned it now.

Jinni was an ex-cop. She'd passed multiple defensive-driving courses before and during her tenure at the Fire-Sky Police Department. And she was heavily pregnant. She would've been driving with extra care and caution down a rain-slick road.

When Marica had interrupted Nicky and Franco's chat with Peter Santibanez at the fertility exhibition, rain had beaded her clothes and hair. She'd smelled like cigarette smoke, but her eyes had been wild.

Nicky pressed her palm against the glass and stared at Marica's smiling face. Demolition derby driving meant taking out your opponents by ramming, sideswiping ... *PIT maneuvers*. She dropped her cup in the trash and strode to the garage elevators.

A crowd of people flowed into the elevator car, and Nicky had to shoulder her way out. Jogging toward the concierge office, she waved down a young man who was wiping raindrops off one of the rental cars. He straightened, rag clutched tightly in his hand, and glanced down at the badge clipped to her belt.

"Can I help you, Officer?"

Nicky peered at his name tag. "You sure can, Benjy. Marica Santibanez's car, the Audi. Can I see it?"

"Last I heard, it was still at the shop."

"Did you see the damage?"

"The front bumper? Sure. It was pretty bad."

"Which shop?" Nicky asked.

"Póncio's. Her dad's."

No way he'd cooperate, and she couldn't get a warrant on a hunch.

A second young man headed over to join the first. They could've been brothers. "Everything okay?"

"She was asking about Mrs. Santibanez's car. The Audi," Benjy said.

"Oh, yeah. She turned right into a cement pillar when she parked it. I heard it was totaled. It's not like her, you know? And that car was her baby." The second guy—Silas, from the name tag—shook his head. "We were working that night. She was really upset, you know?"

"Show me the pillar," Nicky said.

The two young men led her to an empty parking spot. Nicky crouched and ran her hand over jagged gouges in the cement column, dislodging a fist-sized chunk of concrete.

"Whoa. I didn't know it was this bad." Silas pulled his phone out and snapped a photo. "Go get the broom and clean this up," he ordered.

"Who died and made you boss?" Benjy grumped before he hunched off.

"Do you have any pictures of the actual accident?" Nicky asked.

"Sure. We keep files on stuff like that for insurance purposes. Company policy. Did you want to see them?" Silas darted a glance at the concierge office. "You know, maybe I should call—"

With a smile, Nicky cut him off. "No need."

He hesitated, then bobbed his head. She followed him to the small office.

"Here you go." He cued up the photos on the computer, then stepped aside. "Um. Let me send my pics." He slanted her a jumpy glance and started fussing with his phone.

She opened each photo in the file, zooming in on each picture. Marica Santibanez must have hit the pillar hard; the damage appeared severe enough to erase any evidence of a PIT maneuver.

Benjy stepped into the office, lugging a five-gallon bucket in one hand and a broom and dustpan in the other. He dropped the bucket in the corner with a heavy thump.

"Hey, go empty that," Silas said.

"Why? It's not full yet."

Nicky swiveled and looked at the bucket, hope exploding. It was at least three-quarters full of trash and debris, the concrete chunk on top.

"What's that?" she asked.

"Stuff we sweep up from the garage."

"Does it have pieces from Marica Santibanez's car?"

Silas snorted. "Probably, because he never empties—"

"Hey. Stop telling me what to do."

"Dump it on the ground," Nicky said.

The two men exchanged glances. Silas clutched his phone tighter. "Uh, I don't think—"

"Now."

"Okay, but I'm not cleaning it up." Benjy spilled out the bucket.

Nicky pulled her flashlight and knelt. She minutely examined each fragment of plastic, metal, glass....

Dark blue paint streaked a large shard of headlamp glass. *Jinni*

Bernal drove a dark blue car. Her breath quickened. This could be the evidence she needed—

"I hope you have a warrant for your search, Sergeant Matthews. If not, you need to leave. Now."

Peter Santibanez, face like granite, stood in the doorway.

CHAPTER FIFTY-EIGHT

NICKY'S UNIT idled about a mile from the freeway off-ramp on what was a locals' road used by tribal employees of the Fire-Sky Resort and Casino. The orange Porsche flew toward her, more than ten miles an hour over the speed limit as it headed back to the hotel. She'd played a hunch that had paid off. Nicky hit her lights and punched the accelerator. What she was doing was reckless, but if what she suspected was true about Jinni Bernal's death, she was also laying down her marker, the Santibanezes be damned.

The Porsche slowed. It drifted to the gravel shoulder of the narrow road and stopped. Nicky pulled in behind the car. It was imperative she follow protocol. It had to be a good stop. Fingers trembling slightly, she punched the license plate into her computer, then started the hard copy of her speeding ticket. She checked her dash cam to make sure it was on. She wasn't mic'ed up—they hadn't implemented that level of security yet—so it would be her word against Marica Santibanez's.

Her actions measured, she opened her door and stepped onto the blacktop. The area she'd stopped Marica in was flat and scrub-filled for miles in all directions. To her right was Scalding Peak, one of the most sacred places of the Fire-Sky People, perhaps except for the Place of

Emergence. Wreathed in clouds, its lower slopes were white with snow. She'd heard that on the north side the tribe's ski resort had even opened early this season. In front of her, heavy rain blurred the Jemez Mountains, and to the left lay the labyrinthian canyons and high mesas of the pueblo. Behind her ran the north-south freeway from Albuquerque to Santa Fe, and farther east was the bowl-shaped canyon that contained the Fire-Sky museum and the winding road where Jinni had been pushed off the road by the woman behind the tinted glass of the driver's side window. The woman who'd stolen Ryan Bernal's little girl. The woman who thought she could get away with murder.

Nicky squared herself and stared through window at the dark silhouette. The road was completely deserted. Weather darkened the afternoon to dusk, and a chill breeze ran over the exposed skin of her neck.

A baby cried, the sound distant and thin, undulating piteously. The cries were joined by deeper sobbing from a mother, a father, wretched and mournful. They fused into the moan of the wind through the chamisa, but the mournful keening stayed in Nicky's head.

Bebe's muffled wails emanated from the car.

She knocked on the window. It dropped with smooth precision, and with it the sound of Bebe's crying amplified and tore at Nicky. Marica Santibanez turned toward her, eyes hidden behind expensive sunglasses, Annette behind her, peering at Nicky with a pinched expression.

"License, registration, and proof of insurance," Nicky said.

"This is harassment," Marica said. The baby screamed and sobbed.

"The speed limit on the road is forty miles an hour. I clocked you at fifty-two." She had to raise her voice to be heard.

"My husband called. He told me what you're doing. You won't get away with it."

Even though Nicky's blood boiled, she kept her expression impassive. Peter Santibanez had ordered security guards to escort her from the garage after he'd made the attendants sweep the debris back into the bucket. He'd taken the bucket and left. Any evidence it contained was lost.

By the book. "Ma'am, could you please step out of the car? I think you're having a difficult time hearing me." Bebe's crying was heartbreaking, but Annette's head and shoulders blocked Nicky's view of the car seat. Marica exited, and Nicky walked her to the space between their vehicles. She handed Nicky her driver's license and proof of insurance.

In full view of her dash cam, Nicky secured the documents to the top of her clipboard and began to fill in the information required for the ticket.

"You murdered Jinni Bernal," Nicky said, voice flat, "because you wanted your husband's child dead."

"How *dare*—"

"Shut up. It was reckless and stupid because there was no guarantee of success, and yet the outcome couldn't have been any better for you." Nicky turned her clipboard and held out the pen. Her hands were shaking. "By signing, you're not admitting guilt but are agreeing to pay the fine. It's your right to challenge the ticket in court. You ended a woman's life and ruined Ryan Bernal's when you took his little girl."

"It's not his—"

"I won't let you get away with it."

"You have nothing. If you did, I'd be under arrest." Marica pushed her sunglasses to the top of her head and met Nicky's gaze with icy brown eyes. "Think of what you're doing. Peter and I can give this child everything she wants. She'll never go without. What could Ryan Bernal give her? He has to work, so he'd hand her over to his mother until she's old enough for daycare. His job has long hours, and it's dangerous—if he still has it. He's falling apart, and it's not the first time. I know about his past. The drinking, the drugs. Why would you want someone like him raising a child?" Something nasty edged into her expression. "Or is this about your friend Savannah?"

Nicky narrowed her eyes: Marica turning to Savannah in church, thanking her for a devasting betrayal of a life-long friendship, every word designed to inflict maximum damage. Truth clicked into place.

"It wasn't Savannah. It was Annette who told you about the baby, wasn't it? I saw Jinni at the resort a week before her death. Did Jinni tell Annette who the father was so she could get in to see your husband? Annette once told me he slept around and how much she pitied you." Marica's expression stiffened, and Nicky reveled that her barb had found its mark. "I don't pity you. I think you sold your soul for a man's wealth and power." She paused, taking a breath to regain her composure. "You're right. I don't have enough evidence. But I'll get it because I'll *never* let this go. *Never.* Bebe is Ryan's daughter."

Marica snatched the clipboard from Nicky's hand and signed. She thrust it back at Nicky, who tore off the ticket and gave it to Marica. The woman crumpled the paper in her fist and turned on her heel to stride back to the car. The baby's cries were now shuddering sobs.

She pulled the car door open, but before she got in, Marica looked over her shoulder, directly into Nicky's eyes.

"She isn't Bebe. Not anymore."

CHAPTER FIFTY-NINE

IT WAS DARK OUTSIDE. Rain had been spitting fitfully since her drive back from the airport to drop off her mom. Nicky sat at her kitchen table, peeling the label of a half-empty beer, missing her mother's presence.

It had been easy to be alone before. What had changed? She rolled the bit of label into a tiny ball and laughed at herself.

Everything.

There was a knock at her door. She looked in the direction of the sound, frowning. It wouldn't be Javier or another of Luna's guards. With the end of the Tioux case, she'd asked Luna to terminate the surveillance. Taking one more swig of beer, grimacing because it had grown warm, Nicky set the unfinished bottle on the table and went to the front door.

Her heart jumped.

"Franco." He stood across the small courtyard, dressed in jeans and a dark ribbed sweater, hands stuck in his pockets. "I thought you were at Ryan's." Nicky stepped outside and pulled the door closed so that only a wedge of light broke the darkness.

"He's gone. His parents decided he needed to be away from here, and they left for Jicarilla."

"Oh. Do you think it'll help?"

"No."

Neither did she. She hesitated. "This can't get back to Ryan, but I want to reinvestigate Jinni's death. I don't think it was an accident."

Franco straightened, gaze intent. "Why not?"

"A hunch and a shard of headlight glass with dark blue paint smear." She explained, ending with "I went to look for Jinni's car in the boneyard this morning. It was gone. I checked the photos of her bumper, and there's nothing a good lawyer couldn't explain away. I've got nothing. No evidence. Nothing."

"There's always something missed. Always a weak link."

Nicky thought about Annette. "Maybe. Still, I messed up. I tipped my hand because I couldn't control my anger. Couldn't mask my emotions when it really counted." She smiled without humor. "And on that note, I need to apolo—"

"Don't." Franco stepped closer, exposing his face to the diffuse hallway light from the crack in the door. "You were right about me, about the way I run. Confession time." He drew in a long breath. "When I was young, I had a hard time dealing with losing, and it didn't matter if it was kickball or checkers. My grandfather used to yell at me, call me names. Right in my face. I was too emotional, too sensitive. I had to toughen up."

He wiped a hand over his mouth. "Most of what he said was borderline abusive. He was a tough old bird himself. Retired Marine from a different era. But the worst thing was my dad didn't step in and stop him. I was just a little kid, and I couldn't understand why. He was supposed to protect me, and he didn't. I didn't realize for years that he must've had it even worse when he was a kid. Yeah."

He cleared his throat. "In college, I made the mistake of breaking down in front of my girlfriend over another guy taking my first-string position as catcher on the baseball team." His mouth curved, and he shook his head. "Her reaction made my grandfather look like an amateur. My masks, as you call them, helped me deal. They got me through the army and really advanced my undercover work at the DEA. Anyway"—he seemed to retreat from her even though he hadn't moved—"we haven't had a chance to talk, and I want to tell you why I left."

"Franco—"

He raised a hand. "I needed to explain all this to my dad. Needed to apologize to him before I told you. Needed some time with him and my mom to heal up, at least a little. Before, when I visited for holidays or leave, I'd laugh and joke like everything was all right, but I couldn't forgive him. I treated him like crap." He pressed fingers into his eyes. "I didn't understand what I really needed was for him to forgive me. You know why I knew that?"

It was hard to talk, her throat was so tight. She shook her head.

Franco quirked up his lips. "Because of the way you're dealing with your mom. The way you're trying to heal your relationship. Work through your problems." He shifted, buried his hands deep in his pockets. "I should've explained to you why I left. I'm sorry."

Nicky stood across from him in the chilly night, absorbing his words, his half smile so familiar. A tiny drop of rain touched her face, then another.

"Why are we doing this out here?" she asked. "You have a key. You could've let yourself in."

"I took those keys and barged into your home without your permission, remember?" he said. "This time, I figured I'd wait and see if you'd invite me inside."

IN THE DARKNESS of her bedroom, Nicky Matthews lay on her bed and stared up at the ceiling, fingers laced and cradling the back of her head. The phone rang, interrupting her contemplation of the slowly rotating fan.

She picked up her cell. Fire-Sky Dispatch. 2:17 A.M. "Matthews."

"Oh, sorry, Sarge. Hit the wrong number. You're not working tonight."

"Do you need me?"

"Dza. Just Old Man Apodaca reporting someone's dancing on his roof again. He thinks it's one of his daughters' boyfriends or ghosts."

"Who you gonna send out?" she asked.

"Er, either Officer Valentine or Waconda. Both on duty tonight."

"Mr. Apodaca lives in Little Aquita." The village on the pueblo with the worst reputation for ghosts and spirits. Native officers tended to shun the place at night. "Save yourself some trouble. Send Valentine."

She hung up on the dispatcher's laugh.

As Nicky rolled over, Franco's arms slid around her bare waist. He pulled her into his body. God, he felt good.

He sighed, not even opening his eyes. "They don't need you?" he asked, voice groggy.

"No, they don't." Nicky tucked her head on his shoulder and snuggled closer. His leg slid over hers.

"Good," he said. "'Cause I do."

ALSO BY CAROL POTENZA

Hearts of the Missing: A Mystery

The Third Warrior: A Nicky Matthews Mystery

Spirit Daughters: A Nicky Matthews Mystery

Unmasked: A De-Extinct Zoo Mystery

Demystifying the Beats: How to write a killer mystery

by Carol Potenza, Jordyn Kross, Ryley Banks, and Erin Krueger

Coming 2023

Sting of Lies

To receive special offers, bonus content, and info on new releases and other great reads, sign up for my newsletter at

www.carolpotenza.com

IF YOU ENJOYED THIS BOOK...

Authors live for honest reviews. They help other readers find their books in a world where millions of books are published each year. So if you enjoyed this story or any other of my books and have just five minutes, leave a quick review at Amazon, Barnes and Noble, Kobo, Google, or even on my website...

Short or long, your words can make all the difference.

Thank you.

ACKNOWLEDGMENTS

I'd like to thank my critique and writing groups for all that they've taught me. I'd like to thank the best editor in the world—I'm going to miss you while you're away. And I'd like to thank my husband, who is incredibly patient and understanding and with whom I want to spend the rest of my heartbeats.

ABOUT THE AUTHOR

Carol Potenza taught biochemistry before transitioning fully to a mystery writer. She loves the combination of her past and present careers because it gave her the ability not only to teach her students about the biochemical effects of poison, but also to use said poisons very creatively in her murder mysteries (along with other diabolical methods). She lives in the beautiful state of New Mexico with her husband, Leos, and extremely grumpy Chihuahua, Hermes.

For more books and updates

www.carolpotenza.com

Lightning Source UK Ltd.
Milton Keynes UK
UKHW031829190922
409120UK00002B/51